The Modern
Jewish Experience

The Modern Jewish Experience

Advisory Editor

Moses Rischin

Editorial Board

Arthur A. Goren

Irving Howe

YIDDISH TALES

ARNO PRESS

A New York Times Company

New York / 1975

Reprint Edition 1975 by Arno Press Inc.

Reprinted from a copy in
   The University of Illinois Library

THE MODERN JEWISH EXPERIENCE
ISBN for complete set: 0-405-06690-2
See last pages of this volume for titles.

Manufactured in the United States of America

————◦◦◦◦————

Library of Congress Cataloging in Publication Data

Frank, Helena, comp. and tr.
   Yiddish tales.

   (The Modern Jewish experience)
   Reprint of the ed. published by the Jewish Publication
Society of America, Philadelphia.
   1. Short stories, Yiddish--Translations into English.
2. Short stories, English--Translations from Yiddish.
I. Title. II. Series.
PZ1.F867Yi4 [PJ5191.E8]   839'.09'301   74-29531
ISBN 0-405-06755-0

YIDDISH TALES

YIDDISH TALES

TRANSLATED BY
HELENA FRANK

PHILADELPHIA
THE JEWISH PUBLICATION SOCIETY OF AMERICA
1912

PREFACE

This little volume is intended to be both companion and complement to "Stories and Pictures," by I. L. Perez, published by the Jewish Publication Society of America, in 1906.

Its object was twofold: to introduce the non-Yiddish reading public to some of the many other Yiddish writers active in Russian Jewry, and—to leave it with a more cheerful impression of Yiddish literature than it receives from Perez alone. Yes, and we have collected, largely from magazines and papers and unbound booklets, forty-eight tales by twenty different authors. This, thanks to such kind helpers as Mr. F. Hieger, of London, without whose aid we should never have been able to collect the originals of these stories, Mr. Morris Meyer, of London, who most kindly gave me the magazines, etc., in which some of them were contained, and Mr. Israel J. Zevin, of New York, that able editor and delightful *feuilletonist,* to whose critical knowledge of Yiddish letters we owe so much.

Some of these writers, Perez, for example, and Sholom-Alechem, are familiar by name to many of us already, while the reputation of others rests, in circles enthusiastic but tragically small, on what they have written in Hebrew.[1] Such are Berdyczewski, Jehalel, Frischmann, Berschadski, and the silver-penned Judah Steinberg. On these last two be peace in the Olom ho-Emess. The Olom ha-Sheker had nothing for them but struggle and suffering and an early grave.

The tales given here are by no means all equal in literary merit, but they have each its special note, its special echo from that strangely fascinating world so often quoted, so little understood (we say it against ourselves), the Russian Ghetto—a world in the passing, but whose more precious elements, shining, for all who care to see them, through every page of these unpretending tales, and mixed with less and less of what has made their misfortune, will surely live on, free, on the one hand, to blend with all and everything akin to them, and free, on the other, to develop along their own lines—and this year here, next year in Jerusalem.

The American sketches by Zevin and S. Libin differ from the others only in their scene of action. Lerner's were drawn from the life in a little town in Bessarabia, the others are mostly Polish. And the folk tale, which is taken from Joshua Meisach's collection, published in Wilna in 1905, with the title Ma'asiyos vun der Baben, oder Nissim ve-Niflo'os, might have sprung from almost any Ghetto of the Old World.

[1] Berschadski's " Forlorn and Forsaken," Frischmann's " Three Who Ate," and Steinberg's " A Livelihood " and " At the Matzes," though here translated from the Yiddish versions, were probably written in Hebrew originally. In the case of the former two, it would seem that the Yiddish version was made by the authors themselves, and the same may be true of Steinberg's tales, too.

We sincerely regret that nothing from the pen of the beloved "Grandfather" of Yiddish story-tellers in print, Abramowitsch (Mendele Mocher Seforim), was found quite suitable for insertion here, his writings being chiefly much longer than the type selected for this book. Neither have we come across anything appropriate to our purpose by another old favorite, J. Dienesohn. We were, however, able to insert three tales by the veteran author Mordecai Spektor, whose simple style and familiar figures go straight to the people's heart.

With regard to the second half of our object, greater cheerfulness, this collection is an utter failure. It has variety, on account of the many different authors, and the originals have wit and humor in plenty, for wit and humor and an almost passionate playfulness are in the very soul of the language, but it is not cheerful, and we wonder now how we ever thought it could be so, if the collective picture given of Jewish life were, despite its fictitious material, to be anything like a true one. The drollest of the tales, "Gymnasiye" (we refer to the originals), is perhaps the saddest, anyhow in point of actuality, seeing that the Russian Government is planning to make education impossible of attainment by more and more of the Jewish youth—children given into its keeping as surely as any others, and for the crushing of whose lives it will have to answer.

Well, we have done our best. Among these tales are favorites of ours which we have not so much as mentioned by name, thus leaving the gentle reader at liberty to make his own.

H. F.

LONDON, MARCH, 1911

ACKNOWLEDGMENT

The Jewish Publication Society of America desires to acknowledge the valuable aid which Mr. A. S. Freidus, of the Department of Jewish Literature, in the New York Public Library, extended to it in compiling the biographical data relating to the authors whose stories appear in English garb in the present volume. Some of the authors that are living in America courteously furnished the Society with the data referring to their own biographies.

The following sources have been consulted for the biographies: The Jewish Encyclopædia; Wiener, History of Yiddish Literature in the Nineteenth Century; Pinnes, Histoire de la Littérature Judéo-Allemande, and the Yiddish version of the same, Die Geschichte vun der jüdischer Literatur; Baal-Mahashabot, Geklibene Schriften; Sefer Zikkaron le-Sofere Yisrael ha-hayyim ittanu ka-Yom; Eisenstadt, Hakme Yisrael be-Amerika; the memoirs preceding the collected works of some of the authors; and scattered articles in European and American Yiddish periodicals.

CONTENTS

CONTENTS

REUBEN ASHER BRAUDES

Born, 1851, in Wilna (Lithuania), White Russia; went to Roumania after the anti-Jewish riots of 1882, and published a Yiddish weekly, Yehudit, in the interest of Zionism; expelled from Roumania; published a Hebrew weekly, Ha-Zeman, in Cracow, in 1891; then co-editor of the Yiddish edition of Die Welt, the official organ of Zionism; Hebrew critic, publicist, and novelist; contributor to Ha-Lebanon (at eighteen), Ha-Shahar, Ha-Boker Or, and other periodicals; chief work, the novel " Religion and Life."

THE MISFORTUNE

OR HOW THE RAV OF PUMPIAN TRIED TO SOLVE A SOCIAL PROBLEM

Pumpian is a little town in Lithuania, a Jewish town. It lies far away from the highway, among villages reached by the Polish Road. The inhabitants of Pumpian are poor people, who get a scanty living from the peasants that come into the town to make purchases, or else the Jews go out to them with great bundles on their shoulders and sell them every sort of small ware, in return for a little corn, or potatoes, etc. Strangers, passing through, are seldom seen there, and if by any chance a strange person arrives, it is a great wonder and rarity. People peep at him through all the little windows, elderly men venture out to bid him welcome, while boys and youths hang about in the street and stare at him. The women and girls blush and glance at him sideways, and he is the one subject of conversation: "Who can that be? People don't just set off and come like that—there must be something behind it." And in the house-of-study, between Afternoon and Evening Prayer, they gather closely round the elder men, who have been to greet the stranger, to find out who and what the latter may be.

Fifty or sixty years ago, when what I am about to tell you happened, communication between Pumpian and the rest of the world was very restricted indeed: there were as yet no railways, there was no telegraph, the postal service was slow and intermittent. People came and went less often, a journey was a great undertaking, and there were not many outsiders to be found even in the larger towns. Every town was a town to itself, apart, and Pumpian constituted a little world of its own, which had nothing to do with the world at large, and lived its own life.

Neither were there so many newspapers then, anywhere, to muddle people's heads every day of the week, stirring up questions, so that people should have something to talk about, and the Jews had no papers of their own at all, and only heard "news" and "what was going on in the world" in the house-of-study or (lehavdil!) in the bath-house. And what sort of news was it *then?* What sort could it be? World-stirring questions hardly existed (certainly Pumpian was ignorant of them): politics, economics, statistics, capital, social problems, all these words, now on the lips of every boy and girl, were then all but unknown even in the great world, let alone among us Jews, and let alone to Reb Nochumtzi, the Pumpian Rav!

And yet Reb Nochumtzi had a certain amount of worldly wisdom of his own.

Reb Nochumtzi was a native of Pumpian, and had inherited his position there from his father. He had been an only son, made much of by his parents (hence the pet name Nochumtzi clinging to him even in his old age), and never let out of their sight. When he had grown up, they connected him by marriage with the tenant of an estate not far from the town, but his father would not hear of his going there "auf Köst," as the custom is. "I cannot be parted from my Nochumtzi even for a minute," explained the old Rav, "I cannot bear him out of my sight. Besides, we study together." And, in point of fact, they did study together day and night. It was evident that the Rav was determined his Nochumtzi should become Rav in Pumpian after his death—and so he became.

He had been Rav some years in the little town, receiving the same five Polish gulden a week salary as his father (on whom be peace!), and he sat and studied and thought. He had nothing much to do in the way of exercising authority: the town was very quiet, the people orderly, there were no quarrels, and it was seldom that parties went "to law" with one another before the Rav; still less often was there a ritual question to settle: the folk were poor, there was no meat cooked in a Jewish house from one Friday to another, when one must have a bit of meat in honor of Sabbath. Fish was a rarity, and in summer time people often had a "milky Sabbath," as well as a milky week. How should there be "questions"? So he sat and studied and thought, and he was very fond indeed of thinking about the world!

It is true that he sat all day in his room, that he had never in all his life been so much as "four ells" outside the town, that it had never so much as occurred to him to drive about a little in any direction, for, after all, whither should he drive? And why drive anywhither? And yet he knew the world, like any other learned man, a disciple of the wise. Everything is in the Torah, and out of the Torah, out of the Gemoreh, and out of

all the other sacred books, Reb Nochumtzi had learned
to know the world also. He knew that "Reuben's ox
gores Simeon's cow," that "a spark from a smith's hammer can burn a wagon-load of hay," that "Reb Eliezer
ben Charsum had a thousand towns on land and a thousand ships on the sea." Ha, that was a fortune! He
must have been nearly as rich as Rothschild (they knew
about Rothschild even in Pumpian!). "Yes, he was a
rich Tano and no mistake!" he reflected, and was
straightway sunk in the consideration of the subject of
rich and poor.

He knew from the holy books that to be rich is a
pure misfortune. King Solomon, who was certainly
a great sage, prayed to God: Resh wo-Osher al-titten
li!—"Give me neither poverty nor *riches!*" He said
that "riches are stored to the hurt of their owner,"
and in the holy Gemoreh there is a passage which says,
"Poverty becomes a Jew as scarlet reins become a white
horse," and once a sage had been in Heaven for a short
time and had come back again, and he said that he had
seen poor people there occupying the principal seats in
the Garden of Eden, and the rich pushed right away,
back into a corner by the door. And as for the books
of exhortation, there are things written that make you
shudder in every limb. The punishments meted out to
the rich by God in that world, the world of truth, are
no joke. For what bit of merit they have, God rewards
them in *this* poor world, the world of vanity, while
yonder, in the world of truth, they arrive stript and
naked, without so much as a taste of Kingdom-come!

"Consequently, the question is," thought Reb Nochumtzi, "why should they, the rich, want to keep this misfortune? Of what use is this misfortune to them? Who so mad as to take such a piece of misfortune into his house and keep it there? How can anyone take the world-to-come in both hands and lose it for the sake of such vanities?"

He thought and thought, and thought it over again:

"What is a poor creature to do when God sends him the misfortune of riches? He would certainly wish to get rid of them, only who would take his misfortune to please him? Who would free another from a curse and take it upon himself?

"But, after all . . . ha?" the Evil Spirit muttered inside him.

"What a fool you are!" thought Reb Nochumtzi again. "If" (and he described a half-circle downward in the air with his thumb), "if troubles come to us, such as an illness (may the Merciful protect us!), or some other misfortune of the kind, it is expressly stated in the Sacred Writings that it is an expiation for sin, a torment sent into the world, so that we may be purified by it, and made fit to go straight to Paradise. And because it is God who afflicts men with these things, we cannot give them away to anyone else, but have to bear with them. Now, such a misfortune as being rich, which is also a visitation of God, must certainly be borne with like the rest.

"And, besides," he reflected further, "the fool who would take the misfortune to himself, doesn't exist!

What healthy man in his senses would get into a sick-bed?"

He began to feel very sorry for Reb Eliezer ben Charsum with his thousand towns and his thousand ships. "To think that such a saint, such a Tano, one of the authors of the holy Mishnah, should incur such a severe punishment!

"But he stood the trial! Despite this great misfortune, he remained a saint and a Tano to the end, and the holy Gemoreh says particularly that he thereby put to shame all the rich people, who go straight to Gehenna."

Thus Reb Nochumtzi, the Pumpian Rav, sat over the Talmud and reflected continually on the problem of great riches. He knew the world through the Holy Scriptures, and was persuaded that riches were a terrible misfortune, which had to be borne, because no one would consent to taking it from another, and bearing it for him.

Again many years passed, and Reb Nochumtzi gradually came to see that poverty also is a misfortune, and out of his own experience.

His Sabbath cloak began to look threadbare (the weekday one was already patched on every side), he had six little children living, one or two of the girls were grown up, and it was time to think of settling them, and they hadn't a frock fit to put on. The five Polish gulden a week salary was not enough to keep them in bread, and the wife, poor thing, wept the whole day through: "Well, there, ich wie ich, it isn't for myself—but the poor children are naked and barefoot."

At last they were even short of bread.

"Nochumtzi! Why don't you speak?" exclaimed his wife with tears in her eyes. Nochumtzi, can't you hear me? I tell you, we're starving! The children are skin and bone, they haven't a shirt to their back, they can hardly keep body and soul together. Think of a way out of it, invent something to help us!"

And Reb Nochumtzi sat and considered.

He was considering the other misfortune—poverty.

"It is equally a misfortune to be really very poor."

And this also he found stated in the Holy Scriptures.

It was King Solomon, the famous sage, who prayed as well: Resh wo-Osher al-titten li, that is, "Give me neither *poverty* nor riches." Aha! poverty is no advantage, either, and what does the holy Gemoreh say but "Poverty diverts a man from the way of God"? In fact, there is a second misfortune in the world, and one he knows very well, one with which he has a practical, working acquaintance, he and his wife and his children.

And Reb Nochum pursued his train of thought:

"So there are two contrary misfortunes in the world: this way it's bad, and that way it's bitter! Is there really no remedy? Can no one suggest any help?"

And Reb Nochumtzi began to pace the room up and down, lost in thought, bending his whole mind to the subject. A whole flight of Bible texts went through his head, a quantity of quotations from the Gemoreh, hundreds of stories and anecdotes from the "Fountain of Jacob," the Midrash, and other books, telling of rich and poor, fortunate and unfortunate people, till his head went round with them all as he thought. Suddenly he stood still in the middle of the room, and began talking to himself:

"Aha! Perhaps I've discovered a plan after all! And a good plan, too, upon my word it is! Once more: it is quite certain that there will always be more poor than rich—lots more! Well, and it's quite certain that every rich man would like to be rid of his misfortune, only that there is no one willing to take it from him— no *one,* not any *one,* of course not. Nobody would be so mad. But we have to find out a way by which *lots and lots* of people should rid him of his misfortune little by little. What do you say to that? Once more: that means that we must take his unfortunate riches and divide them among a quantity of poor! That will be a good thing for both parties: he will be easily rid of his great misfortune, and they would be helped, too, and the petition of King Solomon would be established, when he said, 'Give me neither poverty nor riches.' It would come true of them all, there would be no riches and no poverty. Ha? What do you think of it? Isn't it really and truly an excellent idea?"

Reb Nochumtzi was quite astonished himself at the plan he had invented, cold perspiration ran down his face, his eyes shone brighter, a happy smile played on his lips. "That's the thing to do!" he explained aloud, sat down by the table, blew his nose, wiped his face, and felt very glad.

"There is only one difficulty about it," occurred to him, when he had quieted down a little from his excitement, "one thing that doesn't fit in. It says particularly in the Torah that there will always be poor people among the Jews, 'the poor shall not cease out of the land.' There must always be poor, and this would make an end of them altogether! Besides, the precept concerning charity would, Heaven forbid, be annulled, the precept which God, blessed is He, wrote in the Torah, and which the holy Gemoreh and all the other holy books make so much of. What is to become of the whole treatise on charity in the Shulchan Aruch? How can we continue to fulfil it?

But a good head is never at a loss! Reb Nochumtzi soon found a way out of the difficulty.

"Never mind!" and he wrinkled his forehead, and pondered on. "There is no fear! Who said that even the whole of the money in the possession of a few unfortunate rich men will be enough to go round? That there will be just enough to help all the Jewish poor? No fear, there will be enough poor left for the exercise of charity. Ai wos? There is another thing: to whom shall be given and to whom not? Ha, that's a detail, too. Of course, one would begin with the learned and the poor scholars and sages, who have to live on the Torah and on Divine Service. The people can just be left to go on as it is. No fear, but it will be all right!"

At last the plan was ready. Reb Nochumtzi thought it over once more, very carefully, found it complete from every point of view, and gave himself up to a feeling of satisfaction and delight.

"Dvoireh!" he called to his wife, "Dvoireh, don't cry! Please God, it will be all right, quite all right. I've thought out a plan. . . A little patience, and it will all come right!"

"Whatever? What sort of plan?"

"There, there, wait and see and hold your tongue! No woman's brain could take it in. You leave it to me, it will be all right!"

And Reb Nochumtzi reflected further:

"Yes, the plan is a good one. Only, how is it to be carried out? With whom am I to begin?"

And he thought of all the householders in Pumpian, but—there was not one single unfortunate man among them! That is, not one of them had money, a real lot of money; there was nobody with whom to discuss his invention to any purpose.

"If so, I shall have to drive to one of the large towns!"

And one Sabbath the beadle gave out in the house-of-study that the Rav begged them all to be present that evening at a convocation.

At the said convocation the Rav unfolded his whole plan to the people, and placed before them the happiness that would result for the whole world, if it were to be realized. But first of all he must journey to a large town, in which there were a great many unfortunate rich people, preferably Wilna, and he demanded of his flock that they should furnish him with the necessary means for getting there.

The audience did not take long to reflect, they agreed to the Rav's proposal, collected a few rubles (for who would not give their last farthing for such an important object?), and on Sunday morning early they hired him a peasant's cart and horse—and the Rav drove away to Wilna.

The Rav passed the drive marshalling his arguments, settling on what he should say, and how he should explain himself, and he was delighted to see how, the more deeply he pondered his plan, the more he thought it out, the more efficient and appropriate it appeared, and the clearer he saw what happiness it would bestow on men all the world over.

The small cart arrived at Wilna.

"Whither are we to drive?" asked the peasant.

"Whither? To a Jew," answered the Rav. "For where is the Jew who will not give me a night's lodging?"

"And I, with my cart and horse?"

The Rav sat perplexed, but a Jew passing by heard the conversation, and explained to him that Wilna is not Pumpian, and that they would have to drive to a post-house, or an inn.

"Be it so!" said the Rav, and the Jew gave him the address of a place to which they should drive.

Wilna! It is certainly not the same thing as Pumpian. Now, for the first time in his life, the Rav saw whole streets of tall houses, of two and three stories, all as it were under one roof, and how fine they are, thought he, with their decorated exteriors!

"Oi, there live the unfortunate people!" said Reb Nochumtzi to himself. "I never saw anything like them before! How can they bear such a misfortune? I shall come to them as an angel of deliverance!"

He had made up his mind to go to the principal Jewish citizen in Wilna, only he must be a good scholar, so as to understand what Reb Nochumtzi had to say to him.

They advised him to go to the president of the Congregation.

Every street along which he passed astonished him separately, the houses, the pavements, the droshkis and carriages, and especially the people, so beautifully got up with gold watch-chains and rings—he was quite bewildered, so that he was afraid he might lose his senses, and forget all his arguments and his reasonings.

At last he arrived at the president's house.

"He lives on the first floor." Another surprise! Reb Nochumtzi was unused to stairs. There was no storied house in all Pumpian! But when you must, you must! One way and another he managed to arrive at the first-floor landing, where he opened the door, and said, all in one breath:

"I am the Pumpian Rav, and have something to say to the president."

The president, a handsome old man, very busy just then with some merchants who had come on business, stood up, greeted him politely, and opening the door of the reception room said to him:

"Please, Rabbi, come in here and wait a little. I shall soon have finished, and then I will come to you here."

Expensive furniture, large mirrors, pictures, softly upholstered chairs, tables, cupboards with shelves full of great silver candlesticks, cups, knives and forks, a beautiful lamp, and many other small objects, all of solid silver, wardrobes with carving in different designs; then, painted walls, a great silver chandelier decorated with cut glass, fascinating to behold! Reb Nochumtzi actually had tears in his eyes, "To think of anyone's being so unfortunate—and to have to bear it!"

"What can I do for you, Pumpian Rav?" inquired the president.

And Reb Nochumtzi, overcome by amazement and enthusiasm, nearly shouted:

"You are so unfortunate!"

The president stared at him, shrugged his shoulders, and was silent.

Then Reb Nochumtzi laid his whole plan before him, the object of his coming.

"I will be frank with you," he said in concluding his long speech, "I had no idea of the extent of the misfortune! To the rescue, men, save yourselves! Take it to heart, think of what it means to have houses like these, and all these riches—it is a most terrible misfortune! Now I see what a reform of the whole world my plan amounts to, what deliverance it will bring to all men!"

The president looked him straight in the face: he saw the man was not mad, but that he had the limited horizon of one born and bred in a small provincial town and in the atmosphere of the house-of-study.

He also saw that it would be impossible to convince him by proofs that his idea was a mistaken one; for a little while he pitied him in silence, then he hit upon an expedient, and said:

"You are quite right, Rabbi! Your plan is really a very good one. But I am only one of many, Wilna is full of such unfortunate people. Everyone of them must be talked to, and have the thing explained to him. Then, the other party must be spoken to as well, I mean the poor people, so that they shall be willing to take their share of the misfortune. That's not such an easy matter as giving a thing away and getting rid of it."

"Of course, of course . . . " agreed Reb Nochumtzi.

"Look here, Rav of Pumpian, I will undertake the more difficult part—let us work together! You shall persuade the rich to give away their misfortune, and I will persuade the poor to take it! Your share of the work will be the easier, because, after all, everybody wants to be rid of his misfortune. Do your part, and as soon as you have finished with the rich, I will arrange for you to be met half-way by the poor. . ."

History does not tell how far the Rav of Pumpian succeeded in Wilna. Only this much is certain, the president never saw him again.

JEHALEL

Pen name of Judah Löb Lewin; born, 1845, in Minsk (Lithuania), White Russia; tutor; treasurer to the Brodski flour mills and their sugar refinery, at Tomaschpol, Podolia, later in Kieff; began to write in 1860; translator of Beaconsfield's Tancred into Hebrew; Talmudist; mystic; first Socialist writer in Hebrew; writer, chiefly in Hebrew, of prose and poetry; contributor to Sholom-Alechem's Jüdische Volksbibliothek, Ha-Shahar, Ha-Meliz, Ha-Zefirah, and other periodicals.

EARTH OF PALESTINE

As my readers know, I wanted to do a little stroke of business—to sell the world-to-come. I must tell you that I came out of it very badly, and might have fallen into some misfortune, if I had had the ware in stock. It fell on this wise: Nowadays everyone is squeezed and stifled; Parnosseh is gone to wrack and ruin, and there is no business—I mean, there *is* business, only not for us Jews. In such bitter times people snatch the bread out of each other's mouths; if it is known that someone has made a find, and started a business, they quickly imitate him; if that one opens a shop, a second does likewise, and a third, and a fourth; if this one makes a contract, the other runs and will do it for less—"Even if I earn nothing, no more will you!"

When I gave out that I had the world-to-come to sell, lots of people gave a start, "Aha! a business!" and before they knew what sort of ware it was, and where it was to be had, they began thinking about a shop—and there was still greater interest shown on the part of certain philanthropists, party leaders, public workers, and such-like. They knew that when I set up trading in the world-to-come, I had announced that my business was only with the poor. Well, they understood that it was likely to be profitable, and might give them the chance óf licking a bone or two. There was very soon a great tararam in our little world, people began inquiring where my goods came from. They surrounded me with spies, who were to find out what I did at night, what I did on Sabbath; they questioned the cook, the market-woman; but in vain, they could not find out how I came by the world-to-come. And there blazed up a fire of jealousy and hatred, and they began to inform, to write letters to the authorities about me. Laban the Yellow and Balaam the Blind (you know them!) made my boss believe that I do business, that is, that I have capital, that is—that is—but my employer investigated the matter, and seeing that my stock in trade was the world-to-come, he laughed, and let me alone. The townspeople among whom it was my lot to dwell, those good people who are a great hand at fishing in troubled waters, as soon as they saw the mud rise, snatched up their implements and set to work, informing by letter that I was dealing in contraband. There appeared a red official and swept out a few corners in my house, but without finding a single specimen bit of the world-to-come, and went away. But I had no peace even then; every day came a fresh letter informing against me. My good brothers never ceased work. The pious, orthodox Jews, the Gemoreh-Köplech, informed, and said I was a swindler, because the world-to-come is a thing that isn't there, that is neither fish, flesh, fowl, nor good red herring, and the whole thing was a delusion; the half-civilized people with long trousers and short earlocks said, on the contrary, that I was making game of religion, so that before long I had enough of it from every side, and made the following resolutions: first, that I would have nothing to do with the world-to-come and such-like things which the Jews did not understand, although they held them very precious; secondly, that I would not let myself in for selling anything. One of my good friends, an experienced merchant, advised me rather to buy than to sell: "There are so many to sell, they will compete with you, inform against you, and behave as no one should. Buying, on the other hand—if you want to buy, you will be esteemed and respected, everyone will flatter you, and be ready to sell to you on credit—everyone is ready to take money, and with very little capital you can buy the best and most expensive ware." The great thing was to get a good name, and then, little by little, by means of credit, one might rise very high.

So it was settled that I should buy. I had a little money on hand for a couple of newspaper articles, for which nowadays they pay; I had a bit of reputation earned by a great many articles in Hebrew, for which I received quite nice complimentary letters; and, in case of need, there is a little money owing to me from certain Jewish booksellers of the Maskilim, for books bought "on commission." Well, I am resolved to buy.

But what shall I buy? I look round and take note of all the things a man can buy, and see that I, as a Jew, may not have them; that which I may buy, no matter where, isn't worth a halfpenny; a thing that is of any value, I can't have. And I determine to take to the old ware which my great-great-grandfathers bought, and made a fortune in. My parents and the whole family wish for it every day. I resolve to buy—you understand me?—earth of Palestine, and I announce both verbally and in writing to all my good and bad brothers that I wish to become a purchaser of the ware.

Oh, what a commotion it made! Hardly was it known that I wished to buy Palestinian earth, than there pounced upon me people of whom I had never thought it possible that they should talk to me, and be in the room with me. The first to come was a kind of Jew with a green shawl, with white shoes, a pale face with a red nose, dark eyes, and yellow earlocks. He commenced unpacking paper and linen bags, out of which he shook a little sand, and he said to me: "That is from Mother Rachel's grave, from the Shunammite's grave, from the graves of Huldah the prophetess and Deborah." Then he shook out the other bags, and mentioned a whole list of men: from the grave of Enoch, Moses our Teacher, Elijah the Prophet, Habakkuk, Ezekiel, Jonah, authors of the Talmud, and holy men as many as there be. He assured me that each kind of sand had its own precious distinction, and had, of course, its special price. I had not had time to examine all the bags of sand, when, aha! I got a letter written on blue paper in Rashi script, in which an unknown well-wisher earnestly warned me against buying of *that* Jew, for neither he nor his father before him had ever been in Palestine, and he had got the sand in K., from the Andreiyeff Hills yonder, and that if I wished for it, *he* had *real* Palestinian earth, from the Mount of Olives, with a document from the Palestinian vicegerent, the Brisk Rebbetzin, to the effect that she had given of this earth even to the eaters of swine's flesh, of whom it is said, "for their worm shall not die," and they also were saved from worms. My Palestinian Jew, after reading the letter, called down all bad dreams upon the head of the Brisk Reb-

betzin, and declared among other things that she herself was a dreadful worm, who, etc. He assured me
that I ought not to send money to the Brisk Rebbetzin,
"May Heaven defend you! it will be thrown away,
as it has been a hundred times already!" and began
once more to praise *his* wares, his earth, saying it was a
marvel. I answered him that I wanted real earth of
Palestine, *earth,* not sand out of little bags.

"Earth, it *is* earth!" he repeated, and became very
angry. "What do you mean by earth? Am I offering
you mud? But that is the way with people nowadays,
when they want something Jewish, there is no pleasing
them! Only" (a thought struck him) "if you want
another sort, perhaps from the field of Machpelah, I can
bring you some Palestinian earth that *is* earth. Meantime give me something in advance, for, besides everything else, I am a Palestinian Jew."

I pushed a coin into his hand, and he went away.
Meanwhile the news had spread, my intention to pur-
chase earth of Palestine had been noised abroad, and the
little town echoed with my name. In the streets, lanes,
and market-place, the talk was all of me and of how
"there is no putting a final value on a Jewish soul: one
thought he was one of *them,* and now he wants to buy
earth of Palestine!" Many of those who met me looked
at me askance, "The same and *not* the same!" In the
synagogue they gave me the best turn at the Reading
of the Law; Jews in shoes and socks wished me "a good
Sabbath" with great heartiness, and a friendly smile:
"Eh-eh-eh! We understand—you are a deep one—you
are one of us after all." In short, they surrounded me,

and nearly carried me on their shoulders, so that I really became something of a celebrity.

Yüdel, the "living orphan," worked the hardest. Yüdel is already a man in years, but everyone calls him the "orphan" on account of what befell him on a time. His history is very long and interesting, I will tell it you in brief.

He has a very distinguished father and a very noble mother, and he is an only child, of a very frolicsome disposition, on account of which his father and his mother frequently disagreed; the father used to punish him and beat him, but the boy hid with his mother. In a word, it came to this, that his father gave him into the hands of strangers, to be educated and put into shape. The mother could not do without him, and fell sick of grief; she became a wreck. Her beautiful house was burnt long ago through the boy's doing: one day, when a child, he played with fire, and there was a conflagration, and the neighbors came and built on the site of her palace, and she, the invalid, lies neglected in a corner. The father, who has left the house, often wished to rejoin her, but by no manner of means can they live together without the son, and so the cast-off child became a "living orphan"; he roams about in the wide world, comes to a place, and when he has stayed there a little while, they drive him out, because wherever he comes, he stirs up a commotion. As is the way with all orphans, he has many fathers, and everyone directs him, hits him, lectures him; he is always in the way, blamed for everything, it's always his fault, so that he has got into the habit of cowering and shrinking at the mere sight of a stick. Wandering about as he does, he has copied the manners and customs of strange people, in every place where he has been; his very character is hardly his own. His father has tried both to threaten and to persuade him into coming back, saying they would then all live together as before, but Yüdel has got to like living from home, he enjoys the scrapes he gets into, and even the blows they earn for him. No matter how people knock him about, pull his hair, and draw his blood, the moment they want him to make friendly advances, there he is again, alert and smiling, turns the world topsyturvy, and won't hear of going home. It is remarkable that Yüdel, who is no fool, and has a head for business, the instant people look kindly on him, imagines they like him, although he has had a thousand proofs to the contrary. He has lately been of such consequence in the eyes of the world that they have begun to treat him in a new way, and they drive him out of every place at once. The poor boy has tried his best to please, but it was no good, they knocked him about till he was covered with blood, took every single thing he had, and empty-handed, naked, hungry, and beaten as he is, they shout at him "Be off!" from every side. Now he lives in narrow streets, in the small towns, hidden away in holes and corners. He very often hasn't enough to eat, but he goes on in his old way, creeps into tight places, dances at all the weddings, loves to meddle, everything concerns him, and where two come together, he is the third.

I have known him a long time, ever since he was a little boy. He always struck me as being very wild, but I saw that he was of a noble disposition, only that he had grown rough from living among strangers. I loved him very much, but in later years he treated me to hot and cold by turns. I must tell you that when Yüdel had eaten his fill, he was always very merry, and minded nothing; but when he had been kicked out by his landlord, and went hungry, then he was angry, and grew violent over every trifle. He would attack me for nothing at all, we quarrelled and parted company, that is, I loved him at a distance. When he wasn't just in my sight, I felt a great pity for him, and a wish to go to him; but hardly had I met him than he was at the old game again, and I had to leave him. Now that I was together with him in my native place, I found him very badly off, he hadn't enough to eat. The town was small and poor, and he had no means of supporting himself. When I saw him in his bitter and dark distress, my heart went out to him. But at such times, as I said before, he is very wild and fanatical. One day, on the Ninth of Ab, I felt obliged to speak out, and tell him that sitting in socks, with his forehead on the ground, reciting Lamentations, would do no good. Yüdel misunderstood me, and thought I was laughing at Jerusalem. He began to fire up, and he spread reports of me in the town, and when he saw me in the distance, he would spit out before me. His anger dated from some time past, because one day I turned him out of my house; he declared that I was the cause of all his misfortunes, and now that I was his neighbor, I had resolved to ruin him; he believed that I hated him and played him false. Why should Yüdel think that?

I don't know. Perhaps he feels one ought to dislike him, or else he is so embittered that he cannot believe in the kindly feelings of others. However that may be, Yüdel continued to speak ill of me, and threw mud at me through the town; crying out all the while that I hadn't a scrap of Jewishness in me.

Now that he heard I was buying Palestinian earth, he began by refusing to believe it, and declared it was a take-in and the trick of an apostate, for how could a person who laughed at socks on the Ninth of Ab really want to buy earth of Palestine? But when he saw the green shawls and the little bags of earth, he went over—a way he has—to the opposite, the exact opposite. He began to worship me, couldn't praise me enough, and talked of me in the back streets, so that the women blessed me aloud. Yüdel was now much given to my company, and often came in to see me, and was most intimate, although there was no special piousness about me. I was just the same as before, but Yüdel took this for the best of signs, and thought it proved me to be of extravagant hidden piety.

"There's a Jew for you!" he would cry aloud in the street. "Earth of Palestine! There's a Jew!"

In short, he filled the place with my Jewishness and my hidden orthodoxy. I looked on with indifference, but after a while the affair began to cost me both time and money.

The Palestinian beggars and, above all, Yüdel and the townsfolk obtained for me the reputation of piety, and there came to me orthodox Jews, treasurers, cabalists, beggar students, and especially the Rebbe's followers;

they came about me like bees. They were never in the
habit of avoiding me, but this was another thing all the
same. Before this, when one of the Rebbe's disciples
came, he would enter with a respectful demeanor, take
off his hat, and, sitting in his cap, would fix his gaze on
my mouth with a sweet smile; we both felt that the one
and only link between us lay in the money that I gave
and he took. He would take it gracefully, put it into
his purse, as it might be for someone else, and thank
me as though he appreciated my kindness. When *I* went
to see *him,* he would place a chair for me, and give me
preserve. But now he came to me with a free and
easy manner, asked for a sip of brandy with a snack to
eat, sat in my room as if it were his own, and looked at
me as if I were an underling, and he had authority over
me; I am the penitent sinner, it is said, and that signi-
fies for him the key to the door of repentance; I have
entered into his domain, and he is my lord and master;
he drinks my health as heartily as though it were his
own, and when I press a coin into his hand, he looks
at it well, to make sure it is worth his while accepting
it. If I happen to visit him, I am on a footing with
all his followers, the Chassidim; his "trustees," and
all his other hangers-on, are my brothers, and come
to me when they please, with all the mud on their boots,
put their hand into my bosom and take out my tobacco-
pouch, and give it as their opinion that the brandy is
weak, not to talk of holidays, especially Purim and
Rejoicing of the Law, when they troop in with a great
noise and vociferation, and drink and dance, and pay
as much attention to me as to the cat.

In fact, all the townsfolk took the same liberties with me. Before, they asked nothing of me, and took me as they found me, now they began to *demand* things of me and to inquire why I didn't do this, and why I did that, and not the other. Shmuelke the bather asked me why I was never seen at the bath on Sabbath. Kalmann the butcher wanted to know why, among the scape-fowls, there wasn't a white one of mine; and even the beadle of the Klaus, who speaks through his nose, and who had never dared approach me, came and insisted on giving me the thirty-nine stripes on the eve of the Day of Atonement: "Eh-eh, if you are a Jew like other Jews, come and lie down, and you shall be given stripes!"

And the Palestinian Jews never ceased coming with their bags of earth, and I never ceased rejecting. One day there came a broad-shouldered Jew from "over there," with his bag of Palestinian earth. The earth pleased me, and a conversation took place between us on this wise:

"How much do you want for your earth?"

"For my earth? From anyone else I wouldn't take less than thirty rubles, but from you, knowing you and *of* you as I do, and as your parents did so much for Palestine, I will take a twenty-five ruble piece. You must know that a person buys this once and for all."

"I don't understand you," I answered. "Twenty-five rubles! How much earth have you there?"

"How much earth have I? About half a quart. There will be enough to cover the eyes and the face. Perhaps you want to cover the whole body, to have it underneath and on the top and at the sides? O, I can bring you

some more, but it will cost you two or three hundred
rubles, because, since the good-for-nothings took to coming to Palestine, the earth has got very expensive.
Believe me, I don't make much by it, it costs me
nearly. . . . "

"I don't understand you, my friend! What's this
about bestrewing the body? What do you mean by it?"

"How do you mean, 'what do you mean by it?'
Bestrewing the body like that of all honest Jews, after
death."

"Ha? After death? To preserve it?"

"Yes, what else?"

"I don't want it for that, I don't mind what happens
to my body after death. I want to buy Palestinian
earth for my lifetime."

"What do you mean? What good can it do you
while you're alive? You are not talking to the point,
or else you are making game of a poor Palestinian
Jew?"

"I am speaking seriously. I want it now, while I
live! What is it you don't understand?"

My Palestinian Jew was greatly perplexed, but he
quickly collected himself, and took in the situation. I
saw by his artful smile that he had detected a strain
of madness in me, and what should he gain by leading
me into the paths of reason? Rather let him profit
by it! And this he proceeded to do, saying with winning
conviction:

"Yes, of course, you are right! How right you are!
May I ever see the like! People are not wrong when
they say, 'The apple falls close to the tree'! You are

drawn to the root, and you love the soil of Palestine, only in a different way, like your holy forefathers, may they be good advocates! You are young, and I am old, and I have heard how they used to bestrew their head-dress with it in their lifetime, so as to fulfil the Scripture verse, 'And have pity on Zion's dust,' and honest Jews shake earth of Palestine into their shoes on the eve of the Ninth of Ab, and at the meal before the fast they dip an egg into Palestinian earth—nu, fein! I never expected so much of you, and I can say with truth, 'There's a Jew for you!' Well, in that case, you will require two pots of the earth, but it will cost you a deal."

"We are evidently at cross-purposes," I said to him. "What are two potfuls? What is all this about bestrewing the body? I want to buy Palestinian earth, earth in Palestine, do you understand? I want to buy, in Palestine, a little bit of earth, a few dessiatines."

"Ha? I didn't quite catch it. What did you say?" and my Palestinian Jew seized hold of his right ear, as though considering what he should do; then he said cheerfully: "Ha—aha! You mean to secure for yourself a burial-place, also for after death! O yes, indeed, you are a holy man and no mistake! Well, you can get that through me, too; give me something in advance, and I shall manage it for you all right at a bargain."

"Why do you go on at me with your 'after death,'" I cried angrily. "I want a bit of earth in Palestine, I want to dig it, and sow it, and plant it . . . "

"Ha? What? Sow it and plant it?! That is . . . that is . . . you only mean . . . may all bad dreams!

. . . " and stammering thus, he scraped all the scattered
earth, little by little, into his bag, gradually got nearer
the door, and—was gone!

It was not long before the town was seething and
bubbling like a kettle on the boil, everyone was upset
as though by some misfortune, angry with me, and still
more with himself: "How could we be so mistaken?
He doesn't want to buy Palestinian earth at all, he
doesn't care what happens to him when he's dead, he
laughs—he only wants to buy earth *in* Palestine, and
set up villages there."

"Eh-eh-eh! He remains one of *them!* He is what
he is—a skeptic!" so they said in all the streets, all
the householders in the town, the women in the market-
place, at the bath, they went about abstracted, and as
furious as though I had insulted them, made fools of
them, taken them in, and all of a sudden they became
cold and distant to me. The pious Jews were seen no
more at my house. I received packages from Palestine
one after the other. One had a black seal, on which
was scratched a black ram's horn, and inside, in large
characters, was a ban from the Brisk Rebbetzin, because
of my wishing to make all the Jews unhappy. Other
packets were from different Palestinian beggars, who tried
to compel me, with fair words and foul, to send them
money for their travelling expenses and for the samples
of earth they enclosed. My fellow-townspeople also got
packages from "over there," warning them against me—
I was a dangerous man, a missionary, and it was a Mitzveh to be revenged on me. There was an uproar, and
no wonder! A letter from Palestine, written in Rashi,

with large seals! In short I was to be put to shame and confusion. Everyone avoided me, nobody came near me. When people were obliged to come to me in money matters or to beg an alms, they entered with deference, and spoke respectfully, in a gentle voice, as to "one of them," took the alms or the money, and were out of the door, behind which they abused me, as usual.

Only Yüdel did not forsake me. Yüdel, the "living orphan," was bewildered and perplexed. He had plenty of work, flew from one house to the other, listening, begging, and talebearing, answering and asking questions; but he could not settle the matter in his own mind: now he looked at me angrily, and again with pity. He seemed to wish not to meet me, and yet he sought occasion to do so, and would look earnestly into my face.

The excitement of my neighbors and their behavior to me interested me very little; but I wanted very much to know the reason why I had suddenly become abhorrent to them? I could by no means understand it.

Once there came a wild, dark night. The sky was covered with black clouds, there was a drenching rain and hail and a stormy wind, it was pitch dark, and it lightened and thundered, as though the world were turning upside down. The great thunder claps and the hail broke a good many people's windows, the wind tore at the roofs, and everyone hid inside his house, or wherever he found a corner. In that dreadful dark night my door opened, and in came—Yüdel, the "living orphan"; he looked as though someone were pushing him from behind, driving him along. He was as white as the wall, cowering, beaten about, helpless as a leaf.

He came in, and stood by the door, holding his hat; he couldn't decide, did not know if he should take it off, or not. I had never seen him so miserable, so despairing, all the time I had known him. I asked him to sit down, and he seemed a little quieted. I saw that he was soaking wet, and shivering with cold, and I gave him hot tea, one glass after the other. He sipped it with great enjoyment. And the sight of him sitting there sipping and warming himself would have been very comic, only it was so very sad. The tears came into my eyes. Yüdel began to brighten up, and was soon Yüdel, his old self, again. I asked him how it was he had come to me in such a state of gloom and bewilderment? He told me the thunder and the hail had broken all the window-panes in his lodging, and the wind had carried away the roof, there was nowhere he could go for shelter; nobody would let him in at night; there was not a soul he could turn to, there remained nothing for him but to lie down in the street and die.

"And so," he said, "having known you so long, I hoped you would take me in, although you are 'one of them,' not at all pious, and, so they say, full of evil intentions against Jews and Jewishness; but I know you are a good man, and will have compassion on me."

I forgave Yüdel his rudeness, because I knew him for an outspoken man, that he was fond of talking, but never did any harm. Seeing him depressed, I offered him a glass of wine, but he refused it.

I understood the reason of his refusal, and started a conversation with him.

"Tell me, Yüdel heart, how is it I have fallen into such bad repute among you that you will not even drink a drop of wine in my house? And why do you say that I am 'one of them,' and not pious? A little while ago you spoke differently of me."

"Ett! It just slipped from my tongue, and the truth is you may be what you please, you are a good man."

"No, Yüdel, don't try to get out of it! Tell me openly (it doesn't concern me, but I am curious to know), why this sudden revulsion of feeling about me, this change of opinion? Tell me, Yüdel, I beg of you, speak freely!"

My gentle words and my friendliness gave Yüdel great encouragement. The poor fellow, with whom not one of "them" has as yet spoken kindly! When he saw that I meant it, he began to scratch his head; it seemed as if in that minute he forgave me all my "heresies," and he looked at me kindly, and as if with pity. Then, seeing that I awaited an answer, he gave a twist to his earlock, and said gently and sincerely:

"You wish me to tell you the truth? You insist upon it? You will not be offended?"

"You know that I never take offence at anything you say. Say anything you like, Yüdel heart, only speak."

"Then I will tell you: the town and everyone else is very angry with you on account of your Palestinian earth: you want to do something new, buy earth and plough it and sow—and where? in our land of Israel, in our Holy Land of Israel!"

"But why, Yüdel dear, when they thought I was buying Palestinian earth to bestrew me after death, was I looked upon almost like a saint?"

"Ê, that's another thing! That showed that you held Palestine holy, for a land whose soil preserves one against being eaten of worms, like any other honest Jew."

"Well, I ask you, Yüdel, what does this mean? When they thought I was buying sand for after my death, I was a holy man, a lover of Palestine, and because I want to buy earth and till it, earth in your Holy Land, our holy earth in the Holy Land, in which our best and greatest counted it a privilege to live, I am a blot on Israel. Tell me, Yüdel, I ask you: *Why,* because one wants to bestrew himself with Palestinian earth after death, is one an orthodox Jew; and when one desires to give oneself wholly to Palestine in life, should one be 'one of them'? Now I ask you—all those Palestinian Jews who came to me with their bags of sand, and were my very good friends, and full of anxiety to preserve my body after death, why have they turned against me on hearing that I wished for a bit of Palestinian earth while I live? Why are they all so interested and such good brothers to the dead, and such bloodthirsty enemies to the living? Why, because I wish to provide for my sad existence, have they noised abroad that I am a missionary, and made up tales against me? Why? I ask you, why, Yüdel, why?"

"You ask me? How should I know? I only know that ever since Palestine was Palestine, people have gone there to die—that I know; but all this ploughing, sowing, and planting the earth, I never heard of in my life before."

"Yes, Yüdel, you are right, because it has been so for a long time, you think so it has to be—that is the real answer to your questions. But why not think back a little? Why should one only go to Palestine to die? Is not Palestinian earth fit to *live* on? On the contrary, it is some of the very best soil, and when we till it and plant it, we fulfil the precept to restore the Holy Land, and we also work for ourselves, toward the realization of an honest and peaceable life. I won't discuss the matter at length with you to-day. It seems that you have quite forgotten what all the holy books say about Palestine, and what a precept it is to till the soil. And another question, touching what you said about Palestine being only there to go and die in. Tell me, those Palestinian Jews who were so interested in my death, and brought earth from over there to bestrew me—tell me, are they also only there to die? Did you notice how broad and stout they were? Ha? And they, they too, when they heard I wanted to live there, fell upon me like wild animals, filling the world with their cries, and made up the most dreadful stories about me. Well, what do you say, Yüdel? I ask you."

"Do I know?" said Yüdel, with a wave of the hand. "Is my head there to think out things like that? But tell me, I beg, what *is* the good to you of buying land in Palestine and getting into trouble all round?"

"You ask, what is the good to me? I want to live, do you hear? I want to *live!*"

"If you can't live without Palestinian earth, why did you not get some before? Did you never want to live till now?"

"Oh, Yüdel, you are right there. I confess that till now I have lived in a delusion, I thought I was living; but—what is the saying?—so long as the thunder is silent . . . "

"Some thunder has struck you!" interrupted Yüdel, looking compassionately into my face.

"I will put it briefly. You must know, Yüdel, that I have been in business here for quite a long time. I worked faithfully, and my chief was pleased with me. I was esteemed and looked up to, and it never occurred to me that things would change; but bad men could not bear to see me doing so well, and they worked hard against me, till one day the business was taken over by my employer's son; and my enemies profited by the opportunity, to cover me with calumnies from head to foot, spreading reports about me which it makes one shudder to hear. This went on till the chief began to look askance at me. At first I got pin-pricks, malicious hints, then things got worse and worse, and at last they began to push me about, and one day they turned me out of the house, and threw me into a hedge. Presently, when I had reviewed the whole situation, I saw that they could do what they pleased with me. I had no one to rely on, my onetime good friends kept aloof from me, I had lost all worth in their eyes; with some because, as is the way with people, they took no trouble to inquire into the reason of my downfall, but, hearing all that was said against me, concluded that I was in the wrong; others, again, because they wished to be agreeable to my enemies; the rest, for reasons without number. In short, reflecting on all this, I saw the game was lost, and there was no saying what might not happen to me! Hitherto I had borne my troubles patiently, with the courage that is natural to me; but now I feel my courage giving way, and I am in fear lest I should fall in my own eyes, in my own estimation, and get to believe that I am worth nothing. And all this because I must needs resort to *them,* and take all the insults they choose to fling at me, and every outcast has me at his mercy. That is why I want to collect my remaining strength, and buy a parcel of land in Palestine, and, God helping, I will become a bit of a householder—do you understand?"

"Why must it be just in Palestine?"

"Because I may not, and I cannot, buy in anywhere else. I have tried to find a place elsewhere, but they were afraid I was going to get the upper hand, so down they came, and made a wreck of it. Over there I shall be proprietor myself—that is firstly, and secondly, a great many relations of mine are buried there, in the country where they lived and died. And although you count me as 'one of them,' I tell you I think a great deal of 'the merits of the fathers,' and that it is very pleasant to me to think of living in the land that will remind me of such dear forefathers. And although it will be hard at first, the recollection of my ancestors and the thought of providing my children with a corner of their own and honestly earned bread will give me strength, till I shall work my way up to something. And I hope I *will* get to something. Remember, Yüdel, I believe and I hope! You will see, Yüdel—you know that our brothers consider Palestinian earth a charm against being eaten by worms, and you think that I laugh at it? No, I believe in it! It is quite, quite true that my Palestinian earth will preserve me from worms, only not after death, no, but alive—from such worms as devour and gnaw at and poison the whole of life!"

Yüdel scratched his nose, gave a rub to the cap on his head, and uttered a deep sigh.

"Yes, Yüdel, you sigh! Now do you know what I wanted to say to you?"

"Ett!" and Yüdel made a gesture with his hand. "What you have to say to me?—ett!"

"Oi, that 'ett!' of yours! Yüdel, I know it! When you have nothing to answer, and you ought to think, and think something out, you take refuge in 'ett!' Just consider for once, Yüdel, I have a plan for you, too. Remember what you were, and what has become of you. You have been knocking about, driven hither and thither, since childhood. You haven't a house, not a corner, you have become a beggar, a tramp, a nobody, despised and avoided, with unpleasing habits, and living a dog's life. You have very good qualities, a clear head, and acute intelligence. But to what purpose do you put them? You waste your whole intelligence on getting in at backdoors and coaxing a bit of bread out of the maidservant, and the mistress is not to know. Can you not devise a means, with that clever brain of yours, how to earn it for yourself? See here, I am going to buy a bit of ground in Palestine, come with me, Yüdel, and you shall work, and be a man like other men. You are what they call a 'living orphan,' because you have many fathers; and don't forget that you have *one* Father who lives, and who is only waiting for you to grow better. Well, how much longer are you going to live among strangers? Till now you haven't thought, and the life suited you, you have grown used to blows and contumely. But now that—that—none will let you in, your eyes must have been opened to see your condition, and you must have begun to wish to be different. Only begin to wish! You see, I have enough to eat, and yet my position has become hateful to me, because I have lost my value, and am in danger of losing my humanity. But you are hungry, and one of these days you will die of starvation out in the street. Yüdel, do just think it over, for if I am right, you will get to be like other people. Your Father will see that you have turned into a man, he will be reconciled with your mother, and you will be 'a father's child,' as you were before. Brother Yüdel, think it over!"

I talked to my Yüdel a long, long time. In the meanwhile, the night had passed. My Yüdel gave a start, as though waking out of a deep slumber, and went away full of thought.

On opening the window, I was greeted by a friendly smile from the rising morning star, as it peeped out between the clouds.

And it began to dawn.

ISAAC LÖB PEREZ

Born, 1851, in Samoscz, Government of Lublin, Russian Poland; Jewish, philosophical, and general literary education; practiced law in Samoscz, a Hasidic town; clerk to the Jewish congregation in Warsaw and as such collector of statistics on Jewish life; began to write at twenty-five; contributor to Zedernbaum's Jüdisches Volksblatt; publisher and editor of Die jüdische Bibliothek (4 vols.), in which he conducted the scientific department, and wrote all the editorials and book reviews, of Literatur and Leben, and of Yom-tov Blättlech; now (1912) co-editor of Der Freind, Warsaw; Hebrew and Yiddish prose writer and poet; allegorist; collected Hebrew works, 1899-1901; collected Yiddish works, 7 vols., Warsaw and New York, 1909-1912 (in course of publication).

A WOMAN'S WRATH

The small room is dingy as the poverty that clings to its walls. There is a hook fastened to the crumbling ceiling, relic of a departed hanging lamp. The old, peeling stove is girded about with a coarse sack, and leans sideways toward its gloomy neighbor, the black, empty fireplace, in which stands an inverted cooking pot with a chipped rim. Beside it lies a broken spoon, which met its fate in unequal contest with the scrapings of cold, stale porridge.

The room is choked with furniture; there is a four-post bed with torn curtains. The pillows visible through their holes have no covers.

There is a cradle, with the large, yellow head of a sleeping child; a chest with metal fittings and an open padlock—nothing very precious left in there, evidently; further, a table and three chairs (originally painted red), a cupboard, now somewhat damaged. Add to these a pail of clean water and one of dirty water, an oven rake with a shovel, and you will understand that a pin could hardly drop onto the floor.

And yet the room contains *him* and *her* beside.

She, a middle-aged Jewess, sits on the chest that fills the space between the bed and the cradle.

To her right is the one grimy little window, to her left, the table. She is knitting a sock, rocking the cradle with her foot, and listens to *him* reading the Talmud at the table, with a tearful, Wallachian, sing-

ing intonation, and swaying to and fro with a series
of nervous jerks. Some of the words he swallows, others
he draws out; now he snaps at a word, and now he skips
it; some he accentuates and dwells on lovingly, others
he rattles out with indifference, like dried peas out of
a bag. And never quiet for a moment. First he draws
from his pocket a once red and whole handkerchief, and
wipes his nose and brow, then he lets it fall into his
lap, and begins twisting his earlocks or pulling at his
thin, pointed, faintly grizzled beard. Again, he lays
a pulled-out hair from the same between the leaves
of his book, and slaps his knees. His fingers coming
into contact with the handkerchief, they seize it, and
throw a corner in between his teeth; he bites it, lays
one foot across the other, and continually shuffles with
both feet.

All the while his pale forehead wrinkles, now in a
perpendicular, now in a horizontal, direction, when the
long eyebrows are nearly lost below the folds of skin.
At times, apparently, he has a sting in the chest, for he
beats his left side as though he were saying the Al-
Chets. Suddenly he leans his head to the left, presses
a finger against his left nostril, and emits an artificial
sneeze, leans his head to the right, and the proceeding
is repeated. In between he takes a pinch of snuff, pulls
himself together, his voice rings louder, the chair creaks,
the table wobbles.

The child does not wake; the sounds are too familiar
to disturb it.

And she, the wife, shrivelled and shrunk before her
time, sits and drinks in delight. She never takes her

eye off her husband, her ear lets no inflection of his voice escape. Now and then, it is true, she sighs. Were he as fit for *this* world as he is for the *other* world, she would have a good time of it here, too—here, too—

"Ma!" she consoles herself, "who talks of honor? Not every one is worthy of both tables!"

She listens. Her shrivelled face alters from minute to minute; she is nervous, too. A moment ago it was eloquent of delight. Now she remembers it is Thursday, there isn't a dreier to spend in preparation for Sabbath. The light in her face goes out by degrees, the smile fades, then she takes a look through the grimy window, glances at the sun. It must be getting late, and there isn't a spoonful of hot water in the house. The needles pause in her hand, a shadow has overspread her face. She looks at the child, it is sleeping less quietly, and will soon wake. The child is poorly, and there is not a drop of milk for it. The shadow on her face deepens into gloom, the needles tremble and move convulsively.

And when she remembers that it is near Passover, that her ear-rings and the festal candlesticks are at the pawnshop, the chest empty, the lamp sold, then the needles perform murderous antics in her fingers. The gloom on her brow is that of a gathering thunder-storm, lightnings play in her small, grey, sunken eyes.

He sits and "learns," unconscious of the charged atmosphere; does not see her let the sock fall and begin wringing her finger-joints; does not see that her forehead is puckered with misery, one eye closed, and the other fixed on him, her learned husband, with a look fit to send a chill through his every limb; does not see her dry lips tremble and her jaw quiver. She controls herself with all her might, but the storm is gathering fury within her. The least thing, and it will explode.

That least thing has happened.

He was just translating a Talmudic phrase with quiet delight, "And thence we derive that—" He was going on with "three,—" but the word "derive" was enough, it was the lighted spark, and her heart was the gunpowder. It was ablaze in an instant. Her determination gave way, the unlucky word opened the floodgates, and the waters poured through, carrying all before them.

"Derived, you say, derived? O, derived may you be, Lord of the World," she exclaimed, hoarse with anger, "derived may you be! Yes! You!" she hissed like a snake. "Passover coming—Thursday—and the child ill—and not a drop of milk is there. Ha?"

Her breath gives out, her sunken breast heaves, her eyes flash.

He sits like one turned to stone. Then, pale and breathless, too, from fright, he gets up and edges toward the door.

At the door he turns and faces her, and sees that hand and tongue are equally helpless from passion; his eyes grow smaller; he catches a bit of handkerchief between his teeth, retreats a little further, takes a deeper breath, and mutters:

"Listen, woman, do you know what Bittul-Torah means? And not letting a husband study in peace, to be always worrying about livelihood, ha? And who feeds the little birds, tell me? Always this want of faith in God, this giving way to temptation, and taking thought for *this* world . . . foolish, ill-natured woman! Not to let a husband study! If you don't take care, you will go to Gehenna."

Receiving no answer, he grows bolder. Her face gets paler and paler, she trembles more and more violently, and the paler she becomes, and the more she trembles, the steadier his voice, as he goes on:

"Gehenna! Fire! Hanging by the tongue! Four death penalties inflicted by the court!"

She is silent, her face is white as chalk.

He feels that he is doing wrong, that he has no call to be cruel, that he is taking a mean advantage, but he has risen, as it were, to the top, and is boiling over. He cannot help himself.

"Do you know," he threatens her, "what Skiloh means? It means stoning, to throw into a ditch and cover up with stones! Srefoh—burning, that is, pouring a spoonful of boiling lead into the inside! Hereg—beheading, that means they cut off your head with a sword! Like this" (and he passes a hand across his neck). "Then Cheneck—strangling! Do you hear? To strangle! Do you understand? And all four for making light of the Torah! For Bittul-Torah!"

His heart is already sore for his victim, but he is feeling his power over her for the first time, and it has gone to his head. Silly woman! He had never known how easy it was to frighten her.

"That comes of making light of the Torah!" he shouts, and breaks off. After all, she might come to her senses at any moment, and take up the broom! He springs back to the table, closes the Gemoreh, and hurries out of the room.

"I am going to the house-of-study!" he calls out over his shoulder in a milder tone, and shuts the door after him.

The loud voice and the noise of the closing door have waked the sick child. The heavy-lidded eyes open, the waxen face puckers, and there is a peevish wail. But she, beside herself, stands rooted to the spot, and does not hear.

"Ha!" comes hoarsely at last out of her narrow chest. "So that's it, is it? Neither this world nor the other. Hanging, he says, stoning, burning, beheading, strangling, hanging by the tongue, boiling lead poured into the inside, he says—for making light of the Torah— Hanging, ha, ha, ha!" (in desperation). "Yes, I'll hang, but *here, here!* And soon! What is there to wait for?"

The child begins to cry louder; still she does not hear.

"A rope! a rope!" she screams, and stares wildly into every corner.

"Where is there a rope? I wish he mayn't find a bone of me left! Let me be rid of *one* Gehenna at any rate! Let him try it, let him be a mother for once, see how he likes it! I've had enough of it! Let it be an atonement! An end, an end! A rope, a rope!!"

Her last exclamation is like a cry for help from out of a conflagration.

She remembers that they *have* a rope somewhere. Yes, under the stove—the stove was to have been tied round against the winter. The rope must be there still.

She runs and finds the rope, the treasure, looks up at the ceiling—the hook that held the lamp—she need only climb onto the table.

She climbs—

But she sees from the table that the startled child, weak as it is, has sat up in the cradle, and is reaching over the side—it is trying to get out—

"Mame, M-mame," it sobs feebly.

A fresh paroxysm of anger seizes her.

She flings away the rope, jumps off the table, runs to the child, and forces its head back into the pillow, exclaiming:

"Bother the child! It won't even let me hang myself! I can't even hang myself in peace! It wants to suck. What is the good? You will suck nothing but poison, poison, out of me, I tell you!"

"There, then, greedy!" she cries in the same breath, and stuffs her dried-up breast into his mouth.

"There, then, suck away—bite!"

THE TREASURE

To sleep, in summer time, in a room four yards square, together with a wife and eight children, is anything but a pleasure, even on a Friday night—and Shmerel the woodcutter rises from his bed, though only half through with the night, hot and gasping, hastily pours some water over his finger-tips, flings on his dressing-gown, and escapes barefoot from the parched Gehenna of his dwelling. He steps into the street—all quiet, all the shutters closed, and over the sleeping town is a distant, serene, and starry sky. He feels as if he were all alone with God, blessed is He, and he says, looking up at the sky, "Now, Lord of the Universe, now is the time to hear me and to bless me with a treasure out of Thy treasure-house!"

As he says this, he sees something like a little flame coming along out of the town, and he knows, That is it! He is about to pursue it, when he remembers it is Sabbath, when one mustn't turn. So he goes after it walking. And as he walks slowly along, the little flame begins to move slowly, too, so that the distance between them does not increase, though it does not shorten, either. He walks on. Now and then an inward voice calls to him: "Shmerel, don't be a fool! Take off the dressing-gown. Give a jump and throw it over the flame!" But he knows it is the Evil Inclination speaking. He throws off the dressing-gown onto his arm, but to spite the Evil Inclination he takes still smaller steps, and rejoices to see that, as soon as he takes these smaller steps, the little flame moves more slowly, too.

Thus he follows the flame, and follows it, till he gradually finds himself outside the town. The road twists and turns across fields and meadows, and the distance between him and the flame grows no longer, no shorter. Were he to throw the dressing-gown, it would not reach the flame. Meantime the thought revolves in his mind: Were he indeed to become possessed of the treasure, he need no longer be a woodcutter, now, in his later years; he has no longer the strength for the work he had once. He would rent a seat for his wife in the women's Shool, so that her Sabbaths and holidays should not be spoiled by their not allowing her to sit here or to sit there. On New Year's Day and the Day of Atonement it is all she can do to stand through the service. Her many children have exhausted her! And he would order her a new dress, and buy her a few strings of pearls. The children should be sent to better Chedorim, and he would cast about for a match for his eldest girl. As it is, the poor child carries her mother's fruit baskets, and never has time so much as to comb her hair thoroughly, and she has long, long plaits, and eyes like a deer.

"It would be a meritorious act to pounce upon the treasure!"

The Evil Inclination again, he thinks. If it is not to be, well, then it isn't! If it were in the week, he would soon know what to do! Or if his Yainkel were there, he would have had something to say. Children nowadays! Who knows what they don't do on Sabbath, as it is! And the younger one is no better: he makes fun of the teacher in Cheder. When the teacher is about to administer a blow, they pull his beard. And who's going to find time to see after them—chopping and sawing a whole day through.

He sighs and walks on and on, now and then glancing up into the sky: "Lord of the Universe, of whom are you making trial? Shmerel Woodcutter? If you do mean to give me the treasure, *give* it me!" It seems to him that the flame proceeds more slowly, but at this very moment he hears a dog bark, and it has a bark he knows—that is the dog in Vissóke. Vissóke is the first village you come to on leaving the town, and he sees white patches twinkle in the dewy morning atmosphere, those are the Vissóke peasant cottages. Then it occurs to him that he has gone a Sabbath day's journey, and he stops short.

"Yes, I have gone a Sabbath day's journey," he thinks, and says, speaking into the air: "You won't lead me astray! It is *not* a God-send! God does not make sport of us—it is the work of a demon." And he feels a little angry with the thing, and turns and hurries toward the town, thinking: "I won't say anything about it at home, because, first, they won't believe me, and if they do, they'll laugh at me. And what have I done to be proud of? The Creator knows how it was, and that is enough for me. Besides, *she* might be angry, who can tell? The children are certainly naked and barefoot, poor little things! Why should they be made to transgress the command to honor one's father?"

No, he won't breathe a word. He won't even ever remind the Almighty of it. If he really has been good, the Almighty will remember without being told.

And suddenly he is conscious of a strange, lightsome, inward calm, and there is a delicious sensation in his limbs. Money is, after all, dross, riches may even lead a man from the right way, and he feels inclined to thank God for not having brought him into temptation by granting him his wish. He would like, if only—to sing a song! "Our Father, our King" is one he remembers from his early years, but he feels ashamed before himself, and breaks off. He tries to recollect one of the cantor's melodies, a Sinai tune—when suddenly he sees that the identical little flame which he left behind him is once more preceding him, and moving slowly townward, townward, and the distance between them neither increases nor diminishes, as though the flame were taking a walk, and he were taking a walk, just taking a little walk in honor of Sabbath. He is glad in his heart and watches it. The sky pales, the stars begin to go out, the east flushes, a narrow pink stream flows lengthwise over his head, and still the flame flickers onward into the town, enters his own street. There is his house. The door, he sees, is open. Apparently he forgot to shut it. And, lo and behold! the flame goes in, the flame goes in at his own house door! He follows, and sees it disappear beneath the bed. All are asleep. He goes softly up to the bed, stoops down, and sees the flame spinning round underneath it, like a top, always in the same place; takes his dressing-gown, and throws it down under the bed, and covers up the flame. No one hears him, and now a golden morning beam steals in through the chink in the shutter.

He sits down on the bed, and makes a vow not to say a word to anyone till Sabbath is over—not half a word, lest it cause desecration of the Sabbath. *She* could never hold her tongue, and the children certainly not; they would at once want to count the treasure, to know how much there was, and very soon the secret would be out of the house and into the Shool, the house-of-study, and all the streets, and people would talk about his treasure, about luck, and people would not say their prayers, or wash their hands, or say grace, as they should, and he would have led his household and half the town into sin. No, not a whisper! And he stretches himself out on the bed, and pretends to be asleep.

And this was his reward: When, after concluding the Sabbath, he stooped down and lifted up the dressing-gown under the bed, there lay a sack with a million of gulden, an almost endless number—the bed was a large one—and he became one of the richest men in the place.

And he lived happily all the years of his life.

Only, his wife was continually bringing up against him: "Lord of the World, how could a man have such a heart of stone, as to sit a whole summer day and not say a word, not a word, not to his own wife, not one single word! And there was I" (she remembers) "crying over my prayer as I said God of Abraham—and crying *so*— for there wasn't a dreier left in the house."

Then he consoles her, and says with a smile:

"Who knows? Perhaps it was all thanks to your 'God of Abraham' that it went off so well."

IT IS WELL

You ask how it is that I remained a Jew? Whose merit it is?

Not through my own merits nor those of my ancestors. I was a six-year-old Cheder boy, my father a countryman outside Wilna, a householder in a small way.

No, I remained a Jew thanks to the Schpol Grandfather.

How do I come to mention the Schpol Grandfather? What has the Schpol Grandfather to do with it, you ask?

The Schpol Grandfather was no Schpol Grandfather then. He was a young man, suffering exile from home and kindred, wandering with a troop of mendicants from congregation to congregation, from friendly inn to friendly inn, in all respects one of them. What difference his heart may have shown, who knows? And after these journeyman years, the time of revelation had not come even yet. He presented himself to the Rabbinical Board in Wilna, took out a certificate, and became a Shochet in a village. He roamed no more, but remained in the neighborhood of Wilna. The Misnagdim, however, have a wonderful *flair,* and they suspected something, began to worry and calumniate him, and finally they denounced him to the Rabbinical authorities as a transgressor of the Law, of the whole Law! What Misnagdim are capable of, to be sure!

As I said, I was then six years old. He used to come to us to slaughter small cattle, or just to spend the night, and I was very fond of him. Whom else, except my father and mother, should I have loved? I had a teacher, a passionate man, a destroyer of souls, and this other was a kind and genial creature, who made you feel happy if he only looked at you. The calumnies did their work, and they took away his certificate. My teacher must have had a hand in it, because he heard of it before anyone, and the next time the Shochet came, he exclaimed "Apostate!" took him by the scruff of his coat, and bundled him out of the house. It cut me to the heart like a knife, only I was frightened to death of the teacher, and never stirred. But a little later, when the teacher was looking away, I escaped and began to run after the Shochet across the road, which, not far from the house, lost itself in a wood that stretched all the way to Wilna. What exactly I proposed to do to help him, I don't know, but something drove me after the poor Shochet. I wanted to say good-by to him, to have one more look into his nice, kindly eyes.

But I ran and ran, and hurt my feet against the stones in the road, and saw no one. I went to the right, down into the wood, thinking I would rest a little on the soft earth of the wood. I was about to sit down, when I heard a voice (it sounded like his voice) farther on in the wood, half speaking and half singing. I went softly towards the voice, and saw him some way off, where he stood swaying to and fro under a tree. I went up to him—he was reciting the Song of Songs. I look closer and see that the tree under which he stands is different from the other trees. The others are still bare of leaves, and this one is green and in full leaf, it shines like the sun, and stretches its flowery branches over the Shochet's head like a tent. And a quantity of birds hop among the twigs and join in singing the Song of Songs. I am so astonished that I stand there with open mouth and eyes, rooted like the trees.

He ends his chant, the tree is extinguished, the little birds are silent, and he turns to me, and says affectionately:

"Listen, Yüdele,"—Yüdel is my name—"I have a request to make of you."

"Really?" I answer joyfully, and I suppose he wishes me to bring him out some food, and I am ready to run and bring him our whole Sabbath dinner, when he says to me:

"Listen, keep what you saw to yourself."

This sobers me, and I promise seriously and faithfully to hold my tongue.

"Listen again. You are going far away, very far away, and the road is a long road."

I wonder, however should I come to travel so far? And he goes on to say:

"They will knock the Rebbe's Torah out of your head, and you will forget Father and Mother, but see you keep to your name! You are called Yüdel—remain a Jew!"

I am frightened, but cry out from the bottom of my heart:

"Surely! As surely may I live!"

Then, because my own idea clung to me, I added: "Don't you want something to eat?"

And before I finished speaking, he had vanished.

The second week after they fell upon us and led me away as a Cantonist, to be brought up among the Gentiles and turned into a soldier.

Time passed, and I forgot everything, as he had foretold. They knocked it all out of my head.

I served far away, deep in Russia, among snows and terrific frosts, and never set eyes on a Jew. There may have been hidden Jews about, but I knew nothing of them, I knew nothing of Sabbath and festival, nothing of any fast. I forgot everything.

But I held fast to my name!

I did not change my coin.

The more I forgot, the more I was inclined to be quit of my torments and trials—to make an end of them by agreeing to a Christian name, but whenever the bad thought came into my head, he appeared before me, the same Shochet, and I heard his voice say to me, "Keep your name, remain a Jew!"

And I knew for certain that it was no empty dream, because every time I saw him *older* and *older,* his beard and earlocks greyer, his face paler. Only his eyes remained the same kind eyes, and his voice, which sounded like a violin, never altered.

Once they flogged me, and he stood by and wiped the cold sweat off my forehead, and stroked my face, and said softly: "Don't cry out! We ought to suffer! Remain a Jew," and I bore it without a cry, without a moan, as though they had been flogging *not*-me.

Once, during the last year, I had to go as a sentry to a public house behind the town. It was evening, and there was a snow-storm. The wind lifted patches of snow, and ground them to needles, rubbed them to dust, and this snow-dust and these snow-needles were whirled through the air, flew into one's face and pricked—you couldn't keep an eye open, you couldn't draw your breath! Suddenly I saw some people walking past me, not far away, and one of them said in Yiddish, "This is the first night of Passover." Whether it was a voice from God, or whether some people really passed me, to this day I don't know, but the words fell upon my heart like lead, and I had hardly reached the tavern and begun to walk up and down, when a longing came over me, a sort of heartache, that is not to be described. I wanted to recite the Haggadah, and not a word of it could I recall! Not even the Four Questions I used to ask my father. I felt it all lay somewhere deep down in my heart. I used to know so much of it, when I was only six years old. I felt, if only I could have recalled one simple word, the rest would have followed and risen out of my memory one after the other, like sleepy birds from beneath the snow. But that one first word is just what I cannot remember! Lord of the Universe, I cried fervently, one word, only one word! As it seems, I made my prayer in a happy hour, for "we were slaves" came into my head just as if it had been thrown down from Heaven. I was overjoyed! I was so full of joy that I felt it brimming over. And then the rest all came back to me, and as I paced up and down on my watch, with my musket on my shoulder, I recited and sang the Haggadah to the snowy world around. I drew it out of me, word after word, like a chain of golden links, like a string of pearls. O, but you won't understand, you couldn't understand, unless you had been taken away there, too!

The wind, meanwhile, had fallen, the snow-storm had come to an end, and there appeared a clear, twinkling sky, and a shining world of diamonds. It was silent all round, and ever so wide, and ever so white, with a sweet, peaceful, endless whiteness. And over this calm, wide, whiteness, there suddenly appeared something still whiter, and lighter, and brighter, wrapped in a robe and a prayer-scarf, the prayer-scarf over its shoulders, and over the prayer-scarf, in front, a silvery white beard; and above the beard, two shining eyes, and above them, a sparkling crown, a cap with gold and silver ornaments. And it came nearer and nearer, and went past me, but as it passed me it said:

"It is well!"

It sounded like a violin, and then the figure vanished.

But it was the same eyes, the same voice.

I took Schpol on my way home, and went to see the Old Man, for the Rebbe of Schpol was called by the people Der Alter, the "Schpol Grandfather."

And I recognized him again, and he recognized me!

WHENCE A PROVERB

"Drunk all the year round, sober at Purim," is a Jewish proverb, and people ought to know whence it comes.

In the days of the famous scholar, Reb Chayyim Vital, there lived in Safed, in Palestine, a young man who (not of us be it spoken!) had not been married a year before he became a widower. God's ways are not to be understood. Such things will happen. But the young man was of the opinion that the world, in as far as he was concerned, had come to an end; that, as there is one sun in heaven, so his wife had been the one woman in the world. So he went and sold all the merchandise in his little shop and all the furniture of his room, and gave the proceeds to the head of the Safed Academy, the Rosh ha-Yeshiveh, on condition that he should be taken into the Yeshiveh and fed with the other scholars, and that he should have a room to himself, where he might sit and learn Torah.

The Rosh ha-Yeshiveh took the money for the Academy, and they partitioned off a little room for the young man with some boards, in a corner of the attic of the house-of-study. They carried in a sack with straw, and vessels for washing, and the young man sat himself down to the Talmud. Except on Sabbaths and holidays, when the householders invited him to dinner, he never set eyes on a living creature. Food sufficient for the day, and a clean shirt in honor of Sabbaths and festivals, were carried up to him by the beadle, and whenever he heard steps on the stair, he used to turn away, and stand with his face to the wall, till whoever it was had gone out again and shut the door.

In a word, he became a Porush, for he lived separate from the world.

At first people thought he wouldn't persevere long, because he was a lively youth by nature; but as week after week went by, and the Porush sat and studied, and the tearful voice in which he intoned the Gemoreh was heard in the street half through the night, or else he was seen at the attic window, his pale face raised towards the sky, then they began to believe in him, and they hoped he might in time become a mighty man in Israel, and perhaps even a wonderworker. They said so to the Rebbe, Chayyim Vital, but he listened, shook his head, and replied, "God grant it may last."

Meantime a little "wonder" really happened. The beadle's little daughter, who used sometimes to carry up the Porush's food for her father, took it into her head that she must have one look at the Porush. What does she? Takes off her shoes and stockings, and carries the food to him barefoot, so noiselessly that she heard her own heart beat. But the beating of her heart frightened her so much that she fell down half the stairs, and was laid up for more than a month in consequence. In her fever she told the whole story, and people began to believe in the Porush more firmly than ever and to wait with increasing impatience till he should become famous.

They described the occurrence to Reb Chayyim Vital, and again he shook his head, and even sighed, and

answered, "God grant he may be victorious!" And
when they pressed him for an explanation of these
words, Reb Chayyim answered, that as the Porush had
left the world, not so much for the sake of Heaven as
on account of his grief for his wife, it was to be feared
that he would be sorely beset and tempted by the
"Other Side," and God grant he might not stumble and
fall.

And Reb Chayyim Vital never spoke without good
reason!

One day the Porush was sitting deep in a book, when
he heard something tapping at the door, and fear came
over him. But as the tapping went on, he rose, forgetting to close his book, went and opened the door—and in
walks a turkey. He lets it in, for it occurs to him that
it would be nice to have a living thing in the room. The
turkey walks past him, and goes and settles down quietly
in a corner. And the Porush wonders what this may
mean, and sits down again to his book. Sitting there,
he remembers that it is going on for Purim. Has someone sent him a turkey out of regard for his study of the
Torah? What shall he do with the turkey? Should
anyone, he reflects, ask him to dinner, supposing it were
to be a poor man, he would send him the turkey on the
eve of Purim, and then he would satisfy himself with
it also. He has not once tasted fowl-meat since he lost
his wife. Thinking thus, he smacked his lips, and his
mouth watered. He threw a glance at the turkey, and
saw it looking at him in a friendly way, as though it
had quite understood his intention, and was very glad to

think it should have the honor of being eaten by a Porush. He could not restrain himself, but was continually lifting his eyes from his book to look at the turkey, till at last he began to fancy the turkey was smiling at him. This startled him a little, but all the same it made him happy to be smiled at by a living creature.

The same thing happened at Minchah and Maariv. In the middle of the Eighteen Benedictions, he could not for the life of him help looking round every minute at the turkey, who continued to smile and smile. Suddenly it seemed to him, he knew that smile well—the Almighty, who had taken back his wife, had now sent him her smile to comfort him in his loneliness, and he began to love the turkey. He thought how much better it would be, if a *rich* man were to invite him at Purim, so that the turkey might live.

And he thought it in a propitious moment, as we shall presently see, but meantime they brought him, as usual, a platter of groats with a piece of bread, and he washed his hands, and prepared to eat.

No sooner, however, had he taken the bread into his hand, and was about to bite into it, than the turkey moved out of its corner, and began peck, peck, peck, towards the bread, by way of asking for some, and as though to say it was hungry, too, and came and stood before him near the table. The Porush thought, "He'd better have some, I don't want to be unkind to him, to tease him," and he took the bread and the platter of porridge, and set it down on the floor before the turkey, who pecked and supped away to its heart's content.

Next day the Porush went over to the Rosh ha-Yeshiveh, and told him how he had come to have a fellow-lodger; he used always to leave some porridge over, and to-day he didn't seem to have had enough. The Rosh ha-Yeshiveh saw a hungry face before him. He said he would tell this to the Rebbe, Chayyim Vital, so that he might pray, and the evil spirit, if such indeed it was, might depart. Meantime he would give orders for two pieces of bread and two plates of porridge to be taken up to the attic, so that there should be enough for both, the Porush and the turkey. Reb Chayyim Vital, however, to whom the story was told in the name of the Rosh ha-Yeshiveh, shook his head, and declared with a deep sigh that this was only the beginning!

Meanwhile the Porush received a double portion and was satisfied, and the turkey was satisfied, too. The turkey even grew fat. And in a couple of weeks or so the Porush had become so much attached to the turkey that he prayed every day to be invited for Purim by a *rich* man, so that he might not be tempted to destroy it.

And, as we intimated, *that* temptation, anyhow, was spared him, for he was invited to dinner by one of the principal householders in the place, and there was not only turkey, but every kind of tasty dish, and wine fit for a king. And the best Purim-players came to entertain the rich man, his family, and the guests who had come to him after their feast at home. And our Porush gave himself up to enjoyment, and ate and drank. Perhaps he even drank rather more than he ate, for the wine was sweet and grateful to the taste, and the warmth of it made its way into every limb.

6

Then suddenly a change came over him.

The Ahasuerus-Esther play had begun. Vashti will not do the king's pleasure and come in to the banquet as God made her. Esther soon finds favor in her stead, she is given over to Hegai, the keeper of the women, to be purified, six months with oil of myrrh and six months with other sweet perfumes. And our Porush grew hot all over, and it was dark before his eyes; then red streaks flew across his field of vision, like tongues of fire, and he was overcome by a strange, wild longing to be back at home, in the attic of the house-of-study— a longing for his own little room, his quiet corner, a longing for the turkey, and he couldn't bear it, and even before they had said grace he jumped up and ran away home.

He enters his room, looks into the corner habitually occupied by the turkey, and stands amazed—the turkey has turned into a woman, a most beautiful woman, such as the world never saw, and he begins to tremble all over. And she comes up to him, and takes him around the neck with her warm, white, naked arms, and the Porush trembles more and more, and begs, "Not here, not here! It is a holy place, there are holy books lying about." Then she whispers into his ear that she is the Queen of Sheba, that she lives not far from the house-of-study, by the river, among the tall reeds, in a palace of crystal, given her by King Solomon. And she draws him along, she wants him to go with her to her palace.

And he hesitates and resists—and he goes.

Next day, there was no turkey, and no Porush, either!

They went to Reb Chayyim Vital, who told them to look for him along the bank of the river, and they found him in a swamp among the tall reeds, more dead than alive.

They rescued him and brought him round, but from that day he took to drink.

And Reb Chayyim Vital said, it all came from his great longing for the Queen of Sheba, that when he drank, he saw her; and they were to let him drink, only not at Purim, because at that time she would have great power over him.

Hence the proverb, "Drunk all the year round, sober at Purim."

MORDECAI SPEKTOR

Born, 1859, in Uman, Government of Kieff, Little Russia; education Hasidic; entered business in 1878; wrote first sketch, A Roman ohn Liebe, in 1882; contributor to Zedernbaum's Jüdisches Volksblatt, 1884-1887; founded, in 1888, and edited Der Hausfreund, at Warsaw; editor of Warsaw daily papers, Unser Leben, and (at present, 1912) Dos neie Leben; writer of novels, historical romances, and sketches in Yiddish; contributor to numerous periodicals; compiled a volume of more than two thousand Jewish proverbs.

AN ORIGINAL STRIKE

I was invited to a wedding.

Not a wedding at which ladies wore low dress, and scattered powder as they walked, and the men were in frock-coats and white gloves, and had waxed moustaches.

Not a wedding where you ate of dishes with outlandish names, according to a printed card, and drank wine dating, according to the label, from the reign of King Sobieski, out of bottles dingy with the dust of yesterday.

No, but a Jewish wedding, where the men, women, and girls wore the Sabbath and holiday garments in which they went to Shool; a wedding where you whet your appetite with sweet-cakes and apple-tart, and sit down to Sabbath fish, with fresh rolls, golden soup, stuffed fowl, and roast duck, and the wine is in large, clear, white bottles; a wedding with a calling to the Reading of the Torah of the bridegroom, a party on the Sabbath preceding the wedding, a good-night-play performed by the musicians, and a bridegroom's-dinner in his native town, with a table spread for the poor.

Reb Yitzchok-Aizik Berkover had made a feast for the poor at the wedding of each of his children, and now, on the occasion of the marriage of his youngest daughter, he had invited all the poor of the little town Lipovietz to his village home, where he had spent all his life.

It is the day of the ceremony under the canopy, two o'clock in the afternoon, and the poor, sent for early in the morning by a messenger, with the three great wagons, are not there. Lipovietz is not more than five versts away—what can have happened? The parents of the bridal couple and the assembled guests wait to proceed with the ceremony.

At last the messenger comes riding on a horse unharnessed from his vehicle, but no poor.

"Why have you come back alone?" demands Reb Yitzchok-Aizik."

"They won't come!" replies the messenger.

"What do you mean by 'they won't come'?" asked everyone in surprise.

"They say that unless they are given a kerbel apiece, they won't come to the wedding."

All laugh, and the messenger goes on:

"There was a wedding with a dinner to the poor in Lipovietz to-day, too, and they have eaten and drunk all they can, and now they've gone on strike, and declare that unless they are promised a kerbel a head, they won't move from the spot. The strike leaders are the Crooked Man with two crutches, Mekabbel the Long, Feitel the Stammerer, and Yainkel Fonfatch; the others would perhaps have come, but these won't let them. So I didn't know what to do. I argued a whole hour, and got nothing by it, so then I unharnessed a horse, and came at full speed to know what was to be done."

We of the company could not stop laughing, but Reb Yitzchok-Aizik was very angry.

"Well, and you bargained with them? Won't they come for less? he asked the messenger.

"Yes, I bargained, and they won't take a kopek less."

"Have their prices gone up so high as all that?" exclaimed Reb Yitzchok-Aizik, with a satirical laugh. "Why did you leave the wagons? We shall do without the tramps, that's all!"

"How could I tell? I didn't know what to do. I was afraid you would be displeased. Now I'll go and fetch the wagons back."

"Wait! Don't be in such a hurry, take time!"

Reb Yitzchok-Aizik began consulting with the company and with himself.

"What an idea! Who ever heard of such a thing? Poor people telling me what to do, haggling with me over my wanting to give them a good dinner and a nice present each, and saying they must be paid in rubles, otherwise it's no bargain, ha! ha! For two guldens each it's not worth their while? It cost them too much to stock the ware? Thirty kopeks wouldn't pay them? I like their impertinence! Mischief take them, I shall do without them!

"Let the musicians play! Where is the beadle? They can begin putting the veil on the bride."

But directly afterwards he waved his hands.

"Wait a little longer. It is still early. Why should it happen to *me,* why should my pleasure be spoilt? Now I've got to marry my youngest daughter without a dinner to the poor! I would have given them half a ruble each, it's not the money I mind, but fancy bargaining with me! Well, there, I have done my part, and if they won't come, I'm sure they're not wanted; afterwards they'll be sorry; they don't get a wedding like this every day. We shall do without them."

"Well, can they put the veil on the bride?" the beadle came and inquired.

"Yes, they can. . . No, tell them to wait a little longer!"

Nearly all the guests, who were tired of waiting, cried out that the tramps could very well be missed.

Reb Yitzchok-Aizik's face suddenly assumed another expression, the anger vanished, and he turned to me and a couple of other friends, and asked if we would drive to the town, and parley with the revolted almsgatherers.

"He has no brains, one can't depend on him," he said, referring to the messenger.

A horse was harnessed to a conveyance, and we drove off, followed by the mounted messenger.

"A revolt—a strike of almsgatherers, how do you like that?" we asked one another all the way. We had heard of workmen striking, refusing to work except for a higher wage, and so forth, but a strike of paupers— paupers insisting on larger alms as pay for eating a free dinner, such a thing had never been known.

In twenty minutes time we drove into Lipovietz.

In the market-place, in the centre of the town, stood the three great peasant wagons, furnished with fresh straw. The small horses were standing unharnessed, eating out of their nose-bags; round the wagons were a hundred poor folk, some dumb, others lame, the greater part blind, and half the town urchins with as many men.

All of them were shouting and making a commotion.

The Crooked One sat on a wagon, and banged it with his crutches; Long Mekabbel, with a red plaster on his neck, stood beside him.

These two leaders of the revolt were addressing the people, the meek of the earth.

"Ha, ha!" exclaimed Long Mekabbel, as he caught sight of us and the messenger, "they have come to beg our acceptance!"

"To beg our acceptance!" shouted the Crooked One, and banged his crutch.

"Why won't you come to the wedding, to the dinner?" we inquired. "Everyone will be given alms."

"How much?" they asked all together.

"We don't know, but you will take what they offer."

"Will they give it us in kerblech? Because, if not, we don't go."

"There will be a hole in the sky if you don't go," cried some of the urchins present.

The almsgatherers threw themselves on the urchins with their sticks, and there was a bit of a row.

Mekabbel the Long, standing on the cart, drew himself to his full height, and began to shout:

"Hush, hush, hush! Quiet, you crazy cripples! One can't hear oneself speak! Let us hear what those have to say who are worth listening to!" and he turned to us with the words:

"You must know, dear Jews, that unless they distribute kerblech among us, we shall not budge. Never you fear! Reb Yitzchok-Aizik won't marry his youngest daughter without us, and where is he to get others of us now? To send to Lunetz would cost him more in conveyances, and he would have to put off the marriage."

"What do they suppose? That because we are poor people they can do what they please with us?" and a new striker hitched himself up by the wheel, blind of one eye, with a tied-up jaw. No one can oblige us to go, even the chief of police and the governor cannot force us—either it's kerblech, or we stay where we are."

"K-ke-kkerb-kkerb-lech!!" came from Feitel the Stammerer.

"Nienblech!" put in Yainkel Fonfatch, speaking through his small nose. "No, more!" called out a couple of merry paupers.

"Kerblech, kerblech!" shouted the rest in concert.

And through their shouting and their speeches sounded such a note of anger and of triumph, it seemed as though they were pouring out all the bitterness of soul collected in the course of their sad and luckless lives.

They had always kept silence, had *had* to keep silence, *had* to swallow the insults offered them along with the farthings, and the dry bread, and the scraped bones, and this was the first time they had been able to retaliate, the first time they had known how it felt to be entreated by the fortunate in all things, and they were determined to use their opportunity of asserting themselves to the full, to take their revenge. In the word kerblech lay the whole sting of their resentment.

And while we talked and reasoned with them, came a second messenger from Reb Yitzchok-Aizik, to say that the paupers were to come at once, and they would be given a ruble each.

There was a great noise and scrambling, the three wagons filled with almsgatherers, one crying out, "O my bad hand!" another, "O my foot!" and a third, "O my poor bones!" The merry ones made antics, and sang in their places, while the horses were put in, and the procession started at a cheerful trot. The urchins gave a great hurrah, and threw little stones after it, with squeals and whistles.

The poor folks must have fancied they were being pelted with flowers and sent off with songs, they looked so happy in the consciousness of their victory.

For the first and perhaps the last time in their lives, they had spoken out, and got their own way.

After the "canopy" and the chicken soup, that is, at "supper," tables were spread for the friends of the family and separate ones for the almsgatherers.

Reb Yitzchok-Aizik and the members of his own household served the poor with their own hands, pressing them to eat and drink.

"Le-Chayyim to you, Reb Yitzchok-Aizik! May you have pleasure in your children, and be a great man, a great rich man!" desired the poor.

"Long life, long life to all of you, brethren! Drink in health, God help All-Israel, and you among them!" replied Reb Yitzchok-Aizik.

After supper the band played, and the almsgatherers, with Reb Yitzchok-Aizik, danced merrily in a ring round the bridegroom.

Then who was so happy as Reb Yitzchok-Aizik? He danced in the ring, the silk skirts of his long coat flapped and flew like eagles' wings, tears of joy fell from his shining eyes, and his spirits rose to the seventh heaven.

He laughed and cried like a child, and exchanged embraces with the almsgatherers.

"Brothers!" he exclaimed as he danced, "let us be merry, let us be Jews! Musicians, give us something cheerful—something gayer, livelier, louder!"

"This is what you call a Jewish wedding!"

"This is how a Jew makes merry!"

So the guests and the almsgatherers clapped their hands in time to the music.

Yes, dear readers, it *was* what I call a Jewish Wedding!

A GLOOMY WEDDING

They handed Gittel a letter that had come by post, she put on her spectacles, sat down by the window, and began to read.

She read, and her face began to shine, and the wrinkled skin took on a little color. It was plain that what she read delighted her beyond measure, she devoured the words, caught her breath, and wept aloud in the fulness of her joy.

"At last, at last! Blessed be His dear Name, whom I am not worthy to mention! I do not know, Gottinyu, how to thank Thee for the mercy Thou hast shown me. Beile! Where is Beile? Where is Yossel? Children! Come, make haste and wish me joy, a great joy has befallen us! Send for Avremele, tell him to come with Zlatke and all the children."

Thus Gittel, while she read the letter, never ceased calling every one into the room, never ceased reading and calling, calling and reading, and devouring the words as she read.

Every soul who happened to be at home came running.

"Good luck to you! Good luck to us all! Moishehle has become engaged in Warsaw, and invites us all to the wedding," Gittel explained. "There, read the letter, Lord of the World, may it be in a propitious hour, may we all have comfort in one another, may we hear nothing but good news of one another and of All-Israel! Read it, read it, children! He writes that he has a very beautiful bride, well-favored, with a large dowry. Lord of the World, I am not worthy of the mercy Thou hast shown me !" repeated Gittel over and over, as she paced the room with uplifted hands, while her daughter Beile took up the letter in her turn. The children and everyone in the house, including the maid from the kitchen, with rolled-up sleeves and wet hands, encircled Beile as she read aloud.

"Read louder, Beiletshke, so that I can hear, so that we can all hear," begged Gittel, and there were tears of happiness in her eyes.

The children jumped for joy to see Grandmother so happy. The word "wedding," which Beile read out of the letter, contained a promise of all delightful things: musicians, pancakes, new frocks and suits, and they could not keep themselves from dancing. The maid, too, was heartily pleased, she kept on singing out, "Oi, what a bride, beautiful as gold !" and did not know what to be doing next—should she go and finish cooking the dinner, or should she pull down her sleeves and make holiday ?

The hiss of a pot boiling over in the kitchen interrupted the letter-reading, and she was requested to go and attend to it forthwith.

"The bride sends us a separate greeting, long life to her, may she live when my bones are dust. Let us go to the provisor, he shall read it; it is written in French."

The provisor, the apothecary's foreman, who lived in the same house, said the bride's letter was not written in French, but in Polish, that she called Gittel her second mother, that she loved her son Moses as her life, that he was her world, that she held herself to be the most fortunate of girls, since God had given her Moses, that Gittel (once more!) was her second mother, and she felt like a dutiful daughter towards her, and hoped that Gittel would love her as her own child.

The bride declared further that she kissed her new sister, Beile, a thousand times, together with Zlatke and their husbands and children, and she signed herself "Your forever devoted and loving daughter Regina."

An hour later all Gittel's children were assembled round her, her eldest son Avremel with his wife, Zlatke and her little ones, Beile's husband, and her son-in-law Yossel. All read the letter with eager curiosity, brandy and spice-cakes were placed on the table, wine was sent for, they drank healths, wished each other joy, and began to talk of going to the wedding.

Gittel, very tired with all she had gone through this day, went to lie down for a while to rest her head, which was all in a whirl, but the others remained sitting at the table, and never stopped talking of Moisheh.

"I can imagine the sort of engagement Moisheh has made, begging his pardon," remarked the daughter-in-law, and wiped her pale lips.

"I should think so, a man who's been a bachelor up to thirty! It's easy to fancy the sort of bride, and the sort of family she has, if they accepted Moisheh as a suitor," agreed the daughter.

"God helping, this ought to make a man of him," sighed Moisheh's elder brother, "he's cost us trouble and worry enough."

"It's your fault," Yossel told him. "If I'd been his elder brother, he would have turned out differently! I should have directed him like a father, and taken him well in hand."

7

"You think so, but when God wishes to punish a man through his own child going astray, nothing is of any use; these are not the old times, when young people feared a Rebbe, and respected their elders. Nowadays the world is topsyturvy, and no sooner has a boy outgrown his childhood than he does what he pleases, and parents are nowhere. What have I left undone to make something out of him, so that he should be a credit to his family? Then, he was left an orphan very early; perhaps he would have obeyed his father (may he enter a lightsome paradise!), but for a brother and his mother, he paid them as much attention as last year's snow, and, if you said anything to him, he answered rudely, and neither coaxing nor scolding was any good. Now, please God, he'll make a fresh start, and give up his antics before it's too late. His poor mother! She's had trouble enough on his account, as we all know."

Beile let fall a tear and said:

"If our father (may he be our kind advocate!) were alive, Moishehle would never have made an engagement like this. Who knows what sort of connections they will be! I can see them, begging his pardon, from here! Is he likely to have asked anyone's advice? He always had a will of his own—did what he wanted to do, never asked his mother, or his sister, or his brother, beforehand. Now he's a bridegroom at thirty if he's a day, and we are all asked to the wedding, are we really? And we shall soon all be running to see the fine sight, such as never was seen before. We are no such fools! He thinks *himself* the clever one now! So he wants us to be at the wedding? Only says it out of politeness."

"We must go, all the same," said Avremel.

"Go and welcome, if you want to—you won't catch _me_ there," answered his sister.

There was a deal more discussion and disputing about not going to the wedding, and only congratulating by telegram, for good manners' sake. Since he had asked no one's advice, and engaged himself without them, let him get married without them, too!

Gittel, up in her bedroom, could not so soon compose herself after the events of the day. What she had experienced was no trifle. Moishehle engaged to be married! She had been through so much on his account in the course of her life, she had loved him, her youngest born, so dearly! He was such a beautiful child that the light of his countenance dazzled you, and bright as the day, so that people opened ears and mouth to hear him talk, and God and men alike envied her the possession of such a boy.

"I counted on making a match for him, as I did with Avremel before him. He was offered the best connections, with the families of the greatest Rabbis. But, no—no—he wanted to go on studying. 'Study here, study there,' said I, 'sixteen years old and a bachelor! If you want to study, can't you study at your father-in-law's, eating Köst? There are books in plenty, thank Heaven, of your father's.' No, no, he wanted to go and study elsewhere, asked nobody's advice, and made off, and for two months I never had a line. I nearly went out of my mind. Then, suddenly, there came a letter, begging my pardon for not having said good-by, and would I forgive him, and send him some money, because he had nothing to eat. It tore my heart to think my Moishehle, who used to make me happy whenever he enjoyed a meal, should hunger. I sent him some money, I went on sending him money for three years, after that he stopped asking for it. I begged him to come home, he made no reply. 'I don't wish to quarrel with Avremel, my sister, and her husband,' he wrote later, 'we cannot live together in peace.' Why? I don't know! Then, for a time, he left off writing altogether, and the messages we got from him sounded very sad. Now he was in Kieff, now in Odessa, now in Charkoff, and they told us he was living like any Gentile, had not the look of a Jew at all. Some said he was living with a Gentile woman, a countess, and would never marry in his life."

Five years ago he had suddenly appeared at home, "to see his mother," as he said. Gittel did not recognize him, he was so changed. The rest found him quite the stranger: he had a "goyish" shaven face, with a twisted moustache, and was got up like a rich Gentile, with a purse full of bank-notes. His family were ashamed to walk abroad with him, Gittel never ceased weeping and imploring him to give up the countess, remain a Jew, stay with his mother, and she, with God's help, would make an excellent match for him, if he would only alter his appearance and ways just a little. Moishehle solemnly assured his mother that he was a Jew, that there was no countess, but that he wouldn't remain at home for a million rubles, first, because he had business elsewhere, and secondly, he had no fancy for his native town, there was nothing there for him to do, and to dispute with his brother and sister about religious piety was not worth his while.

So Moishehle departed, and Gittel wept, wondering why he was different from the other children, seeing they all had the same mother, and she had lived and suffered for all alike. Why would he not stay with her at home? What would he have wanted for there? God be praised, not to sin with her tongue, thanks to God first, and then to *him* (a lightsome paradise be his!), they were provided for, with a house and a few thousand rubles, all that was necessary for their comfort, and a little ready money besides. The house alone, not to sin with her tongue, would bring in enough to make a living. Other people envy us, but it doesn't happen to please him, and he goes wandering about the world—without a wife and without a home—a man twenty and odd years old, and without a home!

The rest of the family were secretly well content to be free of such a poor creature—"the further off, the better—the shame is less."

A letter from him came very seldom after this, and for the last two years he had dropped out altogether. Nobody was surprised, for everyone was convinced that Moisheh would never come to anything. Some told that he was in prison, others knew that he had gone abroad and was being pursued, others, that he had hung himself because he was tired of life, and that before his death he had repented of all his sins, only it was too late.

His relations heard all these reports, and were careful to keep them from his mother, because they were not sure that the bad news was true.

Gittel bore the pain at her heart in silence, weeping at times over her Moishehle, who had got into bad ways—and now, suddenly, this precious letter with its precious news: Her Moishehle is about to marry, and invites them to the wedding!

Thus Gittel, lying in bed in her own room, recalled everything she had suffered through her undutiful son, only now—now everything was forgotten and forgiven, and her mother's heart was full of love for her Moishehle, just as in the days when he toddled about at her apron, and pleased his mother and everyone else.

All her thoughts were now taken up with getting ready to attend the wedding; the time was so short—there were only three weeks left. When her other children were married, Gittel began her preparations three months ahead, and now there were only three weeks.

Next day she took out her watered silk dress, with the green satin flowers, and hung it up to air, examined it, lest there should be a hook missing. After that she polished her long ear-rings with chalk, her pearls, her rings, and all her other ornaments, and bought a new yellow silk kerchief for her head, with a large flowery pattern in a lighter shade.

A week before the journey to Warsaw they baked spice-cakes, pancakes, and almond-rolls to take with her, "from the bridegroom's side," and ordered a wig for the bride. When her eldest son was married, Gittel had also given the bride silver candlesticks for Friday evenings, and presented her with a wig for the Veiling Ceremony.

And before she left, Gittel went to her husband's grave, and asked him to be present at the wedding as a good advocate for the newly-married pair.

Gittel started for Warsaw in grand style, and cheerful and happy, as befits a mother going to the wedding of her favorite son. All those who accompanied her to the station declared that she looked younger and prettier by twenty years, and made a beautiful bridegroom's mother.

Besides wedding presents for the bride, Gittel took with her money for wedding expenses, so that she might play her part with becoming lavishness, and people should not think her Moishehle came, bless and preserve us, of a low-born family—to show that he was none so forlorn but he had, God be praised and may it be for a hundred and twenty years to come! a mother, and a sister, and brothers, and came of a well-to-do family. She would show them that she could be as fine a bridegroom's mother as anyone, even, thank God, in Warsaw. Moishehle was her last child, and she grudged him nothing. Were *he* (may he be a good intercessor!) alive, he would certainly have graced the wedding better, and spent more money, but she would spare nothing to make a good figure on the occasion. She would treat every connection of the bride to a special dance-tune, give the musicians a whole five-ruble-piece for their performance of the Vivat, and two dreierlech for the Kosher-Tanz, beside something for the Rav, the cantor, and the beadle, and alms for the poor—what should she save for? She has no more children to marry off —blessed be His dear Name, who had granted her life to see her Moishehle's wedding!

Thus happily did Gittel start for Warsaw.

One carriage after another drove up to the wedding-reception room in Dluga Street, Warsaw, ladies and their daughters, all in evening dress, and smartly attired gentlemen, alighted and went in.

The room was full, the band played, ladies and gentlemen were dancing, and those who were not, talked of the bride and bridegroom, and said how fortunate they considered Regina, to have secured such a presentable young man, lively, educated, and intelligent, with quite a fortune, which he had made himself, and a good business. Ten thousand rubles dowry with the perfection of a husband was a rare thing nowadays, when a poor professional man, a little doctor without practice, asked fifteen thousand. It was true, they said, that Regina was a pretty girl and a credit to her parents, but how many pretty, bright girls had more money than Regina, and sat waiting?

It was above all the mothers of the young ladies present who talked low in this way among themselves.

The bride sat on a chair at the end of the room, ladies and young girls on either side of her; Gittel, the bridegroom's mother in her watered silk dress, with the large green satin flowers, was seated between two ladies with dresses cut so low that Gittel could not bear to look at them—women with husbands and children daring to show themselves like that at a wedding! Then she could not endure the odor of their bare skin, the powder, pomade, and perfumes with which they were smeared, sprinkled, and wetted, even to their hair. All these strange smells tickled Gittel's nose, and went to her

head like a fume. She sat between the two ladies, feeling
cramped and shut in, unable to stir, and would gladly
have gone away. Only whither? Where should she, the
bridegroom's mother, be sitting, if not near the bride,
at the upper end of the room? But all the ladies sitting
there are half-naked. Should she sit near the door?
That would never do. And Gittel remained sitting, in
great embarrassment, between the two women, and
looked on at the reception, and saw nothing but a room
full of *decolletées,* ladies and girls.

Gittel felt more and more uncomfortable, it made her
quite faint to look at them.

"One can get over the girls, young things, because a
girl has got to please, although no Jewish daughter ought
to show herself to everyone like that, but what are
you to do with present-day children, especially in a
dissolute city like Warsaw? But young women, and
women who have husbands and children, and no need,
thank God, to please anyone, how are they not ashamed
before God and other people and their own children,
to come to a wedding half-naked, like loose girls in a
public house? Jewish daughters, who ought not to be
seen uncovered by the four walls of their room, to come
like that to a wedding! To a Jewish wedding! . . .
Tpfu, tpfu, I'd like to spit at this newfangled world,
may God not punish me for these words! It is enough
to make one faint to see such a display among Jews!"

After the ceremony under the canopy, which was
erected in the centre of the room, the company sat down
to the table, and Gittel was again seated at the top,
between the two women before mentioned, whose perfumes went to her head.

She felt so queer and so ill at ease that she could not partake of the dinner, her mouth seemed locked, and the tears came in her eyes.

When they rose from table, Gittel sought out a place removed from the "upper end," and sat down in a window, but presently the bride's mother, also in *decolleté,* caught sight of her, and went and took her by the hand.

"Why are you sitting here, Mechuteneste? Why are you not at the top?"

"I wanted to rest myself a little."

"Oh, no, no, come and sit there," said the lady, led her away by force, and seated her between the two ladies with the perfumes.

Long, long did she sit, feeling more and more sick and dizzy. If only she could have poured out her heart to some one person, if she could have exchanged a single word with anybody during that whole evening, it would have been a relief, but there was no one to speak to. The music played, there was dancing, but Gittel could see nothing more. She felt an oppression at her heart, and became covered with perspiration, her head grew heavy, and she fell from her chair.

"The bridegroom's mother has fainted!" was the outcry through the whole room. "Water, water!"

They fetched water, discovered a doctor among the guests, and he led Gittel into another room, and soon brought her round.

The bride, the bridegroom, the bride's mother, and the two ladies ran in:

"What can have caused it? Lie down! How do you feel now? Perhaps you would like a sip of lemonade?" they all asked.

"Thank you, I want nothing, I feel better already, leave me alone for a while. I shall soon recover myself, and be all right."

So Gittel was left alone, and she breathed more easily, her head stopped aching, she felt like one let out of prison, only there was a pain at her heart. The tears which had choked her all day now began to flow, and she wept abundantly. The music never ceased playing, she heard the sound of the dancers' feet and the directions of the master of ceremonies; the floor shook, Gittel wept, and tried with all her might to keep from sobbing, so that people should not hear and come in and disturb her. She had not wept so since the death of her husband, and this was the wedding of her favorite son!

By degrees she ceased to weep altogether, dried her eyes, and sat quietly talking to herself of the many things that passed through her head.

"Better that *he* (may he enter a lightsome paradise!) should have died than lived to see what I have seen, and the dear delight which I have had, at the wedding of my youngest child! Better that I myself should not have lived to see his marriage canopy. Canopy, indeed! Four sticks stuck up in the middle of the room to make fun with, for people to play at being married, like monkeys! Then at table: no Seven Blessings, not a Jewish word, not a Jewish face, no Minyan to be seen, only shaven Gentiles upon Gentiles, a roomful of naked women and girls that make you sick to look at them.

Moishehle had better have married a poor orphan, I shouldn't have been half so ashamed or half so unhappy."

Gittel called to mind the sort of a bridegroom's mother she had been at the marriage of her eldest son, and the satisfaction she had felt. Four hundred women had accompanied her to the Shool when Avremele was called to the Reading of the Law as a bridegroom, and they had scattered nuts, almonds, and raisins down upon him as he walked; then the party before the wedding, and the ceremony of the canopy, and the procession with the bride and bridegroom to the Shool, the merry home-coming, the golden soup, the bridegroom brought at supper time to the sound of music, the cantor and his choir, who sang while they sat at table, the Seven Blessings, the Vivat played for each one separately, the Kosher-Tanz, the dance round the bridegroom—and the whole time it had been Gittel here and Gittel there: "Good luck to you, Gittel, may you be happy in the young couple and in all your other children, and live to dance at the wedding of your youngest" (it was a delight and no mistake!). "Where is Gittel?" she hears them cry. "The uncle, the aunt, a cousin have paid for a dance for the Mechuteneste on the bridegroom's side! Play, musicians all!" The company make way for her, and she dances with the uncle, the aunt, and the cousin, and all the rest clap their hands. She is tired with dancing, but still they call "Gittel"! An old friend sings a merry song in her honor. "Play, musicians all!" And Gittel dances on, the company clap their hands, and wish her all that is good, and she is penetrated with genuine happiness and the joy of the occasion. Then, then, when the guests begin to depart, and the mothers of bridegroom and bride whisper together about the forthcoming Veiling Ceremony, she sees the bride in her wig, already a wife, her daughter-in-law! Her jam pancakes and almond-rolls are praised by all, and what cakes are left over from the Veiling Ceremony are either snatched one by one, or else they are seized wholesale by the young people standing round the table, so that she should not see, and they laugh and tease her. That is the way to become a mother-in-law! And here, of course, the whole of the pancakes and sweet-cakes and almond-rolls which she brought have never so much as been unpacked, and are to be thrown away or taken home again, as you please! A shame! No one came to her for cakes. The wig, too, may be thrown away or carried back—Moishehle told her it was not required, it wouldn't quite do. The bride accepted the silver candlesticks with embarrassment, as though Gittel had done something to make her feel awkward, and some girls who were standing by smiled, "Regina has been given candlesticks for the candle-blessing on Fridays—ha, ha, ha!"

The bridal couple with the girl's parents came in to ask how she felt, and interrupted the current of her thoughts.

"We shall drive home now, people are leaving," they said.

"The wedding is over," they told her, "everything in life comes to a speedy end."

Gittel remembered that when Avremel was married, the festivities had lasted a whole week, till over the second cheerful Sabbath, when the bride, the new daughter-in-law, was led to the Shool!

The day after the wedding Gittel drove home, sad, broken in spirit, as people return from the cemetery where they have buried a child, where they have laid a fragment of their own heart, of their own life, under the earth.

Driving home in the carriage, she consoled herself with this at least:

"A good thing that Beile and Zlatke, Avremel and Yossel were not there. The shame will be less, there will be less talk, nobody will know what I am suffering."

Gittel arrived the picture of gloom.

When she left for the wedding, she had looked suddenly twenty years younger, and now she looked twenty years older than before!

POVERTY

I was living in Mezkez at the time, and Seinwill Bookbinder lived there too.

But Heaven only knows where he is now! Even then his continual pallor augured no long residence in Mezkez, and he was a Yadeschlever Jew with a wife and six small children, and he lived by binding books.

Who knows what has become of him! But that is not the question—I only want to prove that Seinwill was a great liar.

If he is already in the other world, may he forgive me—and not be very angry with me, if he is still living in Mezkez!

He was an orthodox and pious Jew, but when you gave him a book to bind, he never kept his word.

When he took a book and even the whole of his pay in advance, he would swear by beard and earlocks, by wife and children, and by the Messiah, that he would bring it back to you by Sabbath, but you had to be at him for weeks before the work was finished and sent in.

Once, on a certain Friday, I remembered that next day, Sabbath, I should have a few hours to myself for reading.

A fortnight before I had given Seinwill a new book to bind for me. It was just a question whether or not he would return it in time, so I set out for his home, with the intention of bringing back the book, finished or not. I had paid him his twenty kopeks in advance, so what excuses could he possibly make? Once for all, I would give him a bit of my mind, and take away the work unfinished—it will be a lesson for him for the next time!

Thus it was, walking along and deciding on what I should say to Seinwill, that I turned into the street to which I had been directed. Once in the said street, I had no need to ask questions, for I was at once shown a little, low house, roofed with mouldered slate.

I stooped a little by way of precaution, and entered Seinwill's house, which consisted of a large kitchen.

Here he lived with his wife and children, and here he worked.

In the great stove that took up one-third of the kitchen there was a cheerful crackling, as in every Jewish home on a Friday.

In the forepart of the oven, on either hand, stood a variety of pots and pipkins, and gossipped together in their several tones. An elder child stood beside them holding a wooden spoon, with which she stirred or skimmed as the case required.

Seinwill's wife, very much occupied, stood by the one four-post bed, which was spread with a clean white sheet, and on which she had laid out various kinds of cakes, of unbaked dough, in honor of Sabbath. Beside her stood a child, its little face red with crying, and hindered her in her work.

"Seinwill, take Chatzkele away! How can I get on with the cakes? Don't you know it's Friday?" she kept calling out, and Seinwill, sitting at his work beside a large table covered with books, repeated every time like an echo:

"Chatzkele, let mother alone!"

And Chatzkele, for all the notice he took, might have been as deaf as the bedpost.

The minute Seinwill saw me, he ran to meet me in a shamefaced way, like a sinner caught in the act; and before I was able to say a word, that is, tell him angrily and with decision that he must give me my book finished or not—never mind about the twenty kopeks, and so on—and thus revenge myself on him, he began to answer, and he showed me that my book was done, it was already in the press, and there only remained the lettering to be done on the back. Just a few minutes more, and he would bring it to my house.

"No, I will wait and take it myself," I said, rather vexed.

Besides, I knew that to stamp a few letters on a book-cover could not take more than a few minutes at most.

"Well, if you are so good as to wait, it will not take long. There is a fire in the oven, I have only just got to heat the screw."

And so saying, he placed a chair for me, dusted it with the flap of his coat, and I sat down to wait. Seinwill really took my book out of the press quite finished except for the lettering on the cover, and began to hurry. Now he is by the oven—from the oven to the corner—and once more to the oven and back to the corner—and so on ten times over, saying to me every time:

"There, directly, directly, in another minute," and back once more across the room.

8

So it went on for about ten minutes, and I began to take quite an interest in this running of his from one place to another, with empty hands, and doing nothing but repeat "Directly, directly, this minute!"

Most of all I wonder why he keeps on looking into the corner—he never takes his eyes off that corner. What is he looking for, what does he expect to see there? I watch his face growing sadder—he must be suffering from something or other—and all the while he talks to himself, "Directly, directly, in one little minute." He turns to me: "I must ask you to wait a little longer. It will be very soon now—in another minute's time. Just because we want it so badly, you'd think she'd rather burst," he said, and he went back to the corner, stooped, and looked into it.

"What are you looking for there every minute?" I ask him.

"Nothing. But directly—Take my advice: why should you sit there waiting? I will bring the book to you myself. When one wants her to, she won't!"

"All right, it's Friday, so I need not hurry. Why should you have the trouble, as I am already here?" I reply, and ask him who is the "she who won't."

"You see, my wife, who is making cakes, is kept waiting by her too, and I, with the lettering to do on the book, I also wait."

"But *what* are you waiting for?"

"You see, if the cakes are to take on a nice glaze while baking, they must be brushed over with a yolk."

"Well, and what has that to do with stamping the letters on the cover of the book?"

"What has that to do with it? Don't you know that the glaze-gold which is used for the letters will not stick to the cover without some white of egg?"

"Yes, I have seen them smearing the cover with white of egg before putting on the letters. Then what?"

"How 'what?' That is why we are waiting for the egg."

"So you have sent out to buy an egg?"

"No, but it will be there directly." He points out to me the corner which he has been running to look into the whole time, and there, on the ground, I see an overturned sieve, and under the sieve, a hen turning round and round and cackling.

"As if she'd rather burst!" continued Seinwill. "Just because we want it so badly, she won't lay. She lays an egg for me nearly every time, and now—just as if she'd rather burst!" he said, and began to scratch his head.

And the hen? The hen went on turning round and round like a prisoner in a dungeon, and cackled louder than ever.

To tell the truth, I had inferred at once that Seinwill was persuaded I should wait for my book till the hen had laid an egg, and as I watched Seinwill's wife, and saw with what anxiety she waited for the hen to lay, I knew that I was right, that Seinwill was indeed so persuaded, for his wife called to him:

"Ask the young man for a kopek and send the child to buy an egg in the market. The cakes are getting cold."

"The young man owes me nothing, a few weeks ago he paid me for the whole job. There is no one to borrow from, nobody will lend me anything, I owe money all around, my very hair is not my own."

When Seinwill had answered his wife, he took another peep into the corner, and said:

"She will not keep us waiting much longer now. She can't cackle forever. Another two minutes!"

But the hen went on puffing out her feathers, pecking and cackling for a good deal more than two minutes. It seemed as if she could not bear to see her master and mistress in trouble, as if she really wished to do them a kindness by laying an egg. But no egg appeared.

I *lent* Seinwill two or three kopeks, which he was to pay me back in work, because Seinwill has never once asked for, or accepted, charity, and the child was sent to the market.

A few minutes later, when the child had come back with an egg, Seinwill's wife had the glistening Sabbath cakes on a shovel, and was placing them gaily in the oven; my book was finished, and the unfortunate hen, released at last from her prison, the sieve, ceased to cackle and to ruffle out her plumage.

SHOLOM-ALECHEM

Pen name of Shalom Rabinovitz; born, 1859, in Pereyaslav, Government of Poltava, Little Russia; Government
Rabbi, at twenty-one, in Lubni, near his native place; has
spent the greater part of his life in Kieff; in Odessa from
1890 to 1893, and in America from 1905 to 1907; Hebrew,
Russian, and Yiddish poet, novelist, humorous short story
writer, critic, and playwright; prolific contributor to Hebrew and Yiddish periodicals; founder of Die jüdische
Volksbibliothek; novels: Stempenyu, Yosele Solovei, etc.;
collected works: first series, Alle Werk, 4 vols., Cracow,
1903-1904; second series, Neueste Werk, 8 vols., Warsaw,
1909-1911.

THE CLOCK

The clock struck thirteen!

Don't imagine I am joking, I am telling you in all seriousness what happened in Mazepevke, in our house, and I myself was there at the time.

We had a clock, a large clock, fastened to the wall, an old, old clock inherited from my grandfather, which had been left him by my great-grandfather, and so forth. Too bad, that a clock should not be alive and able to tell us something beside the time of day! What stories we might have heard as we sat with it in the room! Our clock was famous throughout the town as the best clock going—"Reb Simcheh's clock"—and people used to come and set their watches by it, because it kept more accurate time than any other. You may believe me that even Reb Lebish, the sage, a philosopher, who understood the time of sunset from the sun itself, and knew the calendar by rote, he said himself—I heard him—that our clock was—well, as compared with his watch, it wasn't worth a pinch of snuff, but as there *were* such things as clocks, our clock *was* a clock. And if Reb Lebish himself said so, you may depend upon it he was right, because every Wednesday, between Afternoon and Evening Prayer, Reb Lebish climbed busily onto the roof of the women's Shool, or onto the top of the hill beside the old house-of-study, and looked out for the minute when the sun should set, in one hand his watch, and in the other the calendar. And when the sun dropt out of sight on the further side of

Mazepevke, Reb Lebish said to himself, "Got him!" and
at once came away to compare his watch with the clocks.
When he came in to us, he never gave us a "good
evening," only glanced up at the clock on the wall, then
at his watch, then at the almanac, and was gone!

But it happened one day that when Reb Lebish came
in to compare our clock with the almanac, he gave a
shout:

"Sim-cheh! Make haste! Where are you?"

My father came running in terror.

"Ha, what has happened, Reb Lebish?"

"Wretch, you dare to ask?" and Reb Lebish held his
watch under my father's nose, pointed at our clock, and
shouted again, like a man with a trodden toe:

"Sim-cheh! Why don't you speak? It is a minute
and a half ahead of the time! Throw it away!"

My father was vexed. What did Reb Lebish mean by
telling him to throw away his clock?

"Who is to prove," said he, "that my clock is a minute
and a half fast? Perhaps it is the other way about, and
your watch is a minute and a half slow? Who is to
tell?"

Reb Lebish stared at him as though he had said that
it was possible to have three days of New Moon, or that
the Seventeenth of Tammuz might possibly fall on the
Eve of Passover, or made some other such wild remark,
enough, if one really took it in, to give one an apoplectic
fit. Reb Lebish said never a word, he gave a deep sigh,
turned away without wishing us "good evening,"
slammed the door, and was gone. But no one minded
much, because the whole town knew Reb Lebish for a

person who was never satisfied with anything: he would tell you of the best cantor that he was a dummy, a log; of the cleverest man, that he was a lumbering animal; of the most appropriate match, that it was as crooked as an oven rake; and of the most apt simile, that it was as applicable as a pea to the wall. Such a man was Reb Lebish.

But let me return to our clock. I tell you, that *was* a clock! You could hear it strike three rooms away: Bom! bom! bom! Half the town went by it, to recite the Midnight Prayers, to get up early for Seliches during the week before New Year and on the ten Solemn Days, to bake the Sabbath loaves on Fridays, to bless the candles on Friday evening. They lighted the fire by it on Saturday evening, they salted the meat, and so all the other things pertaining to Judaism. In fact, our clock was the town clock. The poor thing served us faithfully, and never tried stopping even for a time, never once in its life had it to be set to rights by a clockmaker. My father kept it in order himself, he had an inborn talent for clock work. Every year on the Eve of Passover, he deliberately took it down from the wall, dusted the wheels with a feather brush, removed from its inward part a collection of spider webs, desiccated flies, which the spiders had lured in there to their destruction, and heaps of black cockroaches, which had gone in of themselves, and found a terrible end. Having cleaned and polished it, he hung it up again on the wall and shone, that is, they both shone: the clock shone because it was cleaned and polished, and my father shone because the clock shone.

And it came to pass one day that something happened.

It was on a fine, bright, cloudless day; we were all sitting at table, eating breakfast, and the clock struck. Now I always loved to hear the clock strike and count the strokes out loud:

"One—two—three—seven—eleven—twelve—thirteen! Oi! *Thirteen?*"

"Thirteen?" exclaimed my father, and laughed. "You're a fine arithmetician (no evil eye!). Whenever did you hear a clock strike thirteen?"

"But I tell you, it *struck* thirteen!"

"I shall give you thirteen slaps," cried my father, angrily, "and then you won't repeat this nonsense again. Goi, a clock *cannot* strike thirteen!"

"Do you know what, Simcheh," put in my mother, "I am afraid the child is right, I fancy I counted thirteen, too."

"There's another witness!" said my father, but it appeared that he had begun to feel a little doubtful himself, for after the meal he went up to the clock, got upon a chair, gave a turn to a little wheel inside the clock, and it began to strike. We all counted the strokes, nodding our head at each one the while: one—two—three—seven—nine—twelve—thirteen.

"Thirteen!" exclaimed my father, looking at us in amaze. He gave the wheel another turn, and again the clock struck thirteen. My father got down off the chair with a sigh. He was as white as the wall, and remained standing in the middle of the room, stared at the ceiling, chewed his beard, and muttered to himself:

"Plague take thirteen! What can it mean? What does it portend? If it were out of order, it would have stopped. Then, what can it be? The inference can only be that some spring has gone wrong."

"Why worry whether it's a spring or not?" said my mother. "You'd better take down the clock and put it to rights, as you've a turn that way."

"Hush, perhaps you're right," answered my father, took down the clock and busied himself with it. He perspired, spent a whole day over it, and hung it up again in its place.

Thank God, the clock was going as it should, and when, near midnight, we all stood round it and counted *twelve,* my father was overjoyed.

"Ha? It didn't strike thirteen then, did it? When I say it is a spring, I know what I'm about."

"I always said you were a wonder," my mother told him. "But there is one thing I don't understand: why does it wheeze so? I don't think it used to wheeze like that."

"It's your fancy," said my father, and listened to the noise it made before striking, like an old man preparing to cough: chil-chil-chil-chil-trrrr . . . and only then: bom!—bom!—bom!— and even the "bom" was not the same as formerly, for the former "bom" had been a cheerful one, and now there had crept into it a melancholy note, as into the voice of an old worn-out cantor at the close of the service for the Day of Atonement, and the hoarseness increased, and the strike became lower and duller, and my father, worried and anxious. It was plain that the affair preyed upon his mind, that he suffered in secret, that it was undermining his health, and yet he could do nothing. We felt that any moment the clock might stop altogether. The imp started playing all kinds of nasty tricks and idle pranks, shook itself sideways, and stumbled like an old man who drags his feet after him. One could see that the clock was about to stop forever! It was a good thing my father understood in time that the clock was about to yield up its soul, and that the fault lay with the balance weights: the weight was too light. And he puts on a jostle, which has the weight of about four pounds. The clock goes on like a song, and my father becomes as cheerful as a newborn man.

But this was not to be for long: the clock began to lose again, the imp was back at his tiresome performances: he moved slowly on one side, quickly on the other, with a hoarse noise, like a sick old man, so that it went to the heart. A pity to see how the clock agonized, and my father, as he watched it, seemed like a flickering, bickering flame of a candle, and nearly went out for grief.

Like a good doctor, who is ready to sacrifice himself for the patient's sake, who puts forth all his energy, tries every remedy under the sun to save his patient, even so my father applied himself to save the old clock, if only it should be possible.

"The weight is too light," repeated my father, and hung something heavier onto it every time, first a frying-pan, then a copper jug, afterwards a flat-iron, a bag of sand, a couple of tiles—and the clock revived every

time and went on, with difficulty and distress, but still
it went—till one night there was a misfortune.

It was on a Friday evening in winter. We had just
eaten our Sabbath supper, the delicious peppered fish
with horseradish, the hot soup with macaroni, the stewed
plums, and said grace as was meet. The Sabbath
candles flickered, the maid was just handing round
fresh, hot, well-dried Polish nuts from off the top of
the stove, when in came Aunt Yente, a dark-favored
little woman without teeth, whose husband had deserted
her, to become a follower of the Rebbe, quite a number
of years ago.

"Good Sabbath!" said Aunt Yente, "I knew you had
some fresh Polish nuts. The pity is that I've nothing
to crack them with, may my husband live no more years
than I have teeth in my mouth! What did you think,
Malkeh, of the fish to-day? What a struggle there was
over them at the market! I asked him about his fish—
Manasseh, the lazy—when up comes Soreh Peril, the
rich: Make haste, give it me, hand me over that little
pike!—Why in such a hurry? say I. God be with you,
the river is not on fire, and Manasseh is not going to
take the fish back there, either. Take my word for
it, with these rich people money is cheap, and sense
is dear. Turns round on me and says: Paupers, she
says, have no business here—a poor man, she says,
shouldn't hanker after good things. What do you think
of such a shrew? How long did she stand by her mother
in the market selling ribbons? She behaves just like
Pessil Peise Avròhom's over her daughter, the one she
married to a great man in Schtrischtch, who took her

just as she was, without any dowry or anything—Jewish luck! They say she has a bad time of it—no evil eye to her days—can't get on with his children. Well, who would be a stepmother? Let them beware! Take Chavvehle! What is there to find fault with in her? And you should see the life her stepchildren lead her! One hears shouting day and night, cursing, squabbling, and fighting."

The candles began to die down, the shadow climbed the wall, scrambled higher and higher, the nuts crackled in our hands, there was talking and telling stories and tales, just for the pleasure of it, one without any reference to the other, but Aunt Yente talked more than anyone.

"Hush!" cried out Aunt Yente, "listen, because not long ago a still better thing happened. Not far from Yampele, about three versts away, some robbers fell upon a Jewish tavern, killed a whole houseful of people, down to a baby in a cradle. The only person left alive was a servant-girl, who was sleeping on the kitchen stove. She heard people screeching, and jumped down, this servant-girl, off the stove, peeped through a chink in the door, and saw, this servant-girl I'm telling you of, saw the master of the house and the mistress lying on the floor, murdered, in a pool of blood, and she went back, this girl, and sprang through a window, and ran into the town screaming: Jews, to the rescue, help, help, help!"

Suddenly, just as Aunt Yente was shouting, "Help, help, help!" we heard *trrraach!—tarrrach!—bom—dzin—dzin—dzin, bomm!!* We were so deep in the story, we only thought at first that robbers had descended upon our house, and were firing guns, and we could not move for terror. For one minute we looked at one another, and then with one accord we began to call out, "Help! help! help!" and my mother was so carried away that she clasped me in her arms and cried:

"My child, my life for yours, woe is me!"

"Ha? What? What is the matter with him? What has happened?" exclaimed my father.

"Nothing! nothing! hush! hush!" cried Aunt Yente, gesticulating wildly, and the maid came running in from the kitchen, more dead than alive.

"Who screamed? What is it? Is there a fire? What is on fire? Where?"

"Fire? fire? Where is the fire?" we all shrieked. "Help! help! Gewalt, Jews, to the rescue, fire, fire!"

"Which fire? what fire? where fire?! Fire take *you*, you foolish girl, and make cinders of you!" scolded Aunt Yente at the maid. "Now *she* must come, as though we weren't enough before! Fire, indeed, says she! Into the earth with you, to all black years! Did you ever hear of such a thing? What are you all yelling for? Do you know what it was that frightened you? The best joke in the world, and there's nobody to laugh with! God be with you, it was the clock falling onto the floor—now you know! You hung every sort of thing onto it, and now it is fallen, weighing at least three pud. And no wonder! A man wouldn't have fared better. Did you ever?!"

It was only then we came to our senses, rose one by one from the table, went to the clock, and saw it lying on its poor face, killed, broken, shattered, and smashed for evermore!

"There is an end to the clock!" said my father, white as the wall. He hung his head, wrung his fingers, and the tears came into his eyes. I looked at my father and wanted to cry, too.

"There now, see, what is the use of fretting to death?" said my mother. "No doubt it was so decreed and written down in Heaven that to-day, at that particular minute, our clock was to find its end, just (I beg to distinguish!) like a human being, may God not punish me for saying so! May it be an Atonement for not remembering the Sabbath, for me, for thee, for our children, for all near and dear to us, and for all Israel. Amen, Selah!"

FISHEL THE TEACHER

Twice a year, as sure as the clock, on the first day of Nisan and the first of Ellul—for Passover and Tabernacles—Fishel the teacher travelled from Balta to Chaschtschevate, home to his wife and children. It was decreed that nearly all his life long he should be the guest of his own family, a very welcome guest, but a passing one. He came with the festival, and no sooner was it over, than back with him to Balta, back to the schooling, the ruler, the Gemoreh, the dull, thick wits, to the being knocked about from pillar to post, to the wandering among strangers, and the longing for home.

On the other hand, when Fishel *does* come home, he is an emperor! His wife Bath-sheba comes out to meet him, pulls at her head-kerchief, blushes red as fire, questions as though in asides, without as yet looking him in the face, "How are you?" and he replies, "How are *you?*" and Froike his son, a boy of thirteen or so, greets him, and the father asks, "Well, Efroim, and how far on are you in the Gemoreh?" and his little daughter Resele, not at all a bad-looking little girl, with a plaited pigtail, hugs and kisses him.

"Tate, what sort of present have you brought me?"

"Printed calico for a frock, and a silk kerchief for mother. There—give mother the kerchief!"

And Fishel takes a silk (suppose a half-silk!) kerchief out of his Tallis-bag, and Bath-sheba grows redder still, and pulls her head-cloth over her eyes, takes up a bit of household work, busies herself all over the place, and ends by doing nothing.

"Bring the Gemoreh, Efroim, and let me hear what you can do!"

And Froike recites his lesson like the bright boy he is, and Fishel listens and corrects, and his heart expands and overflows with delight, his soul rejoices— a bright boy, Froike, a treasure!

"If you want to go to the bath, there is a shirt ready for you!"

Thus Bath-sheba as she passes him, still not venturing to look him in the face, and Fishel has a sensation of unspeakable comfort, he feels like a man escaped from prison and back in a lightsome world, among those who are near and dear to him. And he sees in fancy a very, very hot bath-house, and himself lying on the highest bench with other Jews, and he perspires and swishes himself with the birch twigs, and can never have enough.

Home from the bath, fresh and lively as a fish, like one newborn, he rehearses the portion of the Law for the festival, puts on the Sabbath cloak and the new girdle, steals a glance at Bath-sheba in her new dress and silk kerchief—still a pretty woman, and so pious and good!—and goes with Froike to the Shool. The air is full of Sholom Alechems, "Welcome, Reb Fishel the teacher, and what are you about?"—"A teacher teaches!"—"What is the news?"—"What should it be? The world is the world!"—"What is going on in Balta?" —" Balta is Balta."

The same formula is repeated every time, every half-year, and Nissel the reader begins to recite the evening prayers, and sends forth his voice, the further the louder, and when he comes to "And Moses declared the set feasts of the Lord unto the children of Israel," it reaches nearly to Heaven. And Froike stands at his father's side, and recites the prayers melodiously, and once more Fishel's heart expands and flows over with joy—a good child, Froike, a good, pious child!

"A happy holiday, a happy holiday!"

"A happy holiday, a happy year!"

At home they find the Passover table spread: the four cups, the bitter herbs, the almond and apple paste, and all the rest of it. The reclining-seats (two small benches with big cushions) stand ready, and Fishel becomes a king. Fishel, robed in white, sits on the throne of his dominion, Bath-sheba, the queen, sits beside him in her new silk kerchief; Efroim, the prince, in a new cap, and the princess Resele with her plait, sit opposite them. Look on with respect! His majesty Fishel is seated on his throne, and has assumed the sway of his kingdom.

The Chaschtschevate scamps, who love to make game of the whole world, not to mention a teacher, maintain that one Passover Eve our Fishel sent his Bath-sheba the following Russian telegram: "Rebyàta sobral dyèngi vezù prigatovi npiyèdu tzàrstvovàtz." Which means: "Have entered my pupils for the next term, am bringing money, prepare the dumplings, I come to reign." The mischief-makers declare that this telegram was seized at Balta station, that Bath-sheba was sought and not found, and that Fishel was sent home with the étape. Dreadful! But I can assure you, there isn't a word of truth in the story, because Fishel never sent a telegram in his life, nobody was ever seen looking for Bath-sheba, and Fishel was never taken anywhere by the étape. That is, he *was* once taken somewhere by the étape, but not on account of a telegram, only on account of a simple passport! And not from Balta, but from Yehupetz, and not at Passover, but in summer-time. He wished, you see, to go to Yehupetz in search of a post as teacher, and forgot his passport. He thought it was in Balta, and he got into a nice mess, and forbade his children and children's children ever to go in search of pupils in Yehupetz.

Since then he teaches in Balta, and comes home for Passover, winds up his work a fortnight earlier, and sometimes manages to hasten back in time for the Great Sabbath. Hasten, did I say? That means when the road *is* a road, when you can hire a conveyance, and when the Bug can either be crossed on the ice or in the ferry-boat. But when, for instance, the snow has begun to melt, and the mud is deep, when there is no conveyance to be had, when the Bug has begun to split the ice, and the ferry-boat has not started running, when a skiff means peril of death, and the festival is upon you—what then? It is just "nit güt."

Fishel the teacher knows the taste of "nit güt." He has had many adventures and mishaps since he became a teacher, and took to faring from Chaschtschevate to Balta and from Balta to Chaschtschevate. He has tried going more than half-way on foot, and helped to push the conveyance besides. He has lain in the mud with a priest, the priest on top, and he below. He has fled before a pack of wolves who were pursuing the vehicle, and afterwards they turned out to be dogs, and not wolves at all. But anything like the trouble on this Passover Eve had never befallen him before.

The trouble came from the Bug, that is, from the Bug's breaking through the ice, and just having its fling when Fishel reached it in a hurry to get home, and really in a hurry, because it was already Friday and Passover Eve, that is, Passover eve fell on a Sabbath that year.

Fishel reached the Bug in a Gentile conveyance Thursday evening. According to his own reckoning, he should have got there Tuesday morning, because he left Balta Sunday after market, the spirit having moved him to go into the market-place to spy after a chance conveyance. How much better it would have been to drive with Yainkel-Shegetz, a Balta carrier, even at the cart-tail, with his legs dangling, and shaken to bits. He would have been home long ago by now, and have forgotten the discomforts of the journey. But he had wanted a cheaper transit, and it is an old saying that cheap things cost dear. Yoneh, the tippler, who procures vehicles in Balta, had said to him: "Take my advice, give two rubles, and you will ride in Yainkel's wagon like a lord, even if you do have to sit behind the wagon. Consider, you're playing with fire, the festival approaches." But as ill-luck would have it, there came along a familiar Gentile from Chaschtschevate.

"Eh, Rabbi, you're not wanting a lift to Chaschtschevate?"

"How much would the fare be?"

He thought to ask how much, and he never thought to ask if it would take him home by Passover, because in a week he could have covered the distance walking behind the cart.

But as Fishel drove out of the town, he soon began to repent of his choice, even though the wagon was large, and he sitting in it in solitary grandeur, like any count. He saw that with a horse that dragged itself along in *that* way, there would be no getting far, for they drove a whole day without getting anywhere in particular, and however much he worried the peasant to know if it were a long way yet, the only reply he got was, "Who can tell?" In the evening, with a rumble and a shout and a crack of the whip, there came up with them Yainkel-Shegetz and his four fiery horses jingling with bells, and the large coach packed with passengers before and behind. Yainkel, catching sight of the teacher in the peasant's cart, gave another loud crack with his whip, ridiculed the peasant, his passenger, and his horse, as only Yainkel-Shegetz knows how, and when a little way off, he turned and pointed at one of the peasant's wheels.

"Hallo, man, look out! There's a wheel turning!"

The peasant stopped the horse, and he and the teacher clambered down together, and examined the wheels. They crawled underneath the cart, and found nothing wrong, nothing at all.

When the peasant understood that Yainkel had made a fool of him, he scratched the back of his neck below his collar, and began to abuse Yainkel and all Jews with curses such as Fishel had never heard before. His voice and his anger rose together:

"May you never know good! May you have a bad
year! May you not see the end of it! Bad luck to
you, you and your horses and your wife and your
daughter and your aunts and your uncles and your
parents-in-law and—and all your cursed Jews!"

It was a long time before the peasant took his seat
again, nor did he cease to fume against Yainkel the
driver and all Jews, until, with God's help, they reached
a village wherein to spend the night.

Next morning Fishel rose with the dawn, recited his
prayers, a portion of the Law, and a few Psalms,
breakfasted on a roll, and was ready to set forward.
Unfortunately, Chfedor (this was the name of his
driver) was *not* ready. Chfedor had sat up late with
a crony and got drunk, and he slept through a whole
day and a bit of the night, and then only started on
his way.

"Well," Fishel reproved him as they sat in the cart,
"well, Chfedor, a nice way to behave, upon my word!
Do you suppose I engaged you for a merrymaking?
What have you to say for yourself, I should like to
know, eh?"

And Fishel addressed other reproachful words to him,
and never ceased casting the other's laziness between
his teeth, partly in Polish, partly in Hebrew, and helping himself out with his hands. Chfedor understood
quite well what Fishel meant, but he answered him not
a word, not a syllable even. No doubt he felt that
Fishel was in the right, and he was silent as a cat,
till, on the fourth day, they met Yainkel-Shegetz,
driving back from Chaschtschevate with a rumble and a

crack of his whip, who called out to them, "You may as well turn back to Balta, the Bug has burst the ice."

Fishel's heart was like to burst, too, but Chfedor, who thought that Yainkel was trying to fool him a second time, started repeating his whole list of curses, called down all bad dreams on Yainkel's hands and feet, and never shut his mouth till they came to the Bug on Thursday evening. They drove straight to Prokop Baranyùk, the ferryman, to inquire when the ferry-boat would begin to run, and the two Gentiles, Chfedor and Prokop, took to sipping brandy, while Fishel proceeded to recite the Afternoon Prayer.

The sun was about to set, and poured a rosy light onto the high hills that stood on either side of the river, and were snow-covered in parts and already green in others, and intersected by rivulets that wound their way with murmuring noise down into the river, where the water foamed with the broken ice and the increasing thaw. The whole of Chaschtschevate lay before him as on a plate, while the top of the monastery sparkled like a light in the setting sun. Standing to recite the Eighteen Benedictions, with his face towards Chaschtschevate, Fishel turned his eyes away and drove out the idle thoughts and images that had crept into his head: Bath-sheba with the new silk kerchief, Froike with the Gemoreh, Resele with her plait, the hot bath and the highest bench, and freshly-baked Matzes, together with nice peppered fish and horseradish that goes up your nose, Passover borshtsh with more Matzes, a heavenly mixture, and all the other good things that desire is

capable of conjuring up—and however often he drove
these fancies away, they returned and crept back into
his brain like summer flies, and disturbed him at his
prayers.

When Fishel had repeated the Eighteen Benedictions
and Olenu, he betook him to Prokop, and entered into
conversation with him about the ferry-boat and the
festival eve, giving him to understand, partly in Polish
and partly in Hebrew and partly with his hands, what
Passover meant to the Jews, and Passover Eve falling
on a Sabbath, and that if, which Heaven forbid, he
had not crossed the Bug by that time to-morrow, he
was a lost man, for, beside the fact that they were on
the lookout for him at home—his wife and children
(Fishel gave a sigh that rent the heart)—he would
not be able to eat or drink for a week, and Fishel
turned away, so that the tears in his eyes should not
be seen.

Prokop Baranyùk quite appreciated Fishel's position,
and replied that he knew to-morrow was a Jewish festival, and even how it was called; he even knew that the
Jews celebrated it by drinking wine and strong brandy;
he even knew that there was yet another festival at
which the Jews drank brandy, and a third when all
Jews were obliged to get drunk, but he had forgotten its
name—

"Well and good," Fishel interrupted him in a lament-
able voice, "but what is to happen? How if I don't
get there?"

To this Prokop made no reply. He merely pointed
with his hand to the river, as much as to say, "See for
yourself!"

And Fishel lifted up his eyes to the river, and saw that which he had never seen before, and heard that which he had never heard in his life. Because you may say that Fishel had never yet taken in anything "out of doors," he had only perceived it accidentally, by the way, as he hurried from Cheder to the house-of-study, and from the house-of-study to Cheder. The beautiful blue Bug between the two lines of imposing hills, the murmur of the winding rivulets as they poured down the hillsides, the roar of the ever-deepening spring-flow, the light of the setting sun, the glittering cupola of the convent, the wholesome smell of Passover-Eve-tide out of doors, and, above all, the being so close to home and not able to get there—all these things lent wings, as it were, to Fishel's spirit, and he was borne into a new world, the world of imagination, and crossing the Bug seemed the merest trifle, if only the Almighty were willing to perform a fraction of a miracle on his behalf.

Such and like thoughts floated in and out of Fishel's head, and lifted him into the air, and so far across the river, he never realized that it was night, and the stars came out, and a cool wind blew in under his cloak to his little prayer-scarf, and Fishel was busy with things that he had never so much as dreamt of: earthly things and Heavenly things, the great size of the beautiful world, the Almighty as Creator of the earth, and so on.

Fishel spent a bad night in Prokop's house—such a night as he hoped never to spend again. The next morning broke with a smile from the bright and cheerful sun. It was a singularly fine day, and so sweetly warm that all the snow left melted into kasha, and

the kasha, into water, and this water poured into the
Bug from all sides; and the Bug became clearer, light
blue, full and smooth, and the large bits of ice that
looked like dreadful wild beasts, like white elephants
hurrying and tearing along as if they were afraid of
being late, grew rarer.

Fishel the teacher recited the Morning Prayer, breakfasted on the last piece of leavened bread left in his
prayer-scarf bag, and went out to the river to see about
the ferry. Imagine his feelings when he heard that the
ferry-boat would not begin running before Sunday afternoon! He clapped both hands to his head, gesticulated
with every limb, and fell to abusing Prokop. Why had
he given him hopes of the ferry-boat's crossing next day?
Whereupon Prokop answered quite coolly that he had
said nothing about crossing with the ferry, he was
talking of taking him across in a small boat! And that
he could still do, if Fishel wished, in a sail-boat,
in a rowboat, in a raft, and the fare was not less than
one ruble.

"A raft, a rowboat, anything you like, only don't let
me spend the festival away from home!"

Thus Fishel, and he was prepared to give him two
rubles then and there, to give his life for the holy
festival, and he began to drive Prokop into getting out
the raft at once, and taking him across in the direction
of Chaschtschevate, where Bath-sheba, Froike, and
Resele are already looking out for him. It may be they
are standing on the opposite hills, that they see him,
and make signs to him, waving their hands, that they
call to him, only one can neither see them nor hear

their voices, because the river is wide, dreadfully wide,
wider than ever!

The sun was already half-way up the deep, blue sky,
when Prokop told Fishel to get into the little trough
of a boat, and when Fishel heard him, he lost all power
in his feet and hands, and was at a loss what to do, for
never in his life had he been in a rowboat, never in
his life had he been in any small boat. And it seemed
to him the thing had only to dip a little to one side,
and all would be over.

"Jump in, and off we'll go!" said Prokop once more,
and with a turn of his oar he brought the boat still
closer in, and took Fishel's bundle out of his hands.

Fishel the teacher drew his coat-skirts neatly together,
and began to perform circles without moving from the
spot, hesitating whether to jump or not. On the one
hand were Passover Eve, Bath-sheba, Froike, Resele, the
bath, the home service, himself as king; on the other,
peril of death, the Destroying Angel, suicide—because
one dip and—good-by, Fishel, peace be upon him!

And Fishel remained circling there with his folded
skirts, till Prokop lost patience and said, another
minute, and he should set out and be off to Chaschtschevate without him. At the beloved word "Chaschtschevate," Fishel called his dear ones to mind, summoned the whole of his courage, and fell into the boat.
I say "fell in," because the instant his foot touched the
bottom of the boat, it slipped, and Fishel, thinking he
was falling, drew back, and this drawing back sent him
headlong forward into the boat-bottom, where he lay
stretched out for some minutes before recovering his

wits, and for a long time after his face was livid, and his hands shook, while his heart beat like a clock, tik-tik-tak, tik-tik-tak!

Prokop meantime sat in the prow as though he were at home. He spit into his hands, gave a stroke with the oar to the left, a stroke to the right, and the boat glided over the shining water, and Fishel's head spun round as he sat. As he sat? No, he hung floating, suspended in the air! One false movement, and that which held him would give way; one lean to the side, and he would be in the water and done with! At this thought, the words came into his mind, "And they sank like lead in the mighty waters," and his hair stood on end at the idea of such a death. How? Not even to be buried with the dead of Israel? And he bethought himself to make a vow to—to do what? To give money in charity? He had none to give—he was a very, very poor man! So he vowed that if God would bring him home in safety, he would sit up whole nights and study, go through the whole of the Talmud in one year, God willing, with God's help.

Fishel would dearly have liked to know if it were much further to the other side, and found himself seated, as though on purpose, with his face to Prokop and his back to Chaschtschevate. And he dared not open his mouth to ask. It seemed to him that his very voice would cause the boat to rock, and one rock—good-by, Fishel! But Prokop opened his mouth of his own accord, and began to speak. He said there was nothing worse when you were on the water than a thaw. It made it impossible, he said, to row straight ahead;

one had to adapt one's course to the ice, to row round and round and backwards.

"There's a bit of ice making straight for us now."

Thus Prokop, and he pulled back and let pass a regular ice-floe, which swam by with a singular rocking motion and a sound that Fishel had never seen or heard before. And then he began to understand what a wild adventure this journey was, and he would have given goodness knows what to be safe on shore, even on the one they had left.

"O, you see that?" asked Prokop, and pointed upstream.

Fishel raised his eyes slowly, was afraid of moving much, and looked and looked, and saw nothing but water, water, and water.

"There's a big one coming down on us now, we must make a dash for it, for it's too late to row back."

So said Prokop, and rowed away with both hands, and the boat glided and slid like a fish through the water, and Fishel felt cold in every limb. He would have liked to question, but was afraid of interfering. However, again Prokop spoke of himself.

"If we don't win by a minute, it will be the worse for us."

Fishel can now no longer contain himself, and asks:

"How do you mean, the worse?"

"We shall be done for," says Prokop.

"Done for?"

"Done for."

"How do you mean, done for?" persists Fishel.

"I mean, it will grind us."

"Grind us?"

"Grind us."

Fishel does not understand what "grind us, grind us" may signify, but it has a sound of finality, of the next world, about it, and Fishel is bathed in a cold sweat, and again the words come into his head, "And they sank like lead in the mighty waters."

And Prokop, as though to quiet our Fishel's mind, tells him a comforting story of how, years ago at this time, the Bug broke through the ice, and the ferry-boat could not be used, and there came to him another person to be rowed across, an excise official from Uman, quite a person of distinction, and offered a large sum; and they had the bad luck to meet two huge pieces of ice, and he rowed to the right, in between the floes, intending to slip through upwards, and he made an involuntary side motion with the boat, and they went flop into the water! Fortunately, he, Prokop, could swim, but the official came to grief, and the fare—money, too.

"It was good-by to my fare!" ended Prokop, with a sigh, and Fishel shuddered, and his tongue dried up, so that he could neither speak nor utter the slightest sound.

In the very middle of the river, just as they were rowing along quite smoothly, Prokop suddenly stopped, and looked—and looked—up the stream; then he laid down the oars, drew a bottle out of his pocket, tilted it into his mouth, sipped out of it two or three times, put it back, and explained to Fishel that he had always to take a few sips of the "bitter drop," otherwise he felt bad when on the water. And he wiped his mouth, took the oars in hand again, and said, having crossed himself three times:

"Now for a race!"

A race? With whom? With what? Fishel did not understand, and was afraid to ask; but again he felt the brush of the Death Angel's wing, for Prokop had gone down onto his knees, and was rowing with might and main. Moreover, he said to Fishel, and pointed to the bottom of the boat:

"Rebbe, lie down!"

Fishel understood that he was to lie down, and did not need to be told twice. For now he had seen a whole host of floes coming down upon them, a world of ice, and he shut his eyes, flung himself face downwards in the boat, and lay trembling like a lamb, and recited in a low voice, "Hear, O Israel!" and the Confession, thought on the graves of Israel, and fancied that now, now he lies in the abyss of the waters, now, now comes a fish and swallows him, like Jonah the prophet when he fled to Tarshish, and he remembers Jonah's prayer, and sings softly and with tears:

"Affofùni màyyim ad nòfesh—the waters have reached unto my soul; tehòm yesovevèni—the deep hath covered me!"

Fishel the teacher sang and wept and thought pitifully of his widowed wife and his orphaned children, and Prokop rowed for all he was worth, and sang *his* little song:

"O thou maiden with the black lashes!"

And Prokop felt the same on the water as on dry land, and Fishel's "Affofùni" and Prokop's "O maiden" blended into one, and a strange song sounded over the Bug, a kind of duet, which had never been heard there before.

"The black year knows why he is so afraid of death, that Jew," so wondered Prokop Baranyùk, "a poor tattered little Jew like him, a creature I would not give this old boat for, and so afraid of death!"

The shore reached, Prokop gave Fishel a shove in the side with his boot, and Fishel started. The Gentile burst out laughing, but Fishel did not hear, Fishel went on reciting the Confession, saying Kaddish for his own soul, and mentally contemplating the graves of Israel!

"Get up, you silly Rebbe! We're there—in Chaschtschevate!"

Slowly, slowly, Fishel raised his head, and gazed around him with red and swollen eyes.

"Chasch-tsche-va-te? ? ? "

"Chaschtschevate! Give me the ruble, Rebbe!"

Fishel crawls out of the boat, and, finding himself really at home, does not know what to do for joy. Shall he run into the town? Shall he go dancing? Shall he first thank and praise God who has brought him safe out of such great peril? He pays the Gentile his fare, takes up his bundle under his arm and is about to run home, the quicker the better, but he pauses a moment first, and turns to Prokop the ferryman:

"Listen, Prokop, dear heart, to-morrow, please God, you'll come and drink a glass of brandy, and taste festival fish at Fishel the teacher's, for Heaven's sake!"

10

"Shall I say no? Am I such a fool?" replied Prokop, licking his lips in anticipation at the thought of the Passover brandy he would sip, and the festival fish he would delectate himself with on the morrow.

And Prokop gets back into his boat, and pulls quietly home again, singing a little song, and pitying the poor Jew who was so afraid of death. "The Jewish faith is the same as the Mahommedan!" and it seems to him a very foolish one. And Fishel is thinking almost the same thing, and pities the Gentile on account of *his* religion. "What knows he, yon poor Gentile, of such holy promises as were made to us Jews, the beloved people!"

And Fishel the teacher hastens uphill, through the Chaschtschevate mud. He perspires with the exertion, and yet he does not feel the ground beneath his feet. He flies, he floats, he is going home, home to his dear ones, who are on the watch for him as for Messiah, who look for him to return in health, to seat himself upon his kingly throne and reign.

Look, Jews, and turn respectfully aside! Fishel the teacher has come home to Chaschtschevate, and seated himself upon the throne of his kingdom!

AN EASY FAST

That which Doctor Tanner failed to accomplish, was effectually carried out by Chayyim Chaikin, a simple Jew in a small town in Poland.

Doctor Tanner wished to show that a man can fast forty days, and he only managed to get through twenty-eight, no more, and that with people pouring spoonfuls of water into his mouth, and giving him morsels of ice to swallow, and holding his pulse—a whole business! Chayyim Chaikin has proved that one can fast more than forty days; not, as a rule, two together, one after the other, but forty days, if not more, in the course of a year.

To fast is all he asks!

Who said drops of water? Who said ice? Not for him! To fast means no food and no drink from one set time to the other, a real four-and-twenty-hours.

And no doctors sit beside him and hold his pulse, whispering, "Hush! Be quiet!"

Well, let us hear the tale!

Chayyim Chaikin is a very poor man, encumbered with many children, and they, the children, support him.

They are mostly girls, and they work in a factory and make cigarette wrappers, and they earn, some one gulden, others half a gulden, a day, and that not every day. How about Sabbaths and festivals and "shtreik" days? One should thank God for everything, even in their out-of-the-way little town strikes are all the fashion!

And out of that they have to pay rent—for a damp corner in a basement.

To buy clothes and shoes for the lot of them! They have a dress each, but they are two to every pair of shoes.

And then food—such as it is! A bit of bread smeared with an onion, sometimes groats, occasionally there is a bit of taran that burns your heart out, so that after eating it for supper, you can drink a whole night.

When it comes to eating, the bread has to be portioned out like cake.

"Oi, dos Essen, dos Essen seiers!"

Thus Chaike, Chayyim Chaikin's wife, a poor, sick creature, who coughs all night long.

"No evil eye," says the father, and he looks at his children devouring whole slices of bread, and would dearly like to take a mouthful himself, only, if he does so, the two little ones, Fradke and Beilke, will go supperless.

And he cuts his portion of bread in two, and gives it to the little ones, Fradke and Beilke.

Fradke and Beilke stretch out their little thin, black hands, look into their father's eyes, and don't believe him: perhaps he is joking? Children are nashers, they play with father's piece of bread, till at last they begin taking bites out of it. The mother sees and exclaims, coughing all the while:

"It is nothing but eating and stuffing!"

The father cannot bear to hear it, and is about to answer her, but he keeps silent—he can't say anything, it is not for him to speak! Who is he in the house? A broken potsherd, the last and least, no good to anyone, no good to them, no good to himself.

Because the fact is he does nothing, absolutely nothing; not because he won't do anything, or because it doesn't befit him, but because there is nothing to do—and there's an end of it! The whole townlet complains of there being nothing to do! It is just a crowd of Jews driven together. Delightful! They're packed like herrings in a barrel, they squeeze each other close, all for love.

"Well-a-day!" thinks Chaikin, "it's something to have children, other people haven't even that. But to depend on one's children is quite another thing and not a happy one!" Not that they grudge him his keep—Heaven forbid! But he cannot take it from them, he really cannot!

He knows how hard they work, he knows how the strength is wrung out of them to the last drop, he knows it well!

Every morsel of bread is a bit of their health and strength—he drinks his children's blood! No, the thought is too dreadful!

"Tatinke, why don't you eat?" ask the children.

"To-day is a fast day with me," answers Chayyim Chaikin.

"Another fast? How many fasts have you?"

"Not so many as there are days in the week."

And Chayyim Chaikin speaks the truth when he says that he has many fasts, and yet there are days on which he eats.

But he likes the days on which he fasts better.

First, they are pleasing to God, and it means a little bit more of the world-to-come, the interest grows, and the capital grows with it.

"Secondly" (he thinks), "no money is wasted on me. Of course, I am accountable to no one, and nobody ever questions me as to how I spend it, but what do I want money for, when I can get along without it?

"And what is the good of feeling one's self a little higher than a beast? A beast eats every day, but I can go without food for one or two days. A man *should* be above a beast!

"O, if a man could only raise himself to a level where he could live without eating at all! But there are one's confounded insides!" So thinks Chayyim Chaikin, for hunger has made a philosopher of him.

"The insides, the necessity of eating, these are the causes of the world's evil! The insides and the necessity of eating have made a pauper of me, and drive my children to toil in the sweat of their brow and risk their lives for a bit of bread!

"Suppose a man had no need to eat! Ai—ai—ai! My children would all stay at home! An end to toil, an end to moil, an end to 'shtreikeven,' an end to the risking of life, an end to factory and factory owners, to rich men and paupers, an end to jealousy and hatred and fighting and shedding of blood! All gone and done with! Gone and done with! A paradise! a paradise!"

So reasons Chayyim Chaikin, and, lost in speculation, he pities the world, and is grieved to the heart to think that God should have made man so little above the beast.

The day on which Chayyim Chaikin fasts is, as I told you, his best day, and a *real* fast day, like the Ninth of Ab, for instance—he is ashamed to confess it—is a festival for him!

You see, it means not to eat, not to be a beast, not to be guilty of the children's blood, to earn the reward of a Mitzveh, and to weep to heart's content on the ruins of the Temple.

For how can one weep when one is full? How can a full man grieve? Only he can grieve whose soul is faint within him! The good year knows how some folk answer it to their conscience, giving in to their insides—afraid of fasting! Buy them a groschen worth of oats, for charity's sake!

Thus would Chayyim Chaikin scorn those who bought themselves off the fast, and dropped a hard coin into the collecting box.

The Ninth of Ab is the hardest fast of all—so the world has it.

Chayyim Chaikin cannot see why. The day is long, is it? Then the night is all the shorter. It's hot out of doors, is it? Who asks you to go loitering about in the sun? Sit in the Shool and recite the prayers, of which, thank God, there are plenty.

"I tell you," persists Chayyim Chaikin, "that the Ninth of Ab is the easiest of the fasts, because it is the best, the very best!

"For instance, take the Day of Atonement fast! It is written, 'And you shall mortify your bodies.' What for? To get a clean bill and a good year.

"It doesn't say that you are to fast on the Ninth of Ab, but you fast of your own accord, because how could you eat on the day when the Temple was wrecked, and Jews were killed, women ripped up, and children dashed to pieces?

"It doesn't say that you are to weep on the Ninth of Ab, but you *do* weep. How could anyone restrain his tears when he thinks of what we lost that day?"

"The pity is, there should be only one Ninth of Ab!" says Chayyim Chaikin.

"Well, and the Seventeenth of Tammuz!" suggests some one.

"And there is only one Seventeenth of Tammuz!" answers Chayyim Chaikin, with a sigh.

"Well, and the Fast of Gedaliah? and the Fast of Esther?" continues the same person.

"Only one of each!" and Chayyim Chaikin sighs again.

Ê, Reb Chayyim, you are greedy for fasts, are you?"

"More fasts, more fasts!" says Chayyim Chaikin, and he takes upon himself to fast on the eve of the Ninth of Ab as well, two days at a stretch.

What do you think of fasting two days in succession? Isn't that a treat? It is hard enough to have to break one's fast after the Ninth of Ab, without eating on the eve thereof as well.

One forgets that one *has* insides, that such a thing exists as the necessity to eat, and one is free of the habit that drags one down to the level of the beast.

The difficulty lies in the drinking! I mean, in the *not* drinking. "If I" (thinks Chayyim Chaikin) "allowed myself one glass of water a day, I could fast a whole week till Sabbath."

You think I say that for fun? Not at all! Chayyim Chaikin is a man of his word. When he says a thing, it's said and done! The whole week preceding the Ninth of Ab he ate nothing, he lived on water.

Who should notice? His wife, poor thing, is sick, the elder children are out all day in the factory, and the younger ones do not understand. Fradke and Beilke only know when they are hungry (and they are always hungry), the heart yearns within them, and they want to eat.

"To-day you shall have an extra piece of bread," says the father, and cuts his own in two, and Fradke and Beilke stretch out their dirty little hands for it, and are overjoyed.

"Tatinke, you are not eating," remark the elder girls at supper, "this is not a fast day!"

"And no more *do* I fast!" replies the father, and thinks: "That was a take-in, but not a lie, because, after all, a glass of water—that is not eating and not fasting, either."

When it comes to the eve of the Ninth of Ab, Chayyim feels so light and airy as he never felt before, not because it is time to prepare for the fast by taking a meal, not because he may eat. On the contrary, he feels that if he took anything solid into his mouth, it would not go down, but stick in his throat.

That is, his heart is very sick, and his hands and feet shake; his body is attracted earthwards, his strength fails, he feels like fainting. But fie, what an idea! To fast a whole week, to arrive at the eve of the Ninth of Ab, and not hold out to the end! Never!

And Chayyim Chaikin takes his portion of bread and potato, calls Fradke and Beilke, and whispers:

"Children, take this and eat it, but don't let Mother see!"

And Fradke and Beilke take their father's share of food, and look wonderingly at his livid face and shaking hands.

Chayyim sees the children snatch at the bread and munch and swallow, and he shuts his eyes, and rises from his place. He cannot wait for the other girls to come home from the factory, but takes his book of Lamentations, puts off his shoes, and drags himself—it is all he can do—to the Shool.

He is nearly the first to arrive. He secures a seat next the reader, on an overturned bench, lying with its feet in the air, and provides himself with a bit of burned-down candle, which he glues with its drippings to the foot of the bench, leans against the corner of the platform, opens his book, "Lament for Zion and all the other towns," and he closes his eyes and sees Zion robed in black, with a black veil over her face, lamenting and weeping and wringing her hands, mourning for her children who fall daily, daily, in foreign lands, for other men's sins.

" And wilt not thou, O Zion, ask of me
    Some tidings of the children from thee reft?
  I bring thee greetings over land and sea,
    From those remaining—from the remnant left!—— "

And he opens his eyes and sees:

A bright sunbeam has darted in through the dull, dusty window-pane, a beam of the sun which is setting yonder behind the town. And though he shuts them again, he still sees the beam, and not only the beam, but the whole sun, the bright, beautiful sun, and no one can see it but him! Chayyim Chaikin looks at the sun and sees it—and that's all! How is it? It must be because he has done with the world and its necessities—he feels happy—he feels light—he can bear anything—he will have an easy fast—do you know, he will have an easy fast, an easy fast!

Chayyim Chaikin shuts his eyes, and sees a strange world, a new world, such as he never saw before. Angels seem to hover before his eyes, and he looks at them, and recognizes his children in them, all his children, big and little, and he wants to say something to them, and cannot speak—he wants to explain to them, that he cannot help it—it is not his fault! How should it, no evil eye! be his fault, that so many Jews are gathered together in one place and squeeze each other, all for love, squeeze each other to death for love? How can he help it, if people desire other people's sweat, other people's blood? if people have not learned to see that one should not drive a man as a horse is driven to work? that a horse is also to be pitied, one of God's creatures, a living thing?——

And Chayyim Chaikin keeps his eyes shut, and sees, sees everything. And everything is bright and light, and curls like smoke, and he feels something is going out of him, from inside, from his heart, and is drawn upward and loses itself from the body, and he feels very light, very, very light, and he gives a sigh—a long, deep sigh—and feels still lighter, and after that he feels nothing at all—absolutely nothing at all—

Yes, he has an easy fast.

When Bäre the beadle, a red-haired Jew with thick lips, came into the Shool in his socks with the worn-down heels, and saw Chayyim Chaikin leaning with his head back, and his eyes open, he was angry, thought Chayyim was dozing, and he began to grumble:

"He ought to be ashamed of himself—reclining like that—came here for a nap, did he?—Reb Chayyim, excuse me, Reb Chayyim!——"

But Chayyim Chaikin did not hear him.

The last rays of the sun streamed in through the Shool window, right onto Chayyim Chaikin's quiet face with the black, shining, curly hair, the black, bushy brows, the half-open, black, kindly eyes, and lit the dead, pale, still, hungry face through and through.

I told you how it would be: Chayyim Chaikin had an easy fast!

THE PASSOVER GUEST

I

"I have a Passover guest for you, Reb Yoneh, such a guest as you never had since you became a householder."

"What sort is he?"

"A real Oriental citron!"

"What does that mean?"

"It means a 'silken Jew,' a personage of distinction. The only thing against him is—he doesn't speak our language."

"What does he speak, then?"

"Hebrew."

"Is he from Jerusalem?"

"I don't know where he comes from, but his words are full of a's."

Such was the conversation that took place between my father and the beadle, a day before Passover, and I was wild with curiosity to see the "guest" who didn't understand Yiddish, and who talked with a's. I had already noticed, in synagogue, a strange-looking individual, in a fur cap, and a Turkish robe striped blue, red, and yellow. We boys crowded round him on all sides, and stared, and then caught it hot from the beadle, who said children had no business "to creep into a stranger's face" like that. Prayers over, everyone greeted the stranger, and wished him a happy Passover, and he, with a sweet smile on his red cheeks set in a round grey beard, replied to each one, "Shalom! Shalom!" instead of our Sholom. This "Shalom! Shalom!" of his sent us boys into fits of laughter. The beadle grew very angry, and pursued us with slaps. We eluded him, and stole deviously back to the stranger, listened to his "Shalom! Shalom!" exploded with laughter, and escaped anew from the hands of the beadle.

I am puffed up with pride as I follow my father and his guest to our house, and feel how all my comrades envy me. They stand looking after us, and every now and then I turn my head, and put out my tongue at them. The walk home is silent. When we arrive, my father greets my mother with "a happy Passover!" and the guest nods his head so that his fur cap shakes. "Shalom! Shalom!" he says. I think of my comrades, and hide my head under the table, not to burst out laughing. But I shoot continual glances at the guest, and his appearance pleases me; I like his Turkish robe, striped yellow, red, and blue, his fresh, red cheeks set in a curly grey beard, his beautiful black eyes that look out so pleasantly from beneath his bushy eyebrows. And I see that my father is pleased with him, too, that he is delighted with him. My mother looks at him as though he were something more than a man, and no one speaks to him but my father, who offers him the cushioned reclining-seat at table.

Mother is taken up with the preparations for the Passover meal, and Rikel the maid is helping her. It is only when the time comes for saying Kiddush that my father and the guest hold a Hebrew conversation. I am proud to find that I understand nearly every word of it. Here it is in full.

My father: "Nu?" (That means, "Won't you please say Kiddush?")

The guest: "Nu-nu!" (meaning, "Say it rather yourself!")

My father: "Nu-O?" ("Why not you?")

The guest: "O-nu?" ("Why should I?")

My father: "I-O!" ("You first!")

The guest: "O-ai!" ("*You* first!")

My father: "È-o-i!" ("I beg of you to say it!")

The guest: "Ai-o-ê!" ("I beg of you!")

My father: "Ai-e-o-nu?" ("Why should you refuse?")

The guest: "Oi-o-e-nu-nu!" ("If you insist, then I must.")

And the guest took the cup of wine from my father's hand, and recited a Kiddush. But what a Kiddush! A Kiddush such as we had never heard before, and shall never hear again. First, the Hebrew—all a's. Secondly, the voice, which seemed to come, not out of his beard, but out of the striped Turkish robe. I thought of my comrades, how they would have laughed, what slaps would have rained down, had they been present at that Kiddush.

Being alone, I was able to contain myself. I asked my father the Four Questions, and we all recited the Haggadah together. And I was elated to think that such a guest was ours, and no one else's.

II

Our sage who wrote that one should not talk at meals (may he forgive me for saying so!) did not know Jewish life. When shall a Jew find time to talk, if not during a meal? Especially at Passover, when there is so much to say before the meal and after it. Rikel the maid handed the water, we washed our hands, repeated the Benediction, mother helped us to fish, and my father turned up his sleeves, and started a long Hebrew talk with the guest. He began with the first question one Jew asks another:

"What is your name?"

To which the guest replied all in a's and all in one breath:

"Ayak Bakar Gashal Damas Hanoch Vassam Za'an Chafaf Tatzatz."

My father remained with his fork in the air, staring in amazement at the possessor of so long a name. I coughed and looked under the table, and my mother said, "Favele, you should be careful eating fish, or you might be choked with a bone," while she gazed at our guest with awe. She appeared overcome by his name, although unable to understand it. My father, who understood, thought it necessary to explain it to her.

"You see, Ayak Bakar, that is our Alef-Bes inverted. It is apparently their custom to name people after the alphabet."

"Alef-Bes! Alef-Bes!" repeated the guest with the sweet smile on his red cheeks, and his beautiful black eyes rested on us all, including Rikel the maid, in the most friendly fashion.

Having learnt his name, my father was anxious to know whence, from what land, he came. I understood this from the names of countries and towns which I caught, and from what my father translated for my mother, giving her a Yiddish version of nearly every phrase. And my mother was quite overcome by every single thing she heard, and Rikel the maid was overcome likewise. And no wonder! It is not every day that a person comes from perhaps two thousand miles away, from a land only to be reached across seven seas and a desert, the desert journey alone requiring forty days and nights. And when you get near to the land, you have to climb a mountain of which the top reaches into the clouds, and this is covered with ice, and dreadful winds blow there, so that there is peril of death! But once the mountain is safely climbed, and the land is reached, one beholds a terrestrial Eden. Spices, cloves, herbs, and every kind of fruit—apples, pears, and oranges, grapes, dates, and olives, nuts and quantities of figs. And the houses there are all built of deal, and roofed with silver, the furniture is gold (here the guest cast a look at our silver cups, spoons, forks, and knives), and brilliants, pearls, and diamonds bestrew the roads, and no one cares to take the trouble of picking them up, they are of no value there. (He was looking at my mother's diamond ear-rings, and at the pearls round her white neck.)

"You hear that?" my father asked her, with a happy face.

"I hear," she answered, and added: "Why don't they bring some over here? They could make money by it. Ask him that, Yoneh!"

My father did so, and translated the answer for my mother's benefit:

"You see, when you arrive there, you may take what you like, but when you leave the country, you must

11

leave everything in it behind, too, and if they shake out of you no matter what, you are done for."

"What do you mean?" questioned my mother, terrified.

"I mean, they either hang you on a tree, or they stone you with stones."

III

The more tales our guest told us, the more thrilling they became, and just as we were finishing the dumplings and taking another sip or two of wine, my father inquired to whom the country belonged. Was there a king there? And he was soon translating, with great delight, the following reply:

"The country belongs to the Jews who live there, and who are called Sefardîm. And they have a king, also a Jew, and a very pious one, who wears a fur cap, and who is called Joseph ben Joseph. He is the high priest of the Sefardîm, and drives out in a gilded carriage, drawn by six fiery horses. And when he enters the synagogue, the Levites meet him with songs."

"There are Levites who sing in your synagogue?" asked my father, wondering, and the answer caused his face to shine with joy.

"What do you think?" he said to my mother. "Our guest tells me that in his country there is a temple, with priests and Levites and an organ."

"Well, and an altar?" questioned my mother, and my father told her:

"He says they have an altar, and sacrifices, he says, and golden vessels—everything just as we used to have it in Jerusalem."

And with these words my father sighs deeply, and
my mother, as she looks at him, sighs also, and I cannot
understand the reason. Surely we should be proud and
glad to think we have such a land, ruled over by a
Jewish king and high priest, a land with Levites and
an organ, with an altar and sacrifices—and bright,
sweet thoughts enfold me, and carry me away as on
wings to that happy Jewish land where the houses are
of pine-wood and roofed with silver, where the furniture
is gold, and diamonds and pearls lie scattered in the
street. And I feel sure, were I really there, I should
know what to do—I should know how to hide things—
they would shake nothing out of *me*. I should certainly
bring home a lovely present for my mother, diamond
ear-rings and several pearl necklaces. I look at the one
mother is wearing, at her ear-rings, and I feel a great
desire to be in that country. And it occurs to me, that
after Passover I will travel there with our guest,
secretly, no one shall know. I will only speak of it
to our guest, open my heart to him, tell him the whole
truth, and beg him to take me there, if only for a little
while. He will certainly do so, he is a very kind and
approachable person, he looks at every one, even at Rikel
the maid, in such a friendly, such a very friendly way!

"So I think, and it seems to me, as I watch our
guest, that he has read my thoughts, and that his
beautiful black eyes say to me:

"Keep it dark, little friend, wait till after Passover,
then we shall manage it!"

IV

I dreamt all night long. I dreamt of a desert, a temple, a high priest, and a tall mountain. I climb the mountain. Diamonds and pearls grow on the trees, and my comrades sit on the boughs, and shake the jewels down onto the ground, whole showers of them, and I stand and gather them, and stuff them into my pockets, and, strange to say, however many I stuff in, there is still room! I stuff and stuff, and still there is room! I put my hand into my pocket, and draw out—not pearls and brilliants, but fruits of all kinds— apples, pears, oranges, olives, dates, nuts, and figs. This makes me very unhappy, and I toss from side to side. Then I dream of the temple, I hear the priests chant, and the Levites sing, and the organ play. I want to go inside and I cannot—Rikel the maid has hold of me, and will not let me go. I beg of her and scream and cry, and again I am very unhappy, and toss from side to side. I wake—and see my father and mother standing there, half dressed, both pale, my father hanging his head, and my mother wringing her hands, and with her soft eyes full of tears. I feel at once that something has gone very wrong, very wrong indeed, but my childish head is incapable of imagining the greatness of the disaster.

The fact is this: our guest from beyond the desert and the seven seas has disappeared, and a lot of things have disappeared with him: all the silver wine-cups, all the silver spoons, knives, and forks; all my mother's ornaments, all the money that happened to be in the house, and also Rikel the maid!

A pang goes through my heart. Not on account of the silver cups, the silver spoons, knives, and forks that have vanished; not on account of mother's ornaments or of the money, still less on account of Rikel the maid, a good riddance! But because of the happy, happy land whose roads were strewn with brilliants, pearls, and diamonds; because of the temple with the priests, the Levites, and the organ; because of the altar and the sacrifices; because of all the other beautiful things that have been taken from me, taken, taken, taken!

I turn my face to the wall, and cry quietly to myself.

GYMNASIYE

A man's worst enemy, I tell you, will never do him the harm he does himself, especially when a woman interferes, that is, a wife. Whom do you think I have in mind when I say that? My own self! Look at me and think. What would you take me for? Just an ordinary Jew. It doesn't say on my nose whether I have money, or not, or whether I am very low indeed, does it?

It may be that I once *had* money, and not only that—money in itself is nothing—but I can tell you, I earned a living, and that respectably and quietly, without worry and flurry, not like some people who like to live in a whirl.

No, my motto is, "More haste, less speed."

I traded quietly, went bankrupt a time or two quietly, and quietly went to work again. But there is a God in the world, and He blessed me with a wife—as she isn't here, we can speak openly—a wife like any other, that is, at first glance she isn't so bad—not at all! In person, (no evil eye!) twice my height; not an ugly woman, quite a beauty, you may say; an intelligent woman, quite a man—and that's the whole trouble! Oi, it isn't good when the wife is a man! The Almighty knew what He was about when, at the creation, he formed Adam first and then Eve. But what's the use of telling her that, when *she* says, "If the Almighty created Adam first and then Eve, that's *His* affair, but if he put more

sense into my heel than into your head, no more am
I to blame for that!"

"What is all this about?" say I.—"It's about that
which should be first and foremost with you," says she
"But I have to be the one to think of everything—even
about sending the boy to the Gymnasiye!"—"Where,"
say I, "is it 'written' that my boy should go to the
Gymnasiye? Can I not afford to have him taught
Torah at home?"—"I've told you a hundred and fifty
times," says she, "that you won't persuade me to go
against the world! And the world," says she, "has
decided that children should go to the Gymnasiye."—"In
my opinion," say I, "the world is mad!"—"And you,"
says she, "are the only sane person in it? A pretty thing
it would be," says she, "if the world were to follow
you!"—"Every man," say I, "should decide on his own
course."—"If my enemies," says she, "and my friends'
enemies, had as little in pocket and bag, in box and
chest, as you have in your head, the world would be
a different place."—"Woe to the man," say I, "who
needs to be advised by his wife!"—"And woe to the
wife," says she, "who has that man to her husband!"—
Now if you can argue with a woman who, when you say
one thing, maintains the contrary, when you give her
one word, treats you to a dozen, and who, if you bid
her shut up, cries, or even, I beg of you, faints—well,
I envy you, that's all! In short, up and down, this way
and that way, she got the best of it—she, not I, because
the fact is, when she wants a thing, it has to be!

Well, what next? Gymnasiye! The first thing was
to prepare the boy for the elementary class in the

Junior Preparatory. I must say, I did not see anything very alarming in that. It seemed to me that anyone of our Cheder boys, an Alef-Bes scholar, could tuck it all into his belt, especially a boy like mine, for whose equal you might search an empire, and not find him. I am a father, not of you be it said! but that boy has a memory that beats everything! To cut a long story short, he went up for examination and—did *not* pass! You ask the reason? He only got a two in arithmetic; they said he was weak at calculation, in the science of mathematics. What do you think of that? He has a memory that beats everything! I tell you, you might search an empire for his like—and they come talking to me about mathematics! Well, he failed to pass, and it vexed me very much. If he *was* to go up for examination, let him succeed. However, being a man and not a woman, I made up my mind to it—it's a misfortune, but a Jew is used to that. Only what was the use of talking to *her* with that bee in her bonnet? Once for all, Gymnasiye! I reason with her. "Tell me," say I, "(may you be well!) what is the good of it? He's safe," say I, "from military service, being an only son, and as for Parnosseh, devil I need it for Parnosseh! What do I care if he *does* become a trader like his father, a merchant like the rest of the Jews? If he is destined to become a rich man, a banker, I don't see that I'm to be pitied."

Thus do I reason with her as with the wall. "So much the better," says she, "if he has *not* been entered for the Junior Preparatory."—"What now?" say I.

"Now," says she, "he can go direct to the Senior Preparatory."

Well, Senior Preparatory, there's nothing so terrible
in that, for the boy has a head, I tell you! You might
search an empire. . . . . And what was the result?
Well, what do you suppose? Another two instead of a
five, not in mathematics this time—a fresh calamity!
His spelling is not what it should be. That is, he can
spell all right, but he gets a bit mixed with the two Russian e's. That is, he puts them in right enough, why
shouldn't he? only not in their proper places. Well,
there's a misfortune for you! I guess I won't find the
way to Poltava fair if the child cannot put the e's
where they belong! When they brought the good news,
she turned the town inside out; ran to the director,
declared that the boy *could* do it; to prove it, let him
be had up again! They paid her as much attention as
if she were last year's snow, put a two, and another
sort of two, and a two with a dash! Call me nut-
crackers, but there was a commotion. "Failed again!"
say I to her. "And if so," say I, "what is to be done?
Are we to commit suicide? A Jew," say I, "is used to
that sort of thing," upon which she fired up and blazed
away and stormed and scolded as only she can. But I
let you off! He, poor child, was in a pitiable state.
Talk of cruelty to animals! Just think: the other boys
in little white buttons, and not he! I reason with him:
"You little fool! What does it matter? Who ever
heard of an examination at which everyone passed?
Somebody must stay at home, mustn't they? Then why
not you? There's really nothing to make such a fuss
about." My wife, overhearing, goes off into a fresh
fury, and falls upon me. "A fine comforter *you* are,"

says she, "who asked you to console him with that sort of nonsense? You'd better see about getting him a proper teacher," says she, "a private teacher, a Russian, for grammar!"

You hear that? Now I must Have two teachers for him—one teacher and a Rebbe are not enough. Up and down, this way and that way, she got the best of it, as usual.

What next? We engaged a second teacher, a Russian this time, not a Jew, preserve us, but a real Gentile, because grammar in the first class, let me tell you, is no trifle, no shredded horseradish! Gra-ma-ti-ke, indeed! The two e's! Well, I was telling about the teacher that God sent us for our sins. It's enough to make one blush to remember the way he treated us, as though we had been the mud under his feet. Laughed at us to our face, he did, devil take him, and the one and only thing he could teach him was: tshasnok, tshasnoka, tshasnoku, tshasnokom. If it hadn't been for *her,* I should have had him by the throat, and out into the street with his blessed grammar. But to *her* it was all right and as it should be. Now the boy will know which e to put. If you'll believe me, they tormented him through that whole winter, for he was not to be had up for slaughter till about Pentecost. Pentecost over, he went up for examination, and this time he brought home no more two's, but a four and a five. There was great joy—we congratulate! we congratulate! Wait a bit, don't be in such a hurry with your congratulations! We don't know yet for certain whether he has got in or not. We shall not know till

August. Why not till August? Why not before? Go
and ask *them*. What is to be done? A Jew is used to
that sort of thing.

August—and I gave a glance out of the corner of my
eye. She was up and doing! From the director to the
inspector, from the inspector to the director! "Why
are you running from Shmunin to Bunin," say I, "like
a poisoned mouse?"

"You asking why?" says she. "Aren't you a native
of this place? You don't seem to know how it is nowadays with the Gymnasiyes and the percentages?" And
what came of it? He did *not* pass! You ask why?
Because he hadn't two fives. If he had had two fives,
then, they say, perhaps he would have got in. You hear
—perhaps! How do you like that *perhaps?* Well, I'll
let you off what I had to bear from her. As for him,
the little boy, it was pitiful. Lay with his face in the
cushion, and never stopped crying till we promised him
another teacher. And we got him a student from the
Gymnasiye itself, to prepare him for the second class,
but after quite another fashion, because the second class
is no joke. In the second, besides mathematics and
grammar, they require geography, penmanship, and I
couldn't for the life of me say what else. I should have
thought a bit of the Maharsho was a more difficult thing
than all their studies put together, and very likely had
more sense in it, too. But what would you have? A Jew
learns to put up with things.

In fine, there commenced a series of "lessons," of
ouròkki. We rose early—the ouròkki! Prayers and
breakfast over—the ouròkki. A whole day—ouròkki.

One heard him late at night drumming it over and
over: Nominative—dative—instrumental—vocative! It
grated so on my ears! I could hardly bear it. Eat?
Sleep? Not he! Taking a poor creature and tormenting
it like that, all for nothing, I call it cruelty to animals!
"The child," say I, "will be ill!" "Bite off your
tongue," says she. I was nowhere, and he went up a
second time to the slaughter, and brought home nothing
but fives! And why not? I tell you, he has a head—
there isn't his like! And such a boy for study as never
was, always at it, day and night, and repeating to himself between whiles! That's all right then, is it? Was
it all right? When it came to the point, and they hung
out the names of all the children who were really
entered, we looked—mine wasn't there! Then there
was a screaming and a commotion. What a shame!
And nothing but fives! *Now* look at her, now see her go,
see her run, see her do this and that! In short, she went
and she ran and she did this and that and the other—
until at last they begged her not to worry them any
longer, that is, to tell you the truth, between ourselves,
they turned her out, yes! And after they had turned
her out, then it was she burst into the house, and showed
for the first time, as it were, what she was worth.
"Pray," said she, "what sort of a father are you? If
you were a good father, an affectionate father, like other
fathers, you would have found favor with the director,
patronage, recommendations, this—that!" Like a
woman, wasn't it? It's not enough, apparently, for me
to have my head full of terms and seasons and fairs
and notes and bills of exchange and "protests" and all

the rest of it. "Do you want me," say I, "to take over your Gymnasiye and your classes, things I'm sick of already?" Do you suppose she listened to what I said? She? Listen? She just kept at it, she sawed and filed and gnawed away like a worm, day and night, day and night! "If your wife," says she, *"were* a wife, and your child, a child—if I were only of *so* much account in this house!"—"Well," say I, "what would happen?"—"You would lie," says she, "nine ells deep in the earth. I," says she, "would bury you three times a day, so that you should never rise again!"

How do you like that? Kind, wasn't it? That (how goes the saying?) was pouring a pailful of water over a husband for the sake of peace. Of course, you'll understand that I was not silent, either, because, after all, I'm no more than a man, and every man has his feelings. I assure you, you needn't envy me, and in the end *she* carried the day, as usual.

Well, what next? I began currying favor, getting up an acquaintance, trying this and that; I had to lower myself in people's eyes and swallow slights, for every one asked questions, and they had every right to do so. "You, no evil eye, Reb Aaron," say they, "are a householder, and inherited a little something from your father. What good year is taking you about to places where a Jew had better not be seen?" Was I to go and tell them I had a wife (may she live one hundred and twenty years!) with this on the brain: Gymnasiye, Gymnasiye, and Gym-na-si-ye? I (much good may it do you!) am, as you see me, no more unlucky than most people, and with God's help I made

my way, and got where I wanted, right up to the nobleman, into his cabinet, yes! And sat down with him
there to talk it over. I thank Heaven, I can talk to any
nobleman, I don't need to have my tongue loosened for
me. "What can I do for you?" he asks, and bids me be
seated. Say I, and whisper into his ear, "My lord,"
say I, "we," say I, "are not rich people, but we have,"
say I, "a boy, and he wishes to study, and I," say I,
"wish it, too, but my wife wishes it very much!" Says
he to me again, "What is it you want?" Say I to him,
and edge a bit closer, "My dear lord," say I, "we," say
I, "are not rich people, but we have," say I, "a small
fortune, and one remarkably clever boy, who," say I,
"wishes to study; and I," say I, "also wish it, but my
wife wishes it *very much!*" and I squeeze that "very
much" so that he may understand. But he's a Gentile
and slow-witted, and he doesn't twig, and this time he
asks angrily, "Then, whatever is it you want?!" I
quietly put my hand into my pocket and quietly take
it out again, and I say quietly: "Pardon me, we," say
I, "are not rich people, but we have a little," say I,
"fortune, and one remarkably clever boy, who," say I,
"wishes to study; and I," say I, "wish it also, but my
wife," say I, "wishes it very much indeed!" and I
take and press into his hand——and this time, yes!
he understood, and went and got a note-book, and
asked my name and my son's name, and which class I
wanted him entered for.

"Oho, lies the wind that way?" think I to myself, and
I give him to understand that I am called Katz, Aaron
Katz, and my son, Moisheh, Moshke we call him, and I

want to get him into the third class. Says he to me,
if I am Katz, and my son is Moisheh, Moshke we call
him, and he wants to get into class three, I am to
bring him in January, and he will certainly be passed.
You hear and understand? Quite another thing!
Apparently the horse trots as we shoe him. The worst
is having to wait. But what is to be done? When they
say, Wait! one waits. A Jew is used to waiting.

January—a fresh commotion, a scampering to and
fro. To-morrow there will be a consultation. The
director and the inspector and all the teachers of the
Gymnasiye will come together, and it's only after the
consultation that we shall know if he is entered or not.
The time for action has come, and my wife is anywhere
but at home. No hot meals, no samovar, no nothing!
She is in the Gymnasiye, that is, not *in* the Gymnasiye,
but *at* it, walking round and round it in the frost, from
first thing in the morning, waiting for them to begin
coming away from the consultation. The frost bites,
there is a tearing east wind, and she paces round and
round the building, and waits. Once a woman, always
a woman! It seemed to me, that when people have
made a promise, it is surely sacred, especially—you
understand? But who would reason with a woman?
Well, she waited one hour, she waited two, waited three,
waited four; the children were all home long ago, and
she waited on. She waited (much good may it do
you!) till she got what she was waiting for. A door
opens, and out comes one of the teachers. She springs
and seizes hold on him. Does he know the result of the
consultation? Why, says he, should he not? They

have passed altogether twenty-five children, twenty-three Christian and two Jewish. Says she, "Who are they?" Says he, "One a Shefselsohn and one a Katz." At the name Katz, my wife shoots home like an arrow from the bow, and bursts into the room in triumph: "Good news! good news! Passed, passed!" and there are tears in her eyes. Of course, I am pleased, too, but I don't feel called upon to go dancing, being a man and not a woman. "It's evidently not much *you* care?" says she to me. "What makes you think that?" say I. —"This," says she, "you sit there cold as a stone! If you knew how impatient the child is, you would have taken him long ago to the tailor's, and ordered his little uniform," says she, "and a cap and a satchel," says she, "and made a little banquet for our friends."— "Why a banquet, all of a sudden?" say I. "Is there a Bar-Mitzveh? Is there an engagement?" I say all this quite quietly, for, after all, I am a man, not a woman. She grew so angry that she stopped talking. And when a woman stops talking, it's a thousand times worse than when she scolds, because so long as she is scolding at least you hear the sound of the human voice. Otherwise it's talk to the wall! To put it briefly, she got her way—she, not I—as usual.

There was a banquet; we invited our friends and our good friends, and my boy was dressed up from head to foot in a very smart uniform, with white buttons and a cap with a badge in front, quite the district-governor! And it did one's heart good to see him, poor child! There was new life in him, he was so happy, and he shone, I tell you, like the July sun! The company

drank to him, and wished him joy: Might he study
in health, and finish the course in health, and go on in
health, till he reached the university! "Ett!" say I,
"we can do with less. Let him only complete the eight
classes at the Gymnasiye," say I, "and, please God, I'll
make a bridegroom of him, with God's help." Cries my
wife, smiling and fixing me with her eye the while,
"Tell him," says she, "that he's wrong! He," says
she, "keeps to the old-fashioned cut." "Tell her from
me," say I, "that I'm blest if the old-fashioned cut
wasn't better than the new." Says she, "Tell him that
he (may he forgive me!) is——" The company burst
out laughing. "Oi, Reb Aaron," say they, "you have
a wife (no evil eye!) who is a Cossack and not a wife
at all!" Meanwhile they emptied their wine-glasses,
and cleared their plates, and we were what is called
"lively." I and my wife were what is called "taken
into the boat," the little one in the middle, and we made
merry till daylight. That morning early we took him
to the Gymnasiye. It was very early, indeed, the door
was shut, not a soul to be seen. Standing outside there
in the frost, we were glad enough when the door opened,
and they let us in. Directly after that the small fry
began to arrive with their satchels, and there was a
noise and a commotion and a chatter and a laughing
and a scampering to and fro—a regular fair! School-
boys jumped over one another, gave each other punches,
pokes, and pinches. As I looked at these young hope-
fuls with the red cheeks, with the merry, laughing eyes,
I called to mind our former narrow, dark, and gloomy
Cheder of long ago years, and I saw that after all she

12

was right; she might be a woman, but she had a man's head on her shoulders! And as I reflected thus, there came along an individual in gilt buttons, who turned out to be a teacher, and asked what I wanted. I pointed to my boy, and said I had come to bring him to Cheder. that is, to the Gymnasiye. He asked to which class? I tell him, the third, and he has only just been entered. He asks his name. Say I, "Katz, Moisheh Katz, that is, Moshke Katz." Says he, "Moshke Katz?" He has no Moshke Katz in the third class. "There is," he says, "a Katz, only not a Moshke Katz, but a Morduch— Morduch Katz." Say I, "What Morduch? Moshke, not Morduch!" "Morduch!" he repeats, and thrusts the paper into my face. I to him, "Moshke." He to me, "Morduch!" In short, Moshke—Morduch, Morduch— Moshke, we hammer away till there comes out a fine tale: that which should have been mine is another's. You see what a kettle of fish? A regular Gentile muddle! They have entered a Katz—yes! But, by mistake, another, not ours. You see how it was: there were two Katz's in our town! What do you say to such luck? I have made a bed, and another will lie in it! No, but you ought to know who the other is, *that* Katz, I mean! A nothing of a nobody, an artisan, a bookbinder or a carpenter, quite a harmless little man, but who ever heard of him? A pauper! And *his* son—yes! And mine—no! Isn't it enough to disgust one, I ask you! And you should have seen that poor boy of mine, when he was told to take the badge off his cap! No bride on her wedding-day need shed more tears than were his! And no matter how I reasoned with him, whether I coaxed or scolded. "You see," I said to her, "what you've done! Didn't I tell you that your Gymnasiye was a slaughter-house for him? I only trust this may have a good ending, that he won't fall ill."—"Let my enemies," said she, "fall ill, if they like. My child," says she, "must enter the Gymnasiye. If he hasn't got in this time, in a year, please God, he *will*. If he hasn't got in," says she, "*here,* he will get in in another town—he *must* get in! Otherwise," says she, "I shall shut an eye, and the earth shall cover me!" You hear what she said? And who, do you suppose, had his way—she or I? When *she* sets her heart on a thing, can there be any question?

Well, I won't make a long story of it. I hunted up and down with him; we went to the ends of the world, wherever there was a town and a Gymnasiye, thither went we! We went up for examination, and were examined, and we passed and passed high, and did *not* get in—and why? All because of the percentage! You may believe, I looked upon my own self as crazy those days! "Wretch! what is this? What is this flying that you fly from one town to another? What good is to come of it? And suppose he does get in, what then?" No, say what you will, ambition is a great thing. In the end it took hold of me, too, and the Almighty had compassion, and sent me a Gymnasiye in Poland, a "commercial" one, where they took in one Jew to every Christian. It came to fifty per cent. But what then? Any Jew who wished his son to enter must bring his Christian with him, and if he passes, that is, the Christian, and one pays his entrance fee, then there is hope.

Instead of one bundle, one has two on one's shoulders, you understand? Besides being worn with anxiety about my own, I had to tremble for the other, because if Esau, which Heaven forbid, fail to pass, it's all over with Jacob. But what I went through before I *got* that Christian, a shoemaker's son, Holiava his name was, is not to be described. And the best of all was this— would you believe that my shoemaker, planted in the earth firmly as Korah, insisted on Bible teaching? There was nothing for it but my son had to sit down beside his, and repeat the Old Testament. How came a son of mine to the Old Testament? Ai, don't ask! He can do everything and understands everything.

With God's help the happy day arrived, and they both passed. Is my story finished? Not quite. When it came to their being entered in the books, to writing out a check, my Christian was not to be found! What has happened? He, the Gentile, doesn't care for his son to be among so many Jews—he won't hear of it! Why should he, seeing that all doors are open to him anyhow, and he can get in where he pleases? Tell him it isn't fair? Much good that would be! "Look here," say I, "how much do you want, Pani Holiava?" Says he, "Nothing!" To cut the tale short—up and down, this way and that way, and friends and people interfering, we had him off to a refreshment place, and ordered a glass, and two, and three, before it all came right! Once he was really in, I cried my eyes out, and thanks be to Him whose Name is blessed, and who has delivered me out of all my troubles! When I got home, a fresh worry! What now? My wife has been reflecting and thinking it over: After all, her only son, the apple of her eye—he would be *there* and we *here!* And if so, what, says she, would life be to her? "Well," say I, "what do you propose doing?"—"What I propose doing?" says she. "Can't you guess? I propose," says she, "to be with him."—"You do?" say I. "And the house? What about the house?"—"The house," says she, "is a house." Anything to object to in that? So she was off to him, and I was left alone at home. And what a home! I leave you to imagine. May such a year be to my enemies! My comfort was gone, the business went to the bad. Everything went to the bad, and we were continually writing letters. I wrote to her, she wrote to me—letters went and letters came. Peace to my beloved wife! Peace to my beloved husband! "For Heaven's sake," I write, "what is to be the end of it? After all, I'm no more than a man! A man without a housemistress!" It was as much use as last year's snow; it was she who had her way, she, and not I, as usual.

To make an end of my story, I worked and worried myself to pieces, made a mull of the whole business, sold out, became a poor man, and carried my bundle over to them. Once there, I took a look round to see where I was in the world, nibbled here and there, just managed to make my way a bit, and entered into a partnership with a trader, quite a respectable man, yes! A well-to-do householder, holding office in the Shool, but at bottom a deceiver, a swindler, a pickpocket, who was nearly the ruin of me! You can imagine what a cheerful state of things it was. Meanwhile I come home one evening, and see my boy come to meet me, looking strangely red in the face, and without a badge on his cap. Say I to him, "Look here, Moshehl, where's your badge?" Says he to me, "Whatever badge?" Say I, "The button." Says he, "Whatever button?" Say I, "The button off your cap." It was a new cap with a new badge, only just bought for the festival! He grows redder than before, and says, "Taken off." Say I, "What do you mean by 'taken off'?" Says he, "I am free." Say I, "What do you mean by 'you are free'?" Says he, "We are *all* free." Say I, "What do you mean by 'we are *all* free'?" Says he, "We are not going back any more." Say I, "What do you mean by 'we are not going back'?" Says he, "We have united in the resolve to stay away." Say I, "What do you mean by *'you'* have united in a resolve? Who are 'you'? What is all this? Bless your grandmother," say I, "do you suppose I have been through all this for you to unite in a resolve? Alas! and alack!" say I, "for you and me and all of us! May it please God not to let this be visited on Jewish heads, because always and everywhere," say I, "Jews are the scapegoats." I speak thus to him and grow angry and reprove him as a father usually does reprove a child. But I have a wife (long life to her!), and she comes running, and washes my head for me, tells me I don't know what is going on in the world, that the world is quite another world to what it used to be, an intelligent world, an open world, a free world, "a world," says she, "in which all are equal, in which there are no rich and no poor, no masters and no servants, no sheep and no shears, no cats, rats, no piggy-wiggy——————" "Te-te-te!" say I, "where have you learned such fine language? a new speech," say I, "with new words. Why not open the hen-house, and let out the hens? Chuck—chuck—chuck, hurrah for freedom!" Upon which she blazes up as if I had poured ten pails of hot water over her. And now for it! As only *they* can! Well, one must sit it out and listen to the end. The worst of it is, there is no end. "Look here," say I, "hush!" say I, "and now let be!" say I, and beat upon my breast. "I have sinned!" say I, "I have transgressed, and now stop," say I, "if you would only be quiet!" But she won't hear, and she won't see. No, she says, she will know why and wherefore and for goodness' sake and exactly, and just how it was, and what it means, and how it happened, and once more and a second time, and all over again from the beginning!

I beg of you—who set the whole thing going? A— woman!

ELIEZER DAVID ROSENTHAL

Born, 1861, in Chotin, Bessarabia; went to Breslau, Germany, in 1880, and pursued studies at the University; returned to Bessarabia in 1882; co-editor of the Bibliothek Dos Leben, published at Odessa, 1904, and Kishineff, 1905; writer of stories.

SABBATH

Friday evening!

The room has been tidied, the table laid. Two Sabbath loaves have been placed upon it, and covered with a red napkin. At the two ends are two metal candlesticks, and between them two more of earthenware, with candles in them ready to be lighted.

On the small sofa that stands by the stove lies a sick man covered up with a red quilt, from under the quilt appears a pale, emaciated face, with red patches on the dried-up cheeks and a black beard. The sufferer· wears a nightcap, which shows part of his black hair and his black earlocks. There is no sign of life in his face, and only a faint one in his great, black eyes.

On a chair by the couch sits a nine-year-old girl with damp locks, which have just been combed out in honor of Sabbath. She is barefoot, dressed only in a shirt and a frock. The child sits swinging her feet, absorbed in what she is doing; but all her movements are gentle and noiseless.

The invalid coughed.

"Kche, kche, kche, kche," came from the sofa.

"What is it, Tate?" asked the little girl, swinging her feet.

The invalid made no reply.

He slowly raised his head with both hands, pulled down the nightcap, and coughed and coughed and coughed, hoarsely at first, then louder, the cough tearing at his sick chest and dinning in the ears. Then he sat up, and went on coughing and clearing his throat, till he had brought up the phlegm.

The little girl continued to be absorbed in her work and to swing her feet, taking very little notice of her sick father.

The invalid smoothed the creases in the cushion, laid his head down again, and closed his eyes. He lay thus for a few minutes, then he said quite quietly:

"Leah!"

"What is it, Tate?" inquired the child again, still swinging her feet.

"Tell . . mother . . . it is . . . time to . . . bless . . . the candles . . . "

The little girl never moved from her seat, but shouted through the open door into the shop:

"Mother, shut up shop! Father says it's time for candle-blessing.

"I'm coming, I'm coming," answered her mother from the shop.

She quickly disposed of a few women customers: sold one a kopek's worth of tea, the other, two kopeks' worth of sugar, the third, two tallow candles. Then she closed the shutters and the street door, and came into the room.

"You've drunk the glass of milk?" she inquired of the sick man.

"Yes . . . I have . . . drunk it," he replied.

"And you, Leahnyu, daughter," and she turned to the child, "may the evil spirit take you! Couldn't you put on your shoes without my telling you? Don't you know it's Sabbath?"

The little girl hung her head, and made no other answer.

Her mother went to the table, lighted the candles, covered her face with her hands, and blessed them.

After that she sat down on the seat by the window to take a rest.

It was only on Sabbath that she could rest from her hard work, toiling and worrying as she was the whole week long with all her strength and all her mind.

She sat lost in thought.

She was remembering past happy days.

She also had known what it is to enjoy life, when her husband was in health, and they had a few hundred rubles. They finished boarding with her parents, they set up a shop, and though he had always been a close frequenter of the house-of-study, a bench-lover, he soon learnt the Torah of commerce. She helped him, and they made a livelihood, and ate their bread in honor. But in course of time some quite new shops were started in the little town, there was great competition, the trade was small, and the gains were smaller, it became necessary to borrow money on interest, on weekly payment, and to pay for goods at once. The interest gradually ate up the capital with the gains. The creditors took what they could lay hands on, and still her husband remained in their debt.

He could not get over this, and fell ill.

The whole bundle of trouble fell upon her: the burden of a livelihood, the children, the sick man, everything, everything, on her.

But she did not lose heart.

"God will help, *he* will soon get well, and will surely find some work. God will not desert us," so she reflected, and meantime she was not sitting idle.

The very difficulty of her position roused her courage, and gave her strength.

She sold her small store of jewelry, and set up a little shop.

Three years have passed since then.

However it may be, God has not abandoned her, and however bitter and sour the struggle for Parnosseh may have been, she had her bit of bread. Only his health did not return, he grew daily weaker and worse.

She glanced at her sick husband, at his pale, emaciated face, and tears fell from her eyes.

During the week she has no time to think how unhappy she is. Parnosseh, housework, attendance on the children and the sick man—these things take up all her time and thought. She is glad when it comes to bedtime, and she can fall, dead tired, onto her bed.

But on Sabbath, the day of rest, she has time to think over her hard lot and all her misery and to cry herself out.

"When will there be an end of my troubles and suffering?" she asked herself, and could give no answer whatever to the question beyond despairing tears. She saw no ray of hope lighting her future, only a great, wide, shoreless sea of trouble.

It flashed across her:

"When he dies, things will be easier."

But the thought of his death only increased her apprehension.

It brought with it before her eyes the dreadfud words:
widow, orphans, poor little fatherless children. . .

These alarmed her more than her present distress.

How can children grow up without a father? Now,
even though he's ill, he keeps an eye on them, tells
them to say their prayers and to study. Who is to
watch over them if he dies?

"Don't punish me, Lord of the World, for my bad
thought," she begged with her whole heart. "I will take
it upon myself to suffer and trouble for all, only don't
let him die, don't let me be called by the bitter name
of widow, don't let my children be called orphans!"

He sits upon his couch, his head a little thrown back
and leaning against the wall. In one hand he holds a
prayer-book—he is receiving the Sabbath into his house.
His pale lips scarcely move as he whispers the words
before him, and his thoughts are far from the prayer.
He knows that he is dangerously ill, he knows what his
wife has to suffer and bear, and not only is he powerless
to help her, but his illness is her heaviest burden, what
with the extra expense incurred on his account and the
trouble of looking after him. Besides which, his weak-
ness makes him irritable, and his anger has more than
once caused her unmerited pain. He sees and knows
it all, and his heart is torn with grief. "Only death
can help us," he murmurs, and while his lips repeat
the words of the prayer-book, his heart makes one request
to God and only one: that God should send kind Death
to deliver him from his trouble and misery.

Suddenly the door opened and a ten-year-old boy came into the room, in a long Sabbath cloak, with two long earlocks, and a prayer-book under his arm.

"A good Sabbath!" said the little boy, with a loud, ringing voice.

It seemed as if he and the holy Sabbath had come into the room together! In one moment the little boy had driven trouble and sadness out of sight, and shed light and consolation round him.

His "good Sabbath!" reached his parents' hearts, awoke there new life and new hopes.

"A good Sabbath!" answered the mother. Her eyes rested on the child's bright face, and her thoughts were no longer melancholy as before, for she saw in his eyes a whole future of happy possibilities.

"A good Sabbath!" echoed the lips of the sick man, and he took a deeper, easier breath. No, he will not die altogether, he will live again after death in the child. He can die in peace, he leaves a Kaddish behind him.

YOM KIPPUR

Erev Yom Kippur, Minchah time!

The Eve of the Day of Atonement, at Afternoon Prayer time.

A solemn and sacred hour for every Jew.

Everyone feels as though he were born again.

All the week-day worries, the two-penny–half-penny interests, seem far, far away; or else they have hidden themselves in some corner. Every Jew feels a noble pride, an inward peace mingled with fear and awe. He knows that the yearly Judgment Day is approaching, when God Almighty will hold the scales in His hand and weigh every man's merits against his transgressions. The sentence given on that day is one of life or death. No trifle! But the Jew is not so terrified as you might think—he has broad shoulders. Besides, he has a certain footing behind the "upper windows," he has good advocates and plenty of them; he has the "binding of Isaac" and a long chain of ancestors and ancestresses, who were put to death for the sanctification of the Holy Name, who allowed themselves to be burnt and roasted for the sake of God's Torah. Nishkoshe! Things are not so bad. The Lord of All may just remember that, and look aside a little. Is He not the Compassionate, the Merciful?

The shadows lengthen and lengthen.

Jews are everywhere in commotion.

Some hurry home straight from the bath, drops of bath-water dripping from beard and earlocks. They have not even dried their hair properly in their haste.

It is time to prepare for the davvening. Some are already on their way to Shool, robed in white. Nearly every Jew carries in one hand a large, well-packed Tallis-bag, which to-day, besides the prayer-scarf, holds the whole Jewish outfit: a bulky prayer-book, a book of Psalms, a Likkute Zevi, and so on; and in the other hand, two wax-candles, one a large one, that is the "light of life," and the other a small one, a shrunken looking thing, which is the "soul-light."

The Tamschevate house-of-study presents at this moment the following picture: the floor is covered with fresh hay, and the dust and the smell of the hay fill the whole building. Some of the men are standing at their prayers, beating their breasts in all seriousness: "We have trespassed, we have been faithless, we have robbed," with an occasional sob of contrition. Others are very busy setting up their wax-lights in boxes filled with sand; one of them, a young man who cannot live without it, betakes himself to the platform and repeats a "Bless ye the Lord." Meantime another comes slyly, and takes out two of the candles standing before the platform, planting his own in their place. Not far from the ark stands the beadle with a strap in his hand, and all the foremost householders go up to him, lay themselves down with their faces to the ground, and the beadle deals them out thirty-nine blows apiece, and not one of them bears him any grudge. Even Reb Groinom, from whom the beadle never hears anything from one Yom Kippur to another but "may you be . . ." and "rascal," "impudence," "brazen face," "spendthrift," "carrion," "dog of all dogs"—and not infrequently Reb Groinom allows himself to apply his right hand to the beadle's cheek, and the latter has to take it all in a spirit of love—this same Reb Groinom now humbly approaches the same poor beadle, lies quietly down with his face to the ground, stretches himself out, and the beadle deliberately counts the strokes up to "thirty-nine Malkes." Covered with hay, Reb Groinom rises slowly, a piteous expression on his face, just as if he had been well thrashed, and he pushes a coin into the Shamash's hand. This is evidently the beadle's day! To-day he can take his revenge on his householders for the insults and injuries of a whole year!

But if you want to be in the thick of it all, you must stand in the anteroom by the door, where people are crowding round the plates for collections. The treasurer sits beside a little table with the directors of the congregation; the largest plate lies before them. To one side of them sits the cantor with his plate, and beside the cantor, several house-of-study youths with theirs. On every plate lies a paper with a written notice: "Visiting the Sick," "Supporting the Fallen," "Clothing the Naked," "Talmud Torah," "Refuge for the Poor," and so forth. Over one plate, marked "The Return to the Land of Israel," presides a modern young man, a Zionist. Everyone wishing to enter the house-of-study must first go to the plates marked "Call to the Torah" and "Seat in the Shool," put in what is his due, and then throw a few kopeks into the other plates.

Berel Tzop bustled up to the plate "Seat in the Shool," gave what was expected of him, popped a few

coppers into the other plates, and prepared to recite
the Afternoon Prayer. He wanted to pause a little
between the words of his prayer, to attend to their
meaning, to impress upon himself that this was the Eve
of the Day of Atonement! But idle thoughts kept
coming into his head, as though on purpose to annoy
him, and his mind was all over the place at once! The
words of the prayers got mixed up with the idea of
oats, straw, wheat, and barley, and however much trouble
he took to drive these idle thoughts away, he did not
succeed. "Blow the great trumpet of our deliverance!"
shouted Berel, and remembered the while that Ivan owed
him ten measures of wheat. " . . . lift up the ensign
to gather our exiles! . . . "—"and I made a mistake in
Stephen's account by thirty kopeks . . . " Berel saw
that it was impossible for him to pray with attention,
and he began to reel off the Eighteen Benedictions,
but not till he reached the Confession could he collect
his scattered thoughts, and realize what he was saying.
When he raised his hands to beat his breast at "We
have trespassed, we have robbed," the hand remained
hanging in the air, half-way. A shudder went through
his limbs, the letters of the words "we have robbed"
began to grow before his eyes, they became gigantic,
they turned strange colors—red, blue, green, and yellow
—now they took the form of large frogs—they got
bigger and bigger, crawled into his eyes, croaked in
his ears: You are a thief, a robber, you have stolen and
plundered! You think nobody saw, that it would all
run quite smoothly, but you are wrong! We shall
stand before the Throne of Glory and cry: You are a
thief, a robber!

Berel stood some time with his hand raised midway in the air.

The whole affair of the hundred rubles rose before his eyes.

A couple of months ago he had gone into the house of Reb Moisheh Chalfon. The latter had just gone out, there was nobody else in the room, nobody had even seen him come in.

The key was in the desk—Berel had looked at it, had hardly touched it—the drawer had opened as though of itself—several hundred-ruble-notes had lain glistening before his eyes! Just that day, Berel had received a very unpleasant letter from the father of his daughter's bridegroom, and to make matters worse, the author of the letter was in the right. Berel had been putting off the marriage for two years, and the Mechutton wrote quite plainly, that unless the wedding took place after Tabernacles, he should return him the contract.

"Return the contract!" the fiery letters burnt into Berel's brain.

He knew his Mechutton well. The Misnaggid! He wouldn't hesitate to tear up a marriage contract, either! And when it's a question of a by no means pretty girl of twenty and odd years! And the kind of bridegroom anybody might be glad to have secured for his daughter! And then to think that only one of those hundred-ruble-notes lying tossed together in that drawer would help him out of all his troubles. And the Evil Inclination whispers in his ear: "Berel, now or never! There will be an end to all your worry! Don't you see, it's a godsend." He, Berel, wrestled with him hard.

He remembers it all distinctly, and he can hear now the faint little voice of the Good Inclination: "Berel, to become a thief in one's latter years! You who so carefully avoided even the smallest deceit! Fie, for shame! If God will, he can help you by honest means too." But the voice of the Good Inclination was so feeble, so husky, and the Evil Inclination suggested in his other ear: "Do you know what? *Borrow* one hundred rubles! Who talks of stealing? You will earn some money before long, and then you can pay him back—it's a charitable loan on his part, only that he doesn't happen to know of it. Isn't it plain to be seen that it's a godsend? If you don't call this Providence, what is? Are you going to take more than you really need? You know your Mechutton? Have you taken a good look at that old maid of yours? You recollect the bridegroom? Well, the Mechutton will be kind and mild as milk. The bridegroom will be a 'silken son-in-law,' the ugly old maid, a young wife—fool! God and men will envy you. . . " And he, Berel, lost his head, his thoughts flew hither and thither, like frightened birds, and—he no longer knew which of the two voices was that of the Good Inclination, and—

No one saw him leave Moisheh Chalfon's house.

And still his hand remains suspended in mid-air, still it does not fall against his breast, and there is a cold perspiration on his brow.

Berel started, as though out of his sleep. He had noticed that people were beginning to eye him as he stood with his hand held at a distance from his person. He hastily rattled through "For the sin, . . ." concluded the Eighteen Benedictions, and went home.

At home, he didn't dawdle, he only washed his hands, recited "Who bringest forth bread," and that was all. The food stuck in his throat, he said grace, returned to Shool, put on the Tallis, and started to intone tunefully the Prayer of Expiation.

The lighted wax-candles, the last rays of the sun stealing in through the windows of the house-of-study, the congregation entirely robed in white and enfolded in the prayer-scarfs, the intense seriousness depicted on all faces, the hum of voices, and the bitter weeping that penetrated from the women's gallery, all this suited Berel's mood, his contrite heart. Berel had recited the Prayer of Expiation with deep feeling; tears poured from his eyes, his own broken voice went right through his heart, every word found an echo there, and he felt it in every limb. Berel stood before God like a little child before its parents: he wept and told all that was in his heavily-laden heart, the full tale of his cares and troubles. Berel was pleased with himself, he felt that he was not saying the words anyhow, just rolling them off his tongue, but he was really performing an act of penitence with his whole heart. He felt remorse for his sins, and God is a God of compassion and mercy, who will certainly pardon him.

"Therefore is my heart sad," began Berel, "that the sin which a man commits against his neighbor cannot be atoned for even on the Day of Atonement, unless he asks his neighbor's forgiveness . . . therefore is my heart broken and my limbs tremble, because even the day of my death cannot atone for this sin."

Berel began to recite this in pleasing, artistic fashion, weeping and whimpering like a spoiled child, and drawling out the words, when it grew dark before his eyes. Berel had suddenly become aware that he was in the position of one about to go in through an open door. He advances, he must enter, it is a question of life and death. And without any warning, just as he is stepping across the threshhold, the door is shut from within with a terrible bang, and he remains standing outside.

And he has read this in the Prayer of Expiation? With fear and fluttering he reads it over again, looking narrowly at every word—a cold sweat covers him—the words prick him like pins. Are these two verses his pitiless judges, are they the expression of his sentence? Is he already condemned? "Ay, ay, you are guilty," flicker the two verses on the page before him, and prayer and tears are no longer of any avail. His heart cried to God: "Have pity, merciful Father! A grown-up girl—what am I to do with her? And his father wanted to break off the engagement. As soon as I have earned the money, I will give it back . . . " But he knew all the time that these were useless subterfuges; the Lord of the Universe can only pardon the sin committed against Himself, the sin committed against man cannot be atoned for even on the Day of Atonement!

Berel took another look at the Prayer of Expiation. The words, "unless he asks his neighbor's forgiveness," danced before his eyes. A ray of hope crept into his despairing heart. One way is left open to him: he can confess to Moisheh Chalfon! But the hope was quickly extinguished. Is that a small matter? What of my

honor, my good name? And what of the match?
"Mercy, O Father," he cried, "have mercy!"

Berel proceeded no further with the Prayer of Expiation. He stood lost in his melancholy thoughts, his
whole life passed before his eyes. He, Berel, had never
licked honey, trouble had been his in plenty, he had
known cares and worries, but God had never abandoned
him. It had frequently happened to him in the course
of his life to think he was lost, to give up all his hope.
But each time God had extricated him unexpectedly
from his difficulty, and not only that, but lawfully,
honestly, Jewishly. And now—he had suddenly lost his
trust in the Providence of His dear Name! "Donkey!"
thus Berel abused himself, "went to look for trouble, did
you? Now you've got it! Sold yourself body and
soul for one hundred rubles! Thief! thief! thief!" It
did Berel good to abuse himself like this, it gave him
a sort of pleasure to aggravate his wounds.

Berel, sunk in his sad reflections, has forgotten where
he is in the world. The congregation has finished the
Prayer of Expiation, and is ready for Kol Nidré. The
cantor is at his post at the reading-desk on the platform,
two of the principal, well-to-do Jews, with Torahs in
their hands, on each side of him. One of them is
Moisheh Chalfon. There is a deep silence in the building. The very last rays of the sun are slanting in
through the window, and mingling with the flames of
the wax-candles. . . .

"With the consent of the All-Present and with the
consent of this congregation, we give leave to pray with
them that have transgressed," startled Berel's ears. It

was Moisheh Chalfon's voice. The voice was low, sweet, and sad. Berel gave a side glance at where Moisheh Chalfon was standing, and it seemed to him that Moisheh Chalfon was doing the same to him, only Moisheh Chalfon was looking not into his eyes, but deep into his heart, and there reading the word Thief! And Moisheh Chalfon is permitting the people to pray together with him, Berel the thief!

"Mercy, mercy, compassionate God!" cried Berel's heart in its despair.

They had concluded Maariv, recited the first four chapters of the Psalms and the Song of Unity, and the people went home, to lay in new strength for the morrow.

There remained only a few, who spent the greater part of the night repeating Psalms, intoning the Mishnah, and so on; they snatched an occasional doze on the bare floor overlaid with a whisp of hay, an old cloak under their head. Berel also stayed the night in the house-of-study. He sat down in a corner, in robe and Tallis, and began reciting Psalms with a pleasing pathos, and he went on until overtaken by sleep. At first he resisted, he took a nice pinch of snuff, rubbed his eyes, collected his thoughts, but it was no good. The covers of the book of Psalms seemed to have been greased, for they continually slipped from his grasp, the printed lines had grown crooked and twisted, his head felt dreadfully heavy, and his eyelids clung together; his nose was forever drooping towards the book of Psalms. He made every effort to keep awake, started up every

time as though he had burnt himself, but sleep was the
stronger of the two. Gradually he slid from the bench
onto the floor; the Psalter slipped finally from between
his fingers, his head dropped onto the hay, and he fell
sweetly asleep . . .

And Berel had a dream:

Yom Kippur, and yet there is a fair in the town,
the kind of fair one calls an "earthquake," a fair such
as Berel does not remember having seen these many
years, so crowded is it with men and merchandise.
There is something of everything—cattle, horses, sheep,
corn, and fruit. All the Tamschevate Jews are strolling
round with their wives and children, there is buying
and selling, the air is full of noise and shouting, the
whole fair is boiling and hissing and humming like a
kettle. One runs this way and one that way, this one
is driving a cow, that one leading home a horse by the
rein, the other buying a whole cart-load of corn. Berel is
all astonishment and curiosity: how is it possible for
Jews to busy themselves with commerce on Yom Kippur? on such a holy day? As far back as he can
remember, Jews used to spend the whole day in Shool,
in linen socks, white robe, and prayer-scarf. They
prayed and wept. And now what has come over them,
that they should be trading on Yom Kippur, as if
it were a common week-day, in shoes and boots (this
last struck him more than anything)? Perhaps it is
all a dream? thought Berel in his sleep. But no, it
is no dream! "Here I am strolling round the fair, wide
awake. And the screaming and the row in my ears,
is that a dream, too? And my having this very minute

been bumped on the shoulder by a Gentile going past
me with a horse—is that a dream? But if the whole
world is taking part in the fair, it's evidently the
proper thing to do . . . " Meanwhile he was watching
a peasant with a horse, and he liked the look of the
horse so much that he bought it and mounted it. And
he looked at it from where he sat astride, and saw the
horse was a horse, but at the selfsame time it was
Moisheh Chalfon as well. Berel wondered: how is it
possible for it to be at once a horse and a man? But
his own eyes told him it was so. He wanted to dis-
mount, but the horse bears him to a shop. Here he
climbed down and asked for a pound of sugar. Berel
kept his eyes on the scales, and—a fresh surprise! Where
they should have been weighing sugar, they were weighing his good and bad deeds. And the two scales were
nearly equally laden, and oscillated up and down in the
air . . .

Suddenly they threw a sheet of paper into the scale
that held his bad deeds. Berel looked to see—it was
the hundred-ruble-note which he had appropriated at
Moisheh Chalfon's! But it was now much larger,
bordered with black, and the letters and numbers were
red as fire. The piece of paper was frightfully heavy,
it was all two men could do to carry it to the weighing-
machine, and when they had thrown it with all their
might onto the scale, something snapped, and the scale
went down, down, down.

At that moment a man sleeping at Berel's head
stretched out a foot, and gave Berel a kick in the head.
Berel awoke.

Not far from him sat a grey-haired old Jew, huddled together, enfolded in a Tallis and robe, repeating Psalms with a melancholy chant and a broken, quavering voice.

Berel caught the words:

"Mark the perfect man, and behold the upright:
For the end of that man is peace.
But the transgressors shall be destroyed together:
The latter end of the wicked shall be cut off . . . "

Berel looked round in a fright: Where is he? He had quite forgotten that he had remained for the night in the house-of-study. He gazed round with sleepy eyes, and they fell on some white heaps wrapped in robes and prayer-scarfs, while from their midst came the low, hoarse, tearful voices of two or three men who had not gone to sleep and were repeating Psalms. Many of the candles were already sputtering, the wax was melting into the sand, the flames rose and fell, and rose again, flaring brightly.

And the pale moon looked in at the windows, and poured her silvery light over the fantastic scene.

Berel grew icy cold, and a dreadful shuddering went through his limbs.

He had not yet remembered that he was spending the night in the house-of-study.

He imagined that he was dead, and astray in limbo. The white heaps which he sees are graves, actual graves, and there among the graves sit a few sinful souls, and bewail and lament their transgressions. And he, Berel, cannot even weep, he is a fallen one, lost forever—he is condemned to wander, to roam everlastingly among the graves.

By degrees, however, he called to mind where he was, and collected his wits.

Only then he remembered his fearful dream.

"No," he decided within himself, "I have lived till now without the hundred rubles, and I will continue to live without them. If the Lord of the Universe wishes to help me, he will do so without them too. My soul and my portion of the world-to-come are dearer to me. Only let Moisheh Chalfon come in to pray, I will tell him the whole truth and avert misfortune."

This decision gave him courage, he washed his hands, and sat down again to the Psalms. Every few minutes he glanced at the window, to see if it were not beginning to dawn, and if Reb Moisheh Chalfon were not coming along to Shool.

The day broke.

With the first sunbeams Berel's fears and terrors began little by little to dissipate and diminish. His resolve to restore the hundred rubles weakened considerably.

"If I don't confess," thought Berel, wrestling in spirit with temptation, "I risk my world-to-come . . . If I do confess, what will my Chantzeh-Leah say to it? *He* writes, either the wedding takes place, or the contract is dissolved! And what shall I do, when his father gets to hear about it? There will be a stain on my character, the marriage contract will be annulled, and I shall be left . . . without my good name and . . . with my ugly old maid . . .

"What is to be done? Help! What is to be done?"

The people began to gather in the Shool. The reader of the Morning Service intoned "He is Lord of the Universe" to the special Yom Kippur tune, a few house-holders and young men supported him, and Berel heard through it all only, Help! What is to be done?

And suddenly he beheld Moisheh Chalfon.

Berel quickly rose from his place, he wanted to make a rush at Moisheh Chalfon. But after all he remained where he was, and sat down again.

"I must first think it over, and discuss it with my Chantzeh-Leah," was Berel's decision.

Berel stood up to pray with the congregation. He was again wishful to pray with fervor, to collect his thoughts, and attend to the meaning of the words, but try as he would, he couldn't! Quite other things came into his head: a dream, a fair, a horse, Moisheh Chalfon, Chantzeh-Leah, oats, barley, *this* world and the next were all mixed up together in his mind, and the words of the prayers skipped about like black patches before his eyes. He wanted to say he was sorry, to cry, but he only made curious grimaces, and could not squeeze out so much as a single tear.

Berel was very dissatisfied with himself. He finished the Morning Prayer, stood through the Additional Service, and proceeded to devour the long Piyyutim.

The question, What is to be done? left him no peace, and he was really reciting the Piyyutim to try and stupefy himself, to dull his brain.

So it went on till U-Nesanneh Toikef.

The congregation began to prepare for U-Nesanneh Toikef, coughed, to clear their throats, and pulled the

Tallesim over their heads. The cantor sat down for a
minute to rest, and unbuttoned his shroud. His face
was pale and perspiring, and his eyes betrayed a great
weariness. From the women's gallery came a sound of
weeping and wailing.

Berel had drawn his Tallis over his head, and started
reciting with earnestness and enthusiasm:

" We will express the mighty holiness of this Day,
  For it is tremendous and awful!
  On which Thy kingdom is exalted,
  And Thy throne established in grace;
  Whereupon Thou art seated in truth.
  Verily, it is Thou who art judge and arbitrator,
  Who knowest all, and art witness, writer, sigillator, re-
      corder and teller;
  And Thou recallest all forgotten things,
  And openest the Book of Remembrance, and the book
      reads itself,
  And every man's handwriting is there . . . "

These words opened the source of Berel's tears, and
he sobbed unaffectedly. Every sentence cut him to the
heart, like a sharp knife, and especially the passage:

"And Thou recallest all forgotten things, and openest
the Book of Remembrance, and the book reads itself,
and every man's handwriting is there . . . " At that
very moment the Book of Remembrance was lying open
before the Lord of the Universe, with the handwritings
of all men. It contains his own as well, the one which
he wrote with his own hand that day when he took away
the hundred-ruble-note. He pictures how his soul flew
up to Heaven while he slept, and entered everything in
the eternal book, and now the letters stood before the

Throne of Glory, and cried, "Berel is a thief, Berel is a robber!" And he has the impudence to stand and pray before God? He, the offender, the transgressor—and the Shool does not fall upon his head?

The congregation concluded U-Nesanneh Toikef, and the cantor began: "And the great trumpet of ram's horn shall be sounded . . . " and still Berel stood with the Tallis over his head.

Suddenly he heard the words:

"And the Angels are dismayed,
Fear and trembling seize hold of them as they proclaim,
As swiftly as birds, and say:
This is the Day of Judgment!"

The words penetrated into the marrow of Berel's bones, and he shuddered from head to foot. The words, "This is the Day of Judgment," reverberated in his ears like a peal of thunder. He imagined the angels were hastening to him with one speed, with one swoop, to seize and drag him before the Throne of Glory, and the piteous wailing that came from the women's court was for him, for his wretched soul, for his endless misfortune.

"No! no! no!" he resolved, "come what may, let him annul the contract, let them point at me with their fingers as at a thief, if they choose, let my Chantzeh-Leah lose her chance! I will take it all in good part, if I may only save my unhappy soul! The minute the Kedushah is over I shall go to Moisheh Chalfon, tell him the whole story, and beg him to forgive me."

The cantor came to the end of U-Nesanneh Toikef, the congregation resumed their seats, Berel also returned to his place, and did not go up to Moisheh Chalfon.

14

"Help, what shall I do, what shall I do?" he thought, as he struggled with his conscience. "Chantzeh-Leah will lay me on the fire . . . she will cry her life out . . . the Mechutton . . . the bridegroom . . . "

The Additional Service and the Afternoon Service were over, people were making ready for the Conclusion Service, Neïleh. The shadows were once more lengthening, the sun was once more sinking in the west. The Shool-Goi began to light candles and lamps, and placed them on the tables and the window-ledges. Jews with faces white from exhaustion sat in the anteroom resting and refreshing themselves with a pinch of snuff, or a drop of hartshorn, and a few words of conversation. Everyone feels more cheerful and in better humor. What had to be done, has been done and well done. The Lord of the Universe has received His due. They have mortified themselves a whole day, fasted continuously, recited prayers, and begged forgiveness!

Now surely the Almighty will do His part, accept the Jewish prayers and have compassion on His people Israel.

Only Berel sits in a corner by himself. He also is wearied and exhausted. He also has fasted, prayed, wept, mortified himself, like the rest. But he knows that the whole of his toil and trouble has been thrown away. He sits troubled, gloomy, and depressed. He knows that they have now reached Neïleh, that he has still time to repent, that the door of Heaven will stand open a little while longer, his repentance may yet pass through . . . otherwise, yet a little while, and the gates of mercy will be shut and . . . too late!

"Oh, open the gate to us, even while it is closing," sounded in Berel's ears and heart . . . yet a little while, and it will be too late!

"No, no!" shrieked Berel to himself, "I will not lose my soul, my world-to-come! Let Chantzeh-Leah burn me and roast me, I will take it all in good part, so that I don't lose my world-to-come!"

Berel rose from his seat, and went up to Moisheh Chalfon.

"Reb Moisheh, a word with you," he whispered into his ear.

"Afterwards, when the prayers are done."

"No, no, no!" shrieked Berel, below his breath, "now, at once!"

Moisheh Chalfon stood up.

Berel led him out of the house-of-study, and aside.

"Reb Moisheh, kind soul, have pity on me and forgive me!" cried Berel, and burst into sobs.

"God be with you, Berel, what has come over you all at once?" asked Reb Moisheh, in astonishment.

"Listen to me, Reb Moisheh!" said Berel, still sobbing. "The hundred rubles you lost a few weeks ago are in my house! . . . God knows the truth, I didn't take them out of wickedness. I came into your house, the key was in the drawer . . . there was no one in the room . . . That day I'd had a letter from my Mechutton that he'd break off his son's engagement if the wedding didn't take place to time. . . My girl is ugly and old . . . the bridegroom is a fine young man . . . a precious stone . . . . I opened the drawer in spite of myself . . . and saw the bank-notes . . . You see how it was? . . . My Mechutton is a Misnaggid . . . a flint-hearted screw . . . I took out the note . . . but it is shortening my years! . . . God knows what I bore and suffered at the time . . . To-night I will bring you the note back . . . Forgive me! . . . Let the Mechutton break off the match, if he chooses, let the woman fret away her years, so long as I am rid of the serpent that is gnawing at my heart, and gives me no peace! I never before touched a ruble belonging to anyone else, and become a thief in my latter years I won't!"

Moisheh Chalfon did not answer him for a little while. He took out his snuff, and had a pinch, then he took out of the bosom of his robe a great red handkerchief, wiped his nose, and reflected a minute or two. Then he said quietly:

"If a match were broken off through me, I should be sorry. You certainly behaved as you should not have, in taking the money without leave, but it is written: Judge not thy neighbor till thou hast stood in his place. You shall keep the hundred rubles. Come to-night and bring me an I. O. U., and begin to repay me little by little."

"What are you, an angel?" exclaimed Berel, weeping.

"God forbid," replied Moisheh Chalfon, quietly, "I am what you are. You are a Jew, and I also am a Jew."

ISAIAH LERNER

Born, 1861, in Zwoniec, Podolia, Southwestern Russia; co-editor of die Bibliothek Dos Leben, published at Odessa, 1904, and Kishineff, 1905.

BERTZI WASSERFÜHRER

I

The first night of Passover. It is already about ten
o'clock. Outside it is dark, wet, cold as the grave. A
fine, close, sleety rain is driving down, a light, sharp,
fitful wind blows, whistles, sighs, and whines, and wan-
ders round on every side, like a returned and sinful soul
seeking means to qualify for eternal bliss. The mud is
very thick, and reaches nearly to the waist.

At one end of the town of Kamenivke, in the Poor
People's Street, which runs along by the bath-house, it
is darkest of all, and muddiest. The houses there are
small, low, and overhanging, tumbled together in such
a way that there is no seeing where the mud begins
and the dwelling ends. No gleam of light, even in the
windows. Either the inhabitants of the street are all
asleep, resting their tired bones and aching limbs, or
else they all lie suffocated in the sea of mud, simply
because the mud is higher than the windows. Whatever
the reason, the street is quiet as a God's-acre, and the
darkness may be felt with the hands.

Suddenly the dead stillness of the street is broken
by the heavy tread of some ponderous creature, walking
and plunging through the Kamenivke mud, and there
appears the tall, broad figure of a man. He staggers
like one tipsy or sick, but he keeps on in a straight line,
at an even pace, like one born and bred and doomed to
die in the familiar mud, till he drags his way to a low,
crouching house at the very end of the street, almost

under the hillside. It grows lighter—a bright flame shines through the little window-panes. He has not reached the door before it opens, and a shaky, tearful voice, full of melancholy, pain, and woe, breaks the hush a second time this night:

"Bertzi, is it you? Are you all right? So late? Has there been another accident? And the cart and the horse, wu senen?"

"All right, all right! A happy holiday!"

His voice is rough, hoarse, and muffled.

She lets him into the passage, and opens the inner door.

But scarcely is he conscious of the light, warmth, and cleanliness of the room, when he gives a strange, wild cry, takes one leap, like a hare, onto the "eating-couch" spread for him on the red-painted, wooden sofa, and— he lies already in a deep sleep.

II

The whole dwelling, consisting of one nice, large, low room, is clean, tidy, and bright. The bits of furniture and all the household essentials are poor, but so clean and polished that one can mirror oneself in them, if one cares to stoop down. The table is laid ready for Passover. The bottles of red wine, the bottle of yellow Passover brandy, and the glass goblets of different colors reflect the light of the thick tallow candles, and shine and twinkle and sparkle. The oven, which stands in the same room, is nearly out, there is one sleepy little bit of fire still flickering. But the pots, ranged round the fire as though to watch over it and encourage it, ex-

hale such delicious, appetizing smells that they would
tempt even a person who had just eaten his fill. But no
one makes a move towards them. All five children lie
stretched in a row on the red-painted, wooden bed.
Even they have not tasted of the precious dishes, of
which they have thought and talked for weeks previous
to the festival. They cried loud and long, waiting for
their father's return, and at last they went sweetly to
sleep. Only one fly is moving about the room: Rochtzi,
Bertzi Wasserführer's wife, and rivers of tears, large,
clear tears, salt with trouble and distress, flow from
her eyes.

III

Although Rochtzi has not seen more than thirty
summers, she looks like an old woman. Once upon a
time she was pretty, she was even known as one of the
prettiest of the Kamenivke girls, and traces of her
beauty are still to be found in her uncommonly large,
dark eyes, and even in her lined face, although the eyes
have long lost their fire, and her cheeks, their color and
freshness. She is dressed in clean holiday attire, but
her eyes are red from the hot, salt tears, and her expression is darkened and sad.

"Such a festival, such a great, holy festival, and then
when it comes. . . " The pale lips tremble and quiver.

How many days and nights, beginning before Purim,
has she sat with her needle between her fingers, so that
the children should have their holiday frocks—and all
depending on her hands and head! How much thought
and care and strength has she spent on preparing the
room, their poor little possessions, and the food? How

many were the days, Sabbaths excepted, on which they went without a spoonful of anything hot, so that they might be able to give a becoming reception to that dear, great, and holy visitor, the Passover? Everything (the Almighty forbid that she should sin with her tongue!) of the best, ready and waiting, and then, after all. . .

He, his sheepskin, his fur cap, and his great boots are soaked with rain and steeped in thick mud, and there, in this condition, lies he, Bertzi Wasserführer, her husband, her Passover "king," like a great black lump, on the nice, clean, white, draped "eating-couch," and snores.

IV

The brief tale I am telling you happened in the days before Kamenivke had joined itself on, by means of the long, tall, and beautiful bridge, to the great high hill that has stood facing it from everlasting, thickly wooded, and watered by quantities of clear, crystal streams, which babble one to another day and night, and whisper with their running tongues of most important things. So long as the bridge had not been flung from one of the giant rocks to the other rock, the Kamenivke people had not been able to procure the good, wholesome water of the wild hill, and had to content themselves with the thick, impure water of the river Smotritch, which has flowed forever round the eminence on which Kamenivke is built. But man, and especially the Jew, gets used to anything, and the Kamenivke people, who are nearly all Grandfather Abraham's grandchildren, had drunk Smotritch water all their lives, and were conscious of no grievance.

But the lot of the Kamenivke water-carriers was hard and bitter. Kamenivke stands high, almost in the air, and the river Smotritch runs deep down in the valley.

In summer, when the ground is dry, it was bearable, for then the Kamenivke water-carrier was merely bathed in sweat as he toiled up the hill, and the Jewish bread-winner has been used to that for ages. But in winter, when the snow was deep and the frost tremendous, when the steep Skossny hill with its clay soil was covered with ice like a hill of glass! Or when the great rains were pouring down, and the town and especially the clay hill are confounded with the deep, thick mud!

Our Bertzi Wasserführer was more alive to the fascinations of this Parnosseh than any other water-carrier. He was, as though in his own despite, a pious Jew and a great man of his word, and he had to carry water for almost all the well-to-do householders. True, that in face of all his good luck he was one of the poorest Jews in the Poor People's Street, only——

V

Lord of the World, may there never again be such a winter as there was then!

Not the oldest man there could recall one like it. The snow came down in drifts, and never stopped. One could and might have sworn on a scroll of the Law, that the great Jewish God was angry with the Kamenivke Jews, and had commanded His angels to shovel down on Kamenivke all the snow that had lain by in all the seven heavens since the sixth day of creation, so that the sinful town might be a ruin and a desolation.

And the terrible, fiery frosts!

Frozen people were brought into the town nearly every day.

Oi, Jews, how Bertzi Wasserführer struggled, what a time he had of it! Enemies of Zion, it was nearly the death of him!

And suddenly the snow began to stop falling, all at once, and then things were worse than ever—there was a sea of water, an ocean of mud.

And Passover coming on with great strides!

For three days before Passover he had not come home to sleep. Who talks of eating, drinking, and sleeping? He and his man toiled day and night, like six horses, like ten oxen.

The last day before Passover was the worst of all. His horse suddenly came to the conclusion that sooner than live such a life, it would die. So it died and vanished somewhere in the depths of the Kamenivke clay.

And Bertzi the water-carrier and his man had to drag the cart with the great water-barrel themselves, the whole day till long after dark.

VI

It is already eleven, twelve, half past twelve at night, and Bertzi's chest, throat, and nostrils continue to pipe and to whistle, to sob and to sigh.

The room is colder and darker, the small fire in the oven went out long ago, and only little stumps of candles remain.

Rochtzi walks and runs about the room, she weeps and wrings her hands.

But now she runs up to the couch by the table, and begins to rouse her husband with screams and cries fit to make one's blood run cold and the hair stand up on one's head:

"No, no, you're not going to sleep any longer, I tell you! Bertzi, do you hear me? Get up, Bertzi, aren't you a Jew?—a man?—the father of children?—Bertzi, have you God in your heart? Bertzi, have you said your prayers? My husband, what about the Seder? I won't have it!—I feel very ill—I am going to faint!—Help!— Water!"

"Have I forgotten somebody's water?—Whose?— Where? . . ."

But Rochtzi is no longer in need of water: she beholds her "king" on his feet, and has revived without it. With her two hands, with all the strength she has, she holds him from falling back onto the couch.

"Don't you see, Bertzi? The candles are burning down, the supper is cold and will spoil. I fancy it's already beginning to dawn. The children, long life to them, went to sleep without any food. Come, please, begin to prepare for the Seder, and I will wake the two elder ones."

Bertzi stands bent double and treble. His breathing is labored and loud, his face is smeared with mud and swollen from the cold, his beard and earlocks are rough and bristly, his eyes sleepy and red. He looks strangely wild and unkempt. Bertzi looks at Rochtzi, at the table, he looks round the room, and sees nothing. But now he looks at the bed: his little children, washed, and in their holiday dresses, are all lying in a row across the bed, and—he remembers everything, and understands what Rochtzi is saying, and what it is she wants him to do.

"Give me some water—I said Minchah and Maariv by the way, while I was at work."

"I'm bringing it already! May God grant you a like happiness! Good health to you! Hershele, get up, my Kaddish, father has come home already! Shmuelkil, my little son, go and ask father the Four Questions."

Bertzi fills a goblet with wine, takes it up in his left hand, places it upon his right hand, and begins:

"Savri Moronon, ve-Rabbonon, ve-Rabbosai—with the permission of the company."—His head goes round.— "Lord of the World!—I am a Jew.—Blessed art Thou, Lord our God, King of the Universe—" It grows dark before his eyes: "The first night of Passover—I ought to make Kiddush—Thou who dost create the fruit of the vine"—his feet fail him, as though they had been cut off—"and I ought to give the Seder—This is the bread of the poor. . . . Lord of the World, you know how it is: I can't do it!—Have mercy!—Forgive me!"

VII

A nasty smell of sputtered-out candles fills the room. Rochtzi weeps. Bertzi is back on the couch and snores.

Different sounds, like the voices of winds, cattle, and wild beasts, and the whirr of a mill, are heard in his snoring. And her weeping—it seems as if the whole room were sighing and quivering and shaking. . . .

EZRIELK THE SCRIBE

Forty days before Ezrielk descended upon this sinful world, his life-partner was proclaimed in Heaven, and the Heavenly Council decided that he was to transcribe the books of the Law, prayers, and Mezuzehs for the Kabtzonivke Jews, and thereby make a living for his wife and children. But the hard word went forth to him that he should not disclose this secret decree to anyone, and should even forget it himself for a goodly number of years. A glance at Ezrielk told one that he had been well lectured with regard to some important matter, and was to tell no tales out of school. Even Minde, the Kabtzonivke Bobbe, testified to this:

"Never in all my life, all the time I've been bringing Jewish children into God's world, have I known a child scream so loud at birth as Ezrielk—a sign that he'd had it well rubbed into him!"

Either the angel who has been sent to fillip little children above the lips when they are being born, was just then very sleepy (Ezrielk was born late at night), or some one had put him out of temper, but one way or another little Ezrielk, the very first minute of his Jewish existence, caught such a blow that his top lip was all but split in two.

After this kindly welcome, when God's angel himself had thus received Ezrielk, slaps, blows, and stripes rained down upon his head, body, and life, all through his days, without pause or ending.

Ezrielk began to attend Cheder when he was exactly three years old. His first teacher treated him very badly, beat him continually, and took all the joy of his childhood from him. By the time this childhood of his had passed, and he came to be married (he began to wear the phylacteries and the prayer-scarf on the day of his marriage), he was a very poor specimen, small, thin, stooping, and yellow as an egg-pudding, his little face dark, dreary, and weazened, like a dried Lender herring. The only large, full things about him were his earlocks, which covered his whole face, and his two blue eyes. He had about as much strength as a fly, he could not even break the wine-glass under the marriage canopy by himself, and had to ask for help of Reb Yainkef Butz, the beadle of the Old Shool.

Among the German Jews a boy like that would have been left unwed till he was sixteen or even seventeen, but our Ezrielk was married at thirteen, for his bride had been waiting for him seventeen years.

It was this way: Reb Seinwill Bassis, Ezrielk's father, and Reb Selig Tachshit, his father-in-law, were Hostre Chassidim, and used to drive every year to spend the Solemn Days at the Hostre Rebbe's. They both (not of you be it spoken!) lost all their children in infancy, and, as you can imagine, they pressed the Rebbe very closely on this important point, left him no peace, till he should bestir himself on their behalf, and exercise all his influence in the Higher Spheres. Once, on the Eve of Yom Kippur, before daylight, after the waving of the scape-fowls, when the Rebbe, long life to him, was in somewhat high spirits, our two Chassidim made another set upon him, but this time they had quite a new plan, and it simply *had* to work out!

"Do you know what? Arrange a marriage between your children! Good luck to you!" The whole company of Chassidim broke some plates, and actually drew up the marriage contract. It was a little difficult to draw up the contract, because they did not know which of our two friends would have the boy (the Rebbe, long life to him, was silent on this head), and which, the girl, but—a learned Jew is never at a loss, and they wrote out the contract with conditions.

For three years running after this their wives bore them each a child, but the children were either both boys or both girls, so that their vow to unite the son of one to a daughter of the other born in the same year could not be fulfilled, and the documents lay on the shelf.

True, the little couples departed for the "real world" within the first month, but the Rebbe consoled the father by saying:

"We may be sure they were not true Jewish children, that is, not true Jewish souls. The true Jewish soul once born into the world holds on, until, by means of various troubles and trials, it is cleansed from every stain. Don't worry, but wait."

The fourth year the Rebbe's words were established: Reb Selig Tachshit had a daughter born to him, and Reb Seinwill Bassis, Ezrielk.

Channehle, Ezrielk's bride, was tall, when they married, as a young fir-tree, beautiful as the sun, clever as the day is bright, and white as snow, with sky-blue,

15

star-like eyes. Her hair was the color of ripe corn—
in a word, she was fair as Abigail and our Mother
Rachel in one, winning as Queen Esther, pious as Leah,
and upright as our Grandmother Sarah.

But although the bride was beautiful, she found no
fault with her bridegroom; on the contrary, she esteemed it a great honor to have him for a husband. All
the Kabtzonivke girls envied her, and every Kabtzonivke
woman who was "expecting" desired with all her heart
that she might have such a son as Ezrielk. The reason
is quite plain: First, what true Jewish maiden looks
for beauty in her bridegroom? Secondly, our Ezrielk
was as full of excellencies as a pomegranate is of seeds.

His teachers had not broken his bones for nothing. The
blows had been of great and lasting good to him. Even
before his wedding, Seinwill Bassis's Ezrielk was deeply
versed in the Law, and could solve the hardest "questions," so that you might have made a Rabbi of him. He
was, moreover, a great scribe. His "in-honor-ofs," and
his "blessed bes" were known, not only in Kabtzonivke,
but all over Kamenivke, and as for his singing—!

When Ezrielk began to sing, poor people forgot their
hunger, thirst, and need, the sick, their aches and pains,
the Kabtzonivke Jews in general, their bitter exile.

He mostly sang unfamiliar tunes and whole "things."

"Where do you get them, Ezrielk?"

The little Ezrielk would open his eyes (he kept them
shut while he sang), his two big blue eyes, and answer
wonderingly:

"Don't you hear how everything sings?"

After a little while, when Ezrielk had been singing so well and so sweetly and so wonderfully that the Kabtzonivke Jews began to feel too happy, people fell athinking, and they grew extremely uneasy and disturbed in their minds:

"It's not all so simple as it looks, there is something behind it. Suppose a not-good one had introduced himself into the child (which God forbid!) ? It would do no harm to take him to the Aleskev Rebbe, long life to him."

As good luck would have it, the Hostre Rebbe came along just then to Kabtzonivke, and, after all, Ezrielk belonged to *him,* he was born through the merit of the Rebbe's miracle-working! So the Chassidim told him the story. The Rebbe, long life to him, sent for him. Ezrielk came and began to sing. The Rebbe listened a long, long time to his sweet voice, which rang out like a hundred thousand crystal and gold bells into every corner of the room.

"Do not be alarmed, he may and he must sing. He gets his tunes there where he got his soul."

And Ezrielk sang cheerful tunes till he was ten years old, that is, till he fell into the hands of the teacher Reb Yainkel Vittiss.

Now, the end and object of Reb Yainkel's teaching was not merely that his pupils should know a lot and know it well. Of course, we know that the Jew only enters this sinful world in order that he may more or less perfect himself, and that it is therefore needful he should, and, indeed, he *must,* sit day and night over the Torah and the Commentaries. Yainkel

Vittiss's course of instruction began and ended with trying to imbue his pupils with a downright, genuine, Jewish-Chassidic enthusiasm.

The first day Ezrielk entered his Cheder, Reb Yainkel lifted his long, thick lashes, and began, while he gazed fixedly at him, to shake his head, saying to himself: "No, no, he won't do like that. There is nothing wrong with the vessel, a goodly vessel, only the wine is still very sharp, and the ferment is too strong. He is too cocky, too lively for me. A wonder, too, for he's been in good hands (tell me, weren't you under both Moisheh-Yusis?), and it's a pity, when you come to think, that such a goodly vessel should be wasted. Yes, he wants treating in quite another way."

And Yainkel Vittiss set himself seriously to the task of shaping and working up Ezrielk.

Reb Yainkel was not in the least concerned when he beat a pupil and the latter cried and screamed at the top of his voice. He knew what he was about, and was convinced that, when one beats and it hurts, even a Jewish child (which must needs get used to blows) may cry and scream, and the more the better; it showed that his method of instruction was taking effect. And when he was thrashing Ezrielk, and the boy cried and yelled, Reb Yainkel would tell him: "That's right, that's the way! Cry, scream—louder still! That's the way to get a truly contrite Jewish heart! You sing too merrily for me—a true Jew should weep even while he sings."

When Ezrielk came to be twelve years old, his teacher declared that he might begin to recite the prayers in Shool before the congregation, as he now had within him that which beseems a good Chassidic Jew.

So Ezrielk began to davven in the Kabtzonivke Old Shool, and a crowd of people, not only from Kabtzonivke, but even from Kamenivke and Ebionivke, used to fill and encircle the Shool to hear him.

Reb Yainkel was not mistaken, he knew what he was saying. Ezrielk was indeed fit to davven: life and the joy of life had vanished from his singing, and the terrorful weeping, the fearful wailing of a nation's two thousand years of misfortune, might be heard and felt in his voice.

Ezrielk was very weakly, and too young to lead the service often, but what a stir he caused when he lifted up his voice in the Shool!

Kabtzonivke, Kamenivke, and Ebionivke will never forget the first U-mipné Chatoénu led by the twelve-year-old Ezrielk, standing before the precentor's desk in a long, wide prayer-scarf.

The men, women, and children who were listening inside and outside the Old Shool felt a shudder go through them, their hair stood on end, and their hearts wept and fluttered in their breasts.

Ezrielk's voice wept and implored, "on account of our sins."

At the time when Ezrielk was distinguishing himself on this fashion with his chanting, the Jewish doctor from Kamenivke happened to be in the place. He saw the crowd round the Old Shool, and he went in. As you may suppose, he was much longer in coming out. He was simply riveted to the spot, and it is said that he rubbed his eyes more than once while he listened

and looked. On coming away, he told them to bring
Ezrielk to see him on the following day, saying that he
wished to see him, and would take no fee.

Next day Ezrielk came with his mother to the doctor's
house.

"A blow has struck me! A thunder has killed me!
Reb Yainkel, do you know what the doctor said?"

"You silly woman, don't scream so! He cannot have
said anything bad about Ezrielk. What is the matter?
Did he hear him intone the Gemoreh, or perhaps sing?
Don't cry and lament like that!"

"Reb Yainkel, what are you talking about? The
doctor said that my Ezrielk is in danger, that he's ill,
that he hasn't a sound organ—his heart, his lungs, are
all sick. Every little bone in him is broken. He mustn't
sing or study—the bath will be his death—he must
have a long cure—he must be sent away for air. God
(he said to me) has given you a precious gift, such as
Heaven and earth might envy. Will you go and bury
it with your own hands?"

"And you were frightened and believed him? Nonsense! I've had Ezrielk in my Cheder two years. Do
I want *him* to come and tell me what goes on there? If
he were a really good doctor, and had one drop of
Jewish blood left in his veins, wouldn't he know that
every true Jew has a sick heart, a bad lung, broken
bones, and deformed limbs, and is well and strong in
spite of it, because the holy Torah is the best medicine
for all sicknesses? Ha, ha, ha! And *he* wants Ezrielk
to give up learning and the bath? Do you know what?
Go home and send Ezrielk to Cheder at once!"

The Kamenivke doctor made one or two more attempts at alarming Ezrielk's parents; he sent his assistant to them more than once, but it was no use, for after what Reb Yainkel had said, nobody would hear of any doctoring.

So Ezrielk continued to study the Talmud and occasionally to lead the service in Shool, like the Chassidic child he was, had a dip nearly every morning in the bath-house, and at thirteen, good luck to him, he was married.

The Hostre Rebbe himself honored the wedding with his presence. The Rebbe, long life to him, was fond of Ezrielk, almost as though he had been his own child. The whole time the saint stayed in Kabtzonivke, Kamenivke, and Ebionivke, Ezrielk had to be near him.

When they told the Rebbe the story of the doctor, he remarked, "Ett! what do *they* know?"

And Ezrielk continued to recite the prayers after his marriage, and to sing as before, and was the delight of all who heard him.

Agreeably to the marriage contract, Ezrielk and his Channehle had a double right to board with their parents "forever"; when they were born and the written engagements were filled in, each was an only child, and both Reb Seinwill and Reb Selig undertook to board them "forever." True, when the parents wedded their "one and only children," they had both of them a houseful of little ones and no Parnosseh (they really hadn't!), but they did not go back upon their word with regard to the "board forever."

Of course, it is understood that the two "everlasting boards" lasted nearly one whole year, and Ezrielk and his wife might well give thanks for not having died of hunger in the course of it, such a bad, bitter year as it was for their poor parents. It was the year of the great flood, when both Reb Seinwill Bassis and Reb Selig Tachshit had their houses ruined.

Ezrielk, Channehle, and their little son had to go and shift for themselves. But the other inhabitants of Kabtzonivke, regardless of this, now began to envy them in earnest: what other couple of their age, with a child and without a farthing, could so easily make a livelihood as they?

Hardly had it come to the ears of the three towns that Ezrielk was seeking a Parnosseh when they were all astir. All the Shools called meetings, and sought for means and money whereby they might entice the wonderful cantor and secure him for themselves. There was great excitement in the Shools. Fancy finding in a little, thin Jewish lad all the rare and precious qualities that go to make a great cantor! The trustees of all the Shools ran about day and night, and a fierce war broke out among them.

The war raged five times twenty-four hours, till the Great Shool in Kamenivke carried the day. Not one of the others could have dreamed of offering him such a salary—three hundred rubles and everything found!

"God is my witness"—thus Ezrielk opened his heart, as he sat afterwards with the company of Hostre Chassidim over a little glass of brandy—"that I find it very hard to leave our Old Shool, where my grandfather

and great-grandfather used to pray. Believe me, brothers, I would not do it, only they give me one hundred
and fifty rubles earnest-money, and I want to pass it
on to my father and father-in-law, so that they may
rebuild their houses. To your health, brothers! Drink
to my remaining an honest Jew, and wish that my head
may not be turned by the honor done to me!"

And Ezrielk began to davven and to sing (again
without a choir) in the Great Shool, in the large town
of Kamenivke. There he intoned the prayers as he had
never done before, and showed who Ezrielk was! The
Old Shool in Kabtzonivke had been like a little box
for his voice.

In those days Ezrielk and his household lived in happiness and plenty, and he and Channehle enjoyed the
respect and consideration of all men. When Ezrielk
led the service, the Shool was filled to overflowing, and
not only with Jews, even the richest Gentiles (I beg to
distinguish!) came to hear him, and wondered how
such a small and weakly creature as Ezrielk, with his
thin chest and throat, could bring out such wonderful
tunes and whole compositions of his own! Money fell
upon the lucky couple, through circumcisions, weddings,
and so on, like snow. Only one thing began, little by
little, to disturb their happiness: Ezrielk took to coughing, and then to spitting blood.

He used to complain that he often felt a kind of pain
in his throat and chest, but they did not consult a
doctor.

"What, a doctor?" fumed Reb Yainkel. "Nonsense!
It hurts, does it? Where's the wonder? A carpenter,

a smith, a tailor, a shoemaker works with his hands, and his hands hurt. Cantors and teachers and match-makers work with their throat and chest, and *these* hurt, they are bound to do so. It is simply hemorrhoids."

So Ezrielk went on intoning and chanting, and the Kamenivke Jews licked their fingers, and nearly jumped out of their skin for joy when they heard him.

Two years passed in this way, and then came a change.

It was early in the morning of the Fast of the Destruction of the Temple, all the windows of the Great Shool were open, and all the tables, benches, and desks had been carried out from the men's hall and the women's hall the evening before. Men and women sat on the floor, so closely packed a pin could not have fallen to the floor between them. The whole street in which was the Great Shool was chuck full with a terrible crowd of men, women, and children, although it just happened to be cold, wet weather. The fact is, Ezrielk's Lamentations had long been famous throughout the Jewish world in those parts, and whoever had ears, a Jewish heart, and sound feet, came that day to hear him. The sad epidemic disease that (not of our days be it spoken!) swallows men up, was devastating Kamenivke and its surroundings that year, and everyone sought a place and hour wherein to weep out his opprest and bitter heart.

Ezrielk also sat on the floor reciting Lamentations, but the man who sat there was not the same Ezrielk, and the voice heard was not his. Ezrielk, with his sugar-sweet, honeyed voice, had suddenly been trans-

formed into a strange being, with a voice that struck
terror into his hearers; the whole people saw, heard,
and felt, how a strange creature was flying about
among them with a fiery sword in his hand. He slashes,
hews, and hacks at their hearts, and with a terrible
voice he cries out and asks: "Sinners! Where is your
holy land that flowed with milk and honey? Slaves!
Where is your Temple? Accursed slaves! You sold
your freedom for money and calumny, for honors and
worldly greatness!"

The people trembled and shook and were all but
entirely dissolved in tears. "Upon Zion and her cities!"
sang out once more Ezrielk's melancholy voice, and
suddenly something snapped in his throat, just as when
the strings of a good fiddle snap when the music is at
its best. Ezrielk coughed, and was silent. A stream of
blood poured from his throat, and he grew white as the
wall.

The doctor declared that Ezrielk had lost his voice
forever, and would remain hoarse for the rest of his
life.

"Nonsense!" persisted Reb Yainkel. "His voice is
breaking—it's nothing more!"

"God will help!" was the comment of the Hostre
saint. A whole year went by, and Ezrielk's voice neither
broke nor returned to him. The Hostre Chassidim
assembled in the house of Elkoneh the butcher to consider and take counsel as to what Ezrielk should take to
in order to earn a livelihood for wife and children. They
thought it over a long, long time, talked and gave their
several opinions, till they hit upon this: Ezrielk had still

one hundred and fifty rubles in store—let him spend one hundred rubles on a house in Kabtzonivke, and begin to traffic with the remainder.

Thus Ezrielk became a trader. He began driving to fairs, and traded in anything and everything capable of being bought or sold.

Six months were not over before Ezrielk was out of pocket. He mortgaged his property, and with the money thus obtained he opened a grocery shop for Channehle. He himself (nothing satisfies a Jew!) started to drive about in the neighborhood, to collect the contributions subscribed for the maintenance of the Hostre Rebbe, long life to him!

Ezrielk was five months on the road, and when, torn, worn, and penniless, he returned home, he found Channehle brought to bed of her fourth child, and the shop bare of ware and equally without a groschen. But Ezrielk was now something of a trader, and is there any strait in which a Jewish trader has not found himself? Ezrielk had soon disposed of the whole of his property, paid his debts, rented a larger lodging, and started trading in several new and more ambitious lines: he pickled gherkins, cabbages, and pumpkins, made beet soup, both red and white, and offered them for sale, and so on. It was Channehle again who had to carry on most of the business, but, then, Ezrielk did not sit with his hands in his pockets. Toward Passover he had Shmooreh Matzes; he baked and sold them to the richest householders in Kamenivke, and before the Solemn Days he, as an expert, tried and recommended cantors and prayer-leaders for the Kamenivke Shools.

When it came to Tabernacles, he trafficked in citrons and "palms."

For three years Ezrielk and his Channehle struggled at their trades, working themselves nearly to death (of Zion's enemies be it spoken!), till, with the help of Heaven, they came to be twenty years old.

By this time Ezrielk and Channehle were the parents of four living and two dead children. Channehle, the once so lovely Channehle, looked like a beaten Hoshanah, and Ezrielk—you remember the picture drawn at the time of his wedding?—well, then try to imagine what he was like now, after those seven years we have described for you! It's true that he was not spitting blood any more, either because Reb Yainkel had been right, when he said that would pass away, or because there was not a drop of blood in the whole of his body.

So that was all right—only, how were they to live? Even Reb Yainkel and all the Hostre Chassidim together could not tell him!

The singing had raised him and lifted him off his feet, and let him fall. And do you know why it was and how it was that everything Ezrielk took to turned out badly? It was because the singing was always there, in his head and his heart. He prayed and studied, singing. He bought and sold, singing. He sang day and night. No one heard him, because he was hoarse, but he sang without ceasing. Was it likely he would be a successful trader, when he was always listening to what Heaven and earth and everything around him were singing, too? He only wished he could have been a slaughterer or a Rav (he was apt enough at study), only, first, Rabbonim and slaughterers don't die every day, and, second, they usually leave heirs to take their places; third, even supposing there were no such heirs, one has to pay "privilege-money," and where is it to come from? No, there was nothing to be done. Only God could and must have pity on him and his wife and children, and help them somehow.

Ezrielk struggled and fought his need hard enough those days. One good thing for him was this—his being a Hostre Chossid; the Hostre Chassidim, although they have been famed from everlasting as the direst poor among the Jews, yet they divide their last mouthful with their unfortunate brethren. But what can the gifts of mortal men, and of such poor ones into the bargain, do in a case like Ezrielk's? And God alone knows what bitter end would have been his, if Reb Shmuel Bär, the Kabtzonivke scribe, had not just then (blessed be the righteous Judge!) met with a sudden death. Our Ezrielk was not long in feeling that he, and only he, should, and, indeed, must, step into Reb Shmuel's shoes. Ezrielk had been an expert at the scribe's work for years and years. Why, his father's house and the scribe's had been nearly under one roof, and whenever Ezrielk, as a child, was let out of Cheder, he would go and sit any length of time in Reb Shmuel's room (something in the occupation attracted him) and watch him write. And the little Ezrielk had more than once tried to make a piece of parchment out of a scrap of skin; and what Jewish boy cannot prepare the veins that are used to sew the phylacteries and the scrolls of the Law? Nor was the scribe's ink a secret to Ezrielk.

So Ezrielk became scribe in Kabtzonivke.

Of course, he did not make a fortune. Reb Shmuel Bär, who had been a scribe all his days, died a very poor man, and left a roomful of hungry, half-naked children behind him, but then—what Jew, I ask you (or has Messiah come?), ever expected to find a Parnosseh with enough, really enough, to eat?

YITZCHOK-YOSSEL BROITGEBER

At the time I am speaking of, the above was about forty years old. He was a little, thin Jew with a long face, a long nose, two large, black, kindly eyes, and one who would sooner be silent and think than talk, no matter what was being said to him. Even when he was scolded for something (and by whom and when and for what was he *not* scolded?), he used to listen with a quiet, startled, but sweet smile, and his large, kindly eyes would look at the other with such wonderment, mingled with a sort of pity, that the other soon stopped short in his abuse, and stood nonplussed before him.

"There, you may talk! You might as well argue with a horse, or a donkey, or the wall, or a log of wood!" and the other would spit and make off.

But if anyone observed that smile attentively, and studied the look in his eyes, he would, to a certainty, have read there as follows:

"O man, man, why are you eating your heart out? Seeing that you don't know, and that you don't understand, why do you undertake to tell me what I ought to do?"

And when he was obliged to answer, he used to do so in a few measured and gentle words, as you would speak to a little, ignorant child, smiling the while, and then he would disappear and start thinking again.

They called him "breadwinner," because, no matter how hard the man worked, he was never able to earn a living. He was a little tailor, but not like the tailors nowadays, who specialize in one kind of garment, for Yitzchok-Yossel made everything: trousers, cloaks, waistcoats, top-coats, fur-coats, capes, collars, bags for prayer-books, "little prayer-scarfs," and so on. Besides, he was a ladies' tailor as well. Summer and winter, day and night, he worked like an ox, and yet, when the Kabtzonivke community, at the time of the great cholera, in order to put an end to the plague, led him, aged thirty, out to the cemetery, and there married him to Malkeh the orphan, she cast him off two weeks later! She was still too young (twenty-eight), she said, to stay with him and die of hunger. She went out into the world, together with a large band of poor, after the great fire that destroyed nearly the whole town, and nothing more was heard of Malkeh the orphan from that day forward. And Yitzchok-Yossel Broitgeber betook himself, with needle and flat-iron, into the women's chamber in the New Shool, the community having assigned it to him as a workroom.

How came it about, you may ask, that so versatile a tailor as Yitzchok-Yossel should be so poor?

Well, if you do, it just shows you didn't know him! Wait and hear what I shall tell you.

The story is on this wise: Yitzchok-Yossel Broitgeber was a tailor who could make anything, and who made nothing at all, that is, since he displayed his imagination in cutting out and sewing on the occasion I am referring to, nobody would trust him.

I can remember as if it were to-day what happened in Kabtzonivke, and the commotion there was in the little town when Yitzchok-Yossel made Reb Yecheskel the teacher a pair of trousers (begging your pardon!) of such fantastic cut that the unfortunate teacher had to wear them as a vest, though he was not then in need of one, having a brand new sheepskin not more than three years old.

And now listen! Binyomin Droibnik the trader's mother died (blessed be the righteous Judge!), and her whole fortune went, according to the Law, to her only son Binyomin. She had to be buried at the expense of the community. If she was to be buried at all, it was the only way. But the whole town was furious with the old woman for having cheated them out of their expectations and taken her whole fortune away with her to the real world. None knew exactly *why,* but it was confidently believed that old "Aunt" Leah had heaps of treasure somewhere in hiding.

It was a custom with us in Kabtzonivke to say, whenever anyone, man or woman, lived long, ate sicknesses by the clock, and still did not die, that it was a sign that he had in the course of his long life gathered great store of riches, that somewhere in a cellar he kept potsful of gold and silver.

The Funeral Society, the younger members, had long been whetting their teeth for "Aunt" Leah's fortune, and now she had died (may she merit Paradise!) and had fooled them.

"What about her money?"

"A cow has flown over the roof and laid an egg!"

In that same night Reb Binyomin's cow (a real cow) calved, and the unfortunate consequence was that she died. The Funeral Society took the calf, and buried "Aunt" Leah at its own expense.

Well, money or no money, inheritance or no inheritance, Reb Binyomin's old mother left him a quilt, a
large, long, wide, wadded quilt. As an article of house
furniture, a quilt is a very useful thing, especially in
a house where there is a wife (no evil eye!) and a
goodly number of children, little and big. Who doesn't
see that? It looks simple enough! Either one keeps
it for oneself and the two little boys (with whom Reb
Binyomin used to sleep), or else one gives it to the
wife and the two little girls (who also sleep all together), or, if not, then to the two bigger boys or the
two bigger girls, who repose on the two bench-beds in
the parlor and kitchen respectively. But this particular
quilt brought such perplexity into Reb Binyomin's
rather small head that he (not of you be it spoken!)
nearly went mad.

"Why I and not she? Why she and not I? Or
they? Or the others? Why they and not I? Why
them and not us? Why the others and not them?
Well, well, what is all this fuss? What did we cover
them with before?"

Three days and three nights Reb Binyomin split his
head and puzzled his brains over these questions, till the
Almighty had pity on his small skull and feeble intelligence, and sent him a happy thought.

"After all, it is an inheritance from one's one and
only mother (peace be upon her!), it is a thing from
Thingland! I must adapt it to some useful purpose,
so that Heaven and earth may envy me its possession!"
And he sent to fetch Yitzchok-Yossel Broitgeber, the
tailor, who could make every kind of garment, and said
to him:

"Reb Yitzchok-Yossel, you see this article?"

"I see it."

"Yes, you see it, but do you understand it, really and truly understand it?"

"I think I do."

"But do you know what this is, ha?"

"A quilt."

"Ha, ha, ha! A quilt? I could have told you that myself. But the stuff, the material?"

"It's good material, beautiful stuff."

"Good material, beautiful stuff? No, I beg your pardon, you are not an expert in this, you don't know the value of merchandise. The real artisan, the true expert, would say: The material is light, soft, and elastic, like a lung, a sound and healthy lung. The stuff—he would say further—is firm, full, and smooth as the best calf's leather. And durable? Why, it's a piece out of the heart of the strongest ox, or the tongue of the Messianic ox itself! Do you know how many winters this quilt has lasted already? But enough! That is not why I have sent for you. We are neither of us, thanks to His blessed Name, do-nothings. The long and short of it is this: I wish to make out of this—you understand me?—out of this material, out of this piece of stuff, a thing, an article, that shall draw everybody to it, a fruit that is worth saying the blessing over, something superfine. An instance: what, for example, tell me, what would you do, if I gave this piece of goods into your hands, and said to you: Reb Yitzchok-Yossel, as you are (without sin be it spoken!) an old workman, a good workman, and, besides that, a good comrade, and a Jew as well, take this material, this stuff, and deal with it as you think best. Only let it be turned into a sort of costume, a sort of garment, so that not only Kabtzonivke, but all Kamenivke, shall be bitten and torn with envy. Eh? What would you turn it into?"

Yitzchok-Yossel was silent, Reb Yitzchok-Yossel went nearly out of his mind, nearly fainted for joy at these last words. He grew pale as death, white as chalk, then burning red like a flame of fire, and sparkled and shone. And no wonder: Was it a trifle? All his life he had dreamed of the day when he should be given a free hand in his work, so that everyone should see who Yitzchok-Yossel is, and at the end came—the trousers, Reb Yecheskel Melammed's trousers! How well, how cleverly he had made them! Just think: trousers and upper garment in one! He had been so overjoyed, he had felt so happy. So sure that now everyone would know who Yitzchok-Yossel Broitgeber is! He had even begun to think and wonder about Malkeh the orphan—poor, unfortunate orphan! Had she ever had one single happy day in her life? Work forever and next to no food, toil till she was exhausted and next to no drink, sleep where she could get it: one time in Elkoneh the butcher's kitchen, another time in Yisroel Dintzis' attic . . . and when at last she got married (good luck to her!), she became the wife of Yitzchok-Yossel Broitgeber! And the wedding took place in the burial-ground. On one side they were digging graves, on the other they were bringing fresh corpses. There was weeping and wailing, and in the middle of it all, the musicians playing and fiddling and singing, and the relations dancing! . . . Good luck! Good luck! The orphan and her breadwinner are being led to the marriage canopy in the graveyard!

He will never forget with what gusto, she, his bride, the first night after their wedding, ate, drank, and slept —the whole of the wedding-supper that had been given them, bridegroom and bride: a nice roll, a glass of brandy, a tea-glass full of wine, and a heaped-up plate of roast meat was cut up and scraped together and eaten (no evil eye!) by *her,* by the bride herself. He had taken great pleasure in watching her face. He had known her well from childhood, and had no need to look at her to know what she was like, but he wanted to see what kind of feelings her face would express during this occupation. When they led him into the bridal chamber—she was already there—the companions of the bridegroom burst into a shout of laughter, for the bride was already snoring. He knew quite well why she had gone to sleep so quickly and comfortably. Was there not sufficient reason? For the first time in her life she had made a good meal and lain down in a bed with bedclothes!

The six groschen candle burnt, the flies woke and began to buzz, the mills clapt, and swung, and groaned, and he, Yitzchok-Yossel Broitgeber, the bridegroom, sat beside the bridal bed on a little barrel of pickled gherkins, and looked at Malkeh the orphan, his bride, his wife, listened to her loud thick snores, and thought.

The town dogs howled strangely. Evidently the wedding in the cemetery had not yet driven away the Angel

of Death. From some of the neighboring houses came
a dreadful crying and screaming of women and children.

Malkeh the orphan heard nothing. She slept sweetly,
and snored as loud (I beg to distinguish!) as Caspar,
the tall, stout miller, the owner of both mills.

Yitzchok-Yossel Broitgeber sits on the little barrel,
looks at her face, and thinks. Her face is dark, rough-
ened, and nearly like that of an old woman. A great,
fat fly knocked against the wick, the candle suddenly
began to burn brighter, and Yitzchok-Yossel saw her
face become prettier, younger, and fresher, and overspread by a smile. That was all the effect of the supper
and the soft bed. Then it was that he had promised
himself, that he had sworn, once and for all, to show
the Kabtzonivke Jews who he is, and then Malkeh the
orphan will have food and a bed every day. He would
have done this long ago, had it not been for those
trousers. The people are so silly, they don't understand! That is the whole misfortune! And it's quite
the other way about: let someone else try and turn
out such an ingenious contrivance! But because it was
he, and not someone else, they laughed and made fun
of him. How Reb Yecheskel, his wife and children, did
abuse him! That was his reward for all his trouble.
And just because they themselves are cattle, horses,
boors, who don't understand the tailor's art! Ha, if
only they understood that tailoring is a noble, refined
calling, limitless and bottomless as (with due distinction!) the holy Torah!

But all is not lost. Who knows? For here comes
Binyomin Droibnik, an intelligent man, a man of brains

and feeling. And think how many years he has been a trader! A retail trader, certainly, a jobber, but still—

"Come, Reb Yitzchok-Yossel, make an end! What will you turn it into?"

"Everything."

"That is to say?"

"A dressing-gown for your Dvoshke,—"

"And then?"

"A morning-gown with tassels,—"

"After that?"

"A coat."

"Well?"

"A dress—"

"And besides that?"

"A pair of trousers and a jacket—"

"Nothing more?"

"Why not? A—"

"For instance?"

"Pelisse, a wadded winter pelisse for you."

"There, there! Just that, and only that!" said Reb Binyomin, delighted.

Yitzchok-Yossel Broitgeber tucked away the quilt under his arm, and was preparing to be off.

"Reb Yitzchok-Yossel! And what about taking my measure? And how about your charge?"

Yitzchok-Yossel dearly loved to take anyone's measure, and was an expert at so doing. He had soon pulled a fair-sized sheet of paper out of one of his deep pockets, folded it into a long paper stick, and begun to measure Reb Binyomin Droibnik's limbs. He did not even omit to note the length and breadth of his feet.

"What do you want with that? Are you measuring me for trousers?"

"Ett, don't you ask! No need to teach a skilled workman his trade!"

"And what about the charge?"

"We shall settle that later."

"No, that won't do with me; I am a trader, you understand, and must have it all pat."

"Five gulden."

"And how much less?"

"How should I know? Well, four."

"Well, and half a ruble?"

"Well, well—"

"Remember, Reb Yitzchok-Yossel, it must be a masterpiece!"

"Trust me!"

For five days and five nights Yitzchok-Yossel set his imagination to work on Binyomin Droibnik's inheritance. There was no eating for him, no drinking, and no sleeping. The scissors squeaked, the needle ran hither and thither, up and down, the inheritance sighed and almost sobbed under the hot iron. But how happy was Yitzchok-Yossel those lightsome days and merry nights? Who could compare with him? Greater than the Kabtzonivke village elder, richer than Yisroel Dintzis, the tax-gatherer, and more exalted than the bailiff himself was Yitzchok-Yossel, that is, in his own estimation. All that he wished, thought, and felt was forthwith created by means of his scissors and iron, his thimble, needle, and cotton. No more putting on of patches, sewing on of pockets, cutting out of "Tefillin-Säcklech" and "little prayer-scarfs," no more doing up of old dresses. Freedom, freedom—he wanted one bit of work of the right sort, and that was all! Ha, now he would show them, the Kabtzonivke cripples and householders, now he would show them who Yitzchok-Yossel Broitgeber is! They would not laugh at him or tease him any more! His fame would travel from one end of the world to the other, and Malkeh the orphan, his bride, his wife, she also would hear of it, and—

She will come back to him! He feels it in every limb. It was not him she cast off, only his bad luck. He will rent a lodging (money will pour in from all sides)—buy a little furniture: a bed, a sofa, a table—in time he will buy a little house of his own—she will come, she has been homeless long enough—it is time she should rest her weary, aching bones—it is high time she should have her own corner!

She will come back, he feels it, she will certainly come home!

The last night! The work is complete. Yitzchok-Yossel spread it out on the table of the women's Shool, lighted a second groschen candle, sat down in front of it with wide open, sparkling eyes, gazed with delight at the product of his imagination and—was wildly happy!

So he sat the whole night.

It was very hard for him to part with his achievement, but hardly was it day when he appeared with it at Reb Binyomin Droibnik's.

"A good morning, a good year, Reb Yitzchok-Yossel! I see by your eyes that you have been successful. Is it true?"

"You can see for yourself, there—"

"No, no, there is no need for me to see it first. Dvoshke, Cheike, Shprintze, Dovid-Hershel, Yitzchok-Yoelik! You understand, I want them all to be present and see."

In a few minutes the whole family had appeared on the scene. Even the four little ones popped up from behind the heaps of ragged covering.

Yitzchok-Yossel untied his parcel and—

"Wuus is duuuusss? ? ? ! ! !"

"A pair of trousers with sleeves!"

JUDAH STEINBERG

Born, 1863, in Lipkany, Bessarabia; died, 1907, in Odessa; education Hasidic; entered business in a small Roumanian village for a short time; teacher, from 1889 in Jedency and from 1896 in Leowo, Bessarabia; removed to Odessa, in 1905, to become correspondent of New York Warheit; writer of fables, stories, and children's tales in Hebrew, and poems in Yiddish; historical drama, Ha-Sotah; collected works in Hebrew, 3 vols., Cracow, 1910-1911 (in course of publication).

A LIVELIHOOD

The two young fellows Maxim Klopatzel and Israel Friedman were natives of the same town in New Bessarabia, and there was an old link existing between them: a mutual detestation inherited from their respective parents. Maxim's father was the chief Gentile of the town, for he rented the corn-fields of its richest inhabitant; and as the lawyer of the rich citizen was a Jew, little Maxim imagined, when his father came to lose his tenantry, that it was owing to the Jews. Little Struli was the only Jewish boy he knew (the children were next door neighbors), and so a large share of their responsibility was laid on Struli's shoulders. Later on, when Klopatzel, the father, had abandoned the plough and taken to trade, he and old Friedman frequently came in contact with each other as rivals.

They traded and traded, and competed one against the other, till they both become bankrupt, when each argued to himself that the other was at the bottom of his misfortune—and their children grew on in mutual hatred.

A little later still, Maxim put down to Struli's account part of the nails which were hammered into his Savior, over at the other end of the town, by the well, where the Government and the Church had laid out money and set up a crucifix with a ladder, a hammer, and all other necessary implements.

And Struli, on his part, had an account to settle with Maxim respecting certain other nails driven in with hammers, and torn scrolls of the Law, and the history of the ten martyrs of the days of Titus, not to mention a few later ones.

Their hatred grew with them, its strength increased with theirs.

When Krushevan began to deal in anti-Semitism, Maxim learned that Christian children were carried off into the Shool, Struli's Shool, for the sake of their blood.

Thenceforth Maxim's hatred of Struli was mingled with fear. He was terrified when he passed the Shool at night, and he used to dream that Struli stood over him in a prayer robe, prepared to slaughter him with a ram's horn trumpet.

This because he had once passed the Shool early one Jewish New Year's Day, had peeped through the window, and seen the ram's horn blower standing in his white shroud, armed with the Shofar, and suddenly a heartrending voice broke out with Min ha-Mezar, and Maxim, taking his feet on his shoulders, had arrived home more dead than alive. There was very nearly a commotion. The priest wanted to persuade him that the Jews had tried to obtain his blood.

So the two children grew into youth as enemies. Their fathers died, and the increased difficulties of their position increased their enmity.

The same year saw them called to military service, from which they had both counted on exemption as the only sons of widowed mothers; only Israel's mother had lately died, bequeathing to the Czar all she had—a soldier; and Maxim's mother had united herself to

a second provider—and there was an end of the two
"only sons!"

Neither of them wished to serve; they were too
intellectually capable, too far developed mentally, too
intelligent, to be turned all at once into Russian soldiers,
and too nicely brought up to march from Port Arthur
to Mukden with only one change of shirt. They both
cleared out, and stowed themselves away till they fell
separately into the hands of the military.

They came together again under the fortress walls
of Mukden.

They ate and hungered sullenly round the same cooking pot, received punches from the same officer, and had
the same longing for the same home.

Israel had a habit of talking in his sleep, and, like
a born Bessarabian, in his Yiddish mixed with a large
portion of Roumanian words.

One night, lying in the barracks among the other
soldiers, and sunk in sleep after a hard day, Struli
began to talk sixteen to the dozen. He called out names,
he quarrelled, begged pardon, made a fool of himself—
all in his sleep.

It woke Maxim, who overheard the homelike names
and phrases, the name of his native town.

He got up, made his way between the rows of sleepers,
and sat down by Israel's pallet, and listened.

Next day Maxim managed to have a large helping
of porridge, more than he could eat, and he found
Israel, and set it before him.

"Maltzimesk!" said the other, thanking him in Roumanian, and a thrill of delight went through Maxim's
frame.

The day following, Maxim was hit by a Japanese bullet, and there happened to be no one beside him at the moment.

The shock drove all the soldier-speech out of his head. "Help, I am killed!" he called out, and fell to the ground.

Struli was at his side like one sprung from the earth, he tore off his Four-Corners, and made his comrade a bandage.

The wound turned out to be slight, for the bullet had passed through, only grazing the flesh of the left arm. A few days later Maxim was back in the company.

"I wanted to see you again, Struli," he said, greeting his comrade in Roumanian.

A flash of brotherly affection and gratitude lighted Struli's Semitic eyes, and he took the other into his arms, and pressed him to his heart.

They felt themselves to be "countrymen," of one and the same native town.

Neither of them could have told exactly when their union of spirit had been accomplished, but each one knew that he thanked God for having brought him together with so near a compatriot in a strange land.

And when the battle of Mukden had made Maxim all but totally blind, and deprived Struli of one foot, they started for home together, according to the passage in the Midrash, "Two men with one pair of eyes and one pair of feet between them." Maxim carried on his shoulders a wooden box, which had now became a burden in common for them, and Struli limped a little in front of him, leaning lightly against his companion, so as to keep him in the smooth part of the road and out of other people's way.

Struli had become Maxim's eyes, and Maxim, Struli's feet; they were two men grown into one, and they provided for themselves out of one pocket, now empty of the last ruble.

They dragged themselves home. "A kasa, a kasa!" whispered Struli into Maxim's ear, and the other turned on him his two glazed eyes looking through a red haze, and set in swollen red lids.

A childlike smile played on his lips:

"A kasa, a kasa!" he repeated, also in a whisper.

Home appeared to their fancy as something holy, something consoling, something that could atone and compensate for all they had suffered and lost. They had seen such a home in their dreams.

But the nearer they came to it in reality, the more the dream faded. They remembered that they were returning as conquered soldiers and crippled men, that they had no near relations and but few friends, while the girls who had coquetted with Maxim before he left would never waste so much as a look on him now he was half-blind; and Struli's plans for marrying and emigrating to America were frustrated: a cripple would not be allowed to enter the country.

All their dreams and hopes finally dissipated, and there remained only one black care, one all-obscuring anxiety: how were they to earn a living?

They had been hoping all the while for a pension, but in their service book was written "on sick-leave." The Russo-Japanese war was distinguished by the fact that the greater number of wounded soldiers went home "on sick-leave," and the money assigned by the Government for their pension would not have been sufficient for even a hundredth part of the number of invalids.

Maxim showed a face with two wide open eyes, to which all the passers-by looked the same. He distinguished with difficulty between a man and a telegraph post, and wore a smile of mingled apprehension and confidence. The sound feet stepped hesitatingly, keeping behind Israel, and it was hard to say which steadied himself most against the other. Struli limped forward, and kept open eyes for two. Sometimes he would look round at the box on Maxim's shoulders, as though he felt its weight as much as Maxim.

Meantime the railway carriages had emptied and refilled, and the locomotive gave a great blast, received an answer from somewhere a long way off, a whistle for a whistle, and the train set off, slowly at first, and then gradually faster and faster, till all that remained of it were puffs of smoke hanging in the air without rhyme or reason.

The two felt more depressed than ever. "Something to eat? Where are we to get a bite?" was in their minds.

Suddenly Yisroel remembered with a start: this was the anniversary of his mother's death—if he could only say one Kaddish for her in a Klaus!

"Is it far from here to a Klaus?" he inquired of a passer-by.

"There is one a little way down that side-street," was the reply.

"Maxim!" he begged of the other, "come with me!"

"Where to?"

"To the synagogue."

Maxim shuddered from head to foot. His fear of a Jewish Shool had not left him, and a thousand foolish terrors darted through his head.

But his comrade's voice was so gentle, so childishly imploring, that he could not resist it, and he agreed to go with him into the Shool.

It was the time for Afternoon Prayer, the daylight and the dark held equal sway within the Klaus, the lamps before the platform increasing the former to the east and the latter to the west. Maxim and Yisroel stood in the western part, enveloped in shadow. The Cantor had just finished "Incense," and was entering upon Ashré, and the melancholy night chant of Minchah and Maariv gradually entranced Maxim's emotional Roumanian heart.

The low, sad murmur of the Cantor seemed to him like the distant surging of a sea, in which men were drowned by the hundreds and suffocating with the water. Then, the Ashré and the Kaddish ended, there was silence. The congregation stood up for the Eighteen Benedictions. Here and there you heard a half-stifled sigh. And now it seemed to Maxim that he was in the hospital at night, at the hour when the groans grow less frequent, and the sufferers fall one by one into a sweet sleep.

Tears started into his eyes without his knowing why. He was no longer afraid, but a sudden shyness had come over him, and he felt, as he watched Yisroel repeating the Kaddish, that the words, which he, Maxim, could not understand, were being addressed to someone unseen, and yet mysteriously present in the darkening Shool.

When the prayers were ended, one of the chief members of the congregation approached the "Mandchurian," and gave Yisroel a coin into his hand.

Yisroel looked round—he did not understand at first what the donor meant by it.

Then it occurred to him—and the blood rushed to his face. He gave the coin to his companion, and explained in a half-sentence or two how they had come by it.

Once outside the Klaus, they both cried, after which they felt better.

"A livelihood!" the same thought struck them both. "We can go into partnership!"

AT THE MATZES

It was quite early in the morning, when Sossye, the scribe's daughter, a girl of seventeen, awoke laughing; a sunbeam had broken through the rusty window, made its way to her underneath the counterpane, and there opened her eyes.

It woke her out of a deep dream which she was ashamed to recall, but the dream came back to her of itself, and made her laugh.

Had she known whom she was going to meet in her dreams, she would have lain down in her clothes, occurs to her, and she laughs aloud.

"Got up laughing!" scolds her mother. "There's a piece of good luck for you! It's a sign of a black year for her (may it be to my enemies!)."

Sossye proceeds to dress herself. She does not want to fall out with her mother to-day, she wants to be on good terms with everyone.

In the middle of dressing she loses herself in thought, with one naked foot stretched out and an open stocking in her hands, wondering how the dream would have ended, if she had not awoke so soon.

Chayyimel, a villager's son, who boards with her mother, passes the open doors leading to Sossye's room, and for the moment he is riveted to the spot. His eyes dance, the blood rushes to his cheeks, he gets all he can by looking, and then hurries away to Cheder without his breakfast, to study the Song of Songs.

And Sossye, fresh and rosy from sleep, her brown eyes glowing under the tumbled gold locks, betakes herself to the kitchen, where her mother, with her usual worried look, is blowing her soul out before the oven into a smoky fire of damp wood.

"Look at the girl standing round like a fool! Run down to the cellar, and fetch me an onion and some potatoes!"

Sossye went down to the cellar, and found the onions and potatoes sprouting.

At sight of a green leaf, her heart leapt. Greenery! greenery! summer is coming! And the whole of her dream came back to her!

"Look, mother, green sprouts!" she cried, rushing into the kitchen.

"A thousand bad dreams on your head! The onions are spoilt, and she laughs! My enemies' eyes will creep out of their lids before there will be fresh greens to eat, and all this, woe is me, is only fit to throw away!"

"Greenery, greenery!" thought Sossye, "summer is coming!"

Greenery had got into her head, and there it remained, and from greenery she went on to remember that to-day was the first Passover-cake baking at Gedalyeh the baker's, and that Shloimeh Shieber would be at work there.

Having begged of her mother the one pair of boots that stood about in the room and fitted everyone, she put them on, and was off to the Matzes.

It was, as we have said, the first day's work at Gedalyeh the baker's, and the sack of Passover flour had

just been opened. Gravely, the flour-boy, a two weeks'
orphan, carried the pot of flour for the Mehereh, and
poured it out together with remembrances of his mother,
who had died in the hospital of injuries received at *their*
hands, and the water-boy came up behind him, and
added recollections of his own.

"The hooligans threw his father into the water off
the bridge—may they pay for it, süsser Gott! May they
live till he is a man, and can settle his account with
them!"

Thus the grey-headed old Henoch, the kneader, and
he kneaded it all into the dough, with thoughts of his
own grandchildren: this one fled abroad, the other in
the regiment, and a third in prison.

The dough stiffens, the horny old hands work it with
difficulty. The dough gets stiffer every year, and the
work harder, it is time for him to go to the asylum!

The dough is kneaded, cut up in pieces, rolled and
riddled—is that a token for the whole Congregation of
Israel? And now appear the round Matzes, which must
wander on a shovel into the heated oven of Shloimeh
Shieber, first into one corner, and then into another, till
another shovel throws them out into a new world,
separated from the old by a screen thoroughly scoured
for Passover, which now rises and now falls. There they
are arranged in columns, a reminder of Pithom and
Rameses. Kuk-ruk, kuk-ruk, ruk-ruk, whisper the still
warm Matzes one to another; they also are remembering,
and they tell the tale of the Exodus after their fashion,
the tale of the flight out of Egypt—only they have seen
more flights than one.

Thus are the Matzes kneaded and baked by the Jews, with "thoughts." The Gentiles call them "blood," and assert that Jews need blood for their Matzes, and they take the trouble to supply us with fresh "thoughts" every year!

But at Gedalyeh the baker's all is still cheerfulness. Girls and boys, in their unspent vigor, surround the tables, there is rolling and riddling and cleaning of clean rolling-pins with pieces of broken glass (from where ever do Jews get so much broken glass?), and the whole town is provided with kosher Matzes. Jokes and silver trills escape the lively young workers, the company is as merry as though the Exodus were to-morrow.

But it won't be to-morrow. Look at them well, because another day you will not find them so merry, they will not seem like the same.

One of the likely lads has left his place, and suddenly appeared at a table beside a pretty, curly-haired girl. He has hurried over his Matzes, and now he wants to help her.

She thanks him for his attention with a rolling-pin over the fingers, and there is such laughter among the spectators that Berke, the old overseer, exclaims, "What impertinence!"

But he cannot finish, because he has to laugh himself. There is a spark in the embers of his being which the girlish merriment around him kindles anew.

And the other lads are jealous of the beaten one. They know very well that no girl would hit a complete stranger, and that the blow only meant, "Impudent boy, why need the world know of anything between us?"

Shloimehle Shieber, armed with the shovels, stands still for a minute trying to distinguish Sossye's voice in the peals of laughter. The Matzes under his care are browning in the oven.

And Sossye takes it into her head to make her Matzes with one pointed corner, so that he may perhaps know them for hers, and laughs to herself as she does so.

There is one table to the side of the room which was not there last year; it was placed there for the formerly well-to-do housemistresses, who last year, when they came to bake their Matzes, gave Yom-tov money to the others. Here all goes on quietly; the laughter of the merry people breaks against the silence, and is swallowed up.

The work grows continually pleasanter and more animated. The riddler stamps two or three Matzes with hieroglyphs at once, in order to show off. Shloimeh at the oven cannot keep pace with him, and grows angry:

"May all bad. . . "

The wish is cut short in his mouth, he has caught a glance of Sossye's through the door of the baking-room, he answers with two, gets three back, Sossye pursing her lips to signify a kiss. Shloimeh folds his hands, which also means something.

Meantime ten Matzes get scorched, and one of Sossye's is pulled in two. "Brennen brennt mir mein Harz," starts a worker singing in a plaintive key.

"Come! hush, hush!" scolds old Berke. "Songs, indeed! What next, you impudent boy?"

"My sorrows be on their head!" sighs a neighbor of Sossye's. "They'd soon be tired of their life, if they were me. I've left two children at home fit to scream their hearts out. The other is at the breast, I have brought it along. It is quiet just now, by good luck."

"What is the use of a poor woman's having children?" exclaims another, evidently "expecting" herself. Indeed, she has a child a year—and a seven-days' mourning a year afterwards.

"Do you suppose I ask for them? Do you think I cry my eyes out for them before God?"

"If she hasn't any, who's to inherit her place at the Matzes-baking—a hundred years hence?"

"All very well for you to talk, *you're* a grass-widow (to no Jewish daughter may it apply!)!"

"May such a blow be to my enemies as he'll surely come back again!"

"It's about time! After three years!"

"Will you shut up, or do you want another beating?"

Sossye went off into a fresh peal of laughter, and the shovel fell out of Shloimeh's hand.

Again he caught a glance, but this time she wrinkled her nose at him, as much as to say, "Fie, you shameless boy! Can't you behave yourself even before other people?"

Hereupon the infant gave account of itself in a small, shrill voice, and the general commotion went on increasing. The overseer scolded, the Matzes-printing-wheel creaked and squeaked, the bits of glass were ground against the rolling-pins, there was a humming of songs and a proclaiming of secrets, followed by bursts of laughter, Sossye's voice ringing high above the rest.

And the sun shone into the room through the small window—a white spot jumped around and kissed everyone there.

Is it the Spirit of Israel delighting in her young men and maidens and whispering in their ears: "What if it *is* Matzes-kneading, and what if it *is* Exile? Only let us be all together, only let us all be merry!"

Or is it the Spring, transformed into a white patch of sunshine, in which all have equal share, and which has not forgotten to bring good news into the house of Gedalyeh the Matzeh-baker?

A beautiful sun was preparing to set, and promised another fine day for the morrow.

"Ding-dong, gul-gul-gul-gul-gul-gul!"

It was the convent bells calling the Christians to confession!

All tongues were silenced round the tables at Gedalyeh the baker's.

A streak of vapor dimmed the sun, and gloomy thoughts settled down upon the hearts of the workers.

"Easter! *Their* Easter is coming on!" and mothers' eyes sought their children.

The white patch of sunshine suddenly gave a terrified leap across the ceiling and vanished in a corner.

"Kik-kik, kik-rik, kik-rik," whispered the hot Matzes. Who is to know what they say?

Who can tell, now that the Jews have baked this year's Matzes, how soon *they* will set about providing them with material for the next?—"thoughts," and broken glass for the rolling-pins.

DAVID FRISCHMANN

Born, 1863, in Lodz, Russian Poland, of a family of merchants; education, Jewish and secular, the latter with special attention to foreign languages and literatures; has spent most of his life in Warsaw; Hebrew critic, editor, poet, satirist, and writer of fairy tales; translator of George Eliot's Daniel Deronda into Hebrew; contributor to Sholom-Alechem's Jüdische Volksbibliothek, Spektor's Hausfreund, and various periodicals; editor of monthly publication Reshafim; collected works in Hebrew, Ketabim Nibharim, 2 vols., Warsaw, 1899-1901, and Reshimot, 4 parts, Warsaw, 1911.

THREE WHO ATE

Once upon a time three people ate. I recall the event as one recalls a dream. Black clouds obscure the men, because it happened long ago.

Only sometimes it seems to me that there are no clouds, but a pillar of fire lighting up the men and their doings, and the fire grows bigger and brighter, and gives light and warmth to this day.

I have only a few words to tell you, two or three words: once upon a time three people ate. Not on a workday or an ordinary Sabbath, but on a Day of Atonement that fell on a Sabbath.

Not in a corner where no one sees or hears, but before all the people in the great Shool, in the principal Shool of the town.

Neither were they ordinary men, these three, but the chief Jews of the community: the Rabbi and his two Dayonim.

The townsfolk looked up to them as if they had been angels, and certainly held them to be saints. And now, as I write these words, I remember how difficult it was for me to understand, and how I sometimes used to think the Rabbi and his Dayonim had done wrong. But even then I felt that they were doing a tremendous thing, that they were holy men with holy instincts, and that it was not easy for them to act thus. Who knows how hard they fought with themselves, who knows how they suffered, and what they endured?

And even if I live many years and grow old, I shall never forget the day and the men, and what was done on it, for they were no ordinary men, but great heroes.

Those were bitter times, such as had not been for long, and such as will not soon return.

A great calamity had descended on us from Heaven, and had spread abroad among the towns and over the country: the cholera had broken out.

The calamity had reached us from a distant land, and entered our little town, and clutched at young and old.

By day and by night men died like flies, and those who were left hung between life and death.

Who can number the dead who were buried in those days! Who knows the names of the corpses which lay about in heaps in the streets!

In the Jewish street the plague made great ravages: there was not a house where there lay not one dead—not a family in which the calamity had not broken out.

In the house where we lived, on the second floor, nine people died in one day. In the basement there died a mother and four children, and in the house opposite we heard wild cries one whole night through, and in the morning we became aware that there was no one left in it alive.

The grave-diggers worked early and late, and the corpses lay about in the streets like dung. They stuck one to the other like clay, and one walked over dead bodies.

The summer broke up, and there came the Solemn Days, and then the most dreadful day of all—the Day of Atonement.

I shall remember that day as long as I live.

The Eve of the Day of Atonement—the reciting of Kol Nidré!

At the desk before the ark there stands, not as usual the precentor and two householders, but the Rabbi and his two Dayonim.

The candles are burning all round, and there is a whispering of the flames as they grow taller and taller. The people stand at their reading-desks with grave faces, and draw on the robes and prayer-scarfs, the Spanish hoods and silver girdles; and their shadows sway this way and that along the walls, and might be the ghosts of the dead who died to-day and yesterday and the day before yesterday. Evidently they could not rest in their graves, and have also come into the Shool.

Hush! . . . the Rabbi has begun to say something, and the Dayonim, too, and a groan rises from the congregation.

"With the consent of the All-Present and with the consent of this congregation, we give leave to pray with them that have transgressed."

And a great fear fell upon me and upon all the people, young and old. In that same moment I saw the Rabbi mount the platform. Is he going to preach? Is he going to lecture the people at a time when they are falling dead like flies? But the Rabbi neither preached nor lectured. He only called to remembrance the souls of those who had died in the course of the last few days. But how long it lasted! How many names he mentioned! The minutes fly one after the other, and the Rabbi has not finished! Will the list of souls never come to an end? Never? And it seems to me the Rabbi had better call out the names of those who are left alive, because they are few, instead of the names of the dead, who are without number and without end.

I shall never forget that night and the praying, because it was not really praying, but one long, loud groan rising from the depth of the human heart, cleaving the sky and reaching to Heaven. Never since the world began have Jews prayed in greater anguish of soul, never have hotter tears fallen from human eyes.

That night no one left the Shool.

After the prayers they recited the Hymn of Unity, and after that the Psalms, and then chapters from the Mishnah, and then ethical books. . .

And I also stand among the congregation and pray, and my eyelids are heavy as lead, and my heart beats like a hammer.

"U-Malochim yechofézun—and the angels fly around."

And I fancy I see them flying in the Shool, up and down, up and down. And among them I see the bad angel with the thousand eyes, full of eyes from head to feet.

That night no one left the Shool, but early in the morning there were some missing—two of the congregation had fallen during the night, and died before our eyes, and lay wrapped in their prayer-scarfs and white robes—nothing was lacking for their journey from the living to the dead.

They kept on bringing messages into the Shool from the Gass, but nobody wanted to listen or to ask questions, lest he should hear what had happened in his own house. No matter how long I live, I shall never forget that night, and all I saw and heard.

But the Day of Atonement, the day that followed, was more awful still.

And even now, when I shut my eyes, I see the whole picture, and I think I am standing once more among the people in the Shool.

It is Atonement Day in the afternoon.

The Rabbi stands on the platform in the centre of the Shool, tall and venerable, and there is a fascination in his noble features. And there, in the corner of the Shool, stands a boy who never takes his eyes off the Rabbi's face.

In truth I never saw a nobler figure.

The Rabbi is old, seventy or perhaps eighty years, but tall and straight as a fir-tree. His long beard is white like silver, but the thick, long hair of his head is whiter still, and his face is blanched, and his lips are pale, and only his large black eyes shine and sparkle like the eyes of a young lion.

I stood in awe of him when I was a little child. I knew he was a man of God, one of the greatest authorities in the Law, whose advice was sought by the whole world.

I knew also that he inclined to leniency in all his decisions, and that none dared oppose him.

The sight I saw that day in Shool is before my eyes
now.

The Rabbi stands on the platform, and his black
eyes gleam and shine in the pale face and in the white
hair and beard.

The Additional Service is over, and the people are
waiting to hear what the Rabbi will say, and one is
afraid to draw one's breath.

And the Rabbi begins to speak.

His weak voice grows stronger and higher every
minute, and at last it is quite loud.

He speaks of the sanctity of the Day of Atonement
and of the holy Torah; of repentance and of prayer,
of the living and of the dead, and of the pestilence that
has broken out and that destroys without pity, without
rest, without a pause—for how long? for how much
longer?

And by degrees his pale cheeks redden and his lips
also, and I hear him say: "And when trouble comes to
a man, he must look to his deeds, and not only to those
which concern him and the Almighty, but to those which
concern himself, to his body, to his flesh, to his own
health."

I was a child then, but I remember how I began to
tremble when I heard these words, because I had understood.

The Rabbi goes on speaking. He speaks of cleanliness
and wholesome air, of dirt, which is dangerous to man,
and of hunger and thirst, which are men's bad angels
when there is a pestilence about, devouring without pity.

And the Rabbi goes on to say:

"And men shall live by My commandments, and not die by them. There are times when one must turn aside from the Law, if by so doing a whole community may be saved."

I stand shaking with fear. What does the Rabbi want? What does he mean by his words? What does he think to accomplish? And suddenly I see that he is weeping, and my heart beats louder and louder. What has happened? Why does he weep? And there I stand in the corner, in the silence, and I also begin to cry.

And to this day, if I shut my eyes, I see him standing on the platform, and he makes a sign with his hand to the two Dayonim to the left and right of him. He and they whisper together, and he says something in their ear. What has happened? Why does his cheek flame, and why are theirs as white as chalk?

And suddenly I hear them talking, but I cannot understand them, because the words do not enter my brain. And yet all three are speaking so sharply and clearly!

And all the people utter a groan, and after the groan I hear the words, "With the consent of the All-Present and with the consent of this congregation, we give leave to eat and drink on the Day of Atonement."

Silence. Not a sound is heard in the Shool, not an eyelid quivers, not a breath is drawn.

And I stand in my corner and hear my heart beating: one—two—one—two. A terror comes over me, and it is black before my eyes. The shadows move to and fro on the wall, and amongst the shadows I see the dead who died yesterday and the day before yesterday and the day before the day before yesterday—a whole people, a great assembly.

And suddenly I grasp what it is the Rabbi asks of us. The Rabbi calls on us to eat, to-day! The Rabbi calls on Jews to eat on the Day of Atonement—not to fast, because of the cholera—because of the cholera—because of the cholera . . . and I begin to cry loudly. And it is not only I—the whole congregation stands weeping, and the Dayonim on the platform weep, and the greatest of all stands there sobbing like a child.

And he implores like a child, and his words are soft and gentle, and every now and then he weeps so that his voice cannot be heard.

"Eat, Jews, eat! To-day we must eat. This is a time to turn aside from the Law. We are to live through the commandments, and not die through them!"

But no one in the Shool has stirred from his place, and there he stands and begs of them, weeping, and declares that he takes the whole responsibility on himself, that the people shall be innocent. But no one stirs. And presently he begins again in a changed voice—he does not beg, he commands:

"I give you leave to eat—I—I—I!"

And his words are like arrows shot from the bow.

But the people are deaf, and no one stirs.

Then he begins again with his former voice, and implores like a child:

"What would you have of me? Why will you torment me till my strength fails? Think you I have not struggled with myself from early this morning till now?"

And the Dayonim also plead with the people.

And of a sudden the Rabbi grows as white as chalk, and lets his head fall on his breast. There is a groan from one end of the Shool to the other, and after the groan the people are heard to murmur among themselves.

Then the Rabbi, like one speaking to himself, says:

"It is God's will. I am eighty years old, and have never yet transgressed a law. But this is also a law, it is a precept. Doubtless the Almighty wills it so! Beadle!"

The beadle comes, and the Rabbi whispers a few words into his ear.

He also confers with the Dayonim, and they nod their heads and agree.

And the beadle brings cups of wine for Sanctification, out of the Rabbi's chamber, and little rolls of bread. And though I should live many years and grow very old, I shall never forget what I saw then, and even now, when I shut my eyes, I see the whole thing: three Rabbis standing on the platform in Shool, and eating before the whole people, on the Day of Atonement!

The three belong to the heroes.

Who shall tell how they fought with themselves, who shall say how they suffered, and what they endured?

"I have done what you wished," says the Rabbi, and his voice does not shake, and his lips do not tremble.

"God's Name be praised!"

And all the Jews ate that day, they ate and wept.

Rays of light beam forth from the remembrance, and spread all around, and reach the table at which I sit and write these words.

Once again: three people ate.

At the moment when the awesome scene in the Shool is before me, there are three Jews sitting in a room opposite the Shool, and they also are eating.

They are the three "enlightened" ones of the place: the tax-collector, the inspector, and the teacher.

The window is wide open, so that all may see; on the table stands a samovar, glasses of red wine, and eatables. And the three sit with playing-cards in their hands, playing Preference, and they laugh and eat and drink.

Do they also belong to the heroes?

MICHA JOSEPH BERDYCZEWSKI

Born, 1865, in Berschad, Podolia, Southwestern Russia; educated in Yeshibah of Volozhin; studied also modern literatures in his youth; has been living alternately in Berlin and Breslau; Hebrew, Yiddish, and German writer, on philosophy, æsthetics, and Jewish literary, spiritual, and timely questions; contributor to Hebrew periodicals; editor of Bet-Midrash, supplement to Bet-Ozar ha-Sifrut; contributed Ueber den Zusammenhang zwischen Ethik und Aesthetik to Berner Studien zur Philosophie und ihrer Geschichte; author of two novels, Mibayit u-Mihuz, and Mahanaim; a book on the Hasidim, Warsaw, 1900; Jüdische Ketobim vun a weiten Korov, Warsaw; Hebrew essays on miscellaneous subjects, eleven parts, Warsaw and Breslau (in course of publication).

MILITARY SERVICE

" They look as if they'd enough of me !"

So I think to myself, as I give a glance at my two
great top-boots, my wide trousers, and my shabby green
uniform, in which there is no whole part left.

I take a bit of looking-glass out of my box, and look
at my reflection. Yes, the military cap on my head *is*
a beauty, and no mistake, as big as Og king of Bashan,
and as bent and crushed as though it had been sat upon
for years together.

Under the cap appears a small, washed-out face, yellow and weazened, with two large black eyes that look
at me somewhat wildly.

I don't recognize myself; I remember me in a grey
jacket, narrow, close-fitting trousers, a round hat, and
a healthy complexion.

I can't make out where I got those big eyes, why
they shine so, why my face should be yellow, and my
nose, pointed.

And yet I know that it is I myself, Chayyim Blumin,
and no other; that I have been handed over for a soldier, and have to serve only two years and eight months,
and not three years and eight months, because I have
a certificate to the effect that I have been through the
first four classes in a secondary school.

Though I know quite well that I am to serve only
two years and eight months, I feel the same as though
it were to be forever; I can't, somehow, believe that

my time will some day expire, and I shall once more be free.

I have tried from the very beginning not to play any tricks, to do my duty and obey orders, so that they should not say, "A Jew won't work—a Jew is too lazy."

Even though I am let off manual labor, because I am on "privileged rights," still, if they tell me to go and clean the windows, or polish the flooring with sand, or clear away the snow from the door, I make no fuss and go. I wash and clean and polish, and try to do the work well, so that they should find no fault with me.

They haven't yet ordered me to carry pails of water.

Why should I not confess it? The idea of having to do that rather frightens me. When I look at the vessel in which the water is carried, my heart begins to flutter: the vessel is almost as big as I am, and I couldn't lift it even if it were empty.

I often think: What shall I do, if to-morrow, or the day after, they wake me at three o'clock in the morning and say coolly:

"Get up, Blumin, and go with Ossadtchok to fetch a pail of water!"

You ought to see my neighbor Ossadtchok! He looks as if he could squash me with one finger. It is as easy for him to carry a pail of water as to drink a glass of brandy. How can I compare myself with him?

I don't care if it makes my shoulder swell, if I could only carry the thing. I shouldn't mind about that. But God in Heaven knows the truth, that I won't be able to lift the pail off the ground, only they won't believe me, they will say:

"Look at the lazy Jew, pretending he is a poor creature that can't lift a pail!"

There—I mind that more than anything.

I don't suppose they *will* send me to fetch water, for, after all, I am on "privileged rights," but I can't sleep in peace: I dream all night that they are waking me at three o'clock, and I start up bathed in a cold sweat.

Drill does not begin before eight in the morning, but they wake us at six, so that we may have time to clean our rifles, polish our boots and leather girdle, brush our coat, and furbish the brass buttons with chalk, so that they should shine like mirrors.

I don't mind the getting up early, I am used to rising long before daylight, but I am always worrying lest something shouldn't be properly cleaned, and they should say that a Jew is so lazy, he doesn't care if his things are clean or not, that he's afraid of touching his rifle, and pay me other compliments of the kind.

I clean and polish and rub everything all I know, but my rifle always seems in worse condition than the other men's. I can't make it look the same as theirs, do what I will, and the head of my division, a corporal, shouts at me, calls me a greasy fellow, and says he'll have me up before the authorities because I don't take care of my arms.

But there is worse than the rifle, and that is the uniform. Mine is *years* old—I am sure it is older than I am. Every day little pieces fall out of it, and the buttons tear themselves out of the cloth, dragging bits of it after them.

I never had a needle in my hand in all my life before, and now I sit whole nights and patch and sew on buttons. And next morning, when the corporal takes hold of a button and gives a pull, to see if it's firmly sewn, a pang goes through my heart: the button is dragged out, and a piece of the uniform follows.

Another whole night's work for me!

After the inspection, they drive us out into the yard and teach us to stand: it must be done so that our stomachs fall in and our chests stick out. I am half as one ought to be, because my stomach is flat enough anyhow, only my chest is weak and narrow and also flat—flat as a board.

The corporal squeezes in my stomach with his knee, pulls me forward by the flaps of the coat, but it's no use. He loses his temper, and calls me greasy fellow, screams again that I am pretending, that I *won't* serve, and this makes my chest fall in more than ever.

I like the gymnastics.

In summer we go out early into the yard, which is very wide and covered with thick grass.

It smells delightfully, the sun warms us through, it feels so pleasant.

The breeze blows from the fields, I open my mouth and swallow the freshness, and however much I swallow, it's not enough, I should like to take in all the air there is. Then, perhaps, I should cough less, and grow a little stronger.

We throw off the old uniforms, and remain in our shirts, we run and leap and go through all sorts of per-

formances with our hands and feet, and it's splendid!
At home I never had so much as an idea of such fun.

At first I was very much afraid of jumping across
the ditch, but I resolved once and for all—I've *got* to
jump it. If the worst comes to the worst, I shall fall
and bruise myself. Suppose I do? What then? Why
do all the others jump it and don't care? One needn't
be so very strong to jump!

And one day, before the gymnastics had begun, I
left my comrades, took heart and a long run, and when
I came to the ditch, I made a great bound, and, lo and
behold, I was over on the other side! I couldn't believe my own eyes that I had done it so easily.

Ever since then I have jumped across ditches, and
over mounds, and down from mounds, as well as any
of them.

Only when it comes to climbing a ladder or swinging myself over a high bar, I know it spells misfortune
for me.

I spring forward, and seize the first rung with my
right hand, but I cannot reach the second with my left.

I stretch myself, and kick out with my feet, but I
cannot reach any higher, not by so much as a vershok,
and so there I hang and kick with my feet, till my right
arm begins to tremble and hurt me. My head goes
round, and I fall onto the grass. The corporal abuses
me as usual, and the soldiers laugh.

I would give ten years of my life to be able to get
higher, if only three or four rungs, but what can I do,
if my arms won't serve me?

Sometimes I go out to the ladder by myself, while the soldiers are still asleep, and stand and look at it: perhaps I can think of a way to manage? But in vain. Thinking, you see, doesn't help you in these cases.

Sometimes they tell one of the soldiers to stand in the middle of the yard with his back to us, and we have to hop over him. He bends down a little, lowers his head, rests his hands on his knees, and we hop over him one at a time. One takes a good run, and when one comes to him, one places both hands on his shoulders, raises oneself into the air, and—over!

I know exactly how it ought to be done; I take the run all right, and plant my hands on his shoulders, only I can't raise myself into the air. And if I do lift myself up a little way, I remain sitting on the soldier's neck, and were it not for his seizing me by the feet, I should fall, and perhaps kill myself.

Then the corporal and another soldier take hold of me by the arms and legs, and throw me over the man's head, so that I may see there is nothing dreadful about it, as though I did not jump right over him because I was afraid, while it is that my arms are so weak, I cannot lean upon them and raise myself into the air.

But when I say so, they only laugh, and don't believe me. They say, "It won't help you; you will have to serve anyhow!"

When, on the other hand, it comes to "theory," the corporal is very pleased with me.

He says, that except himself no one knows "theory" as I do.

He never questions me now, only when one of the others doesn't know something, he turns to me:

"Well, Blumin, *you* tell me!"

I stand up without hurrying, and am about to answer, but he is apparently not pleased with my way of rising from my seat, and orders me to sit down again.

"When your superior speaks to you," says he, "you ought to jump up as though the seat were hot," and he looks at me angrily, as much as to say, "You may know theory, but you'll please to know your manners as well, and treat me with proper respect."

"Stand up again and answer!"

I start up as though I felt a prick from a needle, and answer the question as he likes it done: smartly, all in one breath, and word for word according to the book.

He, meanwhile, looks at the primer, to make sure I am not leaving anything out, but as he reads very slowly, he cannot catch me up, and when I have got to the end, he is still following with his finger and reading. And when he has finished, he gives me a pleased look, and says enthusiastically "Right!" and tells me to sit down again.

"Theory," he says, "that you *do* know!"

Well, begging his pardon, it isn't much to know. And yet there are soldiers who are four years over it, and don't know it then. For instance, take my comrade Ossadtchok; he says that, when it comes to "theory", he would rather go and hang or drown himself. He says, he would rather have to carry three pails of water than sit down to "theory."

I tell him, that if he would learn to read, he could study the whole thing by himself in a week; but he won't listen.

"Nobody," he says, "will ever ask *my* advice."

One thing always alarmed me very much: However was I to take part in the manœuvres?

I cannot lift a single pud (I myself only weigh two pud and thirty pounds), and if I walk three versts, my feet hurt, and my heart beats so violently that I think it's going to burst my side.

At the manœuvres I should have to carry as much as fifty pounds' weight, and perhaps more: a rifle, a cloak, a knapsack with linen, boots, a uniform, a tent, bread, and onions, and a few other little things, and should have to walk perhaps thirty to forty versts a day.

But when the day and the hour arrived, and the command was given "Forward, march!" when the band struck up, and two thousand men set their feet in motion, something seemed to draw me forward, and I went. At the beginning I found it hard, I felt weighted to the earth, my left shoulder hurt me so, I nearly fainted. But afterwards I got very hot, I began to breathe rapidly and deeply, my eyes were starting out of my head like two cupping-glasses, and I not only walked, I ran, so as not to fall behind—and so I ended by marching along with the rest, forty versts a day.

Only I did not sing on the march like the others First, because I did not feel so very cheerful, and second, because I could not breathe properly, let alone sing.

At times I felt burning hot, but immediately afterwards I would grow light, and the marching was easy,

I seemed to be carried along rather than to tread the earth, and it appeared to me as though another were marching in my place, only that my left shoulder ached, and I was hot.

I remember that once it rained a whole night long, it came down like a deluge, our tents were soaked through, and grew heavy. The mud was thick. At three o'clock in the morning an alarm was sounded, we were ordered to fold up our tents and take to the road again. So off we went.

It was dark and slippery. It poured with rain. I was continually stepping into a puddle, and getting my boot full of water. I shivered and shook, and my teeth chattered with cold. That is, I was cold one minute and hot the next. But the marching was no difficulty to me, I scarcely felt that I was on the march, and thought very little about it. Indeed, I don't know what I *was* thinking about, my mind was a blank.

We marched, turned back, and marched again. Then we halted for half an hour, and turned back again.

And this went on a whole night and a whole day.

Then it turned out that there had been a mistake: it was not we who ought to have marched, but another regiment, and we ought not to have moved from the spot. But there was no help for it then.

It was night. We had eaten nothing all day. The rain poured down, the mud was ankle-deep, there was no straw on which to pitch our tents, but we managed somehow. And so the days passed, each like the other. But I got through the manœuvres, and was none the worse.

Now I am already an old soldier; I have hardly another year and a half to serve—about sixteen months. I only hope I shall not be ill. It seems I got a bit of a chill at the manœuvres, I cough every morning, and sometimes I suffer with my feet. I shiver a little at night till I get warm, and then I am very hot, and I feel very comfortable lying abed. But I shall probably soon be all right again.

They say, one may take a rest in the hospital, but I haven't been there yet, and don't want to go at all, especially now I am feeling better. The soldiers are sorry for me, and sometimes they do my work, but not just for love. I get three pounds of bread a day, and don't eat more than one pound. The rest I give to my comrade Ossadtchok. He eats it all, and his own as well, and then he could do with some more. In return for this he often cleans my rifle, and sometimes does other work for me, when he sees I have no strength left.

I am also teaching him and a few other soldiers to read and write, and they are very pleased.

My corporal also comes to me to be taught, but he never gives me a word of thanks.

The superior of the platoon, when he isn't drunk, and is in good humor, says "you" to me instead of "thou," and sometimes invites me to share his bed— I can breathe easier there, because there is more air, and I don't cough so much, either.

Only it sometimes happens that he comes back from town tipsy, and makes a great to-do: How do I, a common soldier, come to be sitting on his bed?

He orders me to get up and stand before him "at attention," and declares he will "have me up" for it.

When, however, he has sobered down, he turns kind again, and calls me to him; he likes me to tell him "stories" out of books.

Sometimes the orderly calls me into the orderly-room, and gives me a report to draw up, or else a list or a calculation to make. He himself writes badly, and is very poor at figures.

I do everything he wants, and he is very glad of my help, only it wouldn't do for him to confess to it, and when I have finished, he always says to me:

"If the commanding officer is not satisfied, he will send you to fetch water."

I know it isn't true, first, because the commanding officer mustn't know that I write in the orderly-room, a Jew can't be an army secretary; secondly, because he is certain to be satisfied: he once gave me a note to write himself, and was very pleased with it.

"If you were not a Jew," he said to me then, "I should make a corporal of you."

Still, my corporal always repeats his threat about the water, so that I may preserve a proper respect for him, although I not only respect him, I tremble before his size. When *he* comes back tipsy from town, and finds me in the orderly-room, he commands me to drag his muddy boots off his feet, and I obey him and drag off his boots.

Sometimes I don't care, and other times it hurts my feelings.

ISAIAH BERSCHADSKI

Pen name of Isaiah Domaschewitski; born, 1871, near Derechin, Government of Grodno (Lithuania), White Russia; died, 1909, in Warsaw; education, Jewish and secular; teacher of Hebrew in Ekaterinoslav, Southern Russia; in business, in Ekaterinoslav and Baku; editor, in 1903, of Ha-Zeman, first in St. Petersburg, then in Wilna; after a short sojourn in Riga removed to Warsaw; writer of novels and short stories, almost exclusively in Hebrew; contributor to Ha-Meliz, Ha-Shiloah, and other periodicals; pen pames besides Berschadski: Berschadi, and Shimoni; collected works in Hebrew, Tefusim u-Zelalim, Warsaw, 1899, and Ketabim Aharonim, Warsaw, 1909.

FORLORN AND FORSAKEN

Forlorn and forsaken she was in her last years. Even when she lay on the bed of sickness where she died, not one of her relations or friends came to look after her; they did not even come to mourn for her or accompany her to the grave. There was not even one of her kin to say the first Kaddish over her resting-place. My wife and I were the only friends she had at the close of her life, no one but us cared for her while she was ill, or walked behind her coffin. The only tears shed at the lonely old woman's grave were ours. I spoke the only Kaddish for her soul, but we, after all, were complete strangers to her!

Yes, we were strangers to her, and she was a stranger to us! We made her acquaintance only a few years before her death, when she was living in two tiny rooms opposite the first house we settled in after our marriage. Nobody ever came to see her, and she herself visited nowhere, except at the little store where she made her necessary purchases, and at the house-of-study near by, where she prayed twice every day. She was about sixty, rather undersized, and very thin, but more lithesome in her movements than is common at that age. Her face was full of creases and wrinkles, and her light brown eyes were somewhat dulled, but her ready smile and quiet glance told of a good heart and a kindly temper. Her simple old gown was always neat, her wig tastefully arranged, her lodging and its furniture clean and tidy—and all this attracted us to her from the first day onward. We were still more taken with her retiring manner, the quiet way in which she kept herself in the background and the slight melancholy of her expression, telling of a life that had held much sadness.

We made advances. She was very willing to become acquainted with us, and it was not very long before she was like a mother to us, or an old aunt. My wife was then an inexperienced "housemistress" fresh to her duties, and found a great help in the old woman, who smilingly taught her how to proceed with the housekeeping. When our first child was born, she took it to her heart, and busied herself with its upbringing almost more than the young mother. It was evident that dandling the child in her arms was a joy to her beyond words. At such moments her eyes would brighten, her wrinkles grew faint, a curiously satisfied smile played round her lips, and a new note of joy came into her voice.

At first sight all this seemed quite simple, because a woman is naturally inclined to care for little children, and it may have been so with her to an exceptional degree, but closer examination convinced me that here lay yet another reason; her attentions to the child, so it seemed, awakened pleasant memories of a long-ago past, when she herself was a young mother caring for children of her own, and looking at this strange child had stirred a longing for those other children, further from her eyes, but nearer to her heart, although perhaps quite unknown to her—who perhaps existed only in her imagination.

And when we were made acquainted with the details of her life, we knew our conjectures to be true. Her history was very simple and commonplace, but very tragic. Perhaps the tragedy of such biographies lies in their being so very ordinary and simple!

She lived quietly and happily with her husband for twenty years after their marriage. They were not rich, but their little house was a kingdom of delight, where no good thing was wanting. Their business was farming land that belonged to a Polish nobleman, a business that knows of good times and of bad, of fat years and lean years, years of high prices and years of low. But on the whole it was a good business and profitable, and it afforded them a comfortable living. Besides, they were used to the country, they could not fancy themselves anywhere else. The very thing that had never entered their head is just what happened. In the beginning of the "eighties" they were obliged to leave the estate they had farmed for ten years, because the lease was up, and the recently promulgated "temporary laws" forbade them to renew it. This was bad for them from a material point of view, because it left them without regular income just when their children were growing up and expenses had increased, but their mental distress was so great, that, for the time, the financial side of the misfortune was thrown into the shade.

When we made her acquaintance, many years had passed since then, many another trouble had come into her life, but one could hear tears in her voice while she told the story of that first misfortune. It was a bitter

Tisho-b'ov for them when they left the house, the gardens, the barns, and the stalls, their whole life, all those things concerning which they had forgotten, and their children had hardly known, that they were not their own possession.

Their town surroundings made them more conscious of their altered circumstances. She herself, the elder children oftener still, had been used to drive into the town now and again, but that was on pleasure trips, which had lasted a day or two at most; they had never tried staying there longer, and it was no wonder if they felt cramped and oppressed in town after their free life in the open.

When they first settled there, they had a capital of about ten thousand rubles, but by reason of inexperience in their new occupation they were worsted in competition with others, and a few turns of bad luck brought them almost to ruin. The capital grew less from year to year; everything they took up was more of a struggle than the last venture; poverty came nearer and nearer, and the father of the family began to show signs of illness, brought on by town life and worry. This, of course, made their material position worse, and the knowledge of it reacted disastrously on his health. Three years after he came to town, he died, and she was left with six children and no means of subsistence. Already during her husband's life they had exchanged their first lodging for a second, a poorer and cheaper one, and after his death they moved into a third, meaner and narrower still, and sold their precious furniture, for which, indeed, there was no place in the new existence. But even so the question of bread and meat was not answered. They still had about six hundred rubles, but, as they were without a trade, it was easy to foresee that the little stock of money would dwindle day by day till there was none of it left—and what then?

The eldest son, Yossef, aged twenty-one, had gone from home a year before his father's death, to seek his fortune elsewhere; but his first letters brought no very good news, and now the second, Avròhom, a lad of eighteen, and the daughter Rochel, who was sixteen, declared their intention to start for America. The mother was against it, begged them with tears not to go, but they did not listen to her. Parting with them, forever most likely, was bad enough in itself, but worst of all was the thought that her children, for whose Jewish education their father had never grudged money even when times were hardest, should go to America, and there, forgetting everything they had learned, become "ganze Goyim." She was quite sure that her husband would never have agreed to his children's being thus scattered abroad, and this encouraged her to oppose their will with more determination. She urged them to wait at least till their elder brother had achieved some measure of success, and could help them. She held out this hope to them, because she believed in her son Yossef and his capacity, and was convinced that in a little time he would become their support.

If only Avròhom and Rochel had not been so impatient (she would lament to us), everything would have turned out differently! They would not have been hustled off to the end of creation, and she would not have been left so lonely in her last years, but—it had apparently been so ordained!

Avròhom and Rochel agreed to defer the journey, but when some months had passed, and Yossef was still wandering from town to town, finding no rest for the sole of his foot, she had to give in to her children and let them go. They took with them two hundred rubles and sailed for America, and with the remaining three hundred rubles she opened a tiny shop. Her expenses were not great now, as only the three younger children were left her, but the shop was not sufficient to support even these. The stock grew smaller month by month, there never being anything over wherewith to replenish it, and there was no escaping the fact that one day soon the shop would remain empty.

And as if this were not enough, there came bad news from the children in America. They did not complain much; on the contrary, they wrote most hopefully about the future, when their position would certainly, so they said, improve; but the mother's heart was not to be deceived, and she felt instinctively that meanwhile they were doing anything but well, while later—who could foresee what would happen later?

One day she got a letter from Yossef, who wrote that, convinced of the impossibility of earning a livelihood within the Pale, he was about to make use of an opportunity that offered itself, and settle in a distant town outside of it. This made her very sad, and she wept over her fate—to have a son living in a Gentile city, where there were hardly any Jews at all. And the next letter from America added sorrow to sorrow. Avròhom and Rochel had parted company, and were living in different towns. She could not bear the thought of her young daughter fending for herself among strangers— a thought that tortured her all the more as she had a peculiar idea of America. She herself could not account for the terror that would seize her whenever she remembered that strange, distant life.

But the worst was nearly over; the turn for the better came soon. She received word from Yossef that he had found a good position in his new home, and in a few weeks he proved his letter true by sending her money. From America, too, the news that came was more cheerful, even joyous. Avròhom had secured steady work with good pay, and before long he wrote for his younger brother to join him in America, and provided him with all the funds he needed for travelling expenses. Rochel had engaged herself to a young man, whose praises she sounded in her letters. Soon after her wedding, she sent money to bring over another brother, and her husband added a few lines, in which he spoke of "his great love for his new relations," and how he "looked forward with impatience to having one of them, his dear brother-in-law, come to live with him."

This was good and cheering news, and it all came within a year's time, but the mother's heart grieved over it more than it rejoiced. Her delight at her daughter's marriage with a good man she loved was anything but unmixed. Melancholy thoughts blended with it, whether she would or not. The occasion was one which a mother's fancy had painted in rainbow colors, on the preparations for which it had dwelt with untold pleasure—and now she had had no share in it at all, and her heart writhed under the disappointment. To make her still sadder, she was obliged to part with two more children. She tried to prevent their going, but they had long ago set their hearts on following their brother and sister to America, and the recent letters had made them more anxious to be off.

So they started, and there remained only the youngest daughter, Rivkeh, a girl of thirteen. Their position was materially not a bad one, for every now and then the old woman received help from her children in America and from her son Yossef, so that she was not even obliged to keep up the shop, but the mother in her was not satisfied, because she wanted to see her children's happiness with her own eyes. The good news that continued to arrive at intervals brought pain as well as pleasure, by reminding her how much less fortunate she was than other mothers, who were counted worthy to live together with their children, and not at a distance from them like her.

The idea that she should go out to those of them who were in America, never occurred to her, or to them, either! But Yossef, who had taken a wife in his new town, and who, soon after, had set up for himself, and was doing very well, now sent for his mother and little sister to come and live with him. At first the mother was unwilling, fearing that she might be in the way of her daughter-in-law, and thus disturb the household peace; even later, when she had assured herself that the young wife was very kind, and there was nothing to be afraid of, she could not make up her mind to go, even though she longed to be with Yossef, her oldest son, who had always been her favorite, and however much she desired to see his wife and her little grandchildren.

Why she would not fulfil his wish and her own, she herself was not clearly conscious; but she shrank from the strange fashion of the life they led, and she never ceased to hope, deep down in her heart, that some day they would come back to her. And this especially with regard to Yossef, who sometimes complained in his letters that his situation was anything but secure, because the smallest circumstance might bring about an edict of expulsion. She quite understood that her son would consider this a very bad thing, but she herself looked at it with other eyes; round about *here,* too, were people who made a comfortable living, and Yossef was no worse than others, that he should not do the same.

Six or seven years passed in this way; the youngest daughter was twenty, and it was time to think of a match for her. Her mother felt sure that Yossef would provide the dowry, but she thought best Rivkeh and her brother should see each other, and she consented readily to let Rivkeh go to him, when Yossef invited her to spend several months as his guest. No sooner had she gone, than the mother realized what it meant, this parting with her youngest and, for the last years, her only child. She was filled with regret at not having gone with her, and waited impatiently for her return. Suddenly she heard that Rivkeh had found favor with a friend of Yossef's, the son of a well-to-do merchant, and that Rivkeh and her brother were equally pleased with him. The two were already engaged, and the wedding was only deferred till she, the mother, should come and take up her abode with them for good.

The longing to see her daughter overcame all her doubts. She resolved to go to her son, and began preparations for the start. These were just completed, when there came a letter from Yossef to say that the situation had taken a sudden turn for the worse, and he and his family might have to leave their town.

This sudden news was distressing and welcome at one and the same time. She was anxious lest the edict of expulsion should harm her son's position, and pleased, on the other hand, that he should at last be coming back, for God would not forsake him here, either; what with the fortune he had, and his aptitude for trade, he would make a living right enough. She waited anxiously, and in a few months had gone through all the mental suffering inherent in a state of uncertainty such as hers, when fear and hope are twined in one.

The waiting was the harder to bear that all this time no letter from Yossef or Rivkeh reached her promptly. And the end of it all was this: news came that the danger was over, and Yossef would remain where he was; but as far as she was concerned, it was best she should do likewise, because trailing about at her age was a serious thing, and it was not worth while her running into danger, and so on.

The old woman was full of grief at remaining thus forlorn in her old age, and she longed more than ever for her children after having hoped so surely that she would be with them soon. She could not understand Yossef's reason for suddenly changing his mind with regard to her coming; but it never occurred to her for one minute to doubt her children's affection. And we, when we had read the treasured bundle of letters from Yossef and Rivkeh, we could not doubt it, either. There was love and longing for the distant mother in every line, and several of the letters betrayed a spirit of bitterness, a note of complaining resentment against the hard times that had brought about the separation from her. And yet we could not help thinking, "Out of sight, out of mind," that which is far from the eyes, weighs lighter at the heart. It was the only explanation we could invent, for why, otherwise, should the mother have to remain alone among strangers?

All these considerations moved me to interfere in the matter without the old woman's knowledge. She could read Yiddish, but could not write it, and before we made friends, her letters to the children were written by a shopkeeper of her acquaintance. But from the time we got to know her, I became her constant secretary, and one day, when writing to Yossef for her, I made use of the opportunity to enclose a letter from myself. I asked his forgiveness for mixing myself up in another's family affairs, and tried to justify the interference by dwelling on our affectionate relations with his mother. I then described, in the most touching words at my command, how hard it was for her to live forlorn, how she pined for the presence of her children and grandchildren, and ended by telling them, that it was their duty to free their mother from all this mental suffering.

There was no direct reply to this letter of mine, but the next one from the son to his mother gave her to understand that there are certain things not to be explained, while the impossibility of explaining them may lead to a misunderstanding. This hint made the position no clearer to us, and the fact of Yossef's not answering me confirmed us in our previous suspicions.

Meanwhile our old friend fell ill, and quickly understood that she would soon die. Among the things she begged me to do after her death and having reference to her burial, there was one particular petition several times repeated: to send a packet of Hebrew books, which had been left by her husband, to her son Yossef, and to inform him of her death by telegram. "My American children"—she explained with a sigh—"have certainly forgotten everything they once learned, forgotten all their Jewishness! But my son Yossef is a different sort; I feel sure of him, that he will say Kaddish after me and read a chapter in the Mishnah, and the books will come in useful for his children— Grandmother's legacy to them."

When I fulfilled the old woman's last wish, I learned how mistaken she had been. The answer to my letter written during her lifetime came now that she was dead. Her children thanked us warmly for our care of her, and they also explained why she and they had remained apart.

She had never known—and it was far better so—by what means her son had obtained the right to live outside the Pale. It was enough that she should have to live *forlorn,* where would have been the good of her knowing that she was *forsaken* as well—that the one of her children who had gone altogether over to "them" was Yossef?

TASHRAK

Pen name of Israel Joseph Zevin; born, 1872, in Gori-Gorki, Government of Mohileff (Lithuania), White Russia; came to New York in 1889; first Yiddish sketch published in Jüdisches Tageblatt, 1893; first English story in The American Hebrew, 1906; associate editor of Jüdisches Tageblatt; writer of sketches, short stories, and biographies, in Hebrew, Yiddish, and English; contributor to Ha-Ibri, Jewish Comment, and numerous Yiddish periodicals; collected works, Geklibene Schriften, 1 vol., New York, 1910, and Tashrak's Beste Erzählungen, 4 vols., New York, 1910.

THE HOLE IN A BEIGEL

When I was a little Cheder-boy, my Rebbe, Bunem-Breine-Gite's, a learned man, who was always tormenting me with Talmudical questions and with riddles, once asked me, "What becomes of the hole in a Beigel, when one has eaten the Beigel?"

This riddle, which seemed to me then very hard to solve, stuck in my head, and I puzzled over it day and night. I often bought a Beigel, took a bite out of it, and immediately replaced the bitten-out piece with my hand, so that the hole should not escape. But when I had eaten up the Beigel, the hole had somehow always disappeared, which used to annoy me very much. I went about preoccupied, thought it over at prayers and at lessons, till the Rebbe noticed that something was wrong with me.

At home, too, they remarked that I had lost my appetite, that I ate nothing but Beigel—Beigel for breakfast, Beigel for dinner, Beigel for supper, Beigel all day long. They also observed that I ate it to the accompaniment of strange gestures and contortions of both my mouth and my hands.

One day I summoned all my courage, and asked the Rebbe, in the middle of a lesson on the Pentateuch:

"Rebbe, when one has eaten a Beigel, what becomes of the hole?"

"Why, you little silly," answered the Rebbe, "what is a hole in a Beigel? Just nothing at all! A bit of emptiness! It's nothing *with* the Beigel and nothing *without* the Beigel!"

Many years have passed since then, and I have not yet been able to satisfy myself as to what is the object of a hole in a Beigel. I have considered whether one could not have Beigels without holes. One lives and learns. And America has taught me this: One *can* have Beigels without holes, for I saw them in a dairy-shop in East Broadway. I at once recited the appropriate blessing, and then I asked the shopman about these Beigels, and heard a most interesting history, which shows how difficult it is to get people to accept anything new, and what sacrifices it costs to introduce the smallest reform.

This is the story:

A baker in an Illinois city took it into his head to make straight Beigels, in the shape of candles. But this reform cost him dear, because the united owners of the bakeries in that city immediately made a set at him and boycotted him.

They argued: "Our fathers' fathers baked Beigels with holes, the whole world eats Beigels with holes, and here comes a bold coxcomb of a fellow, upsets the order of the universe, and bakes Beigels *without* holes! Have you ever heard of such impertinence? It's just revolution! And if a person like this is allowed to go on, he will make an end of everything: to-day it's Beigels without holes, to-morrow it will be holes without Beigels! Such a thing has never been known before!"

And because of the hole in a Beigel, a storm broke out in that city that grew presently into a civil war. The "bosses" fought on, and dragged the bakers'-hands Union after them into the conflict. Now the Union contained two parties, of which one declared that a hole and a Beigel constituted together a private affair, like religion, and that everyone had a right to bake Beigels as he thought best, and according to his conscience. The other party maintained, that to sell Beigels without holes was against the constitution, to which the first party replied that the constitution should be altered, as being too ancient, and contrary to the spirit of the times. At this the second party raised a clamor, crying that the rules could not be altered, because they were Toras-Lokshen and every letter, every stroke, every dot was a law in itself! The city papers were obliged to publish daily accounts of the meetings that were held to discuss the hole in a Beigel, and the papers also took sides, and wrote fiery polemical articles on the subject. The quarrel spread through the city, until all the inhabitants were divided into two parties, the Beigel-with-a-hole party and the Beigel-without-a-hole party. Children rose against their parents, wives against their husbands, engaged couples severed their ties, families were broken up, and still the battle raged—and all on account of the hole in a Beigel!

AS THE YEARS ROLL ON

Rosalie laid down the cloth with which she had been dusting the furniture in her front parlor, and began tapping the velvet covering of the sofa with her fingers. The velvet had worn threadbare in places, and there was a great rent in the middle.

Had the rent been at one of the ends, it could have been covered with a cushion, but there it was, by bad luck, in the very centre, and making a shameless display of itself: Look, here I am! See what a rent!

Yesterday she and her husband had invited company. The company had brought children, and you never have children in the house without having them leave some mischief behind them.

To-day the sun was shining more brightly than ever, and lighting up the whole room. Rosalie took the opportunity to inspect her entire set of furniture. Eight years ago, when she was given the set at her marriage, how happy, she had been! Everything was so fresh and new.

She had noticed before that the velvet was getting worn, and the polish of the chairs disappearing, and the seats losing their spring, but to-day all this struck her more than formerly. The holes, the rents, the damaged places, stared before them with such malicious mockery—like a poor man laughing at his own evil plight.

Rosalie felt a painful melancholy steal over her. Now she could not but see that her furniture was old, that she would soon be ashamed to invite people into her parlor. And her husband will be in no hurry to present her with a new one—he has grown so parsimonious of late!

She replaced the holland coverings of the sofa and chairs, and went out to do her bedroom. There, on a chair, lay her best dress, the one she had put on yesterday for her guests.

She considered the dress: that, too, was frayed in places; here and there even drawn together and sewn over. The bodice was beyond ironing out again—and this was her best dress. She opened the wardrobe, for she wanted to make a general survey of her belongings. It was such a light day, one could see even in the back rooms. She took down one dress after another, and laid them out on the made beds, observing each with a critical eye. Her sense of depression increased the while, and she felt as though stone on stone were being piled upon her heart.

She began to put the clothes back into the wardrobe, and she hung up every one of them with a sigh. When she had finished with the bedroom, she went into the dining-room, and stood by the sideboard on which were set out her best china service and colored plates. She looked them over. One little gold-rimmed cup had lost its handle, a bowl had a piece glued in at the side. On the top shelf stood the statuette of a little god with a broken bow and arrow in his hand, and here there was one little goblet missing out of a whole service.

As soon as everything was in order, Rosalie washed her face and hands, combed up her hair, and began to look at herself in a little hand-glass, but the bath-room, to which she had retired, was dark, and she betook herself back into the front parlor, towel in hand, where she could see herself in the big looking-glass on the wall. Time, which had left traces on the furniture, on the contents of the wardrobe, and on the china, had not spared the woman, though she had been married only eight years. She looked at the crow's-feet by her eyes, and the lines in her forehead, which the worrying thoughts of this day had imprinted there even more sharply than usual. She tried to smile, but the smile in the glass looked no more attractive than if she had given her mouth a twist. She remembered that the only way to remain young is to keep free from care. But how is one to set about it? She threw on a scarlet Japanese kimono, and stuck an artificial flower into her hair, after which she lightly powdered her face and neck. The scarlet kimono lent a little color to her cheeks, and another critical glance at the mirror convinced her that she was still a comely woman, only no more a young one.

The bloom of youth had fled, never to return. Verfallen! And the desire to live was stronger than ever, even to live her life over again from the beginning, sorrows and all.

She began to reflect what she should cook for supper. There was time enough, but she must think of something new: her husband was tired of her usual dishes. He said her cooking was old-fashioned, that it was always the same thing, day in and day out. His taste was evidently getting worn-out, too.

And she wondered what she could prepare, so as to win back her husband's former good temper and affectionate appreciation.

At one time he was an ardent young man, with a fiery tongue. He had great ideals, and he strove high. He talked of making mankind happy, more refined, more noble and free. He had dreamt of a world without tears and troubles, of a time when men should live as brothers, and jealousy and hatred should be unknown. In those days he loved with all the warmth of his youth, and when he talked of love, it was a delight to listen. The world grew to have another face for her then, life, another significance, Paradise was situated on the earth.

Gradually his ideals lost their freshness, their shine wore off, and he became a business man, racking his brain with speculations, trying to grow rich without the necessary qualities and capabilities, and he was left at last with prematurely grey hair as the only result of his efforts.

Eight years after their marriage he was as worn as their furniture in the front parlor.

Rosalie looked out of the window. It was even much brighter outside than indoors. She saw people going up and down the street with different anxieties reflected in their faces, with wrinkles telling different histories of the cares of life. She saw old faces, and the young faces of those who seemed to have tasted of age ere they reached it. "Everything is old and worn and shabby," whispered a voice in her ear.

A burst of childish laughter broke upon her meditations. Round the corner came with a rush a lot of little boys with books under their arms, their faces full of the zest of life, and dancing and jumping till the whole street seemed to be jumping and dancing, too. Elder people turned smilingly aside to make way for them. Among the children Rosalie espied two little girls, also with books under their arms, her little girls! And the mother's heart suddenly brimmed with joy, a delicious warmth stole into her limbs and filled her being.

Rosalie went to the door to meet her two children on their return from school, and when she had given each little face a motherly kiss, she felt a breath of freshness and new life blowing round her.

She took off their cloaks, and listened to their childish prattle about their teachers and the day's lessons.

The clear voices rang through the rooms, awaking sympathetic echoes in every corner. The home wore a new aspect, and the sun shone even more brightly than before and in more friendly, kindly fashion.

The mother spread a little cloth at the edge of the table, gave them milk and sandwiches, and looked at them as they ate—each child the picture of the mother, her eyes, her hair, her nose, her look, her gestures— they ate just as she would do.

And Rosalie feels much better and happier. She doesn't care so much now about the furniture being old, the dresses worn, the china service not being whole, about the wrinkles round her eyes and in her forehead. She only minds about her husband's being so worn-out, so absent-minded that he cannot take pleasure in the children as she can.

DAVID PINSKI

Born, 1872, in Mohileff (Lithuania), White Russia; refused admission to Gymnasium in Moscow under percentage
restrictions; 1889-1891, secretary to Bene Zion in Vitebsk;
1891-1893, student in Vienna; 1893, co-editor of Spektor's
Hausfreund and Perez's Yom-tov Blättlech; 1893, first sketch
published in New York Arbeiterzeitung; 1896, studied philosophy in Berlin; 1899, came to New York, and edited Das
Abendblatt, a daily, and Der Arbeiter, a weekly; 1912,
founder and co-editor of Die Yiddishe Wochenschrift; author
of short stories, sketches, an essay on the Yiddish drama,
and ten dramas, among them Yesurun, Eisik Scheftel, Die
Mutter, Die Familie Zwie, Der Oitzer, Der eibiger Jüd
(first part of a series of Messiah dramas), Der stummer
Moschiach, etc.; one volume of collected dramas, Dramen,
Warsaw, 1909.

REB SHLOIMEH

The seventy-year-old Reb Shloimeh's son, whose home was in the country, sent his two boys to live with their grandfather and acquire town, that is, Gentile, learning.

"Times have changed," considered Reb Shloimeh; "it can't be helped!" and he engaged a good teacher for the children, after making inquiries here and there.

"Give me a teacher who can tell the whole of *their* Law, as the saying goes, standing on one leg!" he would say to his friends, with a smile.

At seventy-one years of age, Reb Shloimeh lived more indoors than out, and he used to listen to the teacher instructing his grandchildren.

"I shall become a doctor in my old age!" he would say, laughing.

The teacher was one day telling his pupils about mathematical geography. Reb Shloimeh sat with a smile on his lips, and laughing in his heart at the little teacher who told "such huge lies" with so much earnestness.

"The earth revolves," said the teacher to his pupils, and Reb Shloimeh smiles, and thinks, "He must have seen it!" But the teacher shows it to be so by the light of reason, and Reb Shloimeh becomes graver, and ceases smiling; he is endeavoring to grasp the proofs; he wants to ask questions, but can find none that will do, and he sits there as if he had lost his tongue.

The teacher has noticed his grave look, and understands that the old man is interested in the lesson, and he begins to tell of even greater wonders. He tells how far the sun is from the earth, how big it is, how many earths could be made out of it—and Reb Shloimeh begins to smile again, and at last can bear it no longer.

"Look here," he exclaimed, "that I cannot and will not listen to! You may tell me the earth revolves— well, be it so! Very well, I'll allow you, that, perhaps, according to reason—even—the size of the earth—the appearance of the earth—do you see?—all that sort of thing. But the sun! Who has measured the sun! Who, I ask you! Have *you* been on it? A pretty thing to say, upon my word!" Reb Shloimeh grew very excited. The teacher took hold of Reb Shloimeh's hand, and began to quiet him. He told him by what means the astronomers had discovered all this, that it was no matter of speculation; he explained the telescope to him, and talked of mathematical calculations, which he, Reb Shloimeh, was not able to understand. Reb Shloimeh had nothing to answer, but he frowned and remained obstinate. "Hê" (he said, and made a contemptuous motion with his hand), "it's nothing to me, not knowing that or being able to understand it! Science, indeed! Fiddlesticks!"

He relapsed into silence, and went on listening to the teacher's "stories." "We even know," the teacher continued, "what metals are to be found in the sun."

"And suppose I won't believe you?" and Reb Shloimeh smiled maliciously.

"I will explain directly," answered the teacher.

"And tell us there's a fair in the sky!" interrupted Reb Shloimeh, impatiently. He was very angry, but the teacher took no notice of his anger.

"Two hundred years ago," began the teacher, "there lived, in England, a celebrated naturalist and mathematician, Isaac Newton. It was told of him that when God said, Let there be light, Newton was born."

"Psh! I should think, very likely!" broke in Reb Shloimeh. "Why not?"

The teacher pursued his way, and gave an explanation of spectral analysis. He spoke at some length, and Reb Shloimeh sat and listened with close attention. "Now do you understand?" asked the teacher, coming to an end.

Reb Shloimeh made no reply, he only looked up from under his brows.

The teacher went on:

"The earth," he said, "has stood for many years. Their exact number is not known, but calculation brings it to several million—"

"Ê," burst in the old man, "I should like to know what next! I thought everyone knew *that*—that even *they*—"

"Wait a bit, Reb Shloimeh," interrupted the teacher, "I will explain directly."

"Ma! It makes me sick to hear you," was the irate reply, and Reb Shloimeh got up and left the room.

All that day Reb Shloimeh was in a bad temper, and went about with knitted brows. He was angry with science, with the teacher, with himself, because he must needs have listened to it all.

"Chatter and foolishness! And there I sit and listen to it!" he said to himself with chagrin. But he remembered the "chatter," something begins to weigh on his heart and brain, he would like to find a something to catch hold of, a proof of the vanity and emptiness of their teaching, to invent some hard question, and stick out a long red tongue at them all—those nowadays barbarians, those nowadays Newtons.

"After all, it's mere child's play," he reflects. "It's ridiculous to take their nonsense to heart."

"Only their proofs, their proofs!" and the feeling of helplessness comes over him once more.

"Ma!" He pulls himself together. "Is it all over with us? Is it all up?! All up?! The earth revolves! Gammon! As to their explanations—very wonderful, to be sure! O, of course, it's all of the greatest importance! Dear me, yes!"

He is very angry, tears the buttons off his coat, puts his hat straight on his head, and spits.

"Apostates, nothing but apostates nowadays," he concludes. Then he remembers the teacher—with what enthusiasm he spoke!

His explanations ring in Reb Shloimeh's head, and prove things, and once more the old gentleman is perplexed.

Preoccupied, cross, with groans and sighs, he went to bed. But he was restless all night, turning from one side to the other, and groaning. His old wife tried to cheer him.

"Such weather as it is to-day," she said, and coughed. "I have a pain in the side, too."

Next morning when the teacher came, Reb Shloimeh inquired with a displeased expression:

"Well, are you going to tell stories again to-day?"

"We shall not take geography to-day," answered the teacher.

"Have your 'astronomers' found out by calculation on which days we may learn geography?" asked Reb Shloimeh, with malicious irony.

"No, that's a discovery of mine!" and the teacher smiled.

"And when have 'your' astronomers decreed the study of geography?" persisted Reb Shloimeh.

"To-morrow."

"To-morrow!" he repeated crossly, and left the room, missing a lesson for the first time.

Next day the teacher explained the eclipses of the sun and moon to his pupils. Reb Shloimeh sat with his chair drawn up to the table, and listened without a movement.

"It is all so exact," the teacher wound up his explanation, "that the astronomers are able to calculate to a minute *when* there will be an eclipse, and have never yet made a mistake."

At these last words Reb Shloimeh nodded in a knowing way, and looked at the pupils as much as to say, "You ask *me* about that!"

The teacher went on to tell of comets, planets, and other suns. Reb Shloimeh snorted, and was continually interrupting the teacher with exclamations. "If you don't believe me, go and measure for yourself!"—"If it is not so, call me a liar!"—"Just so!"—"Within one yard of it!"

Reb Shloimeh repaid his Jewish education with interest. There were not many learned men in the town like Reb Shloimeh. The Rabbis without flattery called him "a full basket," and Reb Shloimeh could not picture to himself the existence of sciences other than "Jewish," and when at last he did picture it, he would not allow that they were right, unfalsified and right. He was so far intelligent, he had received a so far enlightened education, that he could understand how among non-Jews also there are great men. He would even have laughed at anyone who had maintained the contrary. But that among non-Jews there should be men as great as any Jewish ones, that he did *not* believe!—let alone, of course, still greater ones.

And now, little by little, Reb Shloimeh began to believe that "their" learning was not altogether insignificant, for he, "the full basket," was not finding it any too easy to master. And what he had to deal with were not empty speculations, unfounded opinions. No, here were mathematical computations, demonstrations which almost anyone can test for himself, which impress themselves on the mind! And Reb Shloimeh is vexed in his soul. He endeavored to cling to his old thoughts, his old conceptions. He so wished to cry out upon the clear reasoning, the simple explanations, with the phrases that are on the lips of every ignorant obstructionist. And yet he felt that he was unjust, and he gave up disputing with the teacher, as he paid close attention to the latter's demonstrations. And the teacher would say quite simply:

"One *can* measure," he would say, "why not? Only it takes a lot of learning."

When the teacher was at the door, Reb Shloimeh stayed him with a question.

"Then," he asked angrily, "the whole of 'your' learning is nothing but astronomy and geography?"

"Oh, no!" said the teacher, "there's a lot besides—a lot!"

"For instance?"

"Do you want me to tell you standing on one leg?"

"Well, yes, 'on one leg,'" he answered impatiently, as though in anger.

"But one can't tell you 'on one leg,'" said the teacher. "If you like, I shall come on Sabbath, and we can have a chat."

"Sabbath?" repeated Reb Shloimeh in a dissatisfied tone.

"Sabbath, because I can't come at any other time," said the teacher.

"Then let it be Sabbath," said Reb Shloimeh, reflectively.

"But soon after dinner," he called after the teacher, who was already outside the door. "And everything else is as right as your astronomy?" he shouted, when the teacher had already gone a little way.

"You will see!" and the teacher smiled.

Never in his whole life had Reb Shloimeh waited for a Sabbath as he waited for this one, and the two days that came before it seemed very long to him; he never relaxed his frown, or showed a cheerful face the whole time. And he was often seen, during those two days, to lift his hands to his forehead. He went about as though there lay upon him a heavy weight, which he wanted to throw off; or as if he had a very disagreeable bit of business before him, and wished he could get it over.

On Sabbath he could hardly wait for the teacher's appearance. "You wanted a lot of asking," he said to him reproachfully.

The old lady went to take her nap, the grandchildren to their play, and Reb Shloimeh took the snuff-box between his fingers, leant against the back of the "grandfather's chair" in which he was sitting, and listened with close attention to the teacher's words.

The teacher talked a long time, mentioned the names of sciences, and explained their meaning, and Reb Shloimeh repeated each explanation in brief. "Physics, then, is the science of—" "That means, then, that we have here—that physiology explains—"

The teacher would help him, and then immediately begin to talk of another branch of science. By the time the old lady woke up, the teacher had given examples of anatomy, physiology, physics, chemistry, zoology, and sociology.

It was quite late; people were coming back from the Afternoon Service, and those who do not smoke on Sabbath, raised their eyes to the sky. But Reb Shloimeh had forgotten in what sort of world he was living. He sat with wrinkled forehead and drawn brows, listening attentively, seeing nothing before him but the teacher's face, only catching up his every word.

"You are still talking?" asked the old lady, in astonishment, rubbing her eyes.

Reb Shloimeh turned his head toward his wife with a dazed look, as though wondering what she meant by her question.

"Oho!" said the old lady, "you only laugh at us women!"

Reb Shloimeh drew his brows closer together, wrinkled his forehead still more, and once more fastened his eyes on the teacher's lips.

"It will soon be time to light the fire," muttered the old lady.

The teacher glanced at the clock. "It's late," he said.

"I should think it was!" broke in the old lady. "Why I was allowed to sleep so long, I'm sure I don't know! People get to talking and even forget about tea."

Reb Shloimeh gave a look out of the window.

"O wa!" he exclaimed, somewhat vexed, "they are already coming out of Shool, the service is over! What a thing it is to sit talking! O wa!"

He sprang from his seat, gave the pane a rub with his hand, and began to recite the Afternoon Prayer. The teacher put on his things, but "Wait!" Reb Shloimeh signed to him with his hand.

Reb Shloimeh finished reciting "Incense."

"When shall you teach the children all that?" he asked then, looking into the prayer-book with a scowl.

"Not for a long time, not so quickly," answered the teacher. "The children cannot understand everything."

"I should think not, anything so wonderful!" replied Reb Shloimeh, ironically, gazing at the prayer-book and beginning "Happy are we." He swallowed the prayers as he said them, half of every word; no matter how he wrinkled his forehead, he could not expel the stranger thoughts from his brain, and fix his attention on the prayers. After the service he tried taking up a book,

but it was no good, his head was a jumble of all the
new sciences. By means of the little he had just learned,
he wanted to understand and know everything, to fashion a whole body out of a single hair, and he thought,
and thought, and thought. . . .

Sunday, when the teacher came, Reb Shloimeh told
him that he wished to have a little talk with him. Meantime he sat down to listen. The hour during which the
teacher taught the children was too long for him, and he
scarcely took his eyes off the clock.

"Do you want another pupil?" he asked the teacher,
stepping with him into his own room. He felt as though
he were getting red, and he made a very angry face.

"Why not?" answered the teacher, looking hard into
Reb Shloimeh's face. Reb Shloimeh looked at the floor,
his brows, as was usual with him in those days, drawn
together.

"You understand me—a pupil—" he stammered, "you
understand—not a little boy—a pupil—an elderly man
—you understand—quite another sort—"

"Well, well, we shall see!" answered the teacher,
smiling.

"I mean myself!" he snapped out with great displeasure, as if he had been forced to confess some very
evil deed. "Well, I have sinned—what do you want of
me?"

"Oh, but I should be delighted!" and the teacher
smiled.

"I always said I meant to be a doctor!" said Reb
Shloimeh, trying to joke. But his features contracted
again directly, and he began to talk about the terms,

and it was arranged that every day for an hour and a half the teacher should read to him and explain the sciences. To begin with, Reb Shloimeh chose physiology, sociology, and mathematical geography.

Days, weeks, and months have gone by, and Reb Shloimeh has become depressed, very depressed. He does not sleep at night, he has lost his appetite, doesn't care to talk to people.

Bad, bitter thoughts oppress him.

For seventy years he had not only known nothing, but, on the contrary, he had known everything wrong, understood head downwards. And it seemed to him that if he had known in his youth what he knew now, he would have lived differently, that his years would have been useful to others.

He could find no stain on his life—it was one long record of deeds of charity; but they appeared to him now so insignificant, so useless, and some of them even mischievous. Looking round him, he saw no traces of them left. The rich man of whom he used to beg donations is no poorer for them, and the pauper for whom he begged them is the same pauper as before. It is true, he had always thought of the paupers as sacks full of holes, and had only stuffed things into them because he had a soft heart, and could not bear to see a look of disappointment, or a tear rolling down the pale cheek of a hungry pauper. His own little world, as he had found it and as it was now, seemed to him much worse than before, in spite of all the good things he had done in it.

Not one good rich man! Not one genuine pauper! They are all just as hungry and their palms itch—there is no easing them. Times get harder, the world gets poorer. Now he understands the reason of it all, now it all lies before him as clear as on a map—he would be able to make every one understand. Only now—now it was getting late—he has no strength left. His spent life grieves him. If he had not been so active, such a "father of the community," it would not have grieved him so much. But he *had* had a great influence in the town, and this influence had been badly, blindly used! And Reb Shloimeh grew sadder day by day.

He began to feel a pain at his heart, a stitch in the side, a burning in his brain, and he was wrapt in his thoughts. Reb Shloimeh was philosophizing.

To be of use to somebody, he reflected, means to leave an impress of good in their life. One ought to help once for all, so that the other need never come for help again. That can be accomplished by wakening and developing a man's intelligence, so that he may always know for himself wherein his help lies.

And in such work he would have spent his life. If he had only understood long ago, ah, how useful he would have been! And a shudder runs through him.

Tears of vexation come more than once into his eyes.

It was no secret in the town that old Reb Shloimeh spent two to three hours daily sitting with the teacher, only what they did together, that nobody knew. They tried to worm something out of the maid, but what was to be got out of a "glomp with two eyes," whose

one reply was, "I don't know." They scolded her for
it. "How can you not know, glomp?" they exclaimed.
"Aren't you sometimes in the room with them?"

"Look here, good people, what's the use of coming to
me?" the maid would cry. "How can I know, sitting
in the kitchen, what they are about? When I bring in
the tea, I see them talking, and I go!"

"Dull beast!" they would reply. Then they left her,
and betook themselves to the grandchildren, who knew
nothing, either.

"They have tea," was their answer to the question,
"What does grandfather do with the teacher?"

"But what do they talk about, sillies?"

"We haven't heard!" the children answered gravely.

They tried the old lady.

"Is it my business?" she answered.

They tried to go in to Reb Shloimeh's house, on the
pretext of some business or other, but that didn't succeed, either. At last, a few near and dear friends asked
Reb Shloimeh himself.

"How people do gossip!" he answered.

"Well, what is it?"

"We just sit and talk!"

There it remained. The matter was discussed all
over the town. Of course, nobody was satisfied. But
he pacified them little by little.

The apostate teacher must turn hot and cold with
him!

They imagined that they were occupied with research,
and that Reb Shloimeh was opening the teacher's eyes
for him—and they were pacified. When Reb Shloimeh

suddenly fell on melancholy, it never came into anyone's head that there might be a connection between this and the conversations. The old lady settled that it was a question of the stomach, which had always troubled him, and that perhaps he had taken a chill. At his age such things were frequent. "But how is one to know, when he won't speak?" she lamented, and wondered which would be best, cod-liver oil or dried raspberries.

Every one else said that he was already in fear of death, and they pitied him greatly. "That is a sickness which no doctor can cure," people said, and shook their heads with sorrowful compassion. They talked to him by the hour, and tried to prevent him from being alone with his thoughts, but it was all no good; he only grew more depressed, and would often not speak at all.

"Such a man, too, what a pity!" they said, and sighed. "He's pining away—given up to the contemplation of death."

"And if you come to think, why should he fear death?" they wondered. "If *he* fears it, what about us? Och! och! och! Have we so much to show in the next world?" And Reb Shloimeh had a lot to show. Jews would have been glad of a tenth part of his world-to-come, and Christians declared that he was a true Christian, with his love for his fellow-men, and promised him a place in Paradise. "Reb Shloimeh is goodness itself," the town was wont to say. His one lifelong occupation had been the affairs of the community. "They are my life and my delight," he would repeat to his intimate friends, "as indispensable to me as water to a fish." He was a member of all the charitable societies. The Talmud Torah was established under his own roof, and pretty nearly maintained at his expense. The town called him the "father of the community," and all unfortunate, poor, and bitter hearts blessed him unceasingly.

Reb Shloimeh was the one person in the town almost without an enemy, perhaps the one in the whole province. Rich men grumbled at him. He was always after their money—always squeezing them for charities. They called him the old fool, the old donkey, but without meaning what they said. They used to laugh at him, to make jokes upon him, of course among themselves; but they had no enmity against him. They all, with a full heart, wished him joy of his tranquil life.

Reb Shloimeh was born, and had spent years, in wealth. After making an excellent marriage, he set up a business. His wife was the leading spirit within doors, the head of the household, and his whole life had been apparently a success.

When he had married his last child, and found himself a grandfather, he retired from business, and lived his last years on the interest of his fortune.

Free from the hate and jealousy of neighbors, pleasant and satisfactory in every respect, such was Reb Shloimeh's life, and for all that he suddenly became melancholy! It can be nothing but the fear of death!

But very soon Reb Shloimeh, as it were with a wave of the hand, dismissed the past altogether.

He said to himself with a groan that what had been was over and done; he would never grow young again, and once more a shudder went through him at the thought, and there came again the pain in his side and caught his breath, but Reb Shloimeh took no notice, and went on thinking. "Something must be done!" he said to himself, in the tone of one who has suddenly lost his whole fortune—the fortune he has spent his life in getting together, and there is nothing for him but to start work again with his five fingers.

And Reb Shloimeh started. He began with the Talmud Torah, where he had already long provided for the children's bodily needs—food and clothing.

Now he would supply them with spiritual things—instruction and education.

He dismissed the old teachers, and engaged young ones in their stead, even for Jewish subjects. Out of the Talmud Torah he wanted to make a little university. He already fancied it a success. He closed his eyes, laid his forehead on his hands, and a sweet, happy smile parted his lips. He pictured to himself the useful people who would go forth out of the Talmud Torah. Now he can die happy, he thinks. But no, he does not want to die! He wants to live! To live and to work, work, work! He will not and cannot see an end to his life! Reb Shloimeh feels more and more cheerful, lively, and fresh—to work——to work—till—

The whole town was in commotion.

There was a perfect din in the Shools, in the streets, in the houses. Hypocrites and crooked men, who had never before been seen or heard of, led the dance.

"To make Gentiles out of the children, forsooth! To turn the Talmud Torah into a school! That we won't allow! No matter if we have to turn the world upside down, no matter what happens!"

Reb Shloimeh heard the cries, and made as though he heard nothing. He thought it would end there, that no one would venture to oppose him further.

"What do you say to that?" he asked the teachers. "Fanaticism has broken out already!"

"It will give trouble," replied the teachers.

"Eh, nonsense!" said Reb Shloimeh, with conviction. But on Sabbath, at the Reading of the Law, he saw that he had been mistaken. The opposition had collected, and they got onto the platform, and all began speaking at once. It was impossible to make out what they were saying, beyond a word here and there, or the fragment of a sentence: "—none of it!" "we won't allow—!" "—made into Gentiles!"

Reb Shloimeh sat in his place by the east wall, his hands on the desk where lay his Pentateuch. He had taken off his spectacles, and glanced at the platform, put them on again, and was once more reading the Pentateuch. They saw this from the platform, and began to shout louder than ever. Reb Shloimeh stood up, took off his prayer-scarf, and was moving toward the door, when he heard some one call out, with a bang of his fist on the platform:

"With the consent of the Rabbis and the heads of the community, and in the name of the Holy Torah, it is resolved to take the children away from the Talmud Torah, seeing that in place of the Torah there is uncleanness——"

Reb Shloimeh grew pale, and felt a rent in his heart.
He stared at the platform with round eyes and open
mouth.

"The children are to be made into Gentiles," shouted
the person on the platform meantime, "and we have
plenty of Gentiles, thank God, already! Thus may they
perish, with their name and their remembrance! We
are not short of Gentiles—there are more every day!
And hatred increases, and God knows what the Jews
are coming to! Whoso has God in his heart, and is
jealous for the honor of the Law, let him see to it
that the children cease going to the place of peril!"

Reb Shloimeh wanted to call out, "Silence, you scoun-
drel!" The words all but rolled off his tongue, but
he contained himself, and moved on.

"The one who obeys will be blessed," proclaimed the
individual on the platform, "and whoso despises the
decree, his end shall be Gehenna, with that of Jeroboam,
the son of Nebat, who sinned and made Israel to sin!"

With these last words the speaker threw a fiery glance
at Reb Shloimeh.

A quiver ran through the Shool, and all eyes were
turned on Reb Shloimeh, expecting him to begin abusing
the speaker. A lively scene was anticipated. But Reb
Shloimeh smiled.

He quietly handed his prayer-scarf to the beadle,
wished the bystanders "good Sabbath," and walked out
of Shool, leaving them all disconcerted.

That Sabbath Reb Shloimeh was the quietest man in
the whole town. He was convinced that the interdict

would have no effect on anyone. "People are not so foolish as all that," he thought, "and they wouldn't treat *him* in that way!" He sat and laid plans for carrying on the education in the Talmud Torah, and he felt so light of heart that he sang to himself for very pleasure.

The old wife, meanwhile, was muttering and moaning. She had all her life been quite content with her husband and everything he did, and had always done her best to help him, hoping that in the world to come she would certainly share his portion of immortality. And now she saw with horror that he was like to throw away his future. But how ever could it be? she wondered, and was bathed in tears: "What has come over you? What has happened to make you like that? They are not just to you, are they, when they say that about taking children and making Gentiles of them?" Reb Shloimeh smiled. "Do you think," he said to her, "that I have gone mad in my old age? Don't be afraid. I'm in my right mind, and you shall not lose your place in Paradise."

But the wife was not satisfied with the reply, and continued to mutter and to weep. There were goings-on in the town, too. The place was aboil with excitement. Of course they talked about Reb Shloimeh; nobody could make out what had come to him all of a sudden.

"That is the teacher's work!" explained one of a knot of talkers.

"And we thought Reb Shloimeh such a sage, such a clever man, so book-learned. How can the teacher (may his name perish!) have talked him over?"

"It's a pity on the children's account!" one would exclaim here and there. "In the Talmud Torah, under his direction, they wanted for nothing, and what's to become of them now! They'll be running wild in the streets!"

"What then? Do you mean it would be better to make Gentiles of them?"

"Well, there! Of course, I understand!" he would hasten to say, penitently. And a resolution was passed, to the effect that the children should not be allowed to attend the Talmud Torah.

Reb Shloimeh stood at his window, and watched the excited groups in the street, saw how the men threw themselves about, rocked themselves, bit their beards, described half-circles with their thumbs, and he smiled.

In the evening the teachers came and told him what had been said in the town, and how all held that the children were not to be allowed to go to the Talmud Torah. Reb Shloimeh was a little disturbed, but he composed himself again and thought:

"Eh, they will quiet down, never mind! They won't do it to *me!*——"

Entering the Talmud Torah on Sunday, he was greeted by four empty walls. Even two orphans, who had no relations or protector in the town, had not come. They had been frightened and talked at and not allowed to attend, and free meals had been secured for all of them, so that they should not starve.

For the moment Reb Shloimeh lost his head. He glanced at the teachers as though ashamed in their presence, and his glance said, "What is to be done now?"

Suddenly he pulled himself together.

"No!" he exclaimed, "they shall not get the better of me," and he ran out of the Talmud Torah, and was gone.

He ran from house to house, to the parents and relations of the children. But they all looked askance at him, and he accomplished nothing: they all kept to it—"No!"

"Come, don't be silly! Send, send the children to the Talmud Torah," he begged. "You will see, you will not regret it!"

And he drew a picture for them of the sort of people the children would become.

But it was no use.

"*We* haven't got to manage the world," they answered him. "We have lived without all that, and our children will live as we are living now. We have no call to make Gentiles of them!"

"We know, we know! People needn't come to us with stories," they would say in another house. "We don't intend to sell our souls!" was the cry in a third.

"And who says I have sold mine?" Reb Shloimeh would ask sharply.

"How should we know? Besides, who was talking of you?" they answered with a sweet smile.

Reb Shloimeh reached home tired and depressed. The old wife had a shock on seeing him.

"Dear Lord!" she exclaimed, wringing her hands. "What is the matter with you? What makes you look like that?"

The teachers, who were there waiting for him, asked no questions: they had only to look at his ghastly appearance to know what had happened.

Reb Shloimeh sank into his arm-chair.

"Nothing," he said, looking sideways, but meaning it for the teachers.

"Nothing is nothing!" and they betook themselves to consoling him. "We will find something else to do, get hold of some other children, or else wait a little—they'll ask to be taken back presently."

Reb Shloimeh did not hear them. He had let his head sink on to his breast, turned his look sideways, and thoughts he could not piece together, fragments of thoughts, went round and round in the drooping head.

"Why? Why?" He asked himself over and over. "To do such a thing to *me!* Well, there you are! There you have it!—You've lived your life—like a man!—"

His heart felt heavy and hurt him, and his brain grew warm, warm. In one minute there ran through his head the impression which his so nearly finished life had made on him of late, and immediately after it all the plans he had thought out for setting to right his whole past life by means of the little bit left him. And now it was all over and done! "Why? Why?" he asked himself without ceasing, and could not understand it.

He felt his old heart bursting with love to all men. It beat more and more strongly, and would not cease from loving; and he would fain have seen everyone so happy, so happy! He would have worked with his last bit of strength, he would have drawn his last breath

for the cause to which he had devoted himself. He is
no longer conscious of the whereabouts of his limbs,
he feels his head growing heavier, his feet cold, and it
is dark before his eyes.

When he came to himself again, he was in bed; on
his head was a bandage with ice; the old wife was
lamenting; the teachers stood not far from the bed,
and talked among themselves. He wanted to lift his
hand and draw it across his forehead, but somehow he
does not feel his hand at all. He looks at it—it lies
stretched out beside him. And Reb Shloimeh understood what had happened to him.

"A stroke!" he thought, "I am finished, done for!"

He tried to give a whistle and make a gesture with
his hand: "Verfallen!" but the lips would not meet
properly, and the hand never moved.

"There you are, done for!" the lips whispered. He
glanced round, and fixed his eyes on the teachers, and
then on his wife, wishing to read in their faces whether
there was danger, whether he was dying, or whether
there was still hope. He looked, and could not make out
anything. Then, whispering, he called one of the
teachers, whose looks had met his, to his side.

The teacher came running.

"Done for, eh?" asked Reb Shloimeh.

"No, Reb Shloimeh, the doctors give hope," the
teacher replied, so earnestly that Reb Shloimeh's spirits
revived.

"Nu, nu," said Reb Shloimeh, as though he meant,
"So may it be! Out of your mouth into God's ears!"

The other teachers all came nearer.

"Good?" whispered Reb Shloimeh, "good, ha? There's a hero for you!" he smiled.

"Never mind," they said cheeringly, "you will get well again, and work, and do many things yet!"

"Well, well, please God!" he answered, and looked away.

And Reb Shloimeh really got better every day. The having lived wisely and the will to live longer saved him.

The first time that he was able to move a hand or lift a foot, a broad, sweet smile spread itself over his face, and a fire kindled in his all but extinguished eyes.

"Good luck to you!" he cried out to those around. He was very cheerful in himself, and began to think once more about doing something or other. "People must be taught, they must be taught, even if the world turn upside down." he thought, and rubbed his hands together with impatience.

"If it's not to be in the Talmud Torah, it must be somewhere else!" And he set to work thinking where it should be. He recalled all the neighbors to his memory, and suddenly grew cheerful.

Not far away there lived a bookbinder, who employed as many as ten workmen. They work sometimes from fifteen to sixteen hours, and have no strength left for study. One must teach *them,* he thinks. The master is not likely to object. Reb Shloimeh was the making of him, he it was who protected him, introduced him into all the best families, and finally set him on his feet.

Reb Shloimeh grows more and more lively, and is continually trying to rise from his couch.

Once out of bed, he could hardly endure to stay in the room, and how happy he felt, when, leaning on a stick, he stept out into the street! He hurried in the direction of the bookbinder's.

He was convinced that people's feelings toward him had changed for the better, that they would rejoice on seeing him.

How he looked forward to seeing a friendly smile on every face! He would have counted himself the happiest of men, if he had been able to hope that now everything was different, and would come right.

But he did not see the smile.

The town looked upon the apoplectic stroke as God's punishment—it was obvious. "Aha!" they had cried on hearing of it, and everyone saw in it another proof, and it also was "obvious"—of the fact that there is a God in the world, and that people cannot do just what they like. The great fanatics overflowed with eloquence, and saw in it an act of Heavenly vengeance. "Serves him right! Serves him right!" they thought. "Whose fault is it?" people replied, when some one reminded them that it was very sad—such a man as he had been, "Who told him to do it? He has himself to thank for his misfortunes."

The town had never ceased talking of him the whole time. Every one was interested in knowing how he was, and what was the matter with him. And when they heard that he was better, that he was getting well, they really were pleased; they were sure that he would give up all his foolish plans, and understand that God had punished him, and that he would be again as before.

But it soon became known that he clung to his wickedness, and people ceased to rejoice.

The Rabbi and his fanatical friends came to see him one day by way of visiting the sick. Reb Shloimeh felt inclined to ask them if they had come to stare at him as one visited by a miracle, but he refrained, and surveyed them with indifference.

"Well, how are you, Reb Shloimeh?" they asked.

"Gentiles!" answered Reb Shloimeh, almost in spite of himself, and smiled.

The Rabbi and the others became confused.

They sat a little while, couldn't think of anything to say, and got up from their seats. Then they stood a bit, wished him a speedy return to health, and went away, without hearing any answer from Reb Shloimeh to their "good night."

It was not long before the whole town knew of the visit, and it began to boil like a kettle.

To commit such sin is to play with destiny. Once you are in, there is no getting out! Give the devil a hair, and he'll snatch at the whole beard.

So when Reb Shloimeh showed himself in the street, they stared at him and shook their heads, as though to say, "Such a man—and gone to ruin!"

Reb Shloimeh saw it, and it cut him to the heart. Indeed, it brought the tears to his eyes, and he began to walk quicker in the direction of the bookbinder's.

At the bookbinder's they received him in friendly fashion, with a hearty "Welcome!" but he fancied that here also they looked at him askance, and therefore he gave a reason for his coming.

"Walking is hard work," he said, "one must have stopping-places."

With this same excuse he went there every day. He would sit for an hour or two, talking, telling stories, and at last he began to tell the "stories" which the teacher had told.

He sat in the centre of the room, and talked away merrily, with a pun here and a laugh there, and interested the workmen deeply. Sometimes they would all of one accord stop working, open their mouths, fix their eyes, and hang on his lips with an intelligent smile.

Or else they stood for a few minutes tense, motionless as statues, till Reb Shloimeh finished, before the master should interpose.

"Work, work—you will hear it all in time!" he would say, in a cross, dissatisfied tone.

And the workmen would unwillingly bend their backs once more over their task, but Reb Shloimeh remained a little thrown out. He lost the thread of what he was telling, began buttoning and unbuttoning his coat, and glanced guiltily at the binder.

But he went his own way nevertheless.

As to his hearers, he was overjoyed with them. When he saw that the workmen began to take interest in every book that was brought them to be bound, he smiled happily, and his eyes sparkled with delight.

And if it happened to be a book treating of the subjects on which they had heard something from Reb

Shloimeh, they threw themselves upon it, nearly tore it to pieces, and all but came to blows as to who should have the binding of it.

Reb Shloimeh began to feel that he was doing something, that he was being really useful, and he was supremely happy.

The town, of course, was aware of Reb Shloimeh's constant visits to the bookbinder's, and quickly found out what he did there.

"He's just off his head!" they laughed, and shrugged their shoulders. They even laughed in Reb Shloimeh's face, but he took no notice of it.

His pleasure, however, came to a speedy end. One day the binder spoke out.

"Reb Shloimeh," he said shortly, "you prevent us from working with your stories. What do you mean by it? You come and interfere with the work."

"But do I disturb?" he asked. "They go on working all the time——"

"And a pretty way of working," answered the bookbinder. "The boys are ready enough at finding an excuse for idling as it is! And why do you choose me? There are plenty of other workshops——"

It was an honest "neck and crop" business, and there was nothing left for Reb Shloimeh but to take up his stick and go.

"Nothing—again!" he whispered.

There was a sting in his heart, a beating in his temples, and his head burned.

"Nothing—again! This time it's all over. I must die—die—a story *with* an end."

Had he been young, he would have known what to do. He would never have begun to think about death, but now—where was the use of living on? What was there to wait for? All over!—all over!—

It was as much as he could do to get home. He sat down in the arm-chair, laid his head back, and thought.

He pictured to himself the last weeks at the book-binder's and the change that had taken place in the workmen; how they had appeared better-mannered, more human, more intelligent. It seemed to him that he had implanted in them the love of knowledge and the inclination to study, had put them in the way of viewing more rightly what went on around them. He had been of some account with them—and all of a sudden—!

"No!" he said to himself. "They will come to me—they must come!" he thought, and fixed his eyes on the door.

He even forgot that they worked till nine o'clock at night, and the whole evening he never took his eyes off the door.

The time flew, it grew later and later, and the book-binders did not come.

At last he could bear it no longer, and went out into the street; perhaps he would see them, and then he would call them in.

It was dark in the street; the gas lamps, few and far between, scarcely gave any light. A chilly autumn night; the air was saturated with moisture, and there was dreadful mud under foot. There were very few passers-by, and Reb Shloimeh remained standing at his door.

When he heard a sound of footsteps or voices, his heart began to beat quicker. His old wife came out three times to call him into the house again, but he did not hear her, and remained standing outside.

The street grew still. There was nothing more to be heard but the rattles of the night-watchmen. Reb Shloimeh gave a last look into the darkness, as though trying to see someone, and then, with a groan, he went indoors.

Next morning he felt very weak, and stayed in bed. He began to feel that his end was near, that he was but a guest tarrying for a day.

"It's all the same, all the same!" he said to himself, thinking quietly about death.

All sorts of ideas went through his head. He thought as it were unconsciously, without giving himself a clear account of what he was thinking of.

A variety of images passed through his mind, scenes out of his long life, certain people, faces he had seen here and there, comrades of his childhood, but they all had no interest for him. He kept his eyes fixed on the door of his room, waiting for death, as though it would come in by the door.

He lay like that the whole day. His wife came in continually, and asked him questions, and he was silent, not taking his eyes off the door, or interrupting the train of his thoughts. It seemed as if he had ceased either to see or to hear. In the evening the teachers began coming.

"Finished!" said Reb Shloimeh, looking at the door. Suddenly he heard a voice he knew, and raised his head.

"We have come to visit the sick," said the voice.

The door opened, and there came in four workmen at once.

At first Reb Shloimeh could not believe his eyes, but soon a smile appeared upon his lips, and he tried to sit up.

"Come, come!" he said joyfully, and his heart beat rapidly with pleasure.

The workmen remained standing some way from the bed, not venturing to approach the sick man, but Reb Shloimeh called them to him.

"Nearer, nearer, children!" he said.

They came a little nearer.

"Come here, to me!" and he pointed to the bed.

They came up to the bed.

"Well, what are you all about?" he asked with a smile.

The workmen were silent.

"Why did you not come last night?" he asked, and looked at them smiling.

The workmen were silent, and shuffled with their feet.

"How are you, Reb Shloimeh?" asked one of them.

"Very well, very well," answered Reb Shloimeh, still smiling. "Thank you, children! Thank you!"

"Sit down, children, sit down." he said after a pause. "I will tell you some more stories."

"It will tire you, Reb Shloimeh," said a workman. "When you are better——"

"Sit down, sit down!" said Reb Shloimeh, impatiently. "That's *my* business!"

The workmen exchanged glances with the teachers and the teachers signed to them *not* to sit down.

"Not to-day, Reb Shloimeh, another time, when you—"

"Sit down, sit down!" interrupted Reb Shloimeh, "Do me the pleasure!"

Once more the workmen exchanged looks with the teachers, and, at a sign from them, they sat down.

Reb Shloimeh began telling them the long story of the human race, he spoke with ardor, and it was long since his voice had sounded as it sounded then.

He spoke for a long, long time.

They interrupted him two or three times, and reminded him that it was bad for him to talk so much. But he only signified with a gesture that they were to let him alone.

"I am getting better," he said, and went on.

At length the workmen rose from their seats.

"Let us go, Reb Shloimeh. It's getting late for us," they begged.

"True, true," he replied, "but to-morrow, do you hear? Look here, children, to-morrow!" he said, giving them his hand.

The workmen promised to come. They moved away a few steps, and then Reb Shloimeh called them back.

"And the others?" he inquired feebly, as though he were ashamed of asking.

"They were lazy, they wouldn't come," was the reply.

"Well, well," he said, in a tone that meant "Well, well, I know, you needn't say any more, but look here, to-morrow!"

"Now I am well again," he whispered as the workmen went out. He could scarcely move a limb, but he was very cheerful, looked at every one with a happy smile, and his eyes shone.

"Now I am well," he whispered when they had been obliged to put him into bed and cover him up. "Now I am well," he repeated, feeling the while that his head was strangely heavy, his heart faint, and that he was very poorly. Before many minutes he had fallen into a state of unconsciousness.

A dreadful, heartbreaking cry recalled him to himself. He opened his eyes. The room was full of people. In many eyes were tears.

"Soon, then," he thought, and began to remember something.

"What o'clock is it?" he asked of the person who stood beside him.

"Five."

"They stop work at nine," he whispered to himself, and called one of the teachers to him.

"When the workmen come, they are to let them in, do you hear!" he said. The teacher promised.

"They will come at nine," added Reb Shloimeh.

In a little while he asked to write his will. After writing the will, he undressed and closed his eyes.

They thought he had fallen asleep, but Reb Shloimeh was not asleep. He lay and thought, not about his past life, but about the future, the future in which men would live. He thought of what man would come to be. He pictured to himself a bright, glad world, in which all men would be equal in happiness, knowledge, and education, and his dying heart beat a little quicker, while his face expressed joy and contentment. He opened his eyes, and saw beside him a couple of teachers.

"And will it really be?" he asked and smiled.

"Yes, Reb Shloimeh," they answered, without knowing to what his question referred, for his face told them it was something good. The smile accentuated itself on his lips.

Once again he lost himself in thought.

He wanted to imagine that happy world, and see with his mind's eye nothing but happy people, educated people, and he succeeded.

The picture was not very distinct. He was imagining a great heap of happiness—happiness with a body and soul, and he felt *himself* so happy.

A sound of lamentation disturbed him.

"Why do they weep?" he wondered. "Every one will have a good time—everyone!"

He opened his eyes; there were already lights burning. The room was packed with people. Beside him stood all his children, come together to take leave of their father.

He fixed his gaze on the little grandchildren, a gaze of love and gladness.

"*They* will see the happy time," he thought.

He was just going to ask the people to stop lamenting, but at that moment his eye caught the workmen of the evening before.

"Come here, come here, children!" and he raised his voice a little, and made a sign with his head. People did not know what he meant. He begged them to send the workmen to him, and it was done.

He tried to sit up; those around helped him.

"Thank you—chilldren—for coming—thank you!" he said. "Stop—weeping!" he implored of the bystanders. "I want to die quietly—I want every one to—to—be as happy—as I am! Live, all of you, in the—hope of a—good time—as I die—in—that hope. Dear chil—dren—" and he turned to the workmen, "I told you—last night—how man has lived so far. How he lives now, you know for yourselves—but the coming time will be a very happy one: all will be happy—all! Only work honestly, and learn! Learn, children! Everything will be all right! All will be hap——"

A sweet smile appeared on his lips, and Reb Shloimeh died.

In the town they—but what else *could* they say in the town of a man who had died without repeating the Confession, without a tremor at his heart, without any sign of repentance? What else *could* they say of a man who spent his last minutes in telling people to learn, to educate themselves? What else *could* they say of a man who left his whole capital to be devoted to educational purposes and schools?

What was to be expected of them, when his own family declared in court that their father was not responsible when he made his last will?

Forgive them, Reb Shloimeh, for they mean well—they know not what they say and do.

S. LIBIN

Pen name of Israel Hurewitz; born, 1872, in Gori-Gorki,
Government of Mohileff (Lithuania), White Russia; assistant to a druggist at thirteen; went to London at twenty, and,
after seven months there, to New York (1893); worked as
capmaker; first sketch, "A Sifz vun a Arbeiterbrust";
contributor to Die Arbeiterzeitung, Das Abendblatt, Die
Zukunft, Vorwärts, etc.; prolific Yiddish playwright and
writer of sketches on New York Jewish life; dramas to the
number of twenty-six produced on the stage; collected works,
Geklibene Skizzen, 1 vol., New York, 1902, and 2 vols., New
York, 1907.

A PICNIC

Ask Shmuel, the capmaker, just for a joke, if he would like to come for a picnic! He'll fly out at you as if you had invited him to a swing on the gallows. The fact is, he and his Sarah once *went* for a picnic, and the poor man will remember it all his days.

It was on a Sabbath towards the end of August. Shmuel came home from work, and said to his wife:

"Sarah, dear!"

"Well, husband?" was her reply.

"I want to have a treat," said Shmuel, as though alarmed at the boldness of the idea.

"What sort of a treat? Shall you go to the swimming-bath to-morrow?"

"Ett! What's the fun of that?"

"Then, what have you thought of by way of an exception? A glass of ice water for supper?"

"Not that, either."

"A whole siphon?"

Shmuel denied with a shake of the head.

"Whatever can it be!" wondered Sarah. "Are you going to fetch a pint of beer?"

"What should I want with beer?"

"Are you going to sleep on the roof?"

"Wrong again!"

"To buy some more carbolic acid, and drive out the bugs?"

"Not a bad idea," observed Shmuel, "but that is not it, either."

"Well, then, whatever is it, for goodness' sake! The moon?" asked Sarah, beginning to lose patience. "What have you been and thought of? Tell me once for all, and have done with it!"

And Shmuel said:

"Sarah, you know, we belong to a lodge."

"Of course I do!" and Sarah gave him a look of mingled astonishment and alarm. "It's not more than a week since you took a whole dollar there, and I'm not likely to have forgotten what it cost you to make it up. What is the matter now? Do they want another?"

"Try again!"

"Out with it!"

"I—want us, Sarah," stammered Shmuel,—"to go for a picnic."

"A picnic!" screamed Sarah. "Is that the only thing you have left to wish for?"

"Look here, Sarah, we toil and moil the whole year through. It's nothing but trouble and worry, trouble and worry. Call that living! When do we ever have a bit of pleasure?"

"Well, what's to be done?" said his wife, in a subdued tone.

"The summer will soon be over, and we haven't set eyes on a green blade of grass. We sit day and night sweating in the dark."

"True enough!" sighed his wife, and Shmuel spoke louder:

"Let us have an outing, Sarah. Let us enjoy ourselves for once, and give the children a breath of fresh air, let us have a change, if it's only for five minutes!"

"What will it cost?" asks Sarah, suddenly, and Shmuel has soon made the necessary calculation.

"A family ticket is only thirty cents, for Yossele, Rivele, Hannahle, and Berele; for Resele and Doletzke I haven't to pay any carfare at all. For you and me, it will be ten cents there and ten back—that makes fifty cents. Then I reckon thirty cents for refreshments to take with us: a pineapple (a damaged one isn't more than five cents), a few bananas, a piece of watermelon, a bottle of milk for the children, and a few rolls—the whole thing shouldn't cost us more than eighty cents at the outside."

"Eighty cents!" and Sarah clapped her hands together in dismay. "Why, you can live on that two days, and it takes nearly a whole day's earning. You can buy an old ice-box for eighty cents, you can buy a pair of trousers—eighty cents!"

"Leave off talking nonsense!" said Shmuel, disconcerted. "Eighty cents won't make us rich. We shall get on just the same whether we have them or not. We must live like human beings one day in the year! Come, Sarah, let us go! We shall see lots of other people, and we'll watch them, and see how *they* enjoy themselves. It will do you good to see the world, to go where there's a bit of life! Listen, Sarah, what have you been to worth seeing since we came to America? Have you seen Brooklyn Bridge, or Central Park, or the Baron Hirsch baths?"

"You know I haven't!" Sarah broke in. "I've no time to go about sight-seeing. I only know the way from here to the market."

"And what do you suppose?" cried Shmuel. "I should be as great a greenhorn as you, if I hadn't been obliged to look everywhere for work. Now I know that America is a great big place. Thanks to the slack times, I know where there's an Eighth Street, and a One Hundred and Thirtieth Street with tin works, and an Eighty-Fourth Street with a match factory. I know every single lane round the World Building. I know where the cable car line stops. But you, Sarah, know nothing at all, no more than if you had just landed. Let us go, Sarah, I am sure you won't regret it!"

"Well, you know best!" said his wife, and this time she smiled. "Let us go!"

And thus it was that Shmuel and his wife decided to join the lodge picnic on the following day.

Next morning they all rose much earlier than usual on a Sunday, and there was a great noise, for they took the children and scrubbed them without mercy. Sarah prepared a bath for Doletzke, and Doletzke screamed the house down. Shmuel started washing Yossele's feet, but as Yossele habitually went barefoot, he failed to bring about any visible improvement, and had to leave the little pair of feet to soak in a basin of warm water, and Yossele cried, too. It was twelve o'clock before the children were dressed and ready to start, and then Sarah turned her attention to her husband, arranged his trousers, took the spots out of his coat with kerosene, sewed a button onto his vest. After that she dressed herself, in her old-fashioned satin wedding dress. At two o'clock they set forth, and took their places in the car.

"Haven't we forgotten anything?" asked Sarah of her husband.

Shmuel counted his children and the traps. "No, nothing, Sarah!" he said.

Doletzke went to sleep, the other children sat quietly in their places. Sarah, too, fell into a doze, for she was tired out with the preparations for the excursion.

All went smoothly till they got some way up town, when Sarah gave a start.

"I don't feel very well—my head is so dizzy," she said to Shmuel.

"I don't feel very well, either," answered Shmuel. "I suppose the fresh air has upset us."

"I suppose it has," said his wife. "I'm afraid for the children."

Scarcely had she spoken when Doletzke woke up, whimpering, and was sick. Yossele, who was looking at her, began to cry likewise. The mother scolded him, and this set the other children crying. The conductor cast a wrathful glance at poor Shmuel, who was so frightened that he dropped the hand-bag with the provisions, and then, conscious of the havoc he had certainly brought about inside the bag by so doing, he lost his head altogether, and sat there in a daze. Sarah was hushing the children, but the look in her eyes told Shmuel plainly enough what to expect once they had left the car. And no sooner had they all reached the ground in safety than Sarah shot out:

"So, nothing would content him but a picnic? Much good may it do him! You're a workman, and workmen have no call to go gadding about!"

Shmuel was already weary of the whole thing, and said nothing, but he felt a tightening of the heart.

He took up Yossele on one arm and Resele on the other, and carried the bag with the presumably smashed-up contents besides.

"Hush, my dears! Hush, my babies!" he said. "Wait a little and mother will give you some bread and sugar. Hush, be quiet!" He went on, but still the children cried.

Sarah carried Doletzke, and rocked her as she walked, while Berele and Hannahle trotted alongside.

"He has shortened my days," said Sarah, "may his be shortened likewise."

Soon afterwards they turned into the park.

"Let us find a tree and sit down in the shade," said Shmuel. "Come, Sarah!"

"I haven't the strength to drag myself a step further," declared Sarah, and she sank down like a stone just inside the gate. Shmuel was about to speak, but a glance at Sarah's face told him she was worn out, and he sat down beside his wife without a word. Sarah gave Doletzke the breast. The other children began to roll about in the grass, laughed and played, and Shmuel breathed easier.

Girls in holiday attire walked about the park, and there were groups under the trees. Here was a handsome girl surrounded by admiring boys, and there a handsome young man encircled by a bevy of girls.

Out of the leafy distance of the park came the melancholy song of a workman; near by stood a man playing on a fiddle. Sarah looked about her and listened, and by degrees her vexation vanished. It is true that her heart was still sore, but it was not with the soreness of anger. She was taking her life to pieces and thinking it over, and it seemed a very hard and bitter one, and when she looked at her husband and thought of his life, she was near crying, and she laid her hands upon his knee.

Shmuel also sat lost in thought. He was thinking about the trees and the roses and the grass, and listening to the fiddle. And he also was sad at heart.

"O Sarah!" he sighed, and he would have said more, but just at that moment it began to spot with rain, and before they had time to move there came a downpour. People started to scurry in all directions, but Shmuel stood like a statue.

"Shlimm-mazel, look after the children!" commanded Sarah. Shmuel caught up two of them, Sarah another two or three, and they ran to a shelter. Doletzke began to cry afresh.

"Mame, hungry!" began Berele.

"Hungry, hungry!" wailed Yossele. "I want to eat!"

Shmuel hastily opened the hand-bag, and then for the first time he saw what had really happened: the bottle had broken, and the milk was flooding the bag; the rolls and bananas were soaked, and the pineapple (a damaged one to begin with) looked too nasty for words. Sarah caught sight of the bag, and was so angry, she was at a loss how to wreak vengeance on her husband. She was ashamed to scream and scold in the presence of other people, but she went up to him, and whispered fervently into his ear, "The same to you, my good man!"

The children continued to clamor for food.

"I'll go to the refreshment counter and buy a glass of milk and a few rolls," said Shmuel to his wife.

"Have you actually some money left?" asked Sarah. "I thought it had all been spent on the picnic."

"There are just five cents over."

"Well, then go and be quick about it. The poor things are starving."

Shmuel went to the refreshment stall, and asked the price of a glass of milk and a few rolls.

"Twenty cents, mister," answered the waiter.

Shmuel started as if he had burnt his finger, and returned to his wife more crestfallen than ever.

"Well, Shlimm-mazel, where's the milk?" inquired Sarah.

"He asked twenty cents."

"Twenty cents for a glass of milk and a roll? Are you Montefiore?" Sarah could no longer contain herself. "They'll be the ruin of us! If you want to go for another picnic, we shall have to sell the bedding."

The children never stopped begging for something to eat.

"But what are we to do?" asked the bewildered Shmuel.

"Do?" screamed Sarah. "Go home, this very minute!"

Shmuel promptly caught up a few children, and they left the park. Sarah was quite quiet on the way home, merely remarking to her husband that she would settle her account with him later.

"I'll pay you out," she said, "for my satin dress, for the hand-bag, for the pineapple, for the bananas, for the milk, for the whole blessed picnic, for the whole of my miserable existence."

"Scold away!" answered Shmuel. "It is you who were right. I don't know what possessed me. A picnic, indeed! You may well ask what next? A poor wretched workman like me has no business to think of anything beyond the shop."

Sarah, when they reached home, was as good as her word. Shmuel would have liked some supper, as he always liked it, even in slack times, but there was no supper given him. He went to bed a hungry man, and all through the night he repeated in his sleep:

"A picnic, oi, a picnic!"

MANASSEH

It was a stifling summer evening. I had just come home from work, taken off my coat, unbuttoned my waistcoat, and sat down panting by the window of my little room.

There was a knock at the door, and without waiting for my reply, in came a woman with yellow hair, and very untidy in her dress.

I judged from her appearance that she had not come from a distance. She had nothing on her head, her sleeves were tucked up, she held a ladle in her hand, and she was chewing something or other.

"I am Manasseh's wife," said she.

"Manasseh Gricklin's?" I asked.

"Yes," said my visitor, "Gricklin's, Gricklin's."

I hastily slipped on a coat, and begged her to be seated.

Manasseh was an old friend of mine, he was a capmaker, and we worked together in one shop.

And I knew that he lived somewhere in the same tenement as myself, but it was the first time I had the honor of seeing his wife.

"Look here," began the woman, "don't you work in the same shop as my husband?"

"Yes, yes," I said.

"Well, and now tell me," and the yellow-haired woman gave a bound like a hyena, "how is it I see you come home from work with all other respectable people, and my husband not? And it isn't the first time, either, that he's gone, goodness knows where, and come home two hours after everyone else. Where's he loitering about?"

"I don't know," I replied gravely.

The woman brandished her ladle in such a way that I began to think she meant murder.

"You don't know?" she exclaimed with a sinister flash in her eyes. "What do you mean by that? Don't you two leave the shop together? How can you help seeing what becomes of him?"

Then I remembered that when Manasseh and I left the shop, he walked with me a few blocks, and then went off in another direction, and that one day, when I asked him where he was going, he had replied, "To some friends."

"He must go to some friends," I said to the woman.

"To some friends?" she repeated, and burst into strange laughter. "Who? Whose? Ours? We're greeners, we are, we have no friends. What friends should he have, poor, miserable wretch?"

"I don't know," I said, "but that is what he told me."

"All right!" said Manasseh's wife. "I'll teach him a lesson he won't forget in a hurry."

With these words she departed.

When she had left the room, I pictured to myself poor consumptive Manasseh being taught a "lesson" by his yellow-haired wife, and I pitied him.

Manasseh was a man of about thirty. His yellowish-white face was set in a black beard; he was very thin, always ailing and coughing, had never learnt to write, and he read only Yiddish—a quiet, respectable man, I might almost say the only hand in the shop who never grudged a fellow-worker his livelihood. He had been only a year in the country, and the others made sport of him, but I always stood up for him, because I liked him very much.

Wherever does he go, now? I wondered to myself, and I resolved to find out.

Next morning I met Manasseh as usual, and at first I intended to tell him of his wife's visit to me the day before; but the poor operative looked so low-spirited, so thoroughly unhappy, that I felt sure his wife had already given him the promised "lesson," and I hadn't the courage to mention her to him just then.

In the evening, as we were going home from the workshop, Manasseh said to me:

"Did my wife come to see you yesterday?"

"Yes, Brother Manasseh," I answered. "She seemed something annoyed with you."

"She has a dreadful temper," observed the workman. "When she is really angry, she's fit to kill a man. But it's her bitter heart, poor thing—she's had so many troubles! We're so poor, and she's far away from her family."

Manasseh gave a deep sigh.

"She asked you where I go other days after work?" he continued.

"Yes."

"Would you like to know?"

"Why not, Mister Gricklin!"

"Come along a few blocks further," said Manasseh, "and I'll show you."

"Come along!" I agreed, and we walked on together.

A few more blocks and Manasseh led me into a narrow street, not yet entirely built in with houses.

Presently he stopped, with a contented smile. I looked round in some astonishment. We were standing alongside a piece of waste ground, with a meagre fencing of stones and burnt wire, and utilized as a garden.

"Just look," said the workman, pointing at the garden, "how delightful it is! One so seldom sees anything of the kind in New York."

Manasseh went nearer to the fence, and his eyes wandered thirstily over the green, flowering plants, just then in full beauty. I also looked at the garden. The things that grew there were unknown to me, and I was ignorant of their names. Only one thing had a familiar look—a few tall, graceful "moons" were scattered here and there over the place, and stood like absent-minded dreamers, or beautiful sentinels. And the roses were in bloom, and their fragrance came in wafts over the fencing.

"You see the 'moons'?" asked Manasseh, in rapt tones, but more to himself than to me. "Look how beautiful they are! I can't take my eyes off them. I am capable of standing and looking at them for hours. They make me feel happy, almost as if I were at home again. There were a lot of them at home!"

The operative sighed, lost himself a moment in thought, and then said:

"When I smell the roses, I think of old days. We had quite a large garden, and I was so fond of it!

When the flowers began to come out, I used to sit there for hours, and could never look at it enough. The roses appeared to be dreaming with their great golden eyes wide open. The cucumbers lay along the ground like pussy-cats, and the stalks and leaves spread ever so far across the beds. The beans fought for room like street urchins, and the pumpkins and the potatoes—you should have seen them! And the flowers were all colors—pink and blue and yellow, and 1 felt as if everything were alive, as if the whole garden were alive—I fancied I heard them talking together, the roses, the potatoes, the beans. I spent whole evenings in my garden. It was dear to me as my own soul. Look, look, look, don't the roses seem as if they were alive?"

But I looked at Manasseh, and thought the consumptive workman had grown younger and healthier. His face was less livid, and his eyes shone with happiness.

"Do you know," said Manasseh to me, as we walked away from the garden, "I had some cuttings of rose-trees at home, in a basket out on the fire-escape, and they had begun to bud."

There was a pause.

"Well," I inquired, "and what happened?"

"My wife laid out the mattress to air on the top of the basket, and they were all crushed."

Manasseh made on outward gesture with his hand, and I asked no more questions.

The poky, stuffy shop in which he worked came into my mind, and my heart was sore for him.

YOHRZEIT FOR MOTHER

The Ginzburgs' first child died of inflammation of the lungs when it was two years and three months old.

The young couple were in the depths of grief and despair—they even thought seriously of committing suicide.

But people do not do everything they think of doing. Neither Ginzburg nor his wife had the courage to throw themselves into the cold and grizzly arms of death. They only despaired, until, some time after, a new-born child bound them once more to life.

It was a little girl, and they named her Dvoreh, after Ginzburg's dead mother.

The Ginzburgs were both free-thinkers in the full sense of the word, and their naming the child after the dead had no superstitious significance whatever.

It came about quite simply.

"Dobinyu," Ginzburg had asked his wife, "how shall we call our daughter?"

"I don't know," replied the young mother.

"No more do I," said Ginzburg.

"Let us call her Dvorehle," suggested Dobe, automatically, gazing at her pretty baby, and very little concerned about its name.

Had Ginzburg any objection to make? None at all, and the child's name was Dvorehle henceforward. When the first child had lived to be a year old, the parents had made a feast-day, and invited guests to celebrate their first-born's first birthday with them.

With the second child it was not so.

The Ginzburgs loved their Dvorehle, loved her painfully, infinitely, but when it came to the anniversary of her birth they made no rejoicings.

I do not think I shall be going too far if I say they did not dare to do so.

Dvorehle was an uncommon child: a bright girlie, sweet-tempered, pretty, and clever, the light of the house, shining into its every corner. She could be a whole world of delight to her parents, this wee Dvorehle. But it was not the delight, not the happiness they had known with the first child, not the same. *That* had been so free, so careless. Now it was different: terrible pictures of death, of a child's death, would rise up in the midst of their joy, and their gladness suddenly ended in a heavy sigh. They would be at the height of enchantment, kissing and hugging the child and laughing aloud, they would be singing to it and romping with it, everything else would be forgotten. Then, without wishing to do so, they would suddenly remember that not so long ago it was another child, also a girl, that went off into just the same silvery little bursts of laughter—and now, where is it?—dead! O how it goes through the heart! The parents turn pale in the midst of their merrymaking, the mother's eyes fill with tears, and the father's head droops.

"Who knows?" sighs Dobe, looking at their little laughing Dvorehle. "Who knows?"

Ginzburg understands the meaning of her question and is silent, because he is afraid to say anything in reply.

It seems to me that parents who have buried their first-born can never be really happy again.

So Dvorehle's first birthday was allowed to pass as it were unnoticed. When it came to her second, it was nearly the same thing, only Dobe said, "Ginzburg, when our daughter is three years old, then we will have great rejoicings!"

They waited for the day with trembling hearts. Their child's third year was full of terror for them, because their eldest-born had died in her third year, and they felt as though it must be the most dangerous one for their second child.

A dreadful conviction began to haunt them both, only they were afraid to confess it one to the other. This conviction, this fixed idea of theirs, was that when Dvorehle reached the age of their eldest child when it died, Death would once more call their household to mind.

Dvorehle grew to be two years and eight months old. O it was a terrible time! And—and the child fell ill, with inflammation of the lungs, just like the other one.

O pictures that arose and stood before the parents! O terror, O calamity! They were free-thinkers, the Ginzburgs, and if any one had told them that they were not free from what they called superstition, that the belief in a Higher Power beyond our understanding still had a root in their being, if you had spoken thus to Ginzburg or to his wife, they would have laughed at you, both of them, out of the depths of a full heart and with laughter more serious than many another's words. But what happened now is wonderful to tell.

Dobe, sitting by the sick child's cot, began to speak, gravely, and as in a dream:

"Who knows? Who knows? Perhaps? Perhaps?" She did not conclude.

"Perhaps what?" asked Ginzburg, impatiently.

"Why should it come like this?" Dobe went on. "The same time, the same sickness?"

"A simple blind coincidence of circumstances," replied her husband.

"But so exactly—one like the other, as if somebody had made it happen on purpose."

Ginzburg understood his wife's meaning, and answered short and sharp:

"Dobe, don't talk nonsense."

Meanwhile Dvorehle's illness developed, and the day came on which the doctor said that a crisis would occur within twenty-four hours. What this meant to the Ginzburgs would be difficult to describe, but each of them determined privately not to survive the loss of their second child.

They sat beside it, not lifting their eyes from its face. They were pale and dazed with grief and sleepless nights, their hearts half-dead within them, they shed no tears, they were so much more dead than alive themselves, and the child's flame of life flickered and dwindled, flickered and dwindled.

A tangle of memories was stirring in Ginzburg's head, all relating to deaths and graves. He lived through the death of their first child with all details —his father's death, his mother's—early in a summer morning—that was—that was—he recalls it—as though it were to-day.

"What is to-day?" he wonders. "What day of the month is it?" And then he remembers, it is the first of May.

"The same day," he murmurs, as if he were talking in his sleep.

"What the same day?" asks Dobe.

"Nothing," says Ginzburg. "I was thinking of something."

He went on thinking, and fell into a doze where he sat.

He saw his mother enter the room with a soft step, take a chair, and sit down by the sick child.

"Mother, save it!" he begs her, his heart is full to bursting, and he begins to cry.

"Isrolik," says his mother, "I have brought a remedy for the child that bears my name."

"Mame! ! !"

He is about to throw himself upon her neck and kiss her, but she motions him lightly aside.

"Why do you never light a candle for my Yohrzeit?" she inquires, and looks at him reproachfully.

"Mame, have pity on us, save the child!"

"The child will live, only you must light me a candle."

"Mame" (he sobs louder), "have pity!"

"Light my candle—make haste, make haste—"

"Ginzburg!" a shriek from his wife, and he awoke with a start.

"Ginzburg, the child is dying! Fly for the doctor."

Ginzburg cast a look at the child, a chill went through him, he ran to the door.

The doctor came in person.

"Our child is dying! Help save it!" wailed the unhappy mother, and he, Ginzburg, stood and shivered as with cold.

The doctor scrutinized the child, and said:

"The crisis is coming on." There was something dreadful in the quiet of his tone.

"What can be done?" and the Ginzburgs wrung their hands.

"Hush! Nothing! Bring some hot water, bottles of hot water!—Champagne!—Where is the medicine? Quick!" commanded the doctor.

Everything was to hand and ready in an instant.

The doctor began to busy himself with the child, the parents stood by pale as death.

"Well," asked Dobe, "what?"

"We shall soon know," said the doctor.

Ginzburg looked round, glided like a shadow into a corner of the room, and lit the little lamp that stood there.

"What is that for?" asked Dobe, in a fright.

"Nothing, Yohrzeit—my mother's," he answered in a strange voice, and his hands never ceased trembling.

"Your child will live," said the doctor, and father and mother fell upon the child's bed with their faces, and wept.

The flame in the lamp burnt brighter and brighter.

SLACK TIMES THEY SLEEP

Despite the fact of the winter nights being long and dark as the Jewish exile, the Breklins go to bed at dusk.

But you may as well know that when it is dusk outside in the street, the Breklins are already "way on" in the night, because they live in a basement, separated from the rest of the world by an air-shaft, and when the sun gathers his beams round him before setting, the first to be summoned are those down the Breklins' shaft, because of the time required for them to struggle out again.

The same thing in the morning, only reversed. People don't usually get up, if they can help it, before it is really light, and so it comes to pass that when other people have left their beds, and are going about their business, the Breklins are still asleep and making the long, long night longer yet.

If you ask me, "How is it they don't wear their sides out with lying in bed?" I shall reply: They *do* rise with aching sides, and if you say, "How can people be so lazy?" I can tell you, They don't do it out of laziness, and they lie awake a great part of the time.

What's the good of lying in bed if one isn't asleep?

There you have it in a nutshell—it's a question of the economic conditions. The Breklins are very poor, their life is a never-ending struggle with poverty, and they have come to the conclusion that the cheapest way of waging it, and especially in winter, is to lie in bed under a great heap of old clothes and rags of every description.

Breklin is a house-painter, and from Christmas to Purim (I beg to distinguish!) work is dreadfully slack. When you're not earning a crooked penny, what are you to do?

In the first place, you must live on "cash," that is, on the few dollars scraped together and put by during the "season," and in the second place, you must cut down your domestic expenses, otherwise the money won't hold out, and then you might as well keep your teeth in a drawer.

But you may neither eat nor drink, nor live at all to mention—if it's winter, the money goes all the same: it's bitterly cold, and you can't do without the stove, and the nights are long, and you want a lamp.

And the Breklins saw that their money would *not* hold out till Purim—that their Fast of Esther would be too long. Coal was beyond them, and kerosene as dear as wine, and yet how could they possibly spend less? How could they do without a fire when it was so cold? Without a lamp when it was so dark? And the Breklins had an "idea"!

Why sit up at night and watch the stove and the lamp burning away their money, when they might get into bed, bury themselves in rags, and defy both poverty and cold? There is nothing in particular to do, anyhow. What should there be, a long winter evening through? Nothing! They only sat and poured out the bitterness in their heart one upon the other, quarrelled, and scolded. They could do that in bed just as well, and save firing and light into the bargain.

So, at the first approach of darkness, the bed was made ready for Mr. Breklin, and his wife put to sleep their only, three-year-old child. Avremele did not understand why he was put to bed so early, but he asked no questions. The room began to feel cold, and the poor little thing was glad to nestle deep into the bedcoverings.

The lamp and the fire were extinguished, the stove would soon go out of itself, and the Breklin family slept.

They slept, and fought against poverty by lying in bed.

It was waging cheap warfare.

Having had his first sleep out, Breklin turns to his wife:

"What do you suppose the time to be now, Yudith?"

Yudith listens attentively.

"It must be past eight o'clock," she says.

"What makes you think so?" asks Breklin.

"Don't you hear the clatter of knives and forks? Well-to-do folk are having supper."

"We also used to have supper about this time, in the Tsisin," said Breklin, and he gave a deep sigh of longing.

"We shall soon forget the good times altogether," says Yudith, and husband and wife set sail once more for the land of dreams.

A few hours later Breklin wakes with a groan.

"What is the matter?" inquires Yudith.

"My sides ache with lying."

"Mine, too," says Yudith, and they both begin yawning.

"What o'clock would it be now?" wonders Breklin, and Yudith listens again.

"About ten o'clock," she tells him.

"No later? I don't believe it. It must be a great deal later than that."

"Well, listen for yourself," persists Yudith, "and you'll hear the housekeeper upstairs scolding somebody. She's putting out the gas in the hall."

"Oi, weh is mir! How the night drags!" sighs Breklin, and turns over onto his other side.

Yudith goes on talking, but as much to herself as to him:

"Upstairs they are still all alive, and we are asleep in bed."

"Weh is mir, weh is mir!" sighs Breklin over and over, and once more there is silence.

The night wears on.

"Are you asleep?" asks Breklin, suddenly.

"I wish I were! Who could sleep through such a long night? I'm lying awake and racking my brains."

"What over?" asks Breklin, interested.

"I'm trying to think," explains Yudith, "what we can have for dinner to-morrow that will cost nothing, and yet be satisfying."

"Oi, weh is mir!" sighs Breklin again, and is at a loss what to advise.

"I wonder" (this time it is Yudith) "what o'clock it is now!"

"It will soon be morning," is Breklin's opinion.

"Morning? Nonsense!" Yudith knows better.

"It must be morning soon!" He holds to it.

"You are very anxious for the morning," says Yudith, good-naturedly, "and so you think it will soon be here, and I tell you, it's not midnight yet."

"What are you talking about? You don't know what you're saying! I shall go out of my mind."

"You know," says Yudith, "that Avremele always wakes at midnight and cries, and he's still fast asleep."

"No, Mame," comes from under Arvemele's heap of rags.

"Come to me, my beauty! So he was awake after all!" and Yudith reaches out her arms for the child.

"Perhaps he's cold," says Breklin.

"Are you cold, sonny?" asks Yudith.

"Cold, Mame!" replies Avremele.

Yudith wraps the coverlets closer and closer round him, and presses him to her side.

And the night wears on.

"O my sides!" groans Breklin.

"Mine, too!" moans Yudith, and they start another conversation.

One time they discuss their neighbors; another time the Breklins try to calculate how long it is since they married, how much they spend a week on an average, and what was the cost of Yudith's confinement.

It is seldom they calculate anything right, but talking helps to while away time, till the basement begins to lighten, whereupon the Breklins jump out of bed, as though it were some perilous hiding-place, and set to work in a great hurry to kindle the stove.

ABRAHAM RAISIN

Born, 1876, in Kaidanov, Government of Minsk (Lithuania), White Russia; traditional Jewish education; self-taught in Russian language; teacher at fifteen, first in Kaidanov, then in Minsk; first poem published in Perez's Jüdische Bibliothek, in 1891; served in the army, in Kovno, for four years; went to Warsaw in 1900, and to New York in 1911; Yiddish lyric poet and novelist; occasionally writes Hebrew; contributor to Spektor's Hausfreund, New York Abendpost, and New York Arbeiterzeitung; co-editor of Das zwanzigste Jahrhundert; in 1903, published and edited, in Cracow, Das jüdische Wort, first to urge the claim of Yiddish as the national Jewish language; publisher and editor, since 1911, of Dos neie Land, in New York; collected works (poems and tales), 4 vols., Warsaw, 1908-1912.

SHUT IN

Lebele is a little boy ten years old, with pale cheeks, liquid, dreamy eyes, and black hair that falls in twisted ringlets, but, of course, the ringlets are only seen when his hat falls off, for Lebele is a pious little boy, who never uncovers his head.

There are things that Lebele loves and never has, or else he has them only in part, and that is why his eyes are always dreamy and troubled, and always full of longing.

He loves the summer, and sits the whole day in Cheder. He loves the sun, and the Rebbe hangs his caftan across the window, and the Cheder is darkened, so that it oppresses the soul. Lebele loves the moon, the night, but at home they close the shutters, and Lebele, on his little bed, feels as if he were buried alive. And Lebele cannot understand people's behaving so oddly.

It seems to him that when the sun shines in at the window, it is a delight, it is so pleasant and cheerful, and the Rebbe goes and curtains it—no more sun! If Lebele dared, he would ask:

"What ails you, Rebbe, at the sun? What harm can it do you?"

But Lebele will never put that question: the Rebbe is such a great and learned man, he must know best. Ai, how dare he, Lebele, disapprove? He is only a little boy. When he is grown up, he will doubtless curtain the window himself. But as things are now,

Lebele is not happy, and feels sadly perplexed at the behavior of his elders.

Late in the evening, he comes home from Cheder. The sun has already set, the street is cheerful and merry, the cockchafers whizz and, flying, hit him on the nose, the ear, the forehead.

He would like to play about a bit in the street, let them have supper without him, but he is afraid of his father. His father is a kind man when he talks to strangers, he is so gentle, so considerate, so confidential. But to him, to Lebele, he is very unkind, always shouting at him, and if Lebele comes from Cheder a few minutes late, he will be angry.

"Where have you been, my fine fellow? Have you business anywhere?"

Now go and tell him that it is not at all so bad out in the street, that it's a pleasure to hear how the cockchafers whirr, that even the hits they give you on the wing are friendly, and mean, "Hallo, old fellow!" Of course it's a wild absurdity! It amuses him, because he is only a little boy, while his father is a great man, who trades in wood and corn, and who always knows the current prices—when a thing is dearer and when it is cheaper. His father can speak the Gentile language, and drive bargains, his father understands the Prussian weights. Is that a man to be thought lightly of? Go and tell him, if you dare, that it's delightful now out in the street.

And Lebele hurries straight home. When he has reached it, his father asks him how many chapters he has mastered, and if he answers five, his father hums

a tune without looking at him; but if he says only
three, his father is angry, and asks:

"How's that? Why so little, ha?"

And Lebele is silent, and feels guilty before his father.

After that his father makes him translate a Hebrew
word.

"Translate *Kimlùnah!*"

"*Kimlùnah* means 'like a passing the night,' " answers
Lebele, terrified.

His father is silent—a sign that he is satisfied—and
they sit down to supper. Lebele's father keeps an eye
on him the whole time, and instructs him how to eat.

"Is that how you hold your spoon?" inquires the
father, and Lebele holds the spoon lower, and the food
sticks in his throat.

After supper Lebele has to say grace aloud and in
correct Hebrew, according to custom. If he mumbles a
word, his father calls out:

"What did I hear? what? once more, 'Wherewith
Thou dost feed and sustain us.' Well, come, say it!
Don't be in a hurry, it won't burn you!"

And Lebele says it over again, although he *is* in a
great hurry, although he longs to run out into the street,
and the words *do* seem to burn him.

When it is dark, he repeats the Evening Prayer by
lamplight; his father is always catching him making
a mistake, and Lebele has to keep all his wits about
him. The moon, round and shining, is already floating
through the sky, and Lebele repeats the prayers, and
looks at her, and longs after the street, and he gets
confused in his praying.

Prayers over, he escapes out of the house, puzzling over some question in the Talmud against the morrow's lesson. He delays there a while gazing at the moon, as she pours her pale beams onto the Gass. But he soon hears his father's voice:

"Come indoors, to bed!"

It is warm outside, there is not a breath of air stirring, and yet it seems to Lebele as though a wind came along with his father's words, and he grows cold, and he goes in like one chilled to the bone, takes his stand by the window, and stares at the moon.

"It is time to close the shutters—there's nothing to sit up for!" Lebele hears his father say, and his heart sinks. His father goes out, and Lebele sees the shutters swing to, resist, as though they were being closed against their will, and presently there is a loud bang. No more moon!—his father has hidden it!

A while after, the lamp has been put out, the room is dark, and all are asleep but Lebele, whose bed is by the window. He cannot sleep, he wants to be in the street, whence sounds come in through the chinks. He tries to sit up in bed, to peer out, also through the chinks, and even to open a bit of the shutter, without making any noise, and to look, look, but without success, for just then his father wakes and calls out:

"What are you after there, eh? Do you want me to come with the strap?"

And Lebele nestles quietly down again into his pillow, pulls the coverlet over his head, and feels as though he were buried alive.

THE CHARITABLE LOAN

The largest fair in Klemenke is "Ulas." The little town waits for Ulas with a beating heart and extravagant hopes. "Ulas," say the Klemenke shopkeepers and traders, "is a Heavenly blessing; were it not for Ulas, Klemenke would long ago have been 'äus Klemenke,' America would have taken its last few remaining Jews to herself."

But for Ulas one must have the wherewithal—the shopkeepers need wares, and the traders, money.

Without the wherewithal, even Ulas is no good! And Chayyim, the dealer in produce, goes about gloomily. There are only three days left before Ulas, and he hasn't a penny wherewith to buy corn to trade with. And the other dealers in produce circulate in the market-place with caps awry, with thickly-rolled cigarettes in their mouths and walking-sticks in their hands, and they are talking hard about the fair.

"In three days it will be lively!" calls out one.

"Pshshsh," cries another in ecstasy, "in three days' time the place will be packed!"

And Chayyim turns pale. He would like to call down a calamity on the fair, he wishes it might rain, snow, or storm on that day, so that not even a mad dog should come to the market-place; only Chayyim knows that Ulas is no weakling, Ulas is not afraid of the strongest wind—Ulas is Ulas!

And Chayyim's eyes are ready to start out of his head. A charitable loan—where is one to get a charitable loan? If only five and twenty rubles!

He asks it of everyone, but they only answer with a merry laugh:

"Are you mad? Money—just before a fair?"

And it seems to Chayyim that he really will go mad.

"Suppose you went across to Loibe-Bäres?" suggests his wife, who takes her full share in his distress.

"I had thought of that myself," answers Chayyim, meditatively.

"But what?" asks the wife.

Chayyim is about to reply, "But I can't go there, I haven't the courage," only that it doesn's suit him to be so frank with his wife, and he answers:

"Devil take him! He won't lend anything!"

"Try! It won't hurt," she persists.

And Chayyim reflects that he has no other resource, that Loibe-Bäres is a rich man, and living in the same street, a neighbor in fact, and that *he* requires no money for the fair, being a dealer in lumber and timber.

"Give me out my Sabbath overcoat!" says Chayyim to his wife, in a resolute tone.

"Didn't I say so?" the wife answers. "It's the best thing you can do, to go to him."

Chayyim placed himself before a half-broken looking-glass which was nailed to the wall, smoothed his beard with both hands, tightened his earlocks, and then took off his hat, and gave it a polish with his sleeve.

"Just look and see if I haven't got any white on my coat off the wall!"

"If you haven't?" the wife answered, and began slapping him with both hands over the shoulders.

"I thought we once had a little clothes-brush. Where is it? ha?"

"Perhaps you dreamt it," replied his wife, still slapping him on the shoulders, and she went on, "Well, I should say you had got some white on your coat!"

"Come, that'll do!" said Chayyim, almost angrily. "I'll go now."

He drew on his Sabbath overcoat with a sigh, and muttering, "Very likely, isn't it, he'll lend me money!" he went out.

On the way to Loibe-Bäres, Chayyim's heart began to fail him. Since the day that Loibe-Bäres came to live at the end of the street, Chayyim had been in the house only twice, and the path Chayyim was treading now was as bad as an examination: the "approach" to him, the light rooms, the great mirrors, the soft chairs, Loibe-Bäres himself with his long, thick beard and his black eyes with their "gevirish" glance, the lady, the merry, happy children, even the maid, who had remained in his memory since those two visits—all these things together terrified him, and he asked himself, "Where are you going to? Are you mad? Home with you at once!" and every now and then he would stop short on the way. Only the thought that Ulas was near, and that he had no money to buy corn, drove him to continue.

"He won't lend anything—it's no use hoping." Chayyim was preparing himself as he walked for the shock of disappointment; but he felt that if he gave way to that extent, he would never be able to open his mouth to make his request known, and he tried to cheer himself:

"If I catch him in a good humor, he will lend! Why should he be afraid of lending me a few rubles over the fair? I shall tell him that as soon as ever I have sold the corn, he shall have the loan back. I will swear it by wife and children, he will believe me—and I will pay it back."

But this does not make Chayyim any the bolder, and he tries another sort of comfort, another remedy against nervousness.

"He isn't a bad man—and, after all, our acquaintance won't date from to-day—we've been living in the same street twenty years—Parabotzker Street—"

And Chayyim recollects that a fortnight ago, as Loibe-Bäres was passing his house on his way to the market-place, and he, Chayyim, was standing in the yard, he gave him the greeting due to a gentleman ("and I could swear I gave him my hand," Chayyim reminded himself). Loibe-Bäres had made a friendly reply, he had even stopped and asked, like an old acquaintance, "Well, Chayyim, and how are you getting on?" And Chayyim strains his memory and remembers further that he answered on this wise:

"I thank you for asking! Heaven forgive me, one does a little bit of business!"

And Chayyim is satisfied with his reply, "I answered him quite at my ease."

Chayyim resolves to speak to him this time even more leisurely and independently, not to cringe before him.

Chayyim could already see Loibe-Bäres' house in the distance. He coughed till his throat was clear, stroked his beard down, and looked at his coat.

"Still a very good coat!" he said aloud, as though trying to persuade himself that the coat was still good, so that he might feel more courage and more proper pride.

But when he got to Loibe-Bäres' big house, when the eight large windows looking onto the street flashed into his eyes, the windows being brightly illuminated from within, his heart gave a flutter.

"Oi, Lord of the World, help!" came of its own accord to his lips. Then he felt ashamed, and caught himself up, "Ett, nonsense!"

As he pushed the door open, the "prayer" escaped him once more, "Help, mighty God! or it will be the death of me!"

Loibe-Bäres was seated at a large table covered with a clean white table-cloth, and drinking while he talked cheerfully with his household.

"There's a Jew come, Tate!" called out a boy of twelve, on seeing Chayyim standing by the door.

"So there is!" called out a second little boy, still more merrily, fixing Chayyim with his large, black, mischievous eyes.

All the rest of those at table began looking at Chayyim, and he thought every moment that he must fall of a heap onto the floor.

"It will look very bad if I fall," he said to himself, made a step forward, and, without saying good evening, stammered out:

"I just happened to be passing, you understand, and I saw you sitting—so I knew you were at home—well, I thought one ought to call—neighbors—"

"Well, welcome, welcome!" said Loibe-Bäres, smiling. "You've come at the right moment. Sit down."

A stone rolled off Chayyim's heart at this reply, and, with a glance at the two little boys, he quietly took a seat.

"Leah, give Reb Chayyim a glass of tea," commanded Loibe-Bäres.

"Quite a kind man!" thought Chayyim. "May the Almighty come to his aid!"

He gave his host a grateful look, and would gladly have fallen onto the Gevir's thick neck, and kissed him.

"Well, and what are you about?" inquired his host.

"Thanks be to God, one lives!"

The maid handed him a glass of tea. He said, "Thank you," and then was sorry: it is not the proper thing to thank a servant. He grew red and bit his lips.

"Have some jelly with it!" Loibe-Bäres suggested.

"An excellent man, an excellent man!" thought Chayyim, astonished. "He is sure to lend."

"You deal in something?" asked Loibe-Bäres.

"Why, yes," answered Chayyim. "One's little bit of business, thank Heaven, is no worse than other people's!"

"What price are oats fetching now?" it occurred to the Gevir to ask.

Oats had fallen of late, but it seemed better to Chayyim to say that they had risen.

"They have risen very much!" he declared in a mercantile tone of voice.

"Well, and have you some oats ready?" inquired the Gevir further.

"I've got a nice lot of oats, and they didn't cost me much, either. I got them quite cheap," replied Chayyim, with more warmth, forgetting, while he spoke, that he hadn't had an ear of oats in his granary for weeks.

"And you are thinking of doing a little speculating?" asked Loibe-Bäres. "Are you not in need of any money?"

"Thanks be to God," replied Chayyim, proudly, "I have never yet been in need of money."

"Why did I say that?" he thought then, in terror at his own words. "How am I going to ask for a loan now?" and Chayyim wanted to back the cart a little, only Loibe-Bäres prevented him by saying:

"So I understand you make a good thing of it, you are quite a wealthy man."

"My wealth be to my enemies!" Chayyim wanted to draw back, but after a glance at Loibe-Bäres' shining face, at the blue jar with the jelly, he answered proudly:

"Thank Heaven, I have nothing to complain of!"

"There goes your charitable loan!" The thought came like a kick in the back of his head. "Why are you boasting like that? Tell him you want twenty-five rubles for Ulas—that he must save you, that you are in despair, that—"

But Chayyim fell deeper and deeper into a contented and happy way of talking, praised his business more and more, and conversed with the Gevir as with an equal.

But he soon began to feel he was one too many, that he should not have sat there so long, or have talked in that way. It would have been better to have talked about the fair, about a loan. Now it is too late:

"I have no need of money!" and Chayyim gave a despairing look at Loibe-Bäres' cheerful face, at the two little boys who sat opposite and watched him with sly, mischievous eyes, and who whispered knowingly to each other, and then smiled more knowingly still!

A cold perspiration covered him. He rose from his chair.

"You are going already?" observed Loibe-Bäres, politely.

"Now perhaps I could ask him!" It flashed across Chayyim's mind that he might yet save himself, but, stealing a glance at the two boys with the roguish eyes that watched him so slyly, he replied with dignity:

"I must! Business! There is no time!" and it seems to him, as he goes toward the door, that the two little boys with the mischievous eyes are putting out their tongues after him, and that Loibe-Bäres himself smiles and says, "Stick your tongues out further, further still!"

Chayyim's shoulders seem to burn, and he makes haste to get out of the house.

THE TWO BROTHERS

It is three months since Yainkele and Berele—two brothers, the first fourteen years old, the second sixteen— have been at the college that stands in the town of X—, five German miles from their birthplace Dalissovke, after which they are called the "Dalissovkers."

Yainkele is a slight, pale boy, with black eyes that peep slyly from beneath the two black eyebrows. Berele is taller and stouter than Yainkele, his eyes are lighter, and his glance is more defiant, as though he would say, "Let me alone, I shall laugh at you all yet!"

The two brothers lodged with a poor relation, a widow, a dealer in second-hand goods, who never came home till late at night. The two brothers had no bed, but a chest, which was broad enough, served instead, and the brothers slept sweetly on it, covered with their own torn clothes; and in their dreams they saw their native place, the little street, their home, their father with his long beard and dim eyes and bent back, and their mother with her long, pale, melancholy face, and they heard the little brothers and sisters quarrelling, as they fought over a bit of herring, and they dreamt other dreams of home, and early in the morning they were homesick, and then they used to run to the Dalissovke Inn, and ask the carrier if there were a letter for them from home.

The Dalissovke carriers were good Jews with soft hearts, and they were sorry for the two poor boys, who

were so anxious for news from home, whose eyes burned,
and whose hearts beat so fast, so loud, but the carriers
were very busy; they came charged with a thousand
messages from the Dalissovke shopkeepers and traders,
and they carried more letters than the post, but with
infinitely less method. Letters were lost, and parcels
were heard of no more, and the distracted carriers
scratched the nape of their neck, and replied to every
question:

"Directly, directly, I shall find it directly—no, I
don't seem to have anything for you—"

That is how they answered the grown people who
came to them; but our two little brothers stood and
looked at Lezer the carrier—a man in a wadded caftan,
summer and winter—with thirsty eyes and aching
hearts; stood and waited, hoping he would notice them
and say something, if only one word. But Lezer was
always busy: now he had gone into the yard to feed the
horse, now he had run into the inn, and entered into
a conversation with the clerk of a great store, who had
brought a list of goods wanted from a shop in Dalissovke.

And the brothers used to stand and stand, till the
elder one, Berele, lost patience. Biting his lips, and all
but crying with vexation, he would just articulate:

"Reb Lezer, is there a letter from father?"

But Reb Lezer would either suddenly cease to exist,
run out into the street with somebody or other, or be
absorbed in a conversation, and Berele hardly expected
the answer which Reb Lezer would give over his
shoulder:

"There isn't one—there isn't one."

"There isn't one!" Berele would say with a deep sigh, and sadly call to Yainkele to come away. Mournfully, and with a broken spirit, they went to where the day's meal awaited them.

"I am sure he loses the letters!" Yainkele would say a few minutes later, as they walked along.

"He is a bad man!" Berele would mutter with vexation.

But one day Lezer handed them a letter and a small parcel.

The letter ran thus:

"Dear Children,

Be good, boys, and learn with diligence. We send you herewith half a cheese and a quarter of a pound of sugar, and a little berry-juice in a bottle.

Eat it in health, and do not quarrel over it.

From me, your father,

CHAYYIM HECHT."

That day Lezer the carrier was the best man in the world in their eyes, they would not have been ashamed to eat him up with horse and cart for very love. They wrote an answer at once—for letter-paper they used to tear out, with fluttering hearts, the first, unprinted pages in the Gemoreh—and gave it that evening to Lezer the carrier. Lezer took it coldly, pushed it into the breast of his coat, and muttered something like "All right!"

"What did he say, Berele?" asked Yainkele, anxiously.

"I think he said 'all right,'" Berele answered doubtfully.

"I think he said so, too," Yainkele persuaded himself. Then he gave a sigh, and added fearfully:

"He may lose the letter!"

"Bite your tongue out!" answered Berele, angrily, and they went sadly away to supper.

And three times a week, early in the morning, when Lezer the carrier came driving, the two brothers flew, not ran, to the Dalissovke Inn, to ask for an answer to their letter; and Lezer the carrier grew more preoccupied and cross, and answered either with mumbled words, which the brothers could not understand, and dared not ask him to repeat, or else not at all, so that they went away with heavy hearts. But one day they heard Lezer the carrier speak distinctly, so that they understood quite well:

"What are you doing here, you two? What do you come plaguing me for? Letter? Fiddlesticks! How much do you pay me? Am I a postman? Eh? Be off with you, and don't worry."

The brothers obeyed, but only in part: their hearts were like lead, their thin little legs shook, and tears fell from their eyes onto the ground. And they went no more to Lezer the carrier to ask for a letter.

"I wish he were dead and buried!" they exclaimed, but they did not mean it, and they longed all the time just to go and look at Lezer the carrier, his horse and cart. After all, they came from Dalissovke, and the two brothers loved them.

One day, two or three weeks after the carrier sent them about their business in the way described, the two brothers were sitting in the house of the poor relation and talking about home. It was summer-time, and a Friday afternoon.

"I wonder what father is doing now," said Yainkele, staring at the small panes in the small window.

"He must be cutting his nails," answered Berele, with a melancholy smile.

"He must be chopping up lambs' feet," imagined Yainkele, "and Mother is combing Chainele, and Chainele is crying."

"Now we've talked nonsense enough!" decided Berele. "How can we know what is going on there?"

"Perhaps somebody's dead!" added Yainkele, in sudden terror.

"Stuff and nonsense!" said Berele. "When people die, they let one know—"

"Perhaps they wrote, and the carrier won't give us the letter—"

"Ai, that's chatter enough!" Berele was quite cross. "Shut up, donkey! You make me laugh," he went on, to reassure Yainkele, "they are all alive and well."

Yainkele became cheerful again, and all at once he gave a bound into the air, and exclaimed with eager eyes:

"Berele, do what I say! Let's write by the post!"

"Right you are!" agreed Berele. "Only I've no money."

"I have four kopeks; they are over from the ten I got last night. You know, at my 'Thursday' they give me ten kopeks for supper, and I have four over.

"And I have one kopek," said Berele, "just enough for a post-card."

"But which of us will write it?" asked Yainkele.

"I," answered Berele, "I am the eldest, I'm a first-born son."

"But I gave four kopeks!"

"A first-born is worth more than four kopeks."

"No! I'll write half, and you'll write half, ha?"

"Very well. Come and buy a card."

And the two brothers ran to buy a card at the post-office.

"There will be no room for anything!" complained Yainkele, on the way home, as he contemplated the small post-card. "We will make little tiny letters, teeny weeny ones!" advised Berele.

"Father won't be able to read them!"

"Never mind! He will put on his spectacles. Come along—quicker!" urged Yainkele. His heart was already full of words, like a sea, and he wanted to pour it out onto the bit of paper, the scrap on which he had spent his entire fortune.

They reached their lodging, and settled down to write. Berele began, and Yainkele stood and looked on.

"Begin higher up! There is room there for a whole line. Why did you put 'to my beloved Father' so low down?" shrieked Yainkele.

"Where am I to put it, then? In the sky, eh?" asked Berele, and pushed Yainkele aside.

"Go away, I will leave you half. Don't confuse me!— You be quiet!" and Yainkele moved away, and stared with terrified eyes at Berele, as he sat there, bent double, and wrote and wrote, knitted his brows, and dipped the pen, and reflected, and wrote again.

"That's enough!" screamed Yainkele, after a few minutes.

"It's not the half yet," answered Berele, writing on.

"But I ought to have more than half!" said Yainkele, crossly. The longing to write, to pour out his heart onto the post-card, was overwhelming him.

But Berele did not even hear: he had launched out into such rhetorical Hebrew expressions as "First of all, I let you know that I am alive and well," which he had learnt in "The Perfect Letter-Writer," and his little bits of news remained unwritten. He had yet to abuse Lezer the carrier, to tell how many pages of the Gemoreh he had learnt, to let them know they were to send another parcel, because they had no "Monday" and no "Wednesday," and the "Tuesday" was no better than nothing.

And Berele writes and writes, and Yainkele can no longer contain himself—he sees that Berele is taking up more than half the card.

"Enough!" He ran forward with a cry, and seized the penholder.

"Three words more!" begged Berele.

"But remember, not more than three!" and Yainkele's eyes flashed. Berele set to work to write the three words; but that which he wished to express required yet ten to fifteen words, and Berele, excited by the fact of writing, pecked away at the paper, and took up yet another bit of the other half.

"You stop!" shrieked Yainkele, and broke into hysterical sobs, as he saw what a small space remained for him.

"Hush! Just 'from me, thy son,'" begged Berele, "nothing else!"

But Yainkele, remembering that he had given a whole vierer toward the post-card, and that they would read so much of Berele at home, and so little of him, flew into a passion, and came and tried to tear away the card from under Berele's hands. "Let me put 'from me, thy son'!" implored Berele.

"It will do *without* 'from me, thy son'!" screamed Yainkele, although he *felt* that one ought to put it. His anger rose, and he began tugging at the card. Berele held tight, but Yainkele gave such a pull that the card tore in two.

"What have you done, villain!" cried Berele, glaring at Yainkele.

"I *meant* to do it!" wailed Yainkele.

"Oh, but why did you?" cried Berele, gazing in despair at the two torn halves of the post-card.

But Yainkele could not answer. The tears choked him, and he threw himself against the wall, tearing his hair. Then Berele gave way, too, and the little room resounded with lamentations.

LOST HIS VOICE

It was in the large synagogue in Klemenke. The week-day service had come to an end. The town cantor who sings all the prayers, even when he prays alone, and who is longer over them than other people, had already folded his prayer-scarf, and was humming the day's Psalm to himself, to a tune. He sang the last words "cantorishly" high:

"And He will be our guide until death." In the last word "death" he tried, as usual, to rise artistically to the higher octave, then to fall very low, and to rise again almost at once into the height; but this time he failed, the note stuck in his throat and came out false.

He got a fright, and in his fright he looked round to make sure no one was standing beside him. Seeing only old Henoch, his alarm grew less, he knew that old Henoch was deaf.

As he went out with his prayer-scarf and phylacteries under his arm, the unsuccessful "death" rang in his ears and troubled him.

"Plague take it," he muttered, "it never once happened to me before."

Soon, however, he remembered that two weeks ago, on the Sabbath before the New Moon, as he stood praying with the choristers before the altar, nearly the same thing had happened to him when he sang "He is our God" as a solo in the Kedushah.

Happily no one remarked it—anyway the "bass" had said nothing to him. And the memory of the unsuccessful "Hear, O Israel" of two weeks ago and of to-day's "unto death" were mingled together, and lay heavily on his heart.

He would have liked to try the note once more as he walked, but the street was just then full of people, and he tried to refrain till he should reach home. Contrary to his usual custom, he began taking rapid steps, and it looked as if he were running away from some-one. On reaching home, he put away his prayer-scarf without saying so much as good morning, recovered his breath after the quick walk, and began to sing, "He shall be our guide until death."

"That's right, you have so little time to sing in! The day is too short for you!" exclaimed the cantoress, angrily. "It grates on the ears enough already!"

"How, it grates?" and the cantor's eyes opened wide with fright, "I sing a note, and you say 'it grates'? How can it grate?"

He looked at her imploringly, his eyes said: "Have pity on me! Don't say, 'it grates'! because if it *does* grate, I am miserable, I am done for!"

But the cantoress was much too busy and preoccupied with the dinner to sympathize and to understand how things stood with her husband, and went on:

"Of course it grates! Why shouldn't it? It deafens me. When you sing in the choir, I have to bear it, but when you begin by yourself—what?"

The cantor had grown as white as chalk, and only just managed to say:

"Grune, are you mad? What are you talking about?"

"What ails the man to-day!" exclaimed Grune, impatiently. "You've made a fool of yourself long enough! Go and wash your hands and come to dinner!"

The cantor felt no appetite, but he reflected that one must eat, if only as a remedy; not to eat would make matters worse, and he washed his hands.

He chanted the grace loud and cantor-like, glancing occasionally at his wife, to see if she noticed anything wrong; but this time she said nothing at all, and he was reassured. "It was my fancy—just my fancy!" he said to himself. "All nonsense! One doesn't lose one's voice so soon as all that!"

Then he remembered that he was already forty years old, and it had happened to the cantor Meyer Lieder, when he was just that age—

That was enough to put him into a fright again. He bent his head, and thought deeply. Then he raised it, and called out loud:

"Grune!"

"Hush! What is it? What makes you call out in that strange voice?" asked Grune, crossly, running in.

"Well, well, let me live!" said the cantor. "Why do you say 'in that strange voice'? Whose voice was it? eh? What is the matter now?"

There was a sound as of tears as he spoke.

"You're cracked to-day! As nonsensical—Well, what do you want?"

"Beat up one or two eggs for me!" begged the cantor, softly.

"Here's a new holiday!" screamed Grune. "On a Wednesday! Have you got to chant the Sabbath prayers? Eggs are so dear now—five kopeks apiece!"

"Grune," commanded the cantor, "they may be one ruble apiece, two rubles, five rubles, one hundred rubles. Do you hear? Beat up two eggs for me, and don't talk!"

"To be sure, you earn so much money!" muttered Grune.

"Then you think it's all over with me?" said the cantor, boldly. "No, Grune!"

He wanted to tell her that he wasn't sure about it yet, there was still hope, it might be all a fancy, perhaps it was imagination, but he was afraid to say all that, and Grune did not understand what he stammered out. She shrugged her shoulders, and only said, "Upon my word!" and went to beat up the eggs.

The cantor sat and sang to himself. He listened to every note as though he were examining some one. Finding himself unable to take the high octave, he called out despairingly:

"Grune, make haste with the eggs!" His one hope lay in the eggs.

The cantoress brought them with a cross face, and grumbled:

"He wants eggs, and we're pinching and starving—"

The cantor would have liked to open his heart to her, so that she should not think the eggs were what he cared about; he would have liked to say, "Grune, I think I'm done for!" but he summoned all his courage and refrained.

"After all, it may be only an idea," he thought.

And without saying anything further, he began to drink up the eggs as a remedy.

When they were finished, he tried to make a few cantor-like trills. In this he succeeded, and he grew more cheerful.

"It will be all right," he thought, "I shall not lose my voice so soon as all that! Never mind Meyer Lieder, he drank! I don't drink, only a little wine now and again, at a circumcision."

His appetite returned, and he swallowed mouthful after mouthful.

But his cheerfulness did not last: the erstwhile unsuccessful "death" rang in his ears, and the worry returned and took possession of him.

The fear of losing his voice had tormented the cantor for the greater part of his life. His one care, his one anxiety had been, what should he do if he were to lose his voice? It had happened to him once already, when he was fourteen years old. He had a tenor voice, which broke all of a sudden. But that time he didn't care. On the contrary, he was delighted, he knew that his voice was merely changing, and that in six months he would get the baritone for which he was impatiently waiting. But when he had got the baritone, he knew that when he lost that, it would be lost indeed —he would get no other voice. So he took great care of it—how much more so when he had his own household, and had taken the office of cantor in Klemenke! Not a breath of wind was allowed to blow upon his throat, and he wore a comforter in the hottest weather.

It was not so much on account of the Klemenke householders—he felt sure they would not dismiss him from his office. Even if he were to lose his voice altogether, he would still receive his salary. It was not brought to him to his house, as it was—he had to go for it every Friday from door to door, and the Klemenke Jews were good-hearted, and never refused anything to the outstretched hand. He took care of his voice, and trembled to lose it, only out of love for the singing. He thought a great deal of the Klemenke Jews—their like was not to be found—but in the interpretation of music they were uninitiated, they had no feeling whatever. And when, standing before the altar, he used to make artistic trills and variations, and take the highest notes, that was for *himself*—he had great joy in it—and also for his eight singers, who were all the world to him. His very life was bound up with them, and when one of them exclaimed, "Oi, cantor! Oi, how you sing!" his happiness was complete.

The singers had come together from various towns and villages, and all their conversations and their stories turned and wrapped themselves round cantors and music. These stories and legends were the cantor's delight, he would lose himself in every one of them, and give a sweet, deep sigh:

"As if music were a trifle! As if a feeling were a toy!" And now that he had begun to fear he was losing his voice, it seemed to him the singers were different people—bad people! They must be laughing at him among themselves! And he began to be on his guard against them, avoided taking a high note in their presence, lest they should find out—and suffered all the more.

And what would the neighboring cantors say? The thought tormented him further. He knew that he had a reputation among them, that he was a great deal thought of, that his voice was much talked of. He saw in his mind's eye a couple of cantors whispering together, and shaking their heads sorrowfully: they are pitying him! "How sad! You have heard? The poor Klemenke cantor——"

The vision quite upset him.

"Perhaps it's only fancy!" he would say to himself in those dreadful moments, and would begin to sing, to try his highest notes. But the terror he was in took away his hearing, and he could not tell if his voice were what it should be or not.

In two weeks time his face grew pale and thin, his eyes were sunk, and he felt his strength going.

"What is the matter with you, cantor?" said a singer to him one day.

"Ha, what is the matter?" asked the cantor, with a start, thinking they had already found out. "You ask what is the matter with me? Then you know something about it, ha!"

"No, I know nothing. That is why I ask you why you look so upset."

"Upset, you say? Nothing more than upset, ha? That's all?"

"The cantor must be thinking out some new piece for the Solemn Days," decided the choir.

Another month went by, and the cantor had not got the better of his fear. Life had become distasteful to him. If he had known for certain that his voice was gone, he would perhaps have been calmer. Verfallen! No one can live forever (losing his voice and dying was one and the same to him), but the uncertainty, the tossing oneself between yes and no, the Olom ha-Tohu of it all, embittered the cantor's existence.

At last, one fine day, the cantor resolved to get at the truth: he could bear it no longer.

It was evening, the wife had gone to the market for meat, and the choir had gone home, only the eldest singer, Yössel "bass," remained with the cantor.

The cantor looked at him, opened his mouth and shut it again; it was difficult for him to say what he wanted to say.

At last he broke out with:

"Yössel!"

"What is it, cantor?"

"Tell me, are you an honest man?"

Yössel "bass" stared at the cantor, and asked:

"What are you asking me to-day, cantor?"

"Brother Yössel," the cantor said, all but weeping, "Brother Yössel!"

That was all he could say.

"Cantor, what is wrong with you?"

"Brother Yössel, be an honest man, and tell me the truth, the truth!"

"I don't understand! What is the matter with you, cantor?"

"Tell me the truth: Do you notice any change in me?"

"Yes, I do," answered the singer, looking at the cantor, and seeing how pale and thin he was. "A very great change——"

"Now I see you are an honest man, you tell me the truth to my face. Do you know when it began?"

"It will soon be a month," answered the singer.

"Yes, brother, a month, a month, but I felt—"

The cantor wiped off the perspiration that covered his forehead, and continued:

"And you think, Yössel, that it's lost now, for good and all?"

"That *what* is lost?" asked Yössel, beginning to be aware that the conversation turned on something quite different from what was in his own mind.

"What? How can you ask? Ah? What should I lose? Money? I have no money—I mean—of course— my voice."

Then Yössel understood everything—he was too much of a musician *not* to understand. Looking compassionately at the cantor, he asked:

"For certain?"

"For certain?" exclaimed the cantor, trying to be cheerful. "Why must it be for certain? Very likely it's all a mistake—let us hope it is!"

Yössel looked at the cantor, and as a doctor behaves to his patient, so did he:

"Take *do!*" he said, and the cantor, like an obedient pupil, drew out *do*.

"Draw it out, draw it out! Four quavers—draw it out!" commanded Yössel, listening attentively.

The cantor drew it out.

"Now, if you please, *re!*"

The cantor sang out *re-re-re.*

The singer moved aside, appeared to be lost in thought, and then said, sadly:

"Gone!"

"Forever?"

"Well, are you a little boy? Are you likely to get another voice? At your time of life, gone is gone!"

The cantor wrung his hands, threw himself down beside the table, and, laying his head on his arms, he burst out crying like a child.

Next morning the whole town had heard of the misfortune—that the cantor had lost his voice.

"It's an ill wind——" quoted the innkeeper, a well-to-do man. "He won't keep us so long with his trills on Sabbath. I'd take a bitter onion for that voice of his, any day!"

LATE

It was in sad and hopeless mood that Antosh watched the autumn making its way into his peasant's hut. The days began to shorten and the evenings to lengthen, and there was no more petroleum in the hut to fill his humble lamp; his wife complained too—the store of salt was giving out; there was very little soap left, and in a few days he would finish his tobacco. And Antosh cleared his throat, spat, and muttered countless times a day:

"No salt, no soap, no tobacco; we haven't got anything. A bad business!"

Antosh had no prospect of earning anything in the village. The one village Jew was poor himself, and had no work to give. Antosh had only *one* hope left. Just before the Feast of Tabernacles he would drive a whole cart-load of fir-boughs into the little town and bring a tidy sum of money home in exchange.

He did this every year, since buying his thin horse in the market for six rubles.

"When shall you have Tabernacles?" he asked every day of the village Jew. "Not yet," was the Jew's daily reply. "But when *shall* you?" Antosh insisted one day.

"In a week," answered the Jew, not dreaming how very much Antosh needed to know precisely.

In reality there were only five more days to Tabernacles, and Antosh had calculated with business accuracy that it would be best to take the fir-boughs into the town two days before the festival. But this was really the first day of it.

He rose early, ate his dry, black bread dipped in salt, and drank a measure of water. Then he harnessed his thin, starved horse to the cart, took his hatchet, and drove into the nearest wood.

He cut down the branches greedily, seeking out the thickest and longest.

"Good ware is easier sold," he thought, and the cart filled, and the load grew higher and higher. He was calculating on a return of three gulden, and it seemed still too little, so that he went on cutting, and laid on a few more boughs. The cart could hold no more, and Antosh looked at it from all sides, and smiled contentedly.

"That will be enough," he muttered, and loosened the reins. But scarcely had he driven a few paces, when he stopped and looked the cart over again.

"Perhaps it's not enough, after all?" he questioned fearfully, cut down five more boughs, laid them onto the already full cart, and drove on.

He drove slowly, pace by pace, and his thoughts travelled slowly too, as though keeping step with the thin horse.

Antosh was calculating how much salt and how much soap, how much petroleum and how much tobacco he could buy for the return for his ware. At length the calculating tired him, and he resolved to put it off till he should have the cash. Then the calculating would be done much more easily.

But when he reached the town, and saw that the booths were already covered with fir-boughs, he felt a pang at his heart. The booths and the houses seemed to be twirling round him in a circle, and dancing. But he consoled himself with the thought that every year, when he drove into town, he found many booths already covered. Some cover earlier, some later. The latter paid the best.

"I shall ask higher prices," he resolved, and all the while fear tugged at his heart. He drove on. Two Jewish women were standing before a house; they pointed at the cart with their finger, and laughed aloud.

"Why do you laugh?" queried Antosh, excitedly.

"Because you are too soon with your fir-boughs," they answered, and laughed again.

"How too soon?" he asked, astonished. "Too soon— too soon—" laughed the women.

"Pfui," Antosh spat, and drove on, thinking, "Berko said himself, 'In a week.' I am only two days ahead."

A cold sweat covered him, as he reflected he might have made a wrong calculation, founded on what Berko had told him. It was possible that he had counted the days badly—had come too late! There is no doubt: all the booths are covered with fir-boughs. He will have no salt, no tobacco, no soap, and no petroleum.

Sadly he followed the slow paces of his languid horse, which let his weary head droop as though out of sympathy for his master.

Meantime the Jews were crowding out of the synagogues in festal array, with their prayer-scarfs and prayer-books in their hands. When they perceived the peasant with the cart of fir-boughs, they looked questioningly one at the other: Had they made a mistake and begun the festival too early?

"What have you there?" some one inquired.

"What?" answered Antosh, taken aback. "Fir-boughs! Buy, my dear friend, I sell it cheap!" he begged in a piteous voice.

The Jews burst out laughing.

'What should we want it for now, fool?" "The festival has begun!" said another. Antosh was confused with his misfortune, he scratched the back of his head, and exclaimed, weeping:

"Buy! Buy! I want salt, soap! I want petroleum."

The group of Jews, who had begun by laughing, were now deeply moved. They saw the poor, starving peasant standing there in his despair, and were filled with a lively compassion.

"A poor Gentile—it's pitiful!" said one, sympathetically. "He hoped to make a fortune out of his fir-boughs, and now!" observed another.

"It would be proper to buy up that bit of fir," said a third, "else it might cause a Chillul ha-Shem." "On a festival?" objected some one else.

"It can always be used for firewood," said another, contemplating the cartful.

"Whether or no! It's a festival——"

"No salt, no soap, no petroleum——" It was the refrain of the bewildered peasant, who did not understand what the Jews were saying among themselves. He could only guess that they were talking about him. "Hold! he doesn't want *money!* He wants ware. Ware without money may be given even on a festival," called out one.

The interest of the bystanders waxed more lively. Among them stood a storekeeper, whose shop was close by. "Give him, Chayyim, a few jars of salt and other things that he wants—even if it comes to a few gulden. We will contribute."

"All right, willingly!" said Chayyim. "A poor Gentile!"

"A precept, a precept! It would be carrying out a religious precept, as surely as I am a Jew!" chimed in every individual member of the crowd.

Chayyim called the peasant to him; all the rest followed. He gave him out of the stores two jars of salt, a bar of soap, a bottle of petroleum, and two packets of tobacco.

The peasant did not know what to do for joy. He could only stammer in a low voice, "Thank you! thank you!"

"And there's a bit of Sabbath loaf," called out one, when he had packed the things away, "take that with you!"

"There's some more!" and a second hand held some out to him.

"More!"

"More!"

"And more!"

They brought Antosh bread and cake from all sides; his astonishment was such that he could scarcely articulate his thanks.

The people were pleased with themselves, and Yainkel Leives, a cheerful man, who was well supplied for the festival, because his daughter's "intended" was staying in his house, brought Antosh a glass of brandy:

"Drink, and drive home, in the name of God!"

Antosh drank the brandy with a quick gulp, bit off a piece of cake, and declared joyfully, "I shall never forget it!"

"Not at all a bad Gentile," remarked someone in the crowd.

"Well, what would you have? Did you expect him to beat you?" queried another, smiling.

The words "to beat" made a melancholy impression on the crowd, and it dispersed in silence.

THE KADDISH

From behind the curtain came low moans, and low words of encouragement from the old and experienced Bobbe. In the room it was dismal to suffocation. The seven children, all girls, between twenty-three and four years old, sat quietly, each by herself, with drooping head, and waited for something dreadful.

At a little table near a great cupboard with books sat the "patriarch" Reb Selig Chanes, a tall, thin Jew, with a yellow, consumptive face. He was chanting in low, broken tones out of a big Gemoreh, and continually raising his head, giving a nervous glance at the curtain, and then, without inquiring what might be going on beyond the low moaning, taking up once again his sad, tremulous chant. He seemed to be suffering more than the woman in childbirth herself.

"Lord of the World!"—it was the eldest daughter who broke the stillness—"Let it be a boy for once! Help, Lord of the World, have pity!"

"Oi, thus might it be, Lord of the World!" chimed in the second.

And all the girls, little and big, with broken heart and prostrate spirit, prayed that there might be born a boy.

Reb Selig raised his eyes from the Gemoreh, glanced at the curtain, then at the seven girls, gave vent to a deep-drawn Oi, made a gesture with his hand, and said with settled despair, "She will give you another sister!"

The seven girls looked at one another in desperation;

their father's conclusion quite crushed them, and they had no longer even the courage to pray.

Only the littlest, the four-year-old, in the torn frock, prayed softly:

"Oi, please God, there will be a little brother."

"I shall die without a Kaddish!" groaned Reb Selig.

The time drags on, the moans behind the curtain grow louder, and Reb Selig and the elder girls feel that soon, very soon, the "grandmother" will call out in despair, "A little girl!" And Reb Selig feels that the words will strike home to his heart like a blow, and he resolves to run away.

He goes out into the yard, and looks up at the sky. It is midnight. The moon swims along so quietly and indifferently, the stars seem to frolic and rock themselves like little children, and still Reb Selig hears, in the "grandmother's" husky voice, "A girl!"

"Well, there will be no Kaddish! Verfallen!" he says, crossing the yard again. "There's no getting it by force!"

But his trying to calm himself is useless; the fear that it should be a girl only grows upon him. He loses patience, and goes back into the house.

But the house is in a turmoil.

"What is it, eh?"

"A little boy! Tate, a boy! Tatinke, as surely may I be well!" with this news the seven girls fall upon him with radiant faces.

"Eh, a little boy?" asked Reb Selig, as though bewildered, "eh? what?"

"A boy, Reb Selig, a Kaddish!" announced the "grandmother." "As soon as I have bathed him, I will show him you!"

"A boy . . . a boy . . . " stammered Reb Selig in the same bewilderment, and he leant against the wall, and burst into tears like a woman.

The seven girls took alarm.

"That is for joy," explained the "grandmother," "I have known that happen before."

"A boy . . a boy!" sobbed Reb Selig, overcome with happiness, "a boy . . . a boy . . . a Kaddish!"

The little boy received the name of Jacob, but he was called, by way of a talisman, Alter.

Reb Selig was a learned man, and inclined to think lightly of such protective measures; he even laughed at his Cheike for believing in such foolishness; but, at heart, he was content to have it so. Who could tell what might not be in it, after all? Women sometimes know better than men.

By the time Alterke was three years old, Reb Selig's cough had become worse, the sense of oppression on his chest more frequent. But he held himself morally erect, and looked death calmly in the face, as though he would say, "Now I can afford to laugh at you—I leave a Kaddish!"

"What do you think, Cheike," he would say to his wife, after a fit of coughing, "would Alterke be able to say Kaddish if I were to die to-day or to-morrow?"

"Go along with you, crazy pate!" Cheike would exclaim in secret alarm. "You are going to live a long while! Is your cough anything new?"

Selig smiled, "Foolish woman, she supposes I am afraid to die. When one leaves a Kaddish, death is a trifle."

Alterke was sitting playing with a prayer-book and imitating his father at prayer, "A num-num—a num-num."

"Listen to him praying!" and Cheike turned delightedly to her husband. "His soul is piously inclined!"

Selig made no reply, he only gazed at his Kaddish with a beaming face. Then an idea came into his head: Alterke will be a Tzaddik, will help him out of all his difficulties in the other world.

"Mame, I want to eat!" wailed Alterke, suddenly.

He was given a piece of the white bread which was laid aside, for him only, every Sabbath.

Alterke began to eat.

"Who bringest forth! Who bringest forth!" called out Reb Selig.

"Tan't!" answered the child.

"It is time you taught him to say grace," observed Cheike.

And Reb Selig drew Alterke to him and began to repeat with him.

"Say: Boruch."

"Bo'uch," repeated the child after his fashion.

"Attoh."

"Attoh."

When Alterke had finished "Who bringest forth," Cheike answered piously Amen, and Reb Selig saw Alterke, in imagination, standing in the synagogue and repeating Kaddish, and heard the congregation answer

Amen, and he felt as though he were already seated in the Garden of Eden.

Another year went by, and Reb Selig was feeling very poorly. Spring had come, the snow had melted, and he found the wet weather more trying than ever before. He could just drag himself early to the synagogue, but going to the afternoon service had become a difficulty, and he used to recite the afternoon and later service at home, and spend the whole evening with Alterke.

It was late at night. All the houses were shut. Reb Selig sat at his little table, and was looking into the corner where Cheike's bed stood, and where Alterke slept beside her. Selig had a feeling that he would die that night. He felt very tired and weak, and with an imploring look he crept up to Alterke's crib, and began to wake him.

The child woke with a start.

"Alterke"—Reb Selig was stroking the little head— "come to me for a little!"

The child, who had had his first sleep out, sprang up, and went to his father.

Reb Selig sat down in the chair which stood by the little table with the open Gemoreh, lifted Alterke onto the table, and looked into his eyes.

"Alterke!"

"What, Tate?"

"Would you like me to die?"

"Like," answered the child, not knowing what "to die" meant, and thinking it must be something nice.

"Will you say Kaddish after me?" asked Reb Selig, in a strangled voice, and he was seized with a fit of coughing.

"Will say!" promised the child.

"Shall you know how?"

"Shall!"

"Well, now, say: Yisgaddal."

"Yisdaddal," repeated the child in his own way.

"Veyiskaddash."

"Veyistaddash."

And Reb Selig repeated the Kaddish with him several times.

The small lamp burnt low, and scarcely illuminated Reb Selig's yellow, corpse-like face, or the little one of Alterke, who repeated wearily the difficult, and to him unintelligible words of the Kaddish. And Alterke, all the while, gazed intently into the corner, where Tate's shadow and his own had a most fantastic and frightening appearance.

AVRÒHOM THE ORCHARD-KEEPER

When he first came to the place, as a boy, and went straight to the house-of-study, and people, having greeted him, asked "Where do you come from?" and he answered, not without pride, "From the Government of Wilna"—from that day until the day he was married, they called him "the Wilner."

In a few years' time, however, when the house-of-study had married him to the daughter of the Psalm-reader, a coarse, undersized creature, and when, after six months' "board" with his father-in-law, he became a teacher, the town altered his name to "the Wilner teacher." Again, a few years later, when he got a chest affection, and the doctor forbade him to keep school, and he began to deal in fruit, the town learnt that his name was Avròhom, to which they added "the orchard-keeper," and his name is "Avròhom the orchard-keeper" to this day.

Avròhom was quite content with his new calling. He had always wished for a business in which he need not have to do with a lot of people in whom he had small confidence, and in whose society he felt ill at ease.

People have a queer way with them, he used to think, they want to be always talking! They want to tell everything, find out everything, answer everything!

When he was a student he always chose out a place in a corner somewhere, where he could see nobody, and nobody could see him; and he used to murmur the day's task to a low tune, and his murmured repetition made him think of the ruin in which Rabbi José, praying there, heard the Bas-Kol mourn, cooing like a dove, over the exile of Israel. And then he longed to float away to that ruin somewhere in the wilderness, and murmur there like a dove, with no one, no one, to interrupt him, not even the Bas-Kol. But his vision would be destroyed by some hard question which a fellow-student would put before him, describing circles with his thumb and chanting to a shrill Gemoreh-tune.

In the orchard, at the end of the Gass, however, which Avròhom hired of the Gentiles, he had no need to exchange empty words with anyone. Avròhom had no large capital, and could not afford to hire an orchard for more than thirty rubles. The orchard was consequently small, and only grew about twenty apple-trees, a few pear-trees, and a cherry-tree. Avròhom used to move to the garden directly after the Feast of Weeks, although that was still very early, the fruit had not yet set, and there was nothing to steal.

But Avròhom could not endure sitting at home any longer, where the wife screamed, the children cried, and there was a continual "fair." What should he want there? He only wished to be alone with his thoughts and imaginings, and his quiet "tunes," which were always weaving themselves inside him, and were nearly stifled.

It is early to go to the orchard directly after the Feast of Weeks, but Avròhom does not mind, he is drawn back to the trees that can think and hear so much, and keep so many things to themselves.

And Avròhom betakes himself to the orchard. He carries with him, besides phylacteries and prayer-scarf, a prayer-book with the Psalms and the "Stations," two volumes of the Gemoreh which he owns, a few works by the later scholars, and the Tales of Jerusalem; he takes his wadded winter garment and a cushion, makes them into a bundle, kisses the Mezuzeh, mutters farewell, and is off to the orchard.

As he nears the orchard his heart begins to beat loudly for joy, but he is hindered from going there at once. In the yard through which he must pass lies a dog. Later on, when Avròhom has got to know the dog, he will even take him into the orchard, but the first time there is a certain risk—one has to know a dog, otherwise it barks, and Avròhom dreads a bark worse than a bite—it goes through one's head! And Avròhom waits till the owner comes out, and leads him through by the hand.

"Back already?" exclaims the owner, laughing and astonished.

"Why not?" murmurs Avròhom, shamefacedly, and feeling that it is, indeed, early.

"What shall you do?" asks the owner, graver. "There is no hut there at all—last year's fell to pieces."

"Never mind, never mind," begs Avròhom, "it will be all right."

"Well, if you want to come!" and the owner shrugs his shoulders, and lets Avròhom into the orchard.

Avròhom immediately lays his bundle on the ground, stretches himself out full length on the grass, and murmurs, "Good! good!"

At last he is silent, and listens to the quiet rustle of the trees. It seems to him that the trees also wonder at his coming so soon, and he looks at them beseechingly, as though he would say:

"Trees—you, too! I couldn't help it . . . it drew me . . ,"

And soon he fancies that the trees have understood everything, and murmur, "Good, good!"

And Avròhom already feels at home in the orchard. He rises from the ground, and goes to every tree in turn, as though to make its acquaintance. Then he considers the hut that stands in the middle of the orchard.

It has fallen in a little certainly, but Avròhom is all the better pleased with it. He is not particularly fond of new, strong things, a building resembling a ruin is somehow much more to his liking. Such a ruin is inwardly full of secrets, whispers, and melodies. There the tears fall quietly, while the soul yearns after something that has no name and no existence in time or space. And Avròhom creeps into the fallen-in hut, where it is dark and where there are smells of another world. He draws himself up into a ball, and remains hid from everyone.

But to remain hid from the world is not so easy. At first it can be managed. So long as the fruit is ripening, he needs no one, and no one needs him. When one of his children brings him food, he exchanges a few words with it, asks what is going on at home, and how the mother is, and he feels he has done his duty, if, when obliged to go home, he spends there Friday night

and Saturday morning. That over, and the hot stew
eaten, he returns to the orchard, lies down under a
tree, opens the Tales of Jerusalem, goes to sleep reading
a fantastical legend, dreams of the Western Wall,
Mother Rachel's Grave, the Cave of Machpelah, and
other holy, quiet places—places where the air is full of
old stories such as are given, in such easy Hebrew, in
the Tales of Jerusalem.

But when the fruit is ripe, and the trees begin to
bend under the burden of it, Avròhom must perforce
leave his peaceful world, and become a trader.

When the first wind begins to blow in the orchard,
and covers the ground thereof with apples and pears,
Avròhom collects them, makes them into heaps, sorts
them, and awaits the market-women with their loud
tongues, who destroy all the peace and quiet of his
Garden of Eden.

On Sabbath he would like to rest, but of a Sabbath
the trade in apples—on tick of course—is very lively
in the orchards. There is a custom in the town to
that effect, and Avròhom cannot do away with it.
Young gentlemen and young ladies come into the
orchard, and hold a sort of revel; they sing and laugh,
they walk and they chatter, and Avròhom must listen
to it all, and bear it, and wait for the night, when he
can creep back into his hut, and need look at no one
but the trees, and hear nothing but the wind, and
sometimes the rain and the thunder.

But it is worse in the autumn, when the fruit is
getting over-ripe, and he can no longer remain in the
orchard. With a bursting heart he bids farewell to

the trees, to the hut in which he has spent so many quiet, peaceful moments. He conveys the apples to a shed belonging to the farm, which he has hired, ever since he had the orchard, for ten gulden a month, and goes back to the Gass.

In the Gass, at that time, there is mud and rain. Town Jews drag themselves along sick and disheartened. They cough and groan. Avròhom stares round him, and fails to recognize the world.

"Bad!" he mutters. "Fê!" and he spits. "Where is one to get to?"

And Avròhom recalls the beautiful legends in the Tales of Jerusalem, he recalls the land of Israel.

There he knows it is always summer, always warm and fine. And every autumn the vision draws him.

But there is no possibility of his being able to go there—he must sell the apples which he has brought from the orchard, and feed the wife and the children he has "outside the land." And all through the autumn and part of the winter, Avròhom drags himself about with a basket of apples on his arm and a yearning in his heart. He waits for the dear summer, when he will be able to go back and hide himself in the orchard, in the hut, and be alone, where the town mud and the town Jews with dulled senses shall be out of sight, and the week-day noise, out of hearing.

HIRSH DAVID NAUMBERG

Born, 1876, in Msczczonow, Government of Warsaw, Russian Poland, of Hasidic parentage; traditional Jewish education in the house of his grandfather; went to Warsaw in 1898; at present (1912) in America; first literary work appeared in 1900; writer of stories, etc., in Hebrew and Yiddish; co-editor of Ha-Zofeh, Der Freind, Ha-Boker; contributor to Ha-Zeman, Heint, Ha-Dor, Ha-Shiloah, etc.; collected works, 5 vols., Warsaw, 1908-1911.

THE RAV AND THE RAV'S SON

The Sabbath midday meal is over, and the Saken
Rav passes his hands across his serene and pious countenance, pulls out both earlocks, straightens his skull-
cap, and prepares to expound a passage of the Torah as
God shall enlighten him. There sit with him at table,
to one side of him, a passing guest, a Libavitch Chossid,
like the Rav himself, a man with yellow beard and earlocks, and a grubby shirt collar appearing above the
grubby yellow kerchief that envelopes his throat; to the
other side of him, his son Sholem, an eighteen-year-old
youth, with a long pale face, deep, rather dreamy eyes,
a velvet hat, but no earlocks, a secret Maskil, who writes
Hebrew verses, and contemplates growing into a great
Jewish author. The Rebbetzin has been suffering two
or three months with rheumatism, and lies in another
room.

The Rav is naturally humble-minded, and it is no
trifle to him to expound the Torah. To take a passage
of the Bible and say, The meaning is this and that, is a
thing he hasn't the cheek to do. It makes him feel
as uncomfortable as if he were telling lies. Up to
twenty-five years of age he was a Misnaggid, but under
the influence of the Saken Rebbetzin, he became a Chossid, bit by bit. Now he is over fifty, he drives to the
Rebbe, and comes home every time with increased faith
in the latter's supernatural powers, and, moreover, with
a strong desire to expound a little of the Torah himself; only, whenever a good idea comes into his head, it

oppresses him, because he has not sufficient self-confidence to express it.

The difficulty for him lies in making a start. He would like to do as the Rebbe does (long life to him!)— give a push to his chair, a look, stern and somewhat angry, at those sitting at table, then a groaning sigh. But the Rav is ashamed to imitate him, or is partly afraid, lest people should catch him doing it. He drops his eyes, holds one hand to his forehead, while the other plays with the knife on the table, and one hardly hears:

"When thou goest forth to war with thine enemy— thine enemy—that is, the inclination to evil, oi, oi,— a—" he nods his head, gathers a little confidence, continues his explanation of the passage, and gradually warms to the part. He already looks the stranger boldly in the face. The stranger twists himself into a correct attitude, nods assent, but cannot for the life of him tear his gaze from the brandy-bottle on the table, and cannot wonder sufficiently at so much being allowed to remain in it at the end of a meal. And when the Rav comes to the fact that to be in "prison" means to have bad habits, and "well-favored woman" means that every bad habit has its good side, the guest can no longer restrain himself, seizes the bottle rather awkwardly, as though in haste, fills up his glass, spills a little onto the cloth, and drinks with his head thrown back, gulping it like a regular tippler, after a hoarse and sleepy "to your health." This has a bad effect on the Rav's enthusiasm, it "mixes his brains," and he turns to his son for help. To tell the truth, he has not much confidence in his son where the Law is concerned, although he loves him dearly, the boy being the only one of his children in whom he may hope, with God's help, to have comfort, and who, a hundred years hence, shall take over from him the office of Rav in Saken. The elder son is rich, but he is a usurer, and his riches give the Rav no satisfaction whatever. He had had one daughter, but she died, leaving some little orphans. Sholem is, therefore, the only one left him. He has a good head, and is quick at his studies, a quiet, well-behaved boy, a little obstinate, a bit opinionated, but that is no harm in a boy, thinks the old man. True, too, that last week people told him tales. Sholem, they said, read heretical books, and had been seen carrying "burdens" on Sabbath. But this the father does not believe, he will not and cannot believe it. Besides, Sholem is certain to have made amends. If a Talmid-Chochom commit a sin by day, it should be forgotten by nightfall, because a Talmid-Chochom makes amends, it says so in the Gemoreh.

However, the Rav is ashamed to give his own exegesis of the Law before his son, and he knows perfectly well that nothing will induce Sholem to drive with him to the Rebbe.

But the stranger and his brandy-drinking have so upset him that he now looks at his son in a piteous sort of way. "Hear me out, Sholem, what harm can it do you?" says his look.

Sholem draws himself up, and pulls in his chair, supports his head with both his hands, and gazes into his father's eyes out of filial duty. He loves his father, but in his heart he wonders at him; it seems to him

his father ought to learn more about his heretical lean-
ings—it is quite time he should—and he continues to
gaze in silence and in wonder, not unmixed with compassion, and never ceases thinking, "Upon my word,
Tate, what a simpleton you are!"

But when the Rav came in the course of his exposition to speak of "death by kissing" (by the Lord),
and told how the righteous, the holy Tzaddikim, die
from the very sweetness of the Blessed One's kiss, a
spark kindled in Sholem's eyes, and he moved in his
chair. One of those wonders had taken place which do
frequently occur, only they are seldom remarked: the
Chassidic exposition of the Torah had suggested to
Sholem a splendid idea for a romantic poem!

It is an old commonplace that men take in, of what
they hear and see, that which pleases them. Sholem is
fascinated. He wishes to die anyhow, so what could
be more appropriate and to the purpose than that his
love should kiss him on his death-bed, while, in that
very instant, his soul departs?

The idea pleased him so immensely that immediately
after grace, the stranger having gone on his way, and
the Rav laid himself down to sleep in the other room,
Sholem began to write. His heart beat violently while
he made ready, but the very act of writing out a poem
after dinner on Sabbath, in the room where his father
settled the cases laid before him by the townsfolk, was
a bit of heroism well worth the risk. He took the
writing-materials out of his locked box, and, the pen
and ink-pot in one hand and a collection of manuscript
verse in the other, he went on tiptoe to the table.

He folded back the table-cover, laid down his writing
apparatus, and took another look around to make sure
no one was in the room. He counted on the fact that
when the Rav awoke from his nap, he always coughed,
and that when he walked he shuffled so with his feet,
and made so much noise with his long slippers, that
one could hear him two rooms off. In short, there was
no need to be anxious.

He grows calmer, reads the manuscript poems, and
his face tells that he is pleased. Now he wants to
collect his thoughts for the new one, but something
or other hinders him. He unfastens the girdle round
his waist, rolls it up, and throws it into the Rav's soft
stuffed chair.

And now that there is nothing to disturb from without, a second and third wonder must take place within:
the Rav's Torah, which was transformed by Sholem's
brain into a theme for romance, must now descend into
his heart, thence to pour itself onto the paper, and
pass, by this means, into the heads of Sholem's friends,
who read his poems with enthusiasm, and have sinful
dreams afterwards at night.

And he begins to imagine himself on his death-bed,
sick and weak, unable to speak, and with staring eyes.
He sees nothing more, but he feels a light, ethereal
kiss on his cheek, and his soul is aware of a sweet voice
speaking. He tries to take out his hands from under
the coverlet, but he cannot—he is dying—it grows
dark.

A still brighter and more unusual gleam comes into
Sholem's eyes, his heart swells with emotion seeking
an outlet, his brain works like running machinery, a

whole dictionary of words, his whole treasure of conceptions and ideas, is turned over and over so rapidly that the mind is unconscious of its own efforts. His poetic instinct is searching for what it needs. His hand works quietly, forming letter on letter, word on word. Now and again Sholem lifts his eyes from the paper and looks round, he has a feeling as though the four walls and the silence were thinking to themselves: "Hush, hush! Disturb not the poet at his work of creation! Disturb not the priest about to offer sacrifice to God."

To the Rav, meanwhile, lying in the other room, there had come a fresh idea for the exposition of the Torah, and he required to look up something in a book. The door of the reception-room opened, the Rav entered, and Sholem had not heard him.

It was a pity to see the Rav's face, it was so contracted with dismay, and a pity to see Sholem's when he caught sight of his father, who, utterly taken aback, dropt into a seat exactly opposite Sholem, and gave a groan—was it? or a cry?

But he did not sit long, he did not know what one should do or say to one's son on such an occasion; his heart and his eyes inclined to weeping, and he retired into his own room. Sholem remained alone with a very sore heart and a soul opprest. He put the writing-materials back into their box, and went out with the manuscript verses tucked away under his Tallis-koton.

He went into the house-of-study, but it looked dreadfully dismal; the benches were pushed about anyhow, a sign that the last worshippers had been in a great hurry to go home to dinner. The beadle was snoring on a seat somewhere in a corner, as loud and as fast as if he were trying to inhale all the air in the building, so that the next congregation might be suffocated. The cloth on the platform reading-desk was crooked and tumbled, the floor was dirty, and the whole place looked as dead as though its Sabbath sleep were to last till the resurrection.

He left the house-of-study, walked home and back again; up and down, there and back, many times over. The situation became steadily clearer to him; he wanted to justify himself, if only with a word, in his father's eyes; then, again, he felt he must make an end, free himself once and for all from the paternal restraint, and become a Jewish author. Only he felt sorry for his father; he would have liked to do something to comfort him. Only what? Kiss him? Put his arms round his neck? Have his cry out before him and say, "Tatishe, you and I, we are neither of us to blame!" Only how to say it so that the old man shall understand? That is the question.

And the Rav sat in his room, bent over a book in which he would fain have lost himself. He rubbed his brow with both hands, but a stone lay on his heart, a heavy stone; there were tears in his eyes, and he was all but crying. He needed some living soul before whom he could pour out the bitterness of his heart, and he had already turned to the Rebbetzin:

"Zelde!" he called quietly.

"A-h," sighed the Rebbetzin from her bed. "I feel bad; my foot aches, Lord of the World! What is it?"

"Nothing, Zelde. How are you getting on, eh?"
He got no further with her; he even mentally repented
having so nearly added to her burden of life.

It was an hour or two before the Rav collected himself, and was able to think over what had happened.
And still he could not, would not, believe that his son,
Sholem, had broken the Sabbath, that he was worthy
of being stoned to death. He sought for some excuse
for him, and found none, and came at last to the conclusion that it was a work of Satan, a special onset of
the Tempter. And he kept on thinking of the Chassidic
legend of a Rabbi who was seen by a Chossid to smoke
a pipe on Sabbath. Only it was an illusion, a deception
of the Evil One. But when, after he had waited some
time, no Sholem appeared, his heart began to beat more
steadily, the reality of the situation made itself felt,
he got angry, and hastily left the house in search of
the Sabbath-breaker, intending to make an example of
him.

Hardly, however, had he perceived his son walking
to and fro in front of the house-of-study, with a look
of absorption and worry, than he stopped short. He
was afraid to go up to his son. Just then Sholem
turned, they saw each other, and the Rav had willy-
nilly to approach him.

"Will you come for a little walk?" asked the Rav
gently, with downcast eyes. Sholem made no reply,
and followed him.

They came to the Eruv, the Rav looked in all his
pockets, found his handkerchief, tied it round his neck,
and glanced at his son with a kind of prayer in his eye.
Sholem tied his handkerchief round his neck.

When they were outside the town, the old man coughed once and again and said:

"What is all this?"

But Sholem was determined not to answer a word, and his father had to summon all his courage to continue:

"What is all this? Eh? Sabbath-breaking! It is—"

He coughed and was silent.

They were walking over a great, broad meadow, and Sholem had his gaze fixed on a horse that was moving about with hobbled legs, while the Rav shaded his eyes with one hand from the beams of the setting sun.

"How can anyone break the Sabbath? Come now, is it right? Is it a thing to do? Just to go and break the Sabbath! I knew Hebrew grammar, and could write Hebrew, too, once upon a time, but break the Sabbath! Tell me yourself, Sholem, what you think! When you have bad thoughts, how is it you don't come to your father? I suppose I am your father, ha?" the old man suddenly fired up. "Am I your father? Tell me—no? Am I perhaps *not* your father?"

"For I *am* his father," he reflected proudly. "That I certainly am, there isn't the smallest doubt about it! The greatest heretic could not deny it!"

"You come to your father," he went on with more decision, and falling into a Gemoreh chant, "and you tell him *all* about it. What harm can it do to tell him? No harm whatever. I also used to be tempted by bad thoughts. Therefore I began driving to the Rebbe of Libavitch. One mustn't let oneself go! Do you hear me, Sholem? One mustn't let oneself go!"

The last words were long drawn out, the Rav emphasizing them with his hands and wrinkling his forehead. Carried away by what he was saying, he now felt all but sure that Sholem had not begun to be a heretic.

"You see," he continued very gently, "every now and then we come to a stumbling-block, but all the same, we should not—"

Meantime, however, the manuscript folio of verses had been slipping out from under Sholem's Four-Corners, and here it fell to the ground. The Rav stood staring, as though startled out of a sweet dream by the cry of "fire." He quivered from top to toe, and seized his earlocks with both hands. For there could be no doubt of the fact that Sholem had now broken the Sabbath a second time—by carrying the folio outside the town limit. And worse still, he had practiced deception, by searching his pockets when they had come to the Eruv, as though to make sure not to transgress by having anything inside them.

Sholem, too, was taken by surprise. He hung his head, and his eyes filled with tears. The old man was about to say something, probably to begin again with "What is all this?" Then he hastily stopt and snatched up the folio, as though he were afraid Sholem might get hold of it first.

"Ha—ha—azoi!" he began panting. "Azoi! A heretic! A Goi."

But it was hard for him to speak. He might not move from where he stood, so long as he held the papers, it being outside the Eruv.   His ankles were giving way, and he sat down to have a look at the manuscript.

"Aha!   Writing!" he exclaimed as he turned the leaves.   "Come here to me," he called to Sholem, who had moved a few steps aside.   Sholem came and stood obediently before him.   "What is this?" asked the Rav, sternly.

"Poems!"

"What do you mean by poems?   What is the good of them?"   He felt that he was growing weak again, and tried to stiffen himself morally.   "What is the good of them, heretic, tell me!"

"They're just meant to read, Tatishe!"

"What do you mean by 'read'?   A Jeroboam son of Nebat, that's what you want to be, is it?   A Jeroboam son of Nebat, to lead others into heresy!   No!   I won't have it!   On no account will I have it!"

The sun had begun to disappear; it was full time to go home; but the Rav did not know what to do with the folio.   He was afraid to leave it in the field, lest Sholem or another should pick it up later, so he got up and began to recite the Afternoon Prayer.   Sholem remained standing in his place, and tried to think of nothing and to do nothing.

The old man finished "Sacrifices," tucked the folio into his girdle, and, without moving a step, looked at Sholem, who did not move either.

"Say the Afternoon Prayer, Shegetz!" commanded the old man.

Sholem began to move his lips.   And the Rav felt, as he went on with the prayer, that this anger was cool-

29

ing down. Before he came to the Eighteen Benedictions, he gave another look at his son, and it seemed madness to think of him as a heretic, to think that Sholem ought by rights to be thrown into a ditch and stoned to death.

Sholem, for his part, was conscious for the first time of his father's will: for the first time in his life, he not only loved his father, but was in very truth subject to him.

The flaming red sun dropt quietly down behind the horizon just before the old man broke down with emotion over "Thou art One," and took the sky and the earth to witness that God is One and His Name is One, and His people Israel one nation on the earth, to whom He gave the Sabbath for a rest and an inheritance. The Rav wept and swallowed his tears, and his eyes were closed. Sholem, on the other hand, could not take his eye off the manuscript that stuck out of his father's girdle, and it was all he could do not to snatch it and run away.

They said nothing on the way home in the dark, they might have been coming from a funeral. But Sholem's heart beat fast, for he knew his father would throw the manuscript into the fire, where it would be burnt, and when they came to the door of their house, he stopped his father, and said in a voice eloquent of tears:

"Give it me back, Tatishe, please give it me back!"

And the Rav gave it him back without looking him in the face, and said:

"Look here, only don't tell Mother! She is ill, she mustn't be upset. She is ill, not of you be it spoken!"

MEYER BLINKIN

Born, 1879, in a village near Pereyaslav, Government of
Poltava, Little Russia, of Hasidic parentage; educated in
Kieff, where he acquired the trade of carpenter in order
to win the right of residence; studied medicine; began to
write in 1906; came to New York in 1908; writer of stories
to the number of about fifty, which have been published in
various periodicals; wrote also Der Sod, and Dr. Makower.

WOMEN

A Prose Poem

Hedged round with tall, thick woods, as though designedly, so that no one should know what happens there, lies the long-drawn-out old town of Pereyaslav.

To the right, connected with Pereyaslav by a wooden bridge, lies another bit of country, named—Pidvorkes.

The town itself, with its long, narrow, muddy streets, with the crowded houses propped up one against the other like tombstones, with their meagre grey walls all to pieces, with the broken window-panes stuffed with rags—well, the town of Pereyaslav was hardly to be distinguished from any other town inhabited by Jews.

Here, too, people faded before they bloomed. Here, too, men lived on miracles, were fruitful and multiplied out of all season and reason. They talked of a livelihood, of good times, of riches and pleasures, with the same appearance of firm conviction, and, at the same time the utter disbelief, with which one tells a legend read in a book.

And they really supposed these terms to be mere inventions of the writers of books and nothing more! For not only were they incapable of a distinct conception of their real meaning, but some had even given up the very hope of ever being able to earn so much as a living, and preferred not to reach out into the world with their thoughts, straining them for nothing, that is, for the sake of a thing so plainly out of the question as a competence. At night the whole town was overspread by a sky which, if not grey with clouds, was of a troubled and washed-out blue. But the people were better off than by day. Tired out, overwrought, exhausted, prematurely aged as they were, they sought and found comfort in the lap of the dreamy, secret, inscrutable night. Their misery was left far behind, and they felt no more grief and pain.

An unknown power hid everything from them as though with a thick, damp, stone wall, and they heard and saw nothing.

They did not hear the weak voices, like the mewing of blind kittens, of their pining children, begging all day for food as though on purpose—as though they knew there was none to give them. They did not hear the sighs and groans of their friends and neighbors, filling the air with the hoarse sound of furniture dragged across the floor; they did not see, in sleep, Death-from-hunger swing quivering, on threads of spider-web, above their heads.

Even the little fires that flickered feverishly on their hearths, and testified to the continued existence of breathing men, even these they saw no longer. Silence cradled everything to sleep, extinguished it, and caused it to be forgotten.

Hardly, however, was it dawn, hardly had the first rays pierced beneath the closed eyelids, before a whole world of misery awoke and came to life again.

The frantic cries of hundreds of starving children, despairing exclamations and imprecations and other

piteous sounds filled the air. One gigantic curse un-
coiled and crept from house to house, from door to
door, from mouth to mouth, and the population began
to move, to bestir themselves, to run hither and thither.

Half-naked, with parched bones and shrivelled skin,
with sunken yet burning eyes, they crawled over one
another like worms in a heap, fastened on to the bites
in each other's mouth, and tore them away—

But this is summer, and they are feeling compara-
tively cheerful, bold, and free in their movements.
They are stifled and suffocated, they are in a melting-
pot with heat and exhaustion, but there are counter-
balancing advantages; one can live for weeks at a time
without heating the stove; indeed, it is pleasanter indoors without fire, and lighting will cost very little,
now the evenings are short.

In winter it was different. An inclement sky, an
enfeebled sun, a sick day, and a burning, biting frost!

People, too, were different. A bitterness came over
them, and they went about anxious and irritable, with
hanging head, possessed by gloomy despair. It never
even occurred to them to tear their neighbor's bite
out of his mouth, so depressed and preoccupied did
they become. The days were months, the evenings
years, and the weeks—oh! the weeks were eternities!

And no one knew of their misery but the winter
wind that tore at their roofs and howled in their all
but smokeless chimneys like one bewitched, like a lost
soul condemned to endless wandering.

But there were bright stars in the abysmal darkness; their one pride and consolation were the Pid-

vorkes, the inhabitants of the aforementioned district of that name. Was it a question of the upkeep of a Reader or of a bath, the support of a burial-society, of a little hospital or refuge, a Rabbi, of providing Sabbath loaves for the poor, flour for the Passover, the dowry of a needy bride—the Pidvorkes were ready! The sick and lazy, the poverty-stricken and hopeless, found in them support and protection. The Pidvorkes! They were an inexhaustible well that no one had ever found to fail them, unless the Pidvorke husbands happened to be present, on which occasion alone one came away with empty hands.

The fair fame of the Pidvorkes extended beyond Pereyaslav to all poor towns in the neighborhood. Talk of husbands—they knew about the Pidvorkes a hundred miles round; the least thing, and they pointed out to their wives how they should take a lesson from the Pidvorke women, and then they would be equally rich and happy.

It was not because the Pidvorkes had, within their border, great, green velvety hills and large gardens full of flowers that they had reason to be proud, or others, to be proud of them; not because wide fields, planted with various kinds of corn, stretched for miles around them, the delicate ears swaying in sunshine and wind; not even because there flowed round the Pidvorkes a river so transparent, so full of the reflection of the sky, you could not decide which was the bluest of the two. Pereyaslav at any rate was not affected by any of these things, perhaps knew nothing of them, and certainly did not wish to know anything, for whoso dares to let his mind dwell on the like, sins against God. Is it a Jewish concern? A townful of men who have a God, and religious duties to perform, with reward and punishment, who have *that* world to prepare for, and a wife and children in *this* one, people must be mad (of the enemies of Zion be it said!) to stare at the sky, the fields, the river, and all the rest of it—things which a man on in years ought to blush to talk about.

No, they are proud of the Pidvorke women, and parade them continually. The Pidvorke women are no more attractive, no taller, no cleverer than others. They, too, bear children and suckle them, one a year, after the good old custom; neither are they more thought of by their husbands. On the contrary, they are the best abused and tormented women going, and herein lies their distinction.

They put up, with the indifference of all women alike, to the belittling to which they are subjected by their husbands; they swallow their contempt by the mouthful without a reproach, and yet they are exceptions, and yet they are distinguished from all other women, as the rushing waters of the Dnieper from the stagnant pools in the marsh.

About five in the morning, when the men-folk turn in bed, and bury their faces in the white feather pillows, emitting at the same time strange, broken sounds through their big, stupid, red noses—at this early hour their wives have transacted half-a-day's business in the market-place. Dressed in short, light skirts with blue aprons, over which depends on their left a large leather pocket for the receiving of coin and the giving

out of change—one cannot be running every minute
to the cash-box—they stand in their shops with miscellaneous ware, and toil hard. They weigh and measure, buy and sell, and all this with wonderful celerity.
There stands one of them by herself in a shop, and
tries to persuade a young, barefoot peasant woman to
buy the printed cotton she offers her, although the
customer only wants a red cotton with a large, flowery
pattern. She talks without a pause, declaring that the
young peasant may depend upon her, she would not
take her in for the world, and, indeed, to no one else
would she sell the article so cheap. But soon her eye
catches two other women pursuing a peasant man, and
before even making out whether he has any wares with
him or not, she leaves her customer and joins them. If
they run, she feels so must she. The peasant is sure
to be wanting grease or salt, and that may mean ten
kopeks' unexpected gain. Meantime she is not likely
to lose her present customer, fascinated as the latter
must be by her flow of speech.

So she leaves her, and runs after the peasant, who
is already surrounded by a score of women, shrieking,
one louder than the other, praising their ware to the
skies, and each trying to make him believe that he and
she are old acquaintances. But presently the tumult increases, there is a cry, "Cheap fowls, who wants cheap
fowls?" Some rich landholder has sent out a supply
of fowls to sell, and all the women swing round towards
the fowls, keeping a hold on the peasant's cart with their
left hand, so that you would think they wanted to
drag peasant, horse, and cart along with them. They

bargain for a few minutes with the seller of fowls, and advise him not to be obstinate and to take their offers, else he will regret it later.

Suddenly a voice thunders, "The peasants are coming!" and they throw themselves as for dear life upon the cart-loads of produce; they run as though to a conflagration, get under each other's feet, their eyes glisten as though they each wanted to pull the whole market aside. There is a shrieking and scolding, until one or another gets the better of the rest, and secures the peasant's wares. Then only does each woman remember that she has customers waiting in her shop, and she runs in with a beaming smile and tells them that, as they have waited so long, they shall be served with the best and the most beautiful of her store.

By eight o'clock in the morning, when the market is over, when they have filled all the bottles left with them by their customers, counted up the change and their gains, and each one has slipped a coin into her knotted handkerchief, so that her husband should not know of its existence (one simply must! One is only human—one is surely not expected to wrangle with *him* about every farthing?)—then, when there is nothing more to be done in the shops, they begin to gather in knots, and every one tells at length the incidents and the happy strokes of business of the day. They have forgotten all the bad luck they wished each other, all the abuse they exchanged, while the market was in progress; they know that "Parnosseh is Parnosseh," and bear no malice, or, if they do, it is only if one has spoken unkindly of another during a period of quiet, on a Sabbath or a holiday.

Each talks with a special enthusiasm, and deep in her sunken eyes with their blue-black rings there burns a proud, though tiny, fire, as she recalls how she got the better of a customer, and sold something which she had all but thrown away, and not only sold it, but better than usual; or else they tell how late their husbands sleep, and then imagine their wives are still in bed, and set about waking them, "It's time to get up for the market," and they at once pretend to be sleepy—then, when they have already been and come back!

And very soon a voice is heard to tremble with pleasant excitement, and a woman begins to relate the following:

"Just you listen to me: I was up to-day when God Himself was still asleep."—"That is not the way to talk, Sheine!" interrupts a second.—"Well, well, well?" (there is a good deal of curiosity). "And what happened?"—"It was this way: I went out quietly, so that no one should hear, not to wake them, because when Lezer went to bed, it was certainly one o'clock. There was a dispute of some sort at the Rabbi's. You can imagine how early it was, because I didn't even want to wake Soreh, otherwise she always gets up when I do (never mind, it won't hurt her to learn from her mother!). And at half past seven, when I saw there were no more peasants coming in to market, I went to see what was going on indoors. I heard my man calling me to wake up: 'Sheine, Sheine, Sheine!' and I go quietly and lean against the bed, and wait to hear what will happen next. 'Look here!—There is no waking her!—Sheine! It's getting-up time and past! Are you deaf or half-witted? What's come to you this morning?' I was so afraid I should laugh. I gave a jump and called out, O woe is me, why ever didn't you wake me sooner? Bandit! It's already eight o'clock!"

Her hearers go off into contented laughter, which grows clearer, softer, more contented still. Each one tells her tale of how *she* was wakened by her husband, and one tells this joke: Once, when her husband had called to rouse her (he also usually woke her *after* market), she answered that on that morning she did not intend to get up for market, that *he* might go for once instead. This apparently pleases them still better, for their laughter renews itself, more spontaneous and hearty even than before. Each makes a witty remark, each feels herself in merry mood, and all is cheerfulness.

They would wax a little more serious only when they came to talk of their daughters. A woman would begin by trying to recall her daughter's age, and beg a second one to help her remember when the girl was born, so that she might not make a mistake in the calculation. And when it came to one that had a daughter of sixteen, the mother fell into a brown study; she felt herself in a very, very critical position, because when a girl comes to that age, one ought soon to marry her. And there is really nothing to prevent it: money enough will be forthcoming, only let the right kind of suitor present himself, one, that is, who shall insist on a well-dowered bride, because otherwise—what sort of a suitor do you call that? She will have enough to live on, they will buy a shop for her, she is quite capable of managing it—only let Heaven send a young man of acceptable parentage, so that one's husband shall have no need to blush with shame when he is asked about his son-in-law's family and connections.

And this is really what they used to do, for when their daughters were sixteen, they gave them in marriage, and at twenty the daughters were "old," much-experienced wives. They knew all about teething, chicken-pox, measles, and more besides, even about croup. If a young mother's child fell ill, she hastened to her bosom crony, who knew a lot more than she, having been married one whole year or two sooner, and got advice as to what should be done.

The other would make close inquiry whether the round swellings about the child's neck increased in size and wandered, that is, appeared at different times and different places, in which case it was positively nothing serious, but only the tonsils. But if they remained in one place and grew larger, the mother must lose no time, but must run to the doctor.

Their daughters knew that they needed to lay by money, not only for a dowry, but because a girl ought to have money of her own. They knew as well as their mothers that a bridegroom would present himself and ask a lot of money (the best sign of his being the right sort!), and they prayed God for the same without ceasing.

No sooner were they quit of household matters than they went over to the discussion of their connections and alliances—it was the greatest pleasure they had.

The fact that their children, especially their daughters, were so discreet that not one (to speak in a good hour and be silent in a bad!) had as yet ever (far be it from the speaker to think of such a thing!) given birth to a bastard, as was known to happen in other places—this was the crowning point of their joy and exultation.

It even made up to them for the other fact, that they never got a good word from their husbands for their hard, unnatural toil.

And as they chat together, throwing in the remark that "the apple never falls far from the tree," that their daughters take after them in everything, the very wrinkles vanish from their shrivelled faces, a spring of refreshment and blessedness wells up in their hearts, they are lifted above their cares, a feeling of relaxation comes over them, as though a soothing balsam had penetrated their strained and weary limbs.

Meantime the daughters have secrets among themselves. They know a quantity of interesting things that have happened in their quarter, but no one else gets to know of them; they are imparted more with the eyes than with the lips, and all is quiet and confidential.

And if the great calamity had not now befallen the Pidvorkes, had it not stretched itself, spread its claws with such an evil might, had the shame not been so deep and dreadful, all might have passed off quietly as always. But the event was so extraordinary, so cruelly unique—such a thing had not happened since girls were girls, and bridegrooms, bridegrooms, in the Pid-

vorkes—that it inevitably became known to all. Not
(preserve us!) to the men—they know of nothing, and
need to know of nothing—only to the women. But
how much can anyone keep to oneself? It will rise
to the surface, and lie like oil on the water.

From early morning on the women have been hissing and steaming, bubbling and boiling over. They
are not thinking of Parnosseh; they have forgotten all
about Parnosseh; they are in such a state, they have
even forgotten about themselves. There is a whole
crowd of them packed like herrings, and all fire and
flame. But the male passer-by hears nothing of what
they say, he only sees the troubled faces and the drooping heads; they are ashamed to look into one another's
eyes, as though they themselves were responsible for
the great affliction. An appalling misfortune, an
overwhelming sense of shame, a yellow-black spot on
their reputation weighs them to the ground. Uncleanness has forced itself into their sanctuary and defiled
it; and now they seek a remedy, and means to save
themselves, like one drowning; they want to heal the
plague spot, to cover it up, so that no one shall find
it out. They stand and think, and wrinkle the brows
so used to anxiety; their thoughts evolve rapidly, and
yet no good result comes of it, no one sees a way of
escape out of the terrifying net in which the worst
of all evil has entangled them. Should a stranger
happen to come upon them now, one who has heard
of them, but never seen them, he would receive a shock.
The whole of Pidvorkes looks quite different, the
women, the streets, the very sun shines differently, with

pale and narrow beams, which, instead of cheering, seem to burden the heart.

The little grey-curled clouds with their ragged edges, which have collected somewhere unbeknown, and race across the sky, look down upon the women, and whisper among themselves. Even the old willows, for whom the news is no novelty, for many more and more complicated mysteries have come to their knowledge, even they look sad, while the swallows, by the depressed and gloomy air with which they skim the water, plainly express their opinion, which is no other than this: God is punishing the Pidvorkes for *their* great sin, what time they carried fire in their beaks, long ago, to destroy the Temple.

God bears long with people's iniquity, but he rewards in full at the last.

The peasants driving slowly to market, unmolested and unobstructed, neither dragged aside nor laid forcible hold of, were singularly disappointed. They began to think the Jews had left the place.

And the women actually forgot for very trouble that it was market-day. They stood with hands folded, and turned feverishly to every newcomer. What does she say to it? Perhaps she can think of something to advise.

No one answered; they could not speak; they had nothing to say; they only felt that a great wrath had been poured out on them, heavy as lead, that an evil spirit had made its way into their life, and was keeping them in a perpetual state of terror; and that, were they now to hold their peace, and not make an end, God

30

Almighty only knows what might come of it! No one felt certain that to-morrow or the day after the same thunderbolt might not fall on another of them.

Somebody made a movement in the crowd, and there was a sudden silence, as though all were preparing to listen to a weak voice, hardly louder than stillness itself. Their eyes widened, their faces were contracted with annoyance and a consciousness of insult. Their hearts beat faster, but without violence. Suddenly there was a shock, a thrill, and they looked round with startled gaze, to see whence it came, and what was happening. And they saw a woman forcing her way frantically through the crowd, her hands working, her lips moving as in fever, her eyes flashing fire, and her voice shaking as she cried: "Come on and see me settle them! First I shall thrash *him,* and then I shall go for *her!* We must make a cinder-heap of them; it's all we can do."

She was a tall, bony woman, with broad shoulders, who had earned for herself the nickname Cossack, by having, with her own hands, beaten off three peasants who wanted to strangle her husband, he, they declared, having sold them by false weight—it was the first time he had ever tried to be of use to her.

"But don't shout so, Breindel!" begged a woman's voice.

"What do you mean by 'don't shout'! Am I going to hold my tongue? Never you mind, I shall take no water into my mouth. I'll teach them, the apostates, to desecrate the whole town!"

"But don't shout so!" beg several more.

Breindel takes no notice. She clenches her right fist, and, fighting the air with it, she vociferates louder than ever:

"What has happened, women? What are you frightened of? Look at them, if they are not all a little afraid! That's what brings trouble. Don't let us be frightened, and we shall spare ourselves in the future. We shall not be in terror that to-morrow or the day after (they had best not live to hear of it, sweet Father in Heaven!) another of us should have this come upon her!"

Breindel's last words made a great impression. The women started as though someone had poured cold water over them without warning. A few even began to come forward in support of Breindel's proposal. Soreh Leoh said: She advised going, but only to him, the bridegroom, and telling him not to give people occasion to laugh, and not to cause distress to her parents, and to agree to the wedding's taking place to-day or to-morrow, before anything happened, and to keep quiet.

"I say, he shall not live to see it; he shall not be counted worthy to have us come begging favors of him!" cried an angry voice.

But hereupon rose that of a young woman from somewhere in the crowd, and all the others began to look round, and no one knew who it was speaking. At first the young voice shook, then it grew firmer and firmer, so that one could hear clearly and distinctly what was said:

"You might as well spare yourselves the trouble of talking about a thrashing; it's all nonsense; besides, why add to her parents' grief by going to them? Isn't it bad enough for them already? If we really want to do something, the best would be to say nothing to anybody, not to get excited, not to ask anybody's help, and let us make a collection out of our own pockets. Never mind! God will repay us twice what we give. Let us choose out two of us, to take him the money quietly, so that no one shall know, because once a whisper of it gets abroad, it will be carried over seven seas in no time; you know that walls have ears, and streets, eyes."

The women had been holding their breath and looking with pleasurable pride at young Malkehle, married only two months ago and already so clever! The great thick wall of dread and shame against which they had beaten their heads had retreated before Malkehle's soft words; they felt eased; the world grew lighter again. Every one felt envious in her heart of hearts of her to whose apt and golden speech they had just listened. Everyone regretted that such an excellent plan had not occurred to herself. But they soon calmed down, for after all it was a sister who had spoken, one of their own Pidvorkes. They had never thought that Malkehle, though she had been considered clever as a girl, would take part in their debate; and they began to work out a plan for getting together the necessary money, only so quietly that not a cock should crow.

And now their perplexities began! Not one of them could give such a great sum, and even if they all clubbed together, it would still be impossible. They could manage one hundred, two hundred, three hundred rubles, but the dowry was six hundred, and now he says, that

unless they give one thousand, he will break off the
engagement. What, says he, there will be a summons
out against him? Very likely! He will just risk it. The
question went round: Who kept a store in a knotted
handkerchief, hidden from her husband? They each
had such a store, but were all the contents put together,
the half of the sum would not be attained, not by a long
way.

And again there arose a tempest, a great confusion of
women's tongues. Part of the crowd started with fiery
eloquence to criticise their husbands, the good-for-nothings, the slouching lazybones; they proved that as their
husbands did nothing to earn money, but spent all their
time "learning," there was no need to be afraid of them;
and if once in a way they wanted some for themselves,
nobody had the right to say them nay. Others said that
the husbands were, after all, the elder, one must and
should ask their advice! They were wiser and knew best,
and why should they, the women (might the words not be
reckoned as a sin!), be wiser than the rest of the world
put together? And others again cried that there was no
need that they should divorce their husbands because a
girl was with child, and the bridegroom demanded the
dowry twice over.

The noise increased, till there was no distinguishing
one voice from another, till one could not make out
what her neighbor was saying: she only knew that
she also must shriek, scold, and speak her mind. And
who knows what would have come of it, if Breindel-
Cossack, with her powerful gab, had not begun to shout,
that she and Malkehle had a good idea, which would

please everyone very much, and put an end to the whole dispute.

All became suddenly dumb; there was a tense silence, as at the first of the two recitals of the Eighteen Benedictions; the women only cast inquiring looks at Malkehle and Breindel, who both felt their cheeks hot. Breindel, who, ever since the wise Malkehle had spoken such golden words, had not left her side, now stepped forward, and her voice trembled with emotion and pleasant excitement as she said: "Malkehle and I think like this: that we ought to go to Chavvehle, she being so wise and so well-educated, a doctor's wife, and tell her the whole story from beginning to end, so that she may advise us, and if you are ashamed to speak to her yourselves, you should leave it to us two, only on the condition that you go with us. Don't be frightened, she is kind; she will listen to us."

A faint smile, glistening like diamond dust, shone on all faces; their eyes brightened and their shoulders straightened, as though just released from a heavy burden. They all knew Chavvehle for a good and gracious woman, who was certain to give them some advice; she did many such kindnesses without being asked; she had started the school, and she taught their children for nothing; she always accompanied her husband on his visits to the sick-room, and often left a coin of her own money behind to buy a fowl for the invalid. It was even said that she had written about them in the newspapers! She was very fond of them. When she talked with them, her manner was simple, as though they were her equals, and she would ask them all about everything, like any plain Jewish housewife. And yet they were conscious of a great distance between them and Chavveh. They would have liked Chavveh to hear nothing of them but what was good, to stand justified in her eyes as (ten times lehavdil) in those of a Christian. They could not have told why, but the feeling was there.

They are proud of Chavveh; it is an honor for them each and all (and who are they that they should venture to pretend to it?) to possess such a Chavveh, who was highly spoken of even by rich Gentiles. Hence this embarrassed smile at the mention of her name; she would certainly advise, but at the same time they avoided each other's look. The wise Malkeh had the same feeling, but she was able to cheer the rest. Never mind! It doesn't matter telling her. She is a Jewish daughter, too, and will keep it to herself. These things happen behind the "high windows" also. Whereupon they all breathed more freely, and went up the hill to Chavveh. They went in serried ranks, like soldiers, shoulder to shoulder, relief and satisfaction reflected in their faces. All who met them made way for them, stood aside, and wondered what it meant. Some of their own husbands even stood and looked at the marching women, but not one dared to go up to them and ask what was doing. Their object grew dearer to them at every step. A settled resolve and a deep sense of good-will to mankind urged them on. They all felt that they were going in a good cause, and would thereby bar the road to all such occurrences in the future.

The way to Chavveh was long. She lived quite out-side the Pidvorkes, and they had to go through the whole market-place with the shops, which stood close to one another, as though they held each other by the hand, and then only through narrow lanes of old thatched peasant huts, with shy little window-panes. But beside nearly every hut stood a couple of acacia-trees, and the foam-white blossoms among the young green leaves gave a refreshing perfume to the neighborhood. Emerging from the streets, they proceeded towards a pretty hill planted with pink flowering quince-trees. A small, clear stream flowed below it to the left, so deceptively clear that it reflected the hillside in all its natural tints. You had to go quite close in order to make sure it was only a delusion, when the stream met your gaze as seriously as though there were no question of *it* at all.

On the top of the hill stood Chavveh's house, adorned like a bride, covered with creepers and quinces, and with two large lamps under white glass shades, upheld in the right hands of two statues carved in white marble. The distance had not wearied them; they had walked and conversed pleasantly by the way, each telling a story somewhat similar to the one that had occasioned their present undertaking.

"Do you know," began Shifreh, the wholesale dealer, "mine tried to play me a trick with the dowry, too? It was immediately before the ceremony, and he insisted obstinately that unless a silver box and fifty rubles were given to him in addition to what had been promised to him, he would not go under the marriage canopy!"

"Well, if it hadn't been Zorah, it would have been Chayyim Treitel," observed some one, ironically.

They all laughed, but rather weakly, just for the sake of laughing; not one of them really wished to part from her husband, even in cases where he disliked her, and they quarrelled. No indignity they suffered at their husbands' hands could hurt them so deeply as a wish on his part to live separately. After all they are man and wife. They quarrel and make it up again.

And when they spied Chavvehle's house in the distance, they all cried out joyfully, with one accord:

"There is Chavvehle's house!" Once more they forgot about themselves; they were filled with enthusiasm for the common cause, and with a pain that will lie forever at their heart should they not do all that sinful man is able.

The wise Malkehle's heart beat faster than anyone's. She had begun to consider how she should speak to Chavvehle, and although apt, incisive phrases came into her head, one after another, she felt that she would never be able to come out with them in Chavvehle's presence; were it not for the other women's being there, she would have felt at her ease.

All of a sudden a voice exclaimed joyfully, "There we are at the house!" All lifted their heads, and their eyes were gladdened by the sight of the tall flowers arranged about a round table, in the shelter of a widely-branching willow, on which there shone a silver samovar. In and out of the still empty tea-glasses there stole beams of the sinking sun, as it dropt lower and lower behind the now dark-blue hill.

"What welcome guests!" Chavveh met them with a sweet smile, and her eyes awoke answering love and confidence in the women's hearts.

Not a glance, not a movement betrayed surprise on Chavvehle's part, any more than if she had been expecting them everyone.

They felt that she was behaving like any sage, and were filled with a sense of guilt towards her.

Chavvehle excused herself to one or two other guests who were present, and led the women into her summer-parlor, for she had evidently understood that what they had come to say was for her ears only.

They wanted to explain at once, but they couldn't, and the two who of áll found it hardest to speak were the selected spokeswomen, Breindel-Cossack and Malkehle the wise. Chavvehle herself tried to lead them out of their embarrassment.

"You evidently have something important to tell me," she said, "for otherwise one does not get a sight of you."

And now it seemed more difficult than ever, it seemed impossible ever to tell the angelic Chavvehle of the bad action about which they had come. They all wished silently that their children might turn out one-tenth as good as she was, and their impulse was to take Chavvehle into their arms, kiss her and hug her, and cry a long, long time on her shoulder; and if she cried with them, it would be so comforting.

Chavvehle was silent. Her great, wide-open blue eyes grew more and more compassionate as she gazed at the faces of her sisters; it seemed as though they were reading for themselves the sorrowful secret the women had come to impart.

And the more they were impressed with her tactful behavior, and the more they felt the kindness of her gaze, the more annoyed they grew with themselves, the more tongue-tied they became. The silence was so intense as to be almost seen and felt. The women held their breath, and only exchanged roundabout glances, to find out what was going on in each other's mind; and they looked first of all at the two who had undertaken to speak, while the latter, although they did not see this, felt as if every one's gaze was fixed upon them, wondering why they were silent and holding all hearts by a thread.

Chavvehle raised her head, and spoke sweetly:

"Well, dear sisters, tell me a little of what it is about. Do you want my help in any matter? I should be so glad——"

"Dear sisters" she called them, and lightning-like it flashed through their hearts that Chavveh was, indeed, their sister. How could they feel otherwise when they had it from Chavveh herself? Was she not one of their own people? Had she not the same God? True, her speech was a little strange to them, and she was not overpious, but how should God be angry with such a Chavveh as this? If it must be, let him punish *them* for her sin; they would willingly suffer in her place.

The sun had long set; the sky was grey, save for one red streak, and the room had grown dark. Chavvehle rose to light the candles, and the women started and wiped their tearful eyes, so that Chavveh should not remark them. Chavveh saw the difficulty they had in opening their hearts to her, and she began to speak to them of different things, offered them refreshment according to their several tastes, and now Malkehle felt a little more courageous, and managed to say:

"No, good, kind Chavvehle, we are not hungry. We have come to consult with you on a very important matter!"

And then Breindel tried hard to speak in a soft voice, but it sounded gruff and rasping:

"First of all, Chavveh, we want you to speak to us in Yiddish, not in Polish. We are all Jewish women, thank God, together!"

Chavvehle, who had nodded her head during the whole of Breindel's speech, made another motion of assent with her silken eyebrows, and replied:

"I will talk Yiddish to you with pleasure, if that is what you prefer."

"The thing is this, Chavvehle," began Shifreh, the wholesale dealer, "it is a shame and a sorrow to tell, but when the thunderbolt has fallen, one must speak. You know Rochel Esther Leoh's. She is engaged, and the wedding was to have been in eight weeks—and now she, the good-for-nothing, is with child—and he, the son of perdition, says now that if he isn't given more than five hundred rubles, he won't take her——"

Chavvehle was deeply troubled by their words. She saw how great was their distress, and found, to her regret, that she had little to say by way of consolation.

"I feel with you," she said, "in your pain. But do not be so dismayed. It is certainly very bad news, but these things will happen, you are not the first——"

She wanted to say more, but did not know how to continue.

"But what are we to do?" asked several voices at once. "That is what we came to you for, dearie, for you to advise us. Are we to give him all the money he asks, or shall they both know as much happiness as we know what to do else? Or are we to hang a stone round our necks and drown ourselves for shame? Give us some advice, dear, help us!"

Then Chavvehle understood that it was not so much the women who were speaking and imploring, as their stricken hearts, their deep shame and grief, and it was with increased sympathy that she answered them:

"What can I say to help you, dear sisters? You have certainly not deserved this blow; you have enough to bear as it is—things ought to have turned out quite differently; but now that the misfortune has happened, one must be brave enough not to lose one's head, and not to let such a thing happen again, so that it should be the first and last time! But what exactly you should do, I cannot tell you, because I don't know! Only if you should want my help or any money, I will give you either with the greatest pleasure."

They understood each other——

The women parted with Chavveh in great gladness, and turned towards home conscious of a definite purpose. Now they all felt they knew just what to do, and were sure it would prevent all further misfortune and disgrace.

They could have sung out for joy, embraced the hill, the stream, the peasant huts, and kissed and fondled them all together. Mind you, they had even now no definite plan of action, it was just Chavvehle's sympathy that had made all the difference—feeling that Chavveh was with them! Wrapped in the evening mist, they stepped vigorously and cheerily homewards.

Gradually the speed and the noise of their march increased, the air throbbed, and at last a high, sharp voice rose above the rest, whereupon they grew stiller, and the women listened.

"I tell you what, we won't beat them. Only on Sabbath we must all come together like one man, break into the house-of-study just before they call up to the Reading of the Law, and not let them read till they have sworn to agree to our sentence of excommunication!

"She is right!"

"Excommunicate him!"

"Tear him in pieces!"

"Let him be dressed in robe and prayer-scarf, and swear by the eight black candles that he——"

"Swear! Swear!"

The noise was dreadful. No one was allowed to finish speaking. They were all aflame with one fire of revenge, hate, and anger, and all alike athirst for justice. Every new idea, every new suggestion was hastily and hotly seized upon by all together, and there was a grinding of teeth and a clenching of fists. Nature herself seemed affected by the tumult, the clouds flew faster, the stars changed their places, the wind whistled, the trees swayed hither and thither, the frogs croaked, there was a great boiling up of the whole concern.

"Women, women," cried one, "I propose that we go to the court of the Shool, climb into the round mill-stones, and all shout together, so that they may know what we have decided."

"Right! Right! To the Shool!" cried a chorus of voices.

A common feeling of triumph running through them, they took each other friendly-wise by the hand, and made gaily for the court of the Shool. When they got into the town, they fell on each other's necks, and kissed each other with tears and joy. They knew their plan was the best and most excellent that could be devised, and would protect them all from further shame and trouble.

The Pidvorkes shuddered to hear their tread.

All the remaining inhabitants, big and little, men and women, gathered in the court of the Shool, and stood with pale faces and beating hearts to see what would happen.

The eyes of the young bachelors rolled uneasily, the girls had their faces on one another's shoulders, and sobbed.

Breindel, agile as a cat, climbed on to the highest millstone, and proclaimed in a voice of thunder:

"Seeing that such and such a thing has happened, a great scandal such as is not to be hid, and such as we do not wish to hide, all we women have decided to excommunicate——"

Such a tumult arose that for a minute or two Breindel could not be heard, but it was not long before everyone knew who and what was meant.

"We also demand that neither he nor his nearest friends shall be called to the Reading of the Law;

that people shall have nothing to do with them till after the wedding!"

"Nothing to do with them! Nothing to do with them!" shook the air.

"That people shall not lend to them nor borrow of them, shall not come within their four ells!" continued the voice from the millstone.

"And *she* shall be shut up till her time comes, so that no one shall see her. Then we will take her to the burial-ground, and the child shall be born in the burial-ground. The wedding shall take place by day, and without musicians——"

"Without musicians!"

"Without musicians!"

"Without musicians!"

"Serve her right!"

"She deserves worse!"

A hundred voices were continually interrupting the speaker, and more women were climbing onto the mill-stones, and shouting the same things.

"On the wedding-day there will be great black candles burning throughout the whole town, and when the bride is seated at the top of the marriage-hall, with her hair flowing loose about her, all the girls shall surround her, and the Badchen shall tell her, 'This is the way we treat one who has not held to her Jewishness, and has blackened all our faces——' "

"Yes!"

"Yes!"

"So it is!"

"The apostates!"

The last words struck the hearers' hearts like poisoned arrows. A deathly pallor, born of unrealized terror at the suggested idea, overspread all their faces, their feelings were in a tumult of shame and suffering. They thirsted and longed after their former life, the time before the calamity disturbed their peace. Weary and wounded in spirit, with startled looks, throbbing pulses, and dilated pupils, and with no more than a faint hope that all might yet be well, they slowly broke the stillness, and departed to their homes.

LÖB SCHAPIRO

Born, about 1880, in the Government of Kieff, Little Russia; came to Chicago in 1906, and to New York for a short time in 1907-1908; now (1912) in business in Switzerland; contributor to Die Zukunft, New York; collected works, Novellen, 1 vol., Warsaw, 1910.

IF IT WAS A DREAM

Yes, it was a terrible dream! But when one is only nine years old, one soon forgets, and Meyer was nine a few weeks before it came to pass.

Yes, and things had happened in the house every now and then to remind one of it, but then Meyer lived more out of doors than indoors, in the wild streets of New York. Tartilov and New York—what a difference! New York had supplanted Tartilov, effaced it from his memory. There remained only a faint occasional recollection of that horrid dream.

If it really *was* a dream!

It was this way: Meyer dreamt that he was sitting in Cheder learning, but more for show's sake than seriously, because during the Days of Penitence, near the close of the session, the Rebbe grew milder, and Cheder less hateful. And as he sat there and learnt, he heard a banging of doors in the street, and through the window saw Jews running to and fro, as if bereft of their senses, flinging themselves hither and thither exactly like leaves in a gale, or as when a witch rises from the ground in a column of dust, and whirls across the road so suddenly and unexpectedly that it makes one's flesh creep. And at the sight of this running up and down in the street, the Rebbe collapsed in his chair white as death, his under lip trembling.

Meyerl never saw him again. He was told later that the Rebbe had been killed, but somehow the news

gave him no pleasure, although the Rebbe used to beat
him; neither did it particularly grieve him. It probably made no great impression on his mind. After all,
what did it mean, exactly? Killed? and the question
slipped out of his head unanswered, together with the
Rebbe, who was gradually forgotten.

And then the real horror began. They were two days
hiding away in the bath-house—he and some other little
boys and a few older people—without food, without
drink, without Father and Mother. Meyer was not
allowed to get out and go home, and once, when he
screamed, they nearly suffocated him, after which he
sobbed and whimpered, unable to stop crying all at
once. Now and then he fell asleep, and when he woke
everything was just the same, and all through the terror
and the misery he seemed to hear only one word, Goyim,
which came to have a very definite and terrible meaning
for him. Otherwise everything was in a maze, and as
far as seeing goes, he really saw nothing at all.

Later, when they came out again, nobody troubled
about him, or came to see after him, and a stranger
took him home. And neither his father nor his mother
had a word to say to him, any more than if he had just
come home from Cheder as on any other day.

Everything in the house was broken, they had twisted
his father's arm and bruised his face. His mother lay
on the bed, her fair hair tossed about, and her eyes
half-closed, her face pale and stained, and something
about her whole appearance so rumpled and sluttish—
it reminded one of a tumbled bedquilt. His father
walked up and down the room in silence, looking at no

one, his bound arm in a white sling, and when Meyerl, conscious of some invisible calamity, burst out crying, his father only gave him a gloomy, irritated look, and continued to span the room as before.

In about three weeks' time they sailed for America. The sea was very rough during the passage, and his mother lay the whole time in her berth, and was very sick. Meyerl was quite fit, and his father did nothing but pace the deck, even when it poured with rain, till they came and ordered him down-stairs.

Meyerl never knew exactly what happened, but once a Gentile on board the ship passed a remark on his father, made fun of him, or something—and his father drew himself up, and gave the other a look—nothing more than a look! And the Gentile got such a fright that he began crossing himself, and he spit out, and his lips moved rapidly. To tell the truth, Meyerl was frightened himself by the contraction of his father's mouth, the grind of his teeth, and by his eyes, which nearly started from his head. Meyerl had never seen him look like that before, but soon his father was once more pacing the deck, his head down, his wet collar turned up, his hands in his sleeves, and his back slightly bent.

When they arrived in New York City, Meyerl began to feel giddy, and it was not long before the whole of Tartilov appeared to him like a dream.

It was in the beginning of winter, and soon the snow fell, the fresh white snow, and it was something like! Meyerl was now a "boy," he went to "school," made snowballs, slid on the slides, built little fires in the middle of the street, and nobody interfered. He went home to eat and sleep, and spent what you may call his "life" in the street.

In their room were cold, piercing draughts, which made it feel dreary and dismal. Meyer's father, a lean, large-boned man, with a dark, brown face and black beard, had always been silent, and it was but seldom he said so much as "Are you there, Tzippe? Do you hear me, Tzippe?" But now his silence was frightening! The mother, on the other hand, used to be full of life and spirits, skipping about the place, and it was "Shloimeh!" here, and "Shloimeh!" there, and her tongue wagging merrily! And suddenly there was an end of it all. The father only walked back and forth over the room, and she turned to look after him like a child in disgrace, and looked and looked as though forever wanting to say something, and never daring to say it. There was something new in her look, something dog-like! Yes, on my word, something like what there was in the eyes of Mishke the dog with which Meyerl used to like playing "over there," in that little town in dreamland. Sometimes Meyerl, waking suddenly in the night, heard, or imagined he heard, his mother sobbing, while his father lay in the other bed puffing at his cigar, but so hard, it was frightening, because it made a little fire every time in the dark, as though of itself, in the air, just over the place where his father's black head must be lying. Then Meyerl's eyes would shut of themselves, his brain was confused, and his mother and the glowing sparks and the whole room sank away from him, and Meyerl dropped off to sleep.

Twice that winter his mother fell ill. The first time it lasted two days, the second, four, and both times the illness was dangerous. Her face glowed like an oven, her lower lip bled beneath her sharp white teeth, and yet wild, terrifying groans betrayed what she was suffering, and she was often violently sick, just as when they were on the sea.

At those times she looked at her husband with eyes in which there was no prayer. Mishke once ran a thorn deep into his paw, and he squealed and growled angrily, and sucked his paw, as though he were trying to swallow it, thorn and all, and the look in his eyes was the look of Meyerl's mother in her pain.

In those days his father, too, behaved differently, for, instead of walking to and fro across the room, he *ran*, puffing incessantly at his cigar, his brow like a thundercloud and occasional lightnings flashing from his eyes. He never looked at his wife, and neither of them looked at Meyerl, who then felt himself utterly wretched and forsaken.

And—it is very odd, but—it was just on these occasions that Meyerl felt himself drawn to his home. In the street things were as usual, but at home it was like being in Shool during the Solemn Days at the blowing of the ram's horn, when so many tall "fathers" stand with prayer-scarfs over their heads, and hold their breath, and when out of the distance there comes, unfolding over the heads of the people, the long, loud blast of the Shofar.

And both times, when his mother recovered, the shadow that lay on their home had darkened, his father was gloomier than ever, and his mother, when she looked at him, had a still more crushed and dog-like expression, as though she were lying outside in the dust of the street.

The snowfalls became rarer, then they ceased altogether, and there came into the air a feeling of something new—what exactly, it would have been hard for Meyerl to say. Anyhow it was something good, very good, for everyone in the street was glad of it, one could see that by their faces, which were more lightsome and gay.

On the Eve of Passover the sky of home cleared a little too, street and house joined hands through the windows, opened now for the first time since winter set in, and this neighborly act of theirs cheered Meyerl's heart.

His parents made preparations for Passover, and poor little preparations they were: there was no Matzesbaking with its merry to-do; a packet of cold, stale Matzes was brought into the house; there was no pail of beet-root soup in the corner, covered with a coarse cloth of unbleached linen; no dusty china service was fetched from the attic, where it had lain many years between one Passover and another; his father brought in a dinner service from the street, one he had bought cheap, and of which the pieces did not match. But the exhilaration of the festival made itself felt for all that, and warmed their hearts. At home, in Tartilov, it had happened once or twice that Meyerl had lain in his little bed with open eyes, staring stock-still, with terror, into the silent blackness of the night, and feeling as if

he were the only living soul in the whole world, that is,
the whole house; and the sudden crow of a cock would
be enough on these occasions to send a warm current of
relief and security through his heart.

His father's face looked a little more cheerful. In the
daytime, while he dusted the cups, his eyes had something pensive in them, but his lips were set so that you
thought: There, now, now they are going to smile!
The mother danced the Matzeh pancakes up and down
in the kitchen, so that they chattered and gurgled in the
frying-pan. When a neighbor came in to borrow a cooking pot, Meyerl happened to be standing beside his
mother. The neighbor got her pot, the women exchanged a few words about the coming holiday, and then
the neighbor said, "So we shall soon be having a rejoicing at your house?" and with a wink and a smile she
pointed at his mother with her finger, whereupon Meyerl
remarked for the first time that her figure had grown
round and full. But he had no time just then to think
it over, for there came a sound of broken china from the
next room, his mother stood like one knocked on the
head, and his father appeared in the door, and said:

"Go!"

His voice sent a quiver through the window-panes,
as if a heavy wagon were just crossing the bridge
outside at a trot, the startled neighbor turned, and
whisked out of the house.

Meyerl's parents looked ill at ease in their holiday
garb, with the faces of mourners. The whole ceremony
of the Passover home service was spoilt by an atmosphere of the last meal on the Eve of the Fast of the

Destruction of the Temple. And when Meyerl, with
the indifferent voice of one hired for the occasion, sang
out the "Why is this night different?" his heart shrank
together; there was the same hush round about him as
there is in Shool when an orphan recites the first
"Sanctification" for his dead parents.

His mother's lips moved, but gave forth no sound;
from time to time she wetted a finger with her tongue,
and turned over leaf after leaf in her service-book, and
from time to time a large, bright tear fell over her
beautiful but depressed face onto the book, or the white
table-cloth, or her dress. His father never looked at her.
Did he see she was crying? Meyerl wondered. Then,
how strangely he was reciting the Haggadah! He
would chant a portion in long-drawn-out fashion, and
suddenly his voice would break, sometimes with a gur-
gle, as though a hand had seized him by the throat and
closed it. Then he would look silently at his book, or
his eye would wander round the room with a vacant
stare. Then he would start intoning again, and again
his voice would break.

They ate next to nothing, said grace to themselves in
a whisper, after which the father said:

"Meyer, open the door!"

Not without fear, and the usual uncertainty as to the
appearance of the Prophet Elijah, whose goblet stood
filled for him on the table, Meyerl opened the door.

"Pour out Thy wrath upon the Gentiles, who do not
know Thee!"

A slight shudder ran down between Meyerl's shoulders, for a strange, quite unfamiliar voice had sounded

through the room from one end to the other, shot up against the ceiling, flung itself down again, and gone flapping round the four walls, like a great, wild bird in a cage. Meyerl hastily turned to look at his father, and felt the hair bristle on his head with fright: straight and stiff as a screwed-up fiddle-string, there stood beside the table a wild figure, in a snow-white robe, with a dark beard, a broad, bony face, and a weird, black flame in the eyes. The teeth were ground together, and the voice would go over into a plaintive roar, like that of a hungry, bloodthirsty animal. His mother sprang up from her seat, trembling in every limb, stared at him for a few seconds, and then threw herself at his feet. Catching hold of the edge of his robe with both hands, she broke into lamentation:

"Shloimeh, Shloimeh, you'd better kill me! Shloimeh! kill me! oi, oi, misfortune!"

Meyerl felt as though a large hand with long finger-nails had introduced itself into his inside, and turned it upside down with one fell twist. His mouth opened widely and crookedly, and a scream of childish terror burst from his throat. Tartilov had suddenly leapt wildly into view, affrighted Jews flew up and down the street like leaves in a storm, the white-faced Rebbe sat in his chair, his under lip trembling, his mother lay on her bed, looking all pulled about like a rumpled counterpane. Meyerl saw all this as clearly and sharply as though he had it before his eyes, he felt and knew that it was not all over, that it was only just beginning, that the calamity, the great calamity, the real calamity, was still to come, and might at any moment descend upon their heads like a thunderbolt, only *what* it was he did not know, or ask himself, and a second time a scream of distraught and helpless terror escaped his throat.

A few neighbors, Italians, who were standing in the passage by the open door, looked on in alarm, and whispered among themselves, and still the wild curses filled the room, one minute loud and resonant, the next with the spiteful gasping of a man struck to death.

"Mighty God! Pour out Thy wrath on the peoples who have no God in their hearts! Pour out Thy wrath upon the lands where Thy Name is unknown! 'He has devoured, devoured my body, he has laid waste, laid waste my house!' "

> "Thy wrath shall pursue them,
> Pursue them—o'ertake them!
> O'ertake them—destroy them,
> From under Thy heavens!"

SHALOM ASCH

Born, 1881, in Kutno, Government of Warsaw, Russian Poland; Jewish education and Hasidic surroundings; began to write in 1900, earliest works being in Hebrew; Sippurim was published in 1903, and A Städtel in 1904; wrote his first drama in 1905; distinguished for realism, love of nature, and description of patriarchal Jewish life in the villages; playwright; dramas: Gott von Nekomoh, Meschiach's Zeiten, etc.; collected works, Schriften, Warsaw, 1908-1912 (in course of publication).

A SIMPLE STORY

Feigele, like all young girls, is fond of dressing and decking herself out.

She has no time for these frivolities during the week, there is work in plenty, no evil eye! and sewing to do; rent is high, and times are bad. The father earns but little, and there is a deal wanting towards her three hundred rubles dowry, beside which her mother trenches on it occasionally, on Sabbath, when the family purse is empty.

"There are as many marriageable young men as dogs, only every dog wants a fat bone," comes into her head.

She dislikes much thinking. She is a young girl and a pretty one. Of course, one shouldn't be conceited, but when she stands in front of the glass, she sees her bright face and rosy cheeks and the fall of her black hair. But she soon forgets it all, as though she were afraid that to rejoice in it might bring her ill-luck.

Sabbath it is quite another thing—there is time and to spare, and on Sabbath Feigele's toilet knows no end.

The mother calls, "There, Feigele, that's enough! You will do very well as you are." But what should old-fashioned women like her know about it? Anything will do for them. Whether you've a hat and jacket on or not, they're just as pleased.

But a young girl like Feigele knows the difference. *He* is sitting out there on the bench, he, Eleazar, with a party of his mates, casting furtive glances, which he thinks nobody sees, and nudging his neighbor, "Look, fire and flame!" and she, Feigele, behaves as though unaware of his presence, walks straight past, as coolly and unconcernedly as you please, and as though Eleazar might look and look his eyes out after her, take his own life, hang himself, for all *she* cares.

But, O Feigele, the vexation and the heartache when one fine day you walk past, and he doesn't look at *you,* but at Malkeh, who has a new hat and jacket that suit her about as well as a veil suits a dog—and yet he looks at her, and you turn round again, and yet again, pretending to look at something else (because it isn't proper), but you just glance over your shoulder, and he is still looking after Malkeh, his whole face shining with delight, and he nudges his mate, as to say, "Do you see?" O Feigele, you need a heart of adamant, if it is not to burst in twain with mortification!

However, no sooner has Malkeh disappeared down a sidewalk, than he gets up from the bench, dragging his mate along with him, and they follow, arm-in-arm, follow Feigele like her shadow, to the end of the avenue, where, catching her eye, he nods a "Good Sabbath!" Feigele answers with a supercilious tip-tilt of her head, as much as to say, "It is all the same to me, I'm sure; I'll just go down this other avenue for a change," and, lo and behold, if she happens to look around, there is Eleazar, too, and he follows, follows like a wearisome creditor.

And then, O Feigele, such a lovely, blissful feeling comes over you. Don't look, take no notice of him, walk ahead stiffly and firmly, with your head high, let him follow and look at you. And he looks, and he follows, he would follow you to the world's end, into the howling desert. Ha, ha, how lovely it feels!

But once, on a Sabbath evening, walking in the gardens with a girl friend, and he following, Feigele turned aside down a dark path, and sat down on a bench behind a bushy tree.

He came and sat down, too, at the other end of the bench.

Evening: the many branching trees overshadow and obscure, it grows dark, they are screened and hidden from view.

A breeze blows, lightly and pleasantly, and cools the air.

They feel it good to be there, their hearts beat in the stillness.

Who will say the first word?

He coughs, ahem! to show that he is there, but she makes no sign, implying that she neither knows who he is, nor what he wants, and has no wish to learn.

They are silent, they only hear their own beating hearts and the wind in the leaves.

"I beg your pardon, do you know what time it is?"

"No, I don't," she replies stiffly, meaning, "I know quite well what you are after, but don't be in such a hurry, you won't get anything the sooner."

The girl beside her gives her a nudge. "Did you hear that?" she giggles.

Feigele feels a little annoyed with her. Does the girl think *she* is the object? And she presently prepares to rise, but remains, as though glued to the seat.

"A beautiful night, isn't it?"

"Yes, a beautiful evening."

And so the conversation gets into swing, with a question from him and an answer from her, on different subjects, first with fear and fluttering of the heart, then they get closer one to another, and become more confidential. When she goes home, he sees her to the door, they shake hands and say, "Till we meet again!"

And they meet a second and a third time, for young hearts attract each other like a magnet. At first, of course, it is accidental, they meet by chance in the company of two other people, a girl friend of hers and a chum of his, and then, little by little, they come to feel that they want to see each other alone, all to themselves, and they fix upon a quiet time and place.

And they met.

They walked away together, outside the town, between the sky and the fields, walked and talked, and again, conscious that the talk was an artificial one, were even more gladly silent. Evening, and the last sunbeams were gliding over the ears of corn on both sides of the way. Then a breeze came along, and the ears swayed and whispered together, as the two passed on between them down the long road. Night was gathering, it grew continually darker, more melancholy, more delightful.

"I have been wanting to know you for a long time, Feigele."

"I know. You followed me like a shadow."

They are silent.

"What are you thinking about, Feigele?"

"What are *you* thinking about, Eleazar?"

And they plunge once more into a deep converse about all sorts of things, and there seems to be no reason why it should ever end.

It grows darker and darker.

They have come to walk closer together.

Now he takes her hand, she gives a start, but his hand steals further and further into hers.

Suddenly, as dropt from the sky, he bends his face, and kisses her on the cheek.

A thrill goes through her, she takes her hand out of his and appears rather cross, but he knows it is put on, and very soon she is all right again, as if the incident were forgotten.

An hour or two go by thus, and every day now they steal away and meet outside the town.

And Eleazar began to frequent her parents' house, the first time with an excuse—he had some work for Feigele. And then, as people do, he came to know when the work would be done, and Feigele behaved as though she had never seen him before, as though not even knowing who he was, and politely begged him to take a seat.

So it came about by degrees that Eleazar was continually in and out of the house, coming and going as he pleased and without stating any pretext whatever.

Feigele's parents knew him for a steady young man, he was a skilled artisan earning a good wage, and they knew quite well why a young man comes to the home of a young girl, but they feigned ignorance, thinking to themselves, "Let the children get to know each other better, there will be time enough to talk it over afterwards."

Evening: a small room, shadows moving on the walls, a new table on which burns a large, bright lamp, and sitting beside it Feigele sewing and Eleazar reading aloud a novel by Shomer.

Father and mother, tired out with a whole day's work, sleep on their beds behind the curtain, which shuts off half the room.

And so they sit, both of them, only sometimes Eleazar laughs aloud, takes her by the hand, and exclaims with a smile, "Feigele!"

"What do you want, silly?"

"Nothing at all, nothing at all."

And she sews on, thinking, "I have got you fast enough, but don't imagine you are taking somebody from the street, just as she is; there are still eighty rubles wanting to make three hundred in the bank."

And she shows him her wedding outfit, the shifts and the bedclothes, of which half lie waiting in the drawers.

They drew closer one to another, they became more and more intimate, so that all looked upon them as engaged, and expected the marriage contract to be drawn up any day. Feigele's mother was jubilant at her daughter's good fortune, at the prospect of such a son-in-law, such a golden son-in-law!

Reb Yainkel, her father, was an elderly man, a worn-out peddler, bent sideways with the bag of junk continually on his shoulder.

Now he, too, has a little bit of pleasure, a taste of joy, for which God be praised!

Everyone rejoices, Feigele most of all, her cheeks look rosier and fresher, her eyes darker and brighter.

She sits at her machine and sews, and the whole room rings with her voice:

" Un was ich hob' gewollt, hob' ich ausgeführt,
　Soll ich azoi leben!
　Ich hob' gewollt a shenem Choson,
　Hot' mir Gott gegeben."

In the evening comes Eleazar.

"Well, what are you doing?"

"What should I be doing? Wait, I'll show you something."

"What sort of thing?"

She rises from her place, goes to the chest that stands in the stove corner, takes something out of it, and hides it under her apron.

"Whatever have you got there?" he laughs.

"Why are you in such a hurry to know?" she asks, and sits down beside him, brings from under her apron a picture in fine woolwork, Adam and Eve, and shows it him, saying:

"There, now you see! It was worked by a girl I know—for me, for us. I shall hang it up in our room, opposite the bed."

"Yours or mine?"

"You wait, Eleazar! You will see the house I shall arrange for you—a paradise, I tell you, just a little paradise! Everything in it will have to shine, so that it will be a pleasure to step inside."

"And every evening when work is done, we two shall sit together, side by side, just as we are doing now," and he puts an arm around her.

"And you will tell me everything, all about everything," she says, laying a hand on his shoulder, while with the other she takes hold of his chin, and looks into his eyes.

They feel so happy, so light at heart.

Everything in the house has taken on an air of kindliness, there is a soft, attractive gloss on every object in the room, on the walls and the table, the familiar things make signs to her, and speak to her as friend to friend.

The two are silent, lost in their own thoughts.

"Look," she says to him, and takes her bank-book out of the chest, "two hundred and forty rubles already. I shall make it up to three hundred, and then you won't have to say, 'I took you just as you were.' "

"Go along with you, you are very unjust, and I'm cross with you, Feigele."

"Why? Because I tell you the truth to your face?" she asks, looking into his face and laughing.

He turns his head away, pretending to be offended.

"You little silly, are you feeling hurt? I was only joking, can't you see?"

So it goes on, till the old mother's face peeps out from behind the curtain, warning them that it is time to go to rest, when the young couple bid each other good-night.

Reb Yainkel, Feigele's father, fell ill.

It was in the beginning of winter, and there was war between winter and summer: the former sent a snowfall, the latter a burst of sun. The snow turned to mud, and between times it poured with rain by the bucketful.

This sort of weather made the old man ill: he became weak in the legs, and took to his bed.

There was no money for food, and still less for firing, and Feigele had to lend for the time being.

The old man lay abed and coughed, his pale, shrivelled face reddened, the teeth showed between the drawn lips, and the blue veins stood out on his temples.

They sent for the doctor, who prescribed a remedy.

The mother wished to pawn their last pillow, but Feigele protested, and gave up part of her wages, and when this was not enough, she pawned her jacket—anything sooner than touch the dowry.

And he, Eleazar, came every evening, and they sat together beside the well-known table in the lamplight.

"Why are you so sad, Feigele?"

"How can you expect me to be cheerful, with father so ill?"

"God will help, Feigele, and he will get better."

"It's four weeks since I put a farthing into the savings-bank."

"What do you want to save for?"

"What do I want to save for?" she asked with a startled look, as though something had frightened her. "Are you going to tell me that you will take me without a dowry?"

"What do you mean by 'without a dowry'? You are worth all the money in the world to me, worth my whole life. What do I want with your money? See here, my five fingers, they can earn all we need. I have two hundred rubles in the bank, saved from my earnings. What do I want with more?"

They are silent for a moment, with downcast eyes. "And your mother?" she asks quietly.

"Will you please tell me, are you marrying my mother or me? And what concern is she of yours?"

Feigele is silent.

"I tell you again, I'll take you *just as you are*—and you'll take me the same, will you?"

She puts the corner of her apron to her eyes, and cries quietly to herself.

There is stillness around. The lamp sheds its brightness over the little room, and casts their shadows onto the walls.

The heavy sleeping of the old people is audible behind the curtain.

And her head lies on his shoulder, and her thick black hair hides his face.

"How kind you are, Eleazar," she whispers through her tears.

And she opens her whole heart to him, tells him how it is with them now, how bad things are, they have pawned everything, and there is nothing left for to-morrow, nothing but the dowry!

He clasps her lovingly, and dries her cheeks with her apron end, saying: "Don't cry, Feigele, don't cry. It will all come right. And to-morrow, mind, you are to go to the postoffice, and take a little of the dowry, as much as you need, until your father, God helping, is well again, and able to earn something, and then . . . "

"And then . . . " she echoes in a whisper.

"And then it will all come right," and his eyes flash into hers. "Just as you are . . . " he whispers.

And she looks at him, and a smile crosses her face.

She feels so happy, so happy.

Next morning she went to the postoffice for the first time with her bank-book, took out a few rubles, and gave them to her mother.

The mother sighed heavily, and took on a grieved expression; she frowned, and pulled her head-kerchief down over her eyes.

Old Reb Yainkel lying in bed turned his face to the wall.

The old man knew where the money came from, he knew how his only child had toiled for those few rubles. Other fathers gave money to their children, and he took it—

It seemed to him as though he were plundering the two young people. He had not long to live, and he was robbing them before he died.

As he thought on this, his eyes glazed, the veins on his temple swelled, and his face became suffused with blood.

His head is buried in the pillow, and turns to the wall, he lies and thinks these thoughts.

He knows that he is in the way of the children's happiness, and he prays that he may die.

And she, Feigele, would like to come into a fortune all at once, to have a lot of money, to be as rich as any great lady.

And then suppose she had a thousand rubles now, this minute, and he came in: "There, take the whole of it, see if I love you! There, take it, and then you needn't say you love me for nothing, just as I am."

They sit beside the father's bed, she and her Eleazar.

Her heart overflows with content, she feels happier than she ever felt before, there are even tears of joy on her cheeks.

She sits and cries, hiding her face with her apron.

He takes her caressingly by the hands, repeating in his kind, sweet voice, "Feigele, stop crying, Feigele, please!"

The father lies turned with his face to the wall, and the beating of his heart is heard in the stillness.

They sit, and she feels confidence in Eleazar, she feels that she can rely upon him.

She sits and drinks in his words, she feels him rolling the heavy stones from off her heart.

The old father has turned round and looked at them, and a sweet smile steals over his face, as though he would say, "Have no fear, children, I agree with you, I agree with all my heart."

And Feigele feels so happy, so happy . . .

The father is still lying ill, and Feigele takes out one ruble after another, one five-ruble-piece after another.

The old man lies and prays and muses, and looks at the children, and holds his peace.

His face gets paler and more wrinkled, he grows weaker, he feels his strength ebbing away.

Feigele goes on taking money out of the savings-bank, the stamps in her book grow less and less, she knows that soon there will be nothing left.

Old Reb Yainkel wishes in secret that he did not require so much, that he might cease to hamper other people!

He spits blood-drops, and his strength goes on diminishing, and so do the stamps in Feigele's book. The day he died saw the last farthing of Feigele's dowry disappear after the others.

Feigele has resumed her seat by the bright lamp, and sews and sews till far into the night, and with every seam that she sews, something is added to the credit of her new account.

This time the dowry must be a larger one, because for every stamp that is added to the account-book there is a new grey hair on Feigele's black head.

A JEWISH CHILD

The mother came out of the bride's chamber, and cast a piercing look at her husband, who was sitting beside a finished meal, and was making pellets of bread crumbs previous to saying grace.

"You go and talk to her! I haven't a bit of strength left!"

"So, Rochel-Leoh has brought up children, has she, and can't manage them! Why! People will be pointing at you and laughing—a ruin to your years!"

"To my years?! A ruin to *yours*! *My* children, are they? Are they not yours, too? Couldn't you stay at home sometimes to care for them and help me to bring them up, instead of trapesing round—the black year knows where and with whom?"

"Rochel, Rochel, what has possessed you to start a quarrel with me now? The bridegroom's family will be arriving directly."

"And what do you expect me to do, Moishehle, eh?! For God's sake! Go in to her, we shall be made a laughing-stock."

The man rose from the table, and went into the next room to his daughter. The mother followed.

On the little sofa that stood by the window sat a girl about eighteen, her face hidden in her hands, her arms covered by her loose, thick, black hair. She was evidently crying, for her bosom rose and fell like a stormy sea. On the bed opposite lay the white silk wedding-dress, the Chuppeh-Kleid, with the black, silk Shool-Kleid, and the black stuff morning-dress, which the tailor who had undertaken the outfit had brought not long ago. By the door stood a woman with a black scarf round her head and holding boxes with wigs.

"Channehle! You are never going to do me this dishonor? to make me the talk of the town?" exclaimed the father. The bride was silent.

"Look at me, daughter of Moisheh Groiss! It's all very well for Genendel Freindel's daughter to wear a wig, but not for the daughter of Moisheh Groiss? Is that it?"

"And yet Genendel Freindel might very well think more of herself than you: she is more educated than you are, and has a larger dowry," put in the mother.

The bride made no reply.

"Daughter, think how much blood and treasure it has cost to help us to a bit of pleasure, and now you want to spoil it for us? Remember, for God's sake, what you are doing with yourself! We shall be excommunicated, the young man will run away home on foot!"

"Don't be foolish," said the mother, took a wig out of a box from the woman by the door, and approached her daughter. "Let us try on the wig, the hair is just the color of yours," and she laid the strange hair on the girl's head.

The girl felt the weight, put up her fingers to her head, met among her own soft, cool, living locks, the strange, dead hair of the wig, stiff and cold, and it flashed through her, Who knows where the head to which this hair belonged is now? A shuddering enveloped her, and as though she had come in contact with something unclean, she snatched off the wig, threw in onto the floor and hastily left the room.

Father and mother stood and looked at each other in dismay.

The day after the marriage ceremony, the bridegroom's mother rose early, and, bearing large scissors, and the wig and a hood which she had brought from her home as a present for the bride, she went to dress the latter for the "breakfast."

But the groom's mother remained outside the room, because the bride had locked herself in, and would open her door to no one.

The groom's mother ran calling aloud for help to her husband, who, together with a dozen uncles and brothers-in-law, was still sleeping soundly after the evening's festivity. She then sought out the bridegroom, an eighteen-year-old boy with his mother's milk still on his lips, who, in a silk caftan and a fur cap, was moving about the room in bewildered fashion, his eyes on the ground, ashamed to look anyone in the face. In the end she fell back on the mother of the bride, and these two went in to her together, having forced open the door between them.

"Why did you lock yourself in, dear daughter. There is no need to be ashamed."

"Marriage is a Jewish institution!" said the groom's mother, and kissed her future daughter-in-law on both cheeks.

The girl made no reply.

"Your mother-in-law has brought you a wig and a hood for the procession to the Shool," said her own mother.

The band had already struck up the "Good Morning" in the next room.

"Come now, Kallehshi, Kalleh-leben, the guests are beginning to assemble."

The groom's mother took hold of the plaits in order to loosen them.

The bride bent her head away from her, and fell on her own mother's neck.

"I can't, Mame-leben! My heart won't let me, Mame-krön!"

She held her hair with both hands, to protect it from the other's scissors.

"For God's sake, my daughter, my life," begged the mother.

"In the other world you will be plunged for this into rivers of fire.   The apostate who wears her own hair after marriage will have her locks torn out with red hot pincers," said the other with the scissors.

A cold shiver went through the girl at these words.

"Mother-life, mother-crown!" she pleaded.

Her hands sought her hair, and the black silky tresses fell through them in waves.   Her hair, the hair which had grown with her growth, and lived with her life, was to be cut off, and she was never, never to have it again— she was to wear strange hair, hair that had grown on another person's head, and no one knows whether that other person was alive or lying in the earth this long time, and whether she might not come any night to one's bedside, and whine in a dead voice:

"Give me back my hair, give me back my hair!"

A frost seized the girl to the marrow, she shivered and shook.

Then she heard the squeak of scissors over her head, tore herself out of her mother's arms, made one snatch at the scissors, flung them across the room, and said in a scarcely human voice:

"My own hair! May God Himself punish me!"

That day the bridegroom's mother took herself off home again, together with the sweet-cakes and the geese which she had brought for the wedding breakfast for her own guests. She wanted to take the bridegroom as well, but the bride's mother said: "I will not give him back to you! He belongs to me already!"

The following Sabbath they led the bride in procession to the Shool wearing her own hair in the face of all the town, covered only by a large hood.

But may all the names she was called by the way find their only echo in some uninhabited wilderness.

A summer evening, a few weeks after the wedding: The young man had just returned from the Stübel, and went to his room. The wife was already asleep, and the soft light of the lamp fell on her pale face, showing here and there among the wealth of silky-black hair that bathed it. Her slender arms were flung round her head, as though she feared that someone might come by night to shear them off while she slept. He had come home excited and irritable: this was the fourth week of his married life, and they had not yet called him up to the Reading of the Law, the Chassidim pursued him, and to-day Chayyim Moisheh had blamed him in the presence of the whole congregation, and had shamed him, because *she,* his wife, went about in her own hair. "You're no better than a clay image," Reb Chayyim Moisheh had told him. "What do you mean by a woman's saying she won't? It is written: 'And he shall rule over thee.'"

And he had come home intending to go to her and say: "Woman, it is a precept in the Torah! If you persist in wearing your own hair, I may divorce you without returning the dowry," after which he would pack up his things and go home. But when he saw his little wife asleep in bed, and her pale face peeping out of the glory of her hair, he felt a great pity for her. He went up to the bed, and stood a long while looking at her, after which he called softly:

"Channehle ... Channehle ... Channehle ..."

She opened her eyes with a frightened start, and looked round in sleepy wonder:

"Nosson, did you call? What do you want?

"Nothing, your cap has slipped off," he said, lifting up the white nightcap, which had fallen from her head.

She flung it on again, and wanted to turn towards the wall.

"Channehle, Channehle, I want to talk to you."

The words went to her heart. The whole time since their marriage he had, so to say, not spoken to her. During the day she saw nothing of him, for he spent it in the house-of-study or in the Stübel. When he came home to dinner, he sat down to the table in silence. When he wanted anything, he asked for it

speaking into the air, and when really obliged to
exchange a word with her, he did so with his eyes fixed
on the ground, too shy to look her in the face. And now
he said he wanted to talk to her, and in such a gentle
voice, and they two alone together in their room!

"What do you want to say to me?" she asked softly.

"Channehle," he began, "please, don't make a fool
of me, and don't make a fool of yourself in people's eyes.
Has not God decreed that we should belong together?
You are my wife and I am your husband, and is it
proper, and what does it look like, a married woman
wearing her own hair?"

Sleep still half dimmed her eyes, and had altogether
clouded her thought and will. She felt helpless, and
her head fell lightly towards his breast.

"Child," he went on still more gently, "I know you
are not so depraved as they say. I know you are a pious
Jewish daughter, and His blessed Name will help us,
and we shall have pious Jewish children. Put away
this nonsense! Why should the whole world be talking
about you? Are we not man and wife? Is not your
shame mine?"

It seemed to her as though *someone,* at once very far
away and very near, had come and was talking to her.
Nobody had ever yet spoken to her so gently and con-
fidingly. And he was her husband, with whom she
would live so long, so long, and there would be children,
and she would look after the house!

She leant her head lightly against him.

"I know you are very sorry to lose your hair, the orna-
ment of your girlhood, I saw you with it when I was a

guest in your home. I know that God gave you grace and loveliness, I know. It cuts me to the heart that your hair must be shorn off, but what is to be done? It is a rule, a law of our religion, and after all we are Jews. We might even, God forbid, have a child conceived to us in sin, may Heaven watch over and defend us."

She said nothing, but remained resting lightly in his arm, and his face lay in the stream of her silky-black hair with its cool odor. In that hair dwelt a soul, and he was conscious of it. He looked at her long and earnestly, and in his look was a prayer, a pleading with her for her own happiness, for her happiness and his.

"Shall I?" . . . he asked, more with his eyes than with his lips.

She said nothing, she only bent her head over his lap.

He went quickly to the drawer, and took out a pair of scissors.

She laid her head in his lap, and gave her hair as a ransom for their happiness, still half-asleep and dreaming. The scissors squeaked over her head, shearing off one lock after the other, and Channehle lay and dreamt through the night.

On waking next morning, she threw a look into the glass which hung opposite the bed. A shock went through her, she thought she had gone mad, and was in the asylum! On the table beside her lay her shorn hair, dead!

She hid her face in her hands, and the little room was filled with the sound of weeping!

A SCHOLAR'S MOTHER

The market lies foursquare, surrounded on every side by low, whitewashed little houses. From the chimney of the one-storied house opposite the well and inhabited by the baker, issues thick smoke, which spreads low over the market-place. Beneath the smoke is a flying to and fro of white pigeons, and a tall boy standing outside the baker's door is whistling to them.

Equally opposite the well are stalls, doors laid across two chairs and covered with fruit and vegetables, and around them women, with head-kerchiefs gathered round their weary, sunburnt faces in the hottest weather, stand and quarrel over each other's wares.

"It's certainly worth my while to stand quarrelling with *you!* A tramp like you keeping a stall!"

Yente, a woman about forty, whose wide lips have just uttered the above, wears a large, dirty apron, and her broad, red face, with the composed glance of the eyes under the kerchief, gives support to her words.

"Do you suppose you have got the Almighty by the beard? He is mine as well as yours!" answers Taube, pulling her kerchief lower about her ears, and angrily stroking down her hair.

A new customer approached Yente's stall, and Taube, standing by idle, passed the time in vituperations.

"What do I want with the money of a fine lady like you? You'll die like the rest of us, and not a dog will say Kaddish for you," she shrieked, and came to a sudden stop, for Taube had intended to bring up the subject of her own son Yitzchokel, when she remembered that it is against good manners to praise one's own.

Yente, measuring out a quarter of pears to her customer, made answer:

"Well, if you were a little superior to what you are, your husband wouldn't have died, and your child wouldn't have to be ashamed of you, as we all know he is."

Whereon Taube flew into a rage, and shouted:

"Hussy! The idea of my son being ashamed of me! May you be a sacrifice for his littlest finger-nail, for you're not worthy to mention his name!"

She was about to burst out weeping at the accusation of having been the cause of her husband's death and of causing her son to be ashamed of her, but she kept back her tears with all her might in order not to give pleasure to Yente.

The sun was dropping lower behind the other end of the little town, Jews were hurrying across the market-place to Evening Prayer in the house-of-study street, and the Cheder-boys, just let out, began to gather round the well.

Taube collected her few little baskets into her arms (the door and the chairs she left in the market-place; nobody would steal them), and with two or three parting curses to the rude Yente, she quietly quitted the scene.

Walking home with her armful of baskets, she thought of her son Yitzchokel.

Yente's stinging remarks pursued her. It was not Yente's saying that she had caused her husband's death that she minded, for everyone knew how hard she had worked during his illness, it was her saying that Yitz-chokel was ashamed of her, that she felt in her "ribs." It occurred to her that when he came home for the night, he never would touch anything in her house.

And thinking this over, she started once more abusing Yente.

"Let her not live to see such a thing, Lord of the World, the One Father!"

It seemed to her that this fancy of hers, that Yitz-chokel was ashamed of her, was all Yente's fault, it was all her doing, the witch!

"My child, my Yitzchokel, what business is he of yours?" and the cry escaped her:

"Lord of the World, take up my quarrel, Thou art a Father to the orphaned, Thou shouldst not forgive her this!"

"Who is that? Whom are you scolding so, Taube?" called out Necheh, the rich man's wife, standing in the door of her shop, and overhearing Taube, as she scolded to herself on the walk home.

"Who should it be, housemistress, who but the hussy, the abortion, the witch," answered Taube, pointing with one finger towards the market-place, and, without so much as lifting her head to look at the person speaking to her, she went on her way.

She remembered, as she walked, how, that morn-ing, when she went into Necheh's kitchen with a fowl, she heard her Yitzchokel's voice in the other room dis-puting with Necheh's boys over the Talmud. She knew that on Wednesdays Yitzchokel ate his "day" at Necheh's table, and she had taken the fowl there that day

on purpose, so that her Yitzchokel should have a good
plate of soup, for her poor child was but weakly.

When she heard her son's voice, she had been about
to leave the kitchen, and yet she had stayed. Her Yitzchokel disputing with Necheh's children? What did
they know as compared with him? Did they come up to
his level? "He will be ashamed of me," she thought
with a start, "when he finds me with a chicken in my
hand. So his mother is a market-woman, they will say,
there's a fine partner for you!" But she had not left
the kitchen. A child who had never cost a farthing,
and she should like to know how much Necheh's children cost their parents! If she had all the money that
Yitzchokel ought to have cost, the money that ought
to have been spent on him, she would be a rich woman
too, and she stood and listened to his voice.

"Oi, *he* should have lived to see Yitzchokel, it would
have made him well." Soon the door opened, Necheh's
boys appeared, and her Yitzchokel with them. His
cheeks flamed.

"Good morning!" he said feebly, and was out at the
door in no time. She knew that she had caused him
vexation, that he was ashamed of her before his companions.

And she asked herself: Her child, her Yitzchokel, who
had sucked her milk, what had Necheh to do with him?
And she had poured out her bitterness of heart upon
Yente's head for this also, that her son had cost her
parents nothing, and was yet a better scholar than
Necheh's children, and once more she exclaimed:

"Lord of the World! Avenge my quarrel, pay her out
for it, let her not live to see another day!"

Passers-by, seeing a woman walking and scolding aloud, laughed.

Night came on, the little town was darkened.

Taube reached home with her armful of baskets, dragged herself up the steps, and opened the door.

"Mame, it's Ma-a-me !" came voices from within.

The house was full of smoke, the children clustered round her in the middle of the room, and never ceased calling out Mame! One child's voice was tearful: "Where have you been all day?" another's more cheerful: "How nice it is to have you back!" and all the voices mingled together into one.

"Be quiet! You don't give me time to draw my breath!" cried the mother, laying down the baskets.

She went to the fireplace, looked about for something, and presently the house was illumined by a smoky lamp.

The feeble shimmer lighted only the part round the hearth, where Taube was kindling two pieces of stick— an old dusty sewing-machine beside a bed, sign of a departed tailor, and a single bed opposite the lamp, strewn with straw, on which lay various fruits, the odor of which filled the room. The rest of the apartment with the remaining beds lay in shadow.

It is a year and a half since her husband, Lezer the tailor, died. While he was still alive, but when his cough had increased, and he could no longer provide for his family, Taube had started earning something on her own account, and the worse the cough, the harder she had to toil, so that by the time she became a widow, she was already used to supporting her whole family.

The eldest boy, Yitzchokel, had been the one consolation of Lezer the tailor's cheerless existence, and Lezer was comforted on his death-bed to think he should leave a good Kaddish behind him.

When he died, the householders had pity on the desolate widow, collected a few rubles, so that she might buy something to traffic with, and, seeing that Yitzchokel was a promising boy, they placed him in the house-of-study, arranged for him to have his daily meals in the houses of the rich, and bade him pass his time over the Talmud.

Taube, when she saw her Yitzchokel taking his meals with the rich, felt satisfied. A weakly boy, what could *she* give him to eat? There, at the rich man's table, he had the best of everything, but it grieved her that he should eat in strange, rich houses—she herself did not know whether she had received a kindness or the reverse, when he was taken off her hands.

One day, sitting at her stall, she spied her Yitzchokel emerge from the Shool-Gass with his Tefillin-bag under his arm, and go straight into the house of Reb Zindel the rich, to breakfast, and a pang went through her heart. She was still on terms, then, with Yente, because immediately after the death of her husband everyone had been kind to her, and she said:

"Believe me, Yente, I don't know myself what it is. What right have I to complain of the householders? They have been very good to me and to my child, made provision for him in rich houses, treated him as if he were *no* market-woman's son, but the child of gentlefolk, and yet every day when I give the other children their dinner, I forget, and lay a plate for my Yitzchokel too, and when I remember that he has his meals at other people's hands, I begin to cry."

"Go along with you for a foolish woman!" answered Yente. "How would he turn out if he were left to you? What is a poor person to give a child to eat, when you come to think of it?"

"You are right, Yente," Taube replied, "but when I portion out the dinner for the others, it cuts me to the heart."

And now, as she sat by the hearth cooking the children's supper, the same feeling came over her, that they had stolen her Yitzchokel away.

When the children had eaten and gone to bed, she stood the lamp on the table, and began mending a shirt for Yitzchokel.

Presently the door opened, and he, Yitzchokel, came in.

Yitzchokel was about fourteen, tall and thin, his pale face telling out sharply against his black cloak beneath his black cap.

"Good evening!" he said in a low tone.

The mother gave up her place to him, feeling that she owed him respect, without knowing exactly why, and it was borne in upon her that she and her poverty together were a misfortune for Yitzchokel.

He took a book out of the case, sat down, and opened it.

The mother gave the lamp a screw, wiped the globe with her apron, and pushed the lamp nearer to him.

"Will you have a glass of tea, Yitzchokel?" she asked softly, wishful to serve him.

"No, I have just had some."

"Or an apple?"

He was silent.

The mother cleaned a plate, laid two apples on it, and a knife, and placed it on the table beside him.

He peeled one of the apples as elegantly as a grown-up man, repeated the blessing aloud, and ate.

When Taube had seen Yitzchokel eat an apple, she felt more like his mother, and drew a little nearer to him.

And Yitzchokel, as he slowly peeled the second apple, began to talk more amiably:

"To-day I talked with the Dayan about going somewhere else. In the house-of-study here, there is nothing to do, nobody to study with, nobody to ask how and where, and in which book, and he advises me to go to the Academy at Makove; he will give me a letter to Reb Chayyim, the headmaster, and ask him to befriend me."

When Taube heard that her son was about to leave her, she experienced a great shock, but the words, Dayan, Rosh-Yeshiveh, mekarev-sein, and other high-sounding bits of Hebrew, which she did not understand, overawed her, and she felt she must control herself. Besides, the words held some comfort for her: Yitzchokel was holding counsel with her, with her—his mother!

"Of course, if the Dayan says so," she answered piously.

"Yes," Yitzchokel continued, "there one can hear lectures with all the commentaries; Reb Chayyim, the author of the book "Light of the Torah," is a well-known scholar, and there one has a chance of getting to be something decent."

His words entirely reassured her, she felt a certain happiness and exaltation, because he was her child, because she was the mother of such a child, such a son, and because, were it not for her, Yitzchokel would not be there at all. At the same time her heart pained her. and she grew sad.

Presently she remembered her husband, and burst out crying:

"If only *he* had lived, if only he could have had this consolation!" she sobbed.

Yitzchokel minded his book.

That night Taube could not sleep, for at the thought of Yitzchokel's departure the heart ached within her.

And she dreamt, as she lay in bed, that some great Rabbis with tall fur caps and long earlocks came in and took her Yitzchokel away from her; her Yitzchokel was wearing a fur cap and locks like theirs, and he held a large book, and he went far away with the Rabbis, and she stood and gazed after him, not knowing, should she rejoice or weep.

Next morning she woke late. Yitzchokel had already gone to his studies. She hastened to dress the children, and hurried to the market-place. At her stall she fell athinking, and fancied she was sitting beside her son, who was a Rabbi in a large town; there he sits in shoes and socks, a great fur cap on his head, and looks into a huge book. She sits at his right hand knitting a sock, the door opens, and there appears Yente carrying a dish, to ask a ritual question of Taube's son.

A customer disturbed her sweet dream.

After this Taube sat up whole nights at the table, by the light of the smoky lamp, rearranging and mending Yitzchokel's shirts for the journey; she recalled with every stitch that she was sewing for Yitzchokel, who was going to the Academy, to sit and study, and who, every Friday, would put on a shirt prepared for him by his mother.

Yitzchokel sat as always on the other side of the table, gazing into a book. The mother would have liked to speak to him, but she did not know what to say.

Taube and Yitzchokel were up before daylight.

Yitzchokel kissed his little brothers in their sleep, and said to his sleeping little sisters, "Remain in health"; one sister woke and began to cry, saying she wanted to go with him. The mother embraced and quieted her softly, then she and Yitzchokel left the room, carrying his box between them.

The street was still fast asleep, the shops were still closed, behind the church belfry the morning star shone coldly forth onto the cold morning dew on the roofs, and there was silence over all, except in the market-place, where there stood a peasant's cart laden with fruit. It was surrounded by women, and Yente's voice was heard from afar:

"Five gulden and ten groschen, and I'll take the lot!"

And Taube, carrying Yitzchokel's box behind him, walked thus through the market-place, and, catching sight of Yente, she looked at her with pride.

They came out behind the town, onto the highroad, and waited for an "opportunity" to come by on its way to Lentschitz, whence Yitzchokel was to proceed to Kutno.

The sky was grey and cold, and mingled in the distance with the dingy mist rising from the fields, and the road, silent and deserted, ran away out of sight.

They sat down beside the barrier, and waited for the "opportunity."

The mother scraped together a few twenty-kopek-pieces out of her pocket, and put them into his bosom, twisted up in his shirt.

Presently a cart came by, crowded with passengers. She secured a seat for Yitzchokel for forty groschen, and hoisted the box into the cart.

"Go in health! Don't forget your mother!" she cried in tears.

Yitzchokel was silent.

She wanted to kiss her child, but she knew it was not the thing for a grown-up boy to be kissed, so she refrained.

Yitzchokel mounted the cart, the passengers made room for him among them.

"Remain in health, mother!" he called out as the cart set off.

"Go in health, my child! Sit and study, and don't forget your mother!" she cried after him.

The cart moved further and further, till it was climbing the hill in the distance.

Taube still stood and followed it with her gaze; and not till it was lost to view in the dust did she turn and walk back to the town.

She took a road that should lead her past the cemetery.

There was a rather low plank fence round it, and the gravestones were all to be seen, looking up to Heaven.

Taube went and hitched herself up onto the fence, and put her head over into the "field," looking for something among the tombs, and when her eyes had discovered a familiar little tombstone, she shook her head:

"Lezer, Lezer! Your son has driven away to the Academy to study Torah!"

Then she remembered the market, where Yente must by now have bought up the whole cart-load of fruit. There would be nothing left for her, and she hurried into the town.

She walked at a great pace, and felt very pleased with herself. She was conscious of having done a great thing, and this dissipated her annoyance at the thought of Yente acquiring all the fruit.

Two weeks later she got a letter from Yitzchokel, and, not being able to read it herself, she took it to Reb Yochanan, the teacher, that he might read it for her.

Reb Yochanan put on his glasses, cleared his throat thoroughly, and began to read:

"Le-Immi ahuvossi hatzenuoh" . . .

"What is the translation?" asked Taube.

"It is the way to address a mother," explained Reb Yochanan, and continued.

Taube's face had brightened, she put her apron to her eyes and wept for joy.

The reader observed this and read on.

34

"What is the translation, the translation, Reb Yochanan?" the woman kept on asking.

"Never mind, it's not for you, you wouldn't understand—it is an exposition of a passage in the Gemoreh."

She was silent, the Hebrew words awed her, and she listened respectfully to the end.

"I salute Immi ahuvossi and Achoissai, Sarah and Goldeh, and Ochi Yakov; tell him to study diligently. I have all my 'days' and I sleep at Reb Chayyim's," gave out Reb Yochanan suddenly in Yiddish.

Taube contented herself with these few words, took back the letter, put it in her pocket, and went back to her stall with great joy.

"This evening," she thought, "I will show it to the Dayan, and let him read it too."

And no sooner had she got home, cooked the dinner, and fed the children, than she was off with the letter to the Dayan.

She entered the room, saw the tall bookcases filled with books covering the walls, and a man with a white beard sitting at the end of the table reading.

"What is it, a ritual question?" asked the Dayan from his place.

"No."

"What then?"

"A letter from my Yitzchokel."

The Dayan rose, came up and looked at her, took the letter, and began to read it silently to himself.

"Well done, excellent, good! The little fellow knows what he is saying," said the Dayan more to himself than to her.

Tears streamed from Taube's eyes.

"If only *he* had lived! if only he had lived!"

"Shechitas chutz . . . Rambam . . . Tossafos is right . . . " went on the Dayan.

"Her Yitzchokel, Taube the market-woman's son," she thought proudly.

"Take the letter," said the Dayan, at last, "I've read it all through."

"Well, and what?" asked the woman.

"What? What do you want then?"

"What does it say?" she asked in a low voice.

"There is nothing in it for you, you wouldn't understand," replied the Dayan, with a smile.

Yitzchokel continued to write home, the Yiddish words were fewer every time, often only a greeting to his mother. And she came to Reb Yochanan, and he read her the Yiddish phrases, with which she had to be satisfied. "The Hebrew words are for the Dayan," she said to herself.

But one day, "There is nothing in the letter for you," said Reb Yochanan.

"What do you mean?"

"Nothing," he said shortly.

"Read me at least what there is."

"But it is all Hebrew, Torah, you won't understand."

"Very well, then, I *won't* understand . . . "

"Go in health, and don't drive me distracted."

Taube left him, and resolved to go that evening to the Dayan.

"Rebbe, excuse me, translate this into Yiddish," she said, handing him the letter.

The Dayan took the letter and read it.

"Nothing there for you," he said.

"Rebbe," said Taube, shyly, "excuse me, translate the Hebrew for me!"

"But it is Torah, an exposition of a passage in the Torah. You won't understand."

"Well, if you would only read the letter in Hebrew, but aloud, so that I may hear what he says."

"But you won't understand one word, it's Hebrew!" persisted the Dayan, with a smile.

"Well, I *won't* understand, that's all," said the woman, "but it's my child's Torah, my child's!"

The Dayan reflected a while, then he began to read aloud.

Presently, however, he glanced at Taube, and remembered he was expounding the Torah to a woman! And he felt thankful no one had heard him.

"Take the letter, there is nothing in it for you," he said compassionately, and sat down again in his place.

"But it is my child's Torah, my Yitzchokel's letter, why mayn't I hear it? What does it matter if I don't understand? It is my own child!"

The Dayan turned coldly away.

When Taube reached home after this interview, she sat down at the table, took down the lamp from the wall, and looked silently at the letter by its smoky light.

She kissed the letter, but then it occurred to her that she was defiling it with her lips, she, a sinful woman!

She rose, took her husband's prayer-book from the bookshelf, and laid the letter between its leaves.

Then with trembling lips she kissed the covers of the book, and placed it once more in the bookcase.

THE SINNER

So that you should not suspect me of taking his part, I will write a short preface to my story.

It is written: "A man never so much as moves his finger, but it has been so decreed from above," and whatsoever a man does, he fulfils God's will—even animals and birds (I beg to distinguish!) carry out God's wishes: whenever a bird flies, it fulfils a precept, because God, blessed is He, formed it to fly, and an ox the same when it lows, and even a dog when it barks— all praise God with their voices, and sing hymns to Him, each after his manner.

And even the wicked who transgresses fulfils God's will in spite of himself, because why? Do you suppose he takes pleasure in transgressing? Isn't he certain to repent? Well, then? He is just carrying out the will of Heaven.

And the Evil Inclination himself! Why, every time he is sent to persuade a Jew to sin, he weeps and sighs: Woe is me, that I should be sent on such an errand!

After this little preface, I will tell you the story itself.

Formerly, before the thing happened, he was called Reb Avròhom, but afterwards they ceased calling him by his name, and said simply the Sinner.

Reb Avròhom was looked up to and respected by the whole town, a God-fearing Jew, beloved and honored by all, and mothers wished they might have children like him.

He sat the whole day in the house-of-study and learned. Not that he was a great scholar, but he was a pious, scrupulously observant Jew, who followed the straight and beaten road, a man without any pride. He used to recite the prayers in Shool together with the strangers by the door, and quite quietly, without any shouting or, one may say, any special enthusiasm. His prayer that rose to Heaven, the barred gates opening before it till it entered and was taken up into the Throne of Glory, this prayer of his did not become a diamond there, dazzling the eye, but a softly glistening pearl.

And how, you ask, did he come to be called the Sinner? On this wise: You must know that everyone, even those who were hardest on him after the affair, acknowledged that he was a great lover of Israel, and I will add that his sin and, Heaven defend us, his coming to such a fall, all proceeded from his being such a lover of Israel, such a patriot.

And it was just the simple Jew, the very common folk, that he loved.

He used to say: A Jew who is a driver, for instance, and busy all the week with his horses and cart, and soaked in materialism for six days at a stretch, so that he only just manages to get in his prayers—when he comes home on Sabbath and sits down to table, and the bed is made, and the candles burning, and his wife and children are round him, and they sing hymns together, well, the driver dozing off over his prayer-book and forgetting to say grace, I tell you, said Reb Avròhom, the Divine Presence rests on his house and rejoices and says, "Happy am I that I chose me out this people," for such a Jew keeps Sabbath, rests himself, and his horse rests, keeps Sabbath likewise, stands in the stable, and is also conscious that it is the holy Sabbath, and when the driver rises from his sleep, he leads the animal out to pasture, waters it, and they all go for a walk with it in the meadow.

And this walk of theirs is more acceptable to God, blessed is He, than repeating "Bless the Lord, O my soul." It may be this was because he himself was of humble origin; he had lived till he was thirteen with his father, a farmer, in an out-of-the-way village, and ignorant even of his letters. True, his father had taken a youth into the house to teach him Hebrew, but Reb Avròhom as a boy was very wild, wouldn't mind his book, and ran all day after the oxen and horses.

He used to lie out in the meadow, hidden in the long grasses, near him the horses with their heads down pulling at the grass, and the view stretched far, far away, into the endless distance, and above him spread the wide sky, through which the clouds made their way, and the green, juicy earth seemed to look up at it and say: "Look, sky, and see how cheerfully I try to obey God's behest, to make the world green with grass!" And the sky made answer: "See, earth, how I try to fulfil God's command, by spreading myself far and wide!" and the few trees scattered over the fields were like witnesses to their friendly agreement. And little Avròhom lay and rejoiced in the goodness and all the work of God. Suddenly, as though he had received a revelation from Heaven, he went home, and asked the youth who was his teacher, "What blessing should one recite on feeling happy at sight of the world?" The youth laughed, and said: "You stupid boy! One says a blessing over bread and water, but as to saying one over *this world*—who ever heard of such a thing?"

Avròhom wondered, "The world is beautiful, the sky so pretty, the earth so sweet and soft, everything is so delightful to look at, and one says no blessing over it all!"

At thirteen he had left the village and come to the town. There, in the house-of-study, he saw the head of the Academy sitting at one end of the table, and around it, the scholars, all reciting in fervent, appealing tones that went to his heart.

The boy began to cry, whereupon the head of the Academy turned, and saw a little boy with a torn hat, crying, and his hair coming out through the holes, and his boots slung over his shoulder, like a peasant lad fresh from the road. The scholars laughed, but the Rosh ha-Yeshiveh asked him what he wanted.

"To learn," he answered in a low, pleading voice.

The Rosh ha-Yeshiveh had compassion on him, and took him as a pupil. Avròhom applied himself earnestly to the Torah, and in a few days could read Hebrew and follow the prayers without help.

And the way he prayed was a treat to watch. You should have seen him! He just stood and talked, as one person talks to another, quietly and affectionately, without any tricks of manner.

Once the Rosh ha-Yeshiveh saw him praying, and said before his whole Academy, "I can learn better than he, but when it comes to praying, I don't reach to his ankles." That is what he said.

So Reb Avròhom lived there till he was grown up, and had married the daughter of a simple tailor. Indeed, he learnt tailoring himself, and lived by his ten fingers. By day he sat and sewed with an open prayer-book before him, and recited portions of the Psalms to himself. After dark he went into the house-of-study, so quietly that no one noticed him, and passed half the night over the Talmud.

Once some strangers came to the town, and spent the night in the house-of-study behind the stove. Suddenly they heard a thin, sweet voice that was like a tune in itself. They started up, and saw him at his book. The small lamp hanging by a cord poured a dim light upon him where he sat, while the walls remained in shadow. He studied with ardor, with enthusiasm, only his enthusiasm was not for beholders, it was all within; he swayed slowly to and fro, and his shadow swayed with him, and he softly chanted the Gemoreh. By degrees his voice rose, his face kindled, and his eyes began to glow, one could see that his very soul was resolving itself into his chanting. The Divine Presence hovered over him, and he drank in its sweetness. And in the middle of his reading, he got up and walked about the room, repeating in a trembling whisper, "Lord of the World! O Lord of the World!"

Then his voice grew as suddenly calm, and he stood still, as though he had dozed off where he stood, for pure delight. The lamp grew dim, and still he stood and stood and never moved.

Awe fell on the travellers behind the stove, and they cried out. He started and approached them, and they had to close their eyes against the brightness of his face, the light that shone out of his eyes! And he stood there quite quietly and simply, and asked in a gentle voice why they had called out. Were they cold? And he took off his cloak and spread it over them.

Next morning the travellers told all this, and declared that no sooner had the cloak touched them than they had fallen asleep, and they had seen and heard nothing more that night. After this, when the whole town had got wind of it, and they found out who it was that night in the house-of-study, the people began to believe that he was a Tzaddik, and they came to him with Petitions, as Chassidim to their Rebbes, asking him to pray for their health and other wants. But when they brought him such a petition, he would smile and say: "Believe me, a little boy who says grace over a piece of bread which his mother has given him, he can help you more than twenty such as I."

Of course, his words made no impression, except that they brought more petitions than ever, upon which he said:

"You insist on a man of flesh and blood such as I being your advocate with God, blessed is He. Hear a parable: To what shall we liken the thing? To the light of the sun and the light of a small lamp. You can rejoice in the sunlight as much as you please, and no one can take your joy from you; the poorest and most humble may revive himself with it, so long as his eyes can behold it, and even though a man should sit, which God forbid, in a dungeon with closed windows, a reflection will make its way in through the chinks, and he shall rejoice in the brightness. But with the poor light of a lamp it is otherwise. A rich man buys a quantity of lamps and illumines his house, while a poor man sits in darkness. God, blessed be He, is the great light that shines for the whole world, reviving and refreshing all His works. The whole world is full of His mercy, and His compassion is over all His creatures. Believe me, you have no need of an advocate with Him; God is your Father, and you are His dear children. How should a child need an advocate with his father?"

The ordinary folk heard and were silent, but our people, the Chassidim, were displeased. And I'll tell you another thing, I was the first to mention it to the Rebbe, long life to him, and he, as is well known, commanded Reb Avròhom to his presence.

So we set to work to persuade Reb Avròhom and talked to him till he had to go with us

The journey lasted four days.

I remember one night, the moon was wandering in a blue ocean of sky that spread ever so far, till it mingled with a cloud, and she looked at us, pitifully and appealingly, as though to ask us if we knew which way she ought to go, to the right or to the left, and presently the cloud came upon her, and she began struggling to get out of it, and a minute or two later she was free again and smiling at us.

Then a little breeze came, and stroked our faces, and we looked round to the four sides of the world, and it seemed as if the whole world were wrapped in a prayer-scarf woven of mercy, and we fell into a slight melancholy, a quiet sadness, but so sweet and pleasant, it felt like on Sabbath at twilight at the Third Meal.

Suddenly Reb Avròhom exclaimed: "Jews, have you said the blessings on the appearance of the new moon?" We turned towards the moon, laid down our bundles, washed our hands in a little stream that ran by the roadside, and repeated the blessings for the new moon.

He stood looking into the sky, his lips scarcely moving, as was his wont. "Sholom Alechem!" he said, turning to me, and his voice quivered like a violin, and his eyes called to peace and unity. Then an awe of Reb Avròhom came over me for the first time, and when we had finished sanctifying the moon our melancholy left us, and we prepared to continue our way.

But still he stood and gazed heavenward, sighing: "Lord of the Universe! How beautiful is the world which Thou hast made by Thy goodness and great mercy, and these are over all Thy creatures. They all love Thee, and are glad in Thee, and Thou art glad in them, and the whole world is full of Thy glory."

I glanced up at the moon, and it seemed that she was still looking at me, and saying, "I'm lost; which way am I to go?"

We arrived Friday afternoon, and had time enough to go to the bath and to greet the Rebbe.

He, long life to him, was seated in the reception-room beside a table, his long lashes low over his eyes, leaning on his left hand, while he greeted incomers with his right. We went up to him, one at a time, shook hands, and said "Sholom Alechem," and he, long life to him, said nothing to us. Reb Avròhom also went up to him, and held out his hand.

A change came over the Rebbe, he raised his eyelids with his fingers, and looked at Reb Avròhom for some time in silence.

And Reb Avròhom looked at the Rebbe, and was silent too.

The Chassidim were offended by such impertinence.

That evening we assembled in the Rebbe's house-of-study, to usher in the Sabbath. It was tightly packed with Jews, one pushing the other, or seizing hold of his girdle, only beside the ark was there a free space left, a semicircle, in the middle of which stood the Rebbe and prayed.

But Reb Avrohom stood by the door among the poor guests, and prayed after his fashion.

"To Kiddush!" called the beadle.

The Rebbe's wife, daughters, and daughters-in-law now appeared, and their jewelry, their precious stones, and their pearls, sparkled and shone.

The Rebbe stood and repeated the prayer of Sanctification.

He was slightly bent, and his grey beard swept his breast. His eyes were screened by his lashes, and he recited the Sanctification in a loud voice, giving to every word a peculiar inflection, to every sign an expression of its own.

"To table!" was called out next.

At the head of the table sat the Rebbe, sons and sons-in-law to the left, relations to the right of him, then the principal aged Jews, then the rich.

The people stood round about.

The Rebbe ate, and began to serve out the leavings, to his sons and sons-in-law first, and to the rest of those sitting at the table after.

Then there was silence, the Rebbe began to expound the Torah. The portion of the week was Numbers, chapter eight, and the Rebbe began:

"When a man's soul is on a low level, enveloped, Heaven defend us, in uncleanness, and the Divine spark within the soul wishes to rise to a higher level, and cannot do so alone, but must needs be helped, it is a Mitzveh to help her, to raise her, and this Mitzveh is specially incumbent on the priest. This is the meaning of 'the seven lamps shall give light over against the candlestick,' by which is meant the holy Torah. The priest must bring the Jew's heart near to the Torah; in this way he is able to raise it. And who is the priest? The righteous in his generation, because since the Temple was destroyed, the saint must be a priest, for thus is the command from above, that he shall be the priest . . ."

"Avròhom!" the Rebbe called suddenly, "Avròhom! Come here, I am calling you."

The other went up to him.

"Avròhom, did you understand? Did you make out the meaning of what I said?

"Your silence," the Rebbe went on, "is an acknowledgment. I must raise you, even though it be against my will and against your will."

There was dead stillness in the room, people waiting to hear what would come next.

"You are silent?" asked the Rebbe, now a little sternly.

"*You* want to be a raiser of souls? Have *you*, bless and preserve us, bought the Almighty for yourself? Do you think that a Jew can approach nearer to God, blessed is He, through *you*? That *you* are the 'handle of the pestle' and the rest of the Jews nowhere? God's grace is everywhere, whichever way we turn, every time we move a limb we feel God! Everyone must seek Him in his own heart, because there it is that He has caused the Divine Presence to rest. Everywhere and always can the Jew draw near to God . . ."

Thus answered Reb Avròhom, but our people, the Rebbe's followers, shut his mouth before he had made an end, and had the Rebbe not held them back, they would have torn him in pieces on the spot.

"Leave him alone!" he commanded the Chassidim.

And to Reb Avròhom he said:

"Avròhom, you have sinned!"

And from that day forward he was called the Sinner, and was shut out from everywhere. The Chassidim kept their eye on him, and persecuted him, and he was not even allowed to pray in the house-of-study.

And I'll tell you what I think: A wicked man, even when he acts according to his wickedness, fulfils God's command. And who knows? Perhaps they were both right!

ISAAC DOB BERKOWITZ

Born, 1885, in Slutzk, Government of Minsk (Lithuania), White Russia; was in America for a short time in 1908; contributor to Die Zukunft; co-editor of Ha-Olam, Wilna; Hebrew and Yiddish writer; collected works: Yiddish, Gesammelte Schriften, Warsaw, 1910; Hebrew, Sippurim, Cracow, 1910.

COUNTRY FOLK

Feivke was a wild little villager, about seven years old, who had tumbled up from babyhood among Gentile urchins, the only Jewish boy in the place, just as his father Mattes, the Kozlov smith, was the only Jewish householder there. Feivke had hardly ever met, or even seen, anyone but the people of Kozlov and their children. Had it not been for his black eyes, with their moody, persistent gaze from beneath the shade of a deep, worn-out leather cap, it would have puzzled anyone to make out his parentage, to know whence that torn and battered face, that red scar across the top lip, those large, black, flat, unchild-like feet. But the eyes explained everything—his mother's eyes.

Feivke spent the whole summer with the village urchins in the neighboring wood, picking mushrooms, climbing the trees, driving wood-pigeons off their high nests, or wading knee-deep in the shallow bog outside to seek the black, slippery bog-worms; or else he found himself out in the fields, jumping about on the top of a load of hay under a hot sky, and shouting to his companions, till he was bathed in perspiration. At other times, he gathered himself away into a dark, cool barn, scrambled at the peril of his life along a round beam under the roof, crunched dried pears, saw how the sun sprinkled the darkness with a thousand sparks, and—thought. He could always think about Mikita, the son of the village elder, who had almost risen to be conductor on a railway train, and who came from a long way off to visit his father, brass buttons to his coat and a purse full of silver rubles, and piped to the village girls of an evening on the most cunning kind of whistle.

How often it had happened that Feivke could not be found, and did not even come home to bed! But his parents troubled precious little about him, seeing that he was growing up a wild, dissolute boy, and the displeasure of Heaven rested on his head.

Feivke was not a timid child, but there were two things he was afraid of: God and davvening. Feivke had never, to the best of his recollection, seen God, but he often heard His name, they threatened him with It, glanced at the ceiling, and sighed. And this embittered somewhat his sweet, free days. He felt that the older he grew, the sooner he would have to present himself before this terrifying, stern, and unfamiliar God, who was hidden somewhere, whether near or far he could not tell. One day Feivke all but ran a danger. It was early on a winter morning; there was a cold, wild wind blowing outside, and indoors there was a black stranger Jew, in a thick sheepskin, breaking open the tin charity boxes. The smith's wife served the stranger with hot potatoes and sour milk, whereupon the stranger piously closed his eyes, and, having reopened them, caught sight of Feivke through the white steam rising from the dish of potatoes—Feivke, huddled up in a corner—and beckoned him nearer.

"Have you begun to learn, little boy?" he questioned, and took his cheek between two pale, cold fingers, which sent a whiff of snuff up Feivke's nose. His mother, standing by the stove, reddened, and made some inaudible answer. The black stranger threw up his eyes, and slowly shook his head inside the wide sheepskin collar. This shaking to and fro of his head boded no good, and Feivke grew strangely cold inside. Then he grew hot all over, and, for several nights after, thousands of long, cold, pale fingers pursued and pinched him in his dreams.

They had never yet taught him to recite his prayers. Kozlov was a lonely village, far from any Jewish settlement. Every Sabbath morning Feivke, snug in bed, watched his father put on a mended black cloak, wrap himself in the Tallis, shut his eyes, take on a bleating voice, and, turning to the wall, commence a series of bows. Feivke felt that his father was bowing before God, and this frightened him. He thought it a very rash proceeding. Feivke, in his father's place, would sooner have had nothing to do with God. He spent most of the time while his father was at his prayers cowering under the coverlet, and only crept out when he heard his mother busy with plates and spoons, and the pungent smell of chopped radishes and onions penetrated to the bedroom.

Winters and summers passed, and Feivke grew to be seven years old, just such a Feivke as we have described. And the last summer passed, and gave way to autumn.

That autumn the smith's wife was brought to bed of a seventh child, and before she was about again, the cold, damp days were upon them, with the misty mornings, when a fish shivers in the water. And the days of her confinement were mingled for the lonely village Jewess with the Solemn Days of that year into a hard and dreary time. She went slowly about the house, as in a fog, without help or hope, and silent as a shadow. That year they all led a dismal life. The elder children, girls, went out to service in the neighboring towns, to make their own way among strangers. The peasants had become sharper and worse than formerly, and the smith's strength was not what it had been. So his wife resolved to send the two men of the family, Mattes and Feivke, to a Minyan this Yom Kippur. Maybe, if *two* went, God would not be able to resist them, and would soften His heart.

One morning, therefore, Mattes the smith washed, donned his mended Sabbath cloak, went to the window, and blinked through it with his red and swollen eyes. It was the Eve of the Day of Atonement. The room was well-warmed, and there was a smell of freshly-stewed carrots. The smith's wife went out to seek Feivke through the village, and brought him home dishevelled and distracted, and all of a glow. She had torn him away from an early morning of excitement and delight such as could never, never be again. Mikita, the son of the village elder, had put his father's brown colt into harness for the first time. The whole contingent of village boys had been present to watch the fiery young animal twisting between the shafts, drawing loud breaths into its dilated and quivering nostrils, looking wildly at the surrounding boys, and stamping impatiently, as though it would have liked to plow away the earth from under its feet. And suddenly it had given a bound and started careering through the village with the cart behind it. There was a glorious noise and commotion! Feivke was foremost among those who, in a cloud of dust and at the peril of their life, had dashed to seize the colt by the reins.

His mother washed him, looked him over from the low-set leather hat down to his great, black feet, stuffed a packet of food into his hands, and said:

"Go and be a good and devout boy, and God will forgive you."

She stood on the threshold of the house, and looked after her two men starting for a distant Minyan. The bearing of seven children had aged and weakened the once hard, obstinate woman, and, left standing alone in the doorway, watching her poor, barefoot, perverse-natured boy on his way to present himself for the first time before God, she broke down by the Mezuzeh and wept.

Silently, step by step, Feivke followed his father between the desolate stubble fields. It was a good ten miles' walk to the large village where the Minyan assembled, and the fear and the wonder in Feivke's heart increased all the way. He did not yet quite understand whither he was being taken, and what was to be done with him there, and the impetus of the brown colt's career through the village had not as yet subsided in his head. Why had Father put on his black mended cloak? Why had he brought a Tallis with him, and a white shirt-like garment? There was certainly some hour of calamity and terror ahead, something was preparing which had never happened before.

They went by the great Kozlov wood, wherein every tree stood silent and sad for its faded and fallen leaves. Feivke dropped behind his father, and stepped aside into the wood. He wondered: Should he run away and hide in the wood? He would willingly stay there for the rest of his life. He would foregather with Nasta, the barrel-maker's son, he of the knocked-out eye; they would roast potatoes out in the wood, and now and again, stolen-wise, milk the village cows for their repast. Let them beat him as much as they pleased, let them kill him on the spot, nothing should induce him to leave the wood again!

But no! As Feivke walked along under the silent trees and through the fallen leaves, and perceived that the whole wood was filled through and through with a soft, clear light, and heard the rustle of the leaves beneath his step, a strange terror took hold of him. The wood had grown so sparse, the trees so discolored, and he should have to remain in the stillness alone, and roam about in the winter wind!

Mattes the smith had stopped, wondering, and was blinking around with his sick eyes.

"Feivke, where are you?"

Feivke appeared out of the wood.

"Feivke, to-day you mustn't go into the wood. To-day God may yet—to-day you must be a good boy," said the smith, repeating his wife's words as they came to his mind, "and you must say Amen."

Feivke hung his head and looked at his great, bare, black feet. "But if I don't know how," he said sullenly.

"It's no great thing to say Amen!" his father replied encouragingly. "When you hear the other people say it, you can say it, too! Everyone must say Amen, then God will forgive them," he added, recalling again his wife and her admonitions.

Feivke was silent, and once more followed his father step by step. What will they ask him, and what is he to answer? It seemed to him now that they were going right over away yonder where the pale, scarcely-tinted sky touched the earth. There, on a hill, sits a great, old God in a large sheepskin cloak. Everyone goes up to him, and He asks them questions, which they have to answer, and He shakes His head to and fro inside the sheepskin collar. And what is he, a wild, ignorant little boy, to answer this great, old God?

Feivke had committed a great many transgressions concerning which his mother was constantly admonishing him, but now he was thinking only of two great transgressions committed recently, of which his mother knew nothing. One with regard to Anishka the beggar. Anishka was known to the village, as far back as it could remember, as an old, blind beggar, who went the round of the villages, feeling his way with a long stick. And one day Feivke and another boy played him a trick: they placed a ladder in his way, and Anishka stumbled and fell, hurting his nose. Some peasants had come up and caught Feivke. Anishka sat in the middle of the road with blood on his face, wept bitterly, and declared that God would not forget his blood that had been spilt. The peasants had given the little Zhydek a sound thrashing, but Feivke felt

now as if that would not count: God would certainly
remember the spilling of Anishka's blood.

Feivke's second hidden transgression had been committed outside the village, among the graves of the
peasants. A whole troop of boys, Feivke in their midst,
had gone pigeon hunting, aiming at the pigeons with
stones, and a stone of Feivke's had hit the naked figure on the cross that stood among the graves. The
Gentile boys had started and taken fright, and those
among them who were Feivke's good friends told him
he had actually hit the son of God, and that the thing
would have consequences; it was one for which people
had their heads cut off.

These two great transgressions now stood before him,
and his heart warned him that the hour had come when
he would be called to account for what he had done to
Anishka and to God's son. Only he did not know what
answer he could make.

By the time they came near the windmill belonging
to the large strange village, the sun had begun to set.
The village river with the trees beside it were visible
a long way off, and, crossing the river, a long high
bridge.

"The Minyan is there," and Mattes pointed his finger
at the thatched roofs shining in the sunset.

Feivke looked down from the bridge into the deep,
black water that lay smooth and still in the shadow
of the trees. The bridge was high and the water deep!
Feivke felt sick at heart, and his mouth was dry.

"But, Tate, I won't be able to answer," he let out in
despair.

"What, not Amen? Eh, eh, you little silly, that is no great matter. Where is the difficulty? One just ups and answers!" said his father, gently, but Feivke heard that the while his father was trying to quiet him, his own voice trembled.

At the other end of the bridge there appeared the great inn with the covered terrace, and in front of the building were moving groups of Jews in holiday garb, with red handkerchiefs in their hands, women in yellow silk head-kerchiefs, and boys in new clothes holding small prayer-books. Feivke remained obstinately outside the crowd, and hung about the stable, his black eyes staring defiantly from beneath the worn-out leather cap. But he was not left alone long, for soon there came to him a smart, yellow-haired boy, with restless little light-colored eyes, and a face like a chicken's, covered with freckles. This little boy took a little bottle with some essence in it out of his pocket, gave it a twist and a flourish in the air, and suddenly applied it to Feivke's nose, so that the strong waters spurted into his nostril. Then he asked:

"To whom do you belong?"

Feivke blew the water out of his nose, and turned his head away in silence.

"Listen, turkey, lazy dog! What are you doing there? Have you said Minchah?"

"N-no ..."

"Is the Jew in a torn cloak there your father?"

"Y-yes ... T-tate ..."

The yellow-haired boy took Feivke by the sleeve.

"Come along, and you'll see what they'll do to your father."

Inside the room into which Feivke was dragged by his new friend, it was hot, and there was a curious, unfamiliar sound. Feivke grew dizzy. He saw Jews bowing and bending along the wall and beating their breasts—now they said something, and now they wept in an odd way. People coughed and spat sobbingly, and blew their noses with their red handkerchiefs. Chairs and stiff benches creaked, while a continual clatter of plates and spoons came through the wall.

In a corner, beside a heap of hay, Feivke saw. his father where he stood, looking all round him, blinking shamefacedly and innocently with his weak, red eyes. Round him was a lively circle of little boys whispering with one another in evident expectation.

"That is his boy, with the lip," said the chicken-face, presenting Feivke.

At the same moment a young man came up to Mattes. He wore a white collar without a tie and with a pointed brass stud. This young man held a whip, which he brandished in the air like a rider about to mount his horse.

"Well, Reb Smith."

"Am I ... I suppose I am to lie down?" asked Mattes, subserviently, still smiling round in the same shy and yet confiding manner.

"Be so good as to lie down."

The young man gave a mischievous look at the boys, and made a gesture in the air with the whip.

Mattes began to unbutton his cloak, and slowly and cautiously let himself down onto the hay, whereupon the young man applied the whip with might and main, and his whole face shone.

"One, two, three! Go on, Rebbe, go on!" urged the boys, and there were shouts of laughter.

Feivke looked on in amaze. He wanted to go and take his father by the sleeve, make him get up and escape, but just then Mattes raised himself to a sitting posture, and began to rub his eyes with the same shy smile.

"Now, Rebbe, this one!" and the yellow-haired boy began to drag Feivke towards the hay. The others assisted. Feivke got very red, and silently tried to tear himself out of the boy's hands, making for the door, but the other kept his hold. In the doorway Feivke glared at him with his obstinate black eyes, and said:

"I'll knock your teeth out!"

"Mine? You? You booby, you lazy thing! This is *our* house! Do you know, on New Year's Eve I went with my grandfather to the town! I shall call Leibrutz. He'll give you something to remember him by!"

And Leibrutz was not long in joining them. He was the inn driver, a stout youth of fifteen, in a peasant smock with a collar stitched in red, otherwise in full array, with linen socks and a handsome bottle of strong waters against faintness in his hands. To judge by the size of the bottle, his sturdy looks belied a peculiarly delicate constitution. He pushed towards Feivke with one shoulder, in no friendly fashion, and looked at him with one eye, while he winked with the other at the freckled grandson of the host.

"Who is the beauty?"

"How should I know? A thief most likely. The Kozlov smith's boy. He threatened to knock out my teeth."

"So, so, dear brother mine!" sang out Leibrutz, with a cold sneer, and passed his five fingers across Feivke's nose. "We must rub a little horseradish under his eyes, and he'll weep like a beaver. Listen, you Kozlov urchin, you just keep your hands in your pockets, because Leibrutz is here! Do you know Leibrutz? Lucky for you that I have a Jewish heart: to-day is Yom Kippur."

But the chicken-faced boy was not pacified.

"Did you ever see such a lip? And then he comes to our house and wants to fight us!"

The whole lot of boys now encircled Feivke with teasing and laughter, and he stood barefooted in their midst, looking at none of them, and reminding one of a little wild animal caught and tormented.

It grew dark, and quantities of soul-lights were set burning down the long tables of the inn. The large building was packed with red-faced, perspiring Jews, in flowing white robes and Tallesim. The Confession was already in course of fervent recital, there was a great rocking and swaying over the prayer-books and a loud noise in the ears, everyone present trying to make himself heard above the rest. Village Jews are simple and ignorant, they know nothing of "silent prayer" and whispering with the lips. They are deprived of prayer in common a year at a time, and are distant from the Lord of All, and when the Awful Day comes, they want to take Him by storm, by violence. The noisiest of all was the prayer-leader himself, the young man with the white collar and no tie. He was from town, and wished to convince the country folk that he was an adept at his profession and to be relied on. Feivke stood in the stifling room utterly confounded. The prayers and the wailful chanting passed over his head like waves, his heart was straitened, red sparks whirled before his eyes. He was in a state of continual apprehension. He saw a snow-white old Jew come out of a corner with a scroll of the Torah wrapped in a white velvet, gold-embroidered cover. How the gold sparkled and twinkled and reflected itself in the illuminated beard of the old man! Feivke thought the moment had come, but he saw it all as through a mist, a long way off, to the sound of the wailful chanting, and as in a mist the scroll and the old man vanished together. Feivke's face and body were flushed with heat, his knees shook, and at the same time his hands and feet were cold as ice.

Once, while Feivke was standing by the table facing the bright flames of the soul-lights, a dizziness came over him, and he closed his eyes. Thousands of little bells seemed to ring in his ears. Then some one gave a loud thump on the table, and there was silence all around. Feivke started and opened his eyes. The sudden stillness frightened him, and he wanted to move away from the table, but he was walled in by men in white robes, who had begun rocking and swaying anew. One of them pushed a prayer-book towards him, with great black letters, which hopped and fluttered to Feivke's eyes like so many little black birds.

He shook visibly, and the men looked at him in silence: "Nu-nu, nu-nu!" He remained for some time squeezed against the prayer-book, hemmed in by the tall, strange men in robes swaying and praying over his head. A cold perspiration broke out over him, and when at last he freed himself, he felt very tired and weak. Having found his way to a corner close to his father, he fell asleep on the floor.

There he had a strange dream. He dreamt that he was a tree, growing like any other tree in a wood, and that he saw Anishka coming along with blood on his face, in one hand his long stick, and in the other a stone—and Feivke recognized the stone with which he had hit the crucifix. And Anishka kept turning his head and making signs to some one with his long stick, calling out to him that here was Feivke. Feivke looked hard, and there in the depths of the wood was God Himself, white all over, like freshly-fallen snow. And God suddenly grew ever so tall, and looked down at Feivke. Feivke felt God looking at him, but he could not see God, because there was a mist before his eyes. And Anishka came nearer and nearer with the stone in his hand. Feivke shook, and cold perspiration oozed out all over him. He wanted to run away, but he seemed to be growing there like a tree, like all the other trees of the wood.

Feivke awoke on the floor, amid sleeping men, and the first thing he saw was a tall, barefoot person all in white, standing over the sleepers with something in his hand. This tall, white figure sank slowly onto its knees, and, bending silently over Mattes the smith, who lay snoring with the rest, it deliberately put a bottle to his nose. Mattes gave a squeal, and sat up hastily.

"Ha, who is it?" he asked in alarm.

It was the young man from town, the prayer-leader, with a bottle of strong smelling-salts.

"It is I," he said with a *dégagé* air, and smiled. "Never mind, it will do you good! You are fasting, and there is an express law in the Chayyé Odom on the subject."

"But why me?" complained Mattes, blinking at him reproachfully. "What have I done to you?"

Day was about to dawn. The air in the room had cooled down; the soul-lights were still playing in the dark, dewy window-panes. A few of the men bedded in the hay on the floor were waking up. Feivke stood in the middle of the room with staring eyes. The young man with the smelling-bottle came up to him with a lively air.

"O you little object! What are you staring at me for? Do you want a sniff? There, then, sniff!"

Feivke retreated into a corner, and continued to stare at him in bewilderment.

No sooner was it day, than the davvening recommenced with all the fervor of the night before, the room was as noisy, and very soon nearly as hot. But it had not the same effect on Feivke as yesterday, and he was no longer frightened of Anishka and the stone—the whole dream had dissolved into thin air. When they once more brought out the scroll of the Law in its white mantle, Feivke was standing by the table, and looked on indifferently while they uncovered the black, shining, crowded letters. He looked indifferently at the young man from town swaying over the Torah, out of which he read fluently, intoning with a strangely free and easy manner, like an adept to whom all this was nothing new. Whenever he stopped reading, he threw back his head, and looked down at the people with a bright, satisfied smile.

The little boys roamed up and down the room in socks, with smelling-salts in their hands, or yawned into their little prayer-books. The air was filled with the dust of the trampled hay. The sun looked in at a window, and the soul-lights grew dim as in a mist. It seemed to Feivke he had been at the Minyan a long, long time, and he felt as though some great misfortune had befallen him. Fear and wonder continued to oppress him, but not the fear and wonder of yesterday. He was tired, his body burning, while his feet were contracted with cold. He got away outside, stretched himself out on the grass behind the inn and dozed, facing the sun. He dozed there through a good part of the day. Bright red rivers flowed before his eyes, and they made his brains ache. Some one, he did not know who, stood over him, and never stopped rocking to and fro and reciting prayers. Then—it was his father bending over him with a rather troubled look, and waking him in a strangely gentle voice:

"Well, Feivke, are you asleep? You've had nothing to eat to-day yet?"

"No ..."

Feivke followed his father back into the house on his unsteady feet. Weary Jews with pale and lengthened noses were resting on the terrace and the benches. The sun was already low down over the village and shining full into the inn windows. Feivke stood by one of the windows with his father, and his head swam from the bright light. Mattes stroked his chin-beard continually, then there was more davvening and more rocking while they recited the Eighteen Benedictions. The Benedictions ended, the young man began to trill, but in a weaker voice and without charm. He was sick of the whole thing, and kept on in the half-hearted way with which one does a favor. Mattes forgot to look at his prayer-book, and, standing in the window, gazed at the tree-tops, which had caught fire in the rays of the setting sun. Nobody was expecting anything of him, when he suddenly gave a sob, so loud and so piteous that all turned and looked at him in astonishment. Some of the people laughed. The prayer-leader had just intoned "Michael on the right hand uttereth praise," out of the Afternoon Service. What was there to cry about in that? All the little boys had assembled round Mattes the smith, and were choking with laughter, and a certain youth, the host's new son-in-law, gave a twitch to Mattes' Tallis:

"Reb Kozlover, you've made a mistake!"

Mattes answered not a word. The little fellow with the freckles pushed his way up to him, and imitating the young man's intonation, repeated, "Reb Kozlover, you've made a mistake!"

Feivke looked wildly round at the bystanders, at his father. Then he suddenly advanced to the freckled boy, and glared at him with his black eyes.

"You, you—kob tebi biessi!" he hissed in Little-Russian.

The laughter and commotion increased; there was an exclamation: "Rascal, in a holy place!" and another: "Aha! the Kozlover smith's boy must be a first-class scamp!" The prayer-leader thumped angrily on his prayer-book, because no one was listening to him.

Feivke escaped once more behind the inn, but the whole company of boys followed him, headed by Leibrutz the driver.

"There he is, the Kozlov lazy booby!" screamed the freckled boy. "Have you ever heard the like? He actually wanted to fight again, and in our house! What do you think of that?"

Leibrutz went up to Feivke at a steady trot and with the gesture of one who likes to do what has to be done calmly and coolly.

"Wait, boys! Hands off! We've got a remedy for him here, for which I hope he will be thankful."

So saying, he deliberately took hold of Feivke from behind, by his two arms, and made a sign to the boy with yellow hair.

"Now for it, Aarontche, give it to the youngster!"

The little boy immediately whipped the smelling-bottle out of his pocket, took out the stopper with a flourish, and held it to Feivke's nose. The next moment Feivke had wrenched himself free, and was making for the chicken-face with nails spread, when he received two smart, sounding boxes on the ears, from two great, heavy, horny hands, which so clouded his brain that for a minute he stood dazed and dumb. Suddenly he made a spring at Leibrutz, fell upon his hand, and fastened his sharp teeth in the flesh. Leibrutz gave a loud yell.

There was a great to-do. People came running out in their robes, women with pale, startled faces called to their children. A few of them reproved Mattes for his son's behavior. Then they dispersed, till there remained behind the inn only Mattes and Feivke. Mattes looked at his boy in silence. He was not a talkative man, and he found only two or three words to say:

"Feivke, Mother there at home—and you—here?"

Again Feivke found himself alone on the field, and again he stretched himself out and dozed. Again, too, the red streams flowed before his eyes, and someone unknown to him stood at his head and recited prayers. Only the streams were thicker and darker, and the davvening over his head was louder, sadder, more penetrating.

It was quite dark when Mattes came out again, took Feivke by the hand, set him on his feet, and said, "Now we are going home."

Indoors everything had come to an end, and the room had taken on a week-day look. The candles were gone, and a lamp was burning above the table, round which sat men in their hats and usual cloaks, no robes to be seen, and partook of some refreshment. There

was no more davvening, but in Feivke's ears was the
same ringing of bells. It now seemed to him that he
saw the room and the men for the first time, and
the old Jew sitting at the head of the table, presiding
over bottles and wine-glasses, and clicking with his
tongue, could not possibly be the old man with the silver-
white beard who had held the scroll of the Law to
his breast.

Mattes went up to the table, gave a cough, bowed
to the company, and said, "A good year!"

The old man raised his head, and thundered so loudly
that Feivke's face twitched as with pain:

"Ha?"

"I said—I am just going—going home—home again
—so I wish—wish you—a good year!"

"Ha, a good year? A good year to you also! Wait,
have a little brandy, ha?"

Feivke shut his eyes. It made him feel bad to have
the lamp burning so brightly and the old man talking so loud. Why need he speak in such a high, rasping voice that it went through one's head like a saw?

"Ha? Is it your little boy who scratched my Aarontche's face? Ha? A rascal is he? Beat him well!
There, give him a little brandy, too—and a bit of cake!
He fasted too, ha? But he can't recite the prayers?
Fie! *You* ought to be beaten! Ha? Are you going
home? Go in health! Ha? Your wife has just been
confined?—Perhaps you need some money for the holidays? Ha? What do you say?"

Mattes and Feivke started to walk home. Mattes
gave a look at the clear sky, where the young half-

moon had floated into view. "Mother will be expecting us," he said, and began to walk quickly. Feivke could hardly drag his feet.

On the tall bridge they were met by a cool breeze blowing from the water. Once across the bridge, Mattes again quickened his pace. Presently he stopped to look around—no Feivke! He turned back and saw Feivke sitting in the middle of the road. The child was huddled up in a silent, shivering heap. His teeth chattered with cold.

"Feivke, what is the matter? Why are you sitting down? Come along home!"

"I won't"—Feivke clattered out with his teeth—"I c-a-n-'t—"

"Did they hit you so hard, Feivke?"

Feivke was silent. Then he stretched himself out on the ground, his hands and feet quivering.

"Cold—."

"Aren't you well, Feivke?"

The child made an effort, sat up, and looked fixedly at his father, with his black, feverish eyes, and suddenly he asked:

"Why did you cry there? Tate, why? Tell me, why?!"

"Where did I cry, you little silly? Why, I just cried—it's Yom Kippur. Mother is fasting, too—get up, Feivke, and come home. Mother will make you a poultice," occurred to him as a happy thought.

"No! Why did you cry, while they were laughing?" Feivke insisted, still sitting in the road and shaking like a leaf. "One mustn't cry when they laugh, one mustn't!"

And he lay down again on the damp ground.

"Feivele, come home, my son!"

Mattes stood over the boy in despair, and looked around for help. From some way off, from the tall bridge, came a sound of heavy footsteps growing louder and louder, and presently the moonlight showed the figure of a peasant.

"Ai, who is that? Matke the smith? What are you doing there? Are you casting spells? Who is that lying on the ground?"

"I don't know myself what I'm doing, kind soul. That is my boy, and he won't come home, or he can't. What am I to do with him?" complained Mattes to the peasant, whom he knew.

"Has he gone crazy? Give him a kick! Ai, you little lazy devil, get up!" Feivke did not move from the spot, he only shivered silently, and his teeth chattered.

"Ach, you devil! What sort of a boy have you there, Matke? A visitation of Heaven! Why don't you beat him more? The other day they came and told tales of him—Agapa said that—"

"I don't know, either, kind soul, what sort of a boy he is," answered Mattes, and wrung his hands in desperation.

Early next morning Mattes hired a conveyance, and drove Feivke to the town, to the asylum for the sick poor. The smith's wife came out and saw them start, and she stood a long while in the doorway by the Mezuzeh.

And on another fine autumn morning, just when the villagers were beginning to cart loads of fresh earth to secure the village against overflowing streams, the village boys told one another the news of Feivke's death.

THE LAST OF THEM

They had been Rabbonim for generations in the Misnagdic community of Mouravanke, old, poverty-stricken Mouravanke, crowned with hoary honor, hidden away in the thick woods. Generation on generation of them had been renowned far and near, wherever a Jewish word was spoken, wherever the voice of the Torah rang out in the warm old houses-of-study.

People talked of them everywhere, as they talk of miracles when miracles are no more, and of consolation when all hope is long since dead—talked of them as great-grandchildren talk of the riches of their great-grandfather, the like of which are now unknown, and of the great seven-branched, old-fashioned lamp, which he left them as an inheritance of times gone by.

For as the lustre of an old, seven-branched lamp shining in the darkness, such was the lustre of the family of the Rabbonim of Mouravanke.

That was long ago, ever so long ago, when Mouravanke lay buried in the dark Lithuanian forests. The old, low, moss-grown houses were still set in wide, green gardens, wherein grew beet-root and onions, while the hop twined itself and clustered thickly along the wooden fencing. Well-to-do Jews still went about in linen pelisses, and smoked pipes filled with dry herbs. People got a living out of the woods, where they burnt pitch the whole week through, and Jewish families ate rye-bread and groats-pottage.

A new baby brought no anxiety along with it. People praised God, carried the pitcher to the well, filled it, and poured a quart of water into the pottage. The newcomer was one of God's creatures, and was assured of his portion along with the others.

And if a Jew had a marriageable daughter, and could not afford a dowry, he took a stick in his hand, donned a white shirt with a broad mangled collar, repeated the "Prayer of the Highway," and set off on foot to Volhynia, that thrice-blessed wonderland, where people talk with a "Chirik," and eat Challeh with saffron even in the middle of the week—with saffron, if not with honey.

There, in Volhynia, on Friday evenings, the rich Jewish householder of the district walks to and fro leisurely in his brightly lit room. In all likelihood, he is a short, plump, hairy man, with a broad, fair beard, a gathered silk sash round his substantial figure, a cheery singsong "Sholom-Alechem" on his mincing, "chiriky" tongue, and a merry crack of the thumb. The Lithuanian guest, teacher or preacher, the shrunk and shrivelled stranger with the piercing black eyes, sits in a corner, merely moving his lips and gazing at the floor— perhaps because he feels ill at ease in the bright, nicely-furnished room; perhaps because he is thinking of his distant home, of his wife and children and his marriageable daughter; and perhaps because it has suddenly all become oddly dear to him, his poor, forsaken native place, with its moiling, poverty-struck Jews, whose week is spent pitch-burning in the forest; with its old, warm houses-of-study; with its celebrated giants of the Torah, bending with a candle in their hand over the great hoary Gemorehs.

And here, at table, between the tasty stuffed fish and the soup, with the rich Volhynian "stuffed monkeys," the brusque, tongue-tied guest is suddenly unable to contain himself, and overflows with talk about his corner in Lithuania.

"Whether we have our Rabbis at home?! N-nu!!"

And thereupon he holds forth grandiloquently, with an ardor and incisiveness born of the love and the longing at his heart. The piercing black eyes shoot sparks, as the guest tells of the great men of Mouravanke, with their fiery intellects, their iron perseverance, who sit over their books by day and by night. From time to time they take an hour and a half's doze, falling with their head onto their fists, their beards sweeping the Gemoreh, the big candle keeping watch overhead and waking them once more to the study of the Torah.

At dawn, when the people begin to come in for the Morning Prayer, they walk round them on tiptoe, giving them their four-ells' distance, and avoid meeting their look, which is apt to be sharp and burning.

"That is the way we study in Lithuania!"

The stout, hairy householder, good-natured and credulous, listens attentively to the wonderful tales, loosens the sash over his pelisse in leisurely fashion, unbuttons his waistcoat across his generous waist, blows out his cheeks, and sways his head from side to side, because— one may believe anything of the Lithuanians!

Then, if once in a long, long while the rich
Volhynian householder stumbled, by some miracle or
other, into Lithuania, sheer curiosity would drive him
to take a look at the Lithuanian celebrity. But he
would stand before him in trembling and astonishment,
as one stands before a high granite rock, the summit of
which can barely be discerned. Is he terrified by the
dark and bushy brows, the keen, penetrating looks, the
deep, stern wrinkles in the forehead that might have
been carved in stone, they are so stiffly fixed? Who
can say? Or is he put out of countenance by the
cold, hard assertiveness of their speech, which bores
into the conscience like a gimlet, and knows of no
mercy?—for from between those wrinkles, from beneath
those dark brows, shines out the everlasting glory of
the Shechinah.

Such were the celebrated Rabbonim of Mouravanke.

They were an old family, a long chain of great men,
generation on generation of tall, well-built, large-boned
Jews, all far on in years, with thick, curly beards. It
was very seldom one of these beards showed a silver
hair. They were stern, silent men, who heard and saw
everything, but who expressed themselves mostly by
means of their wrinkles and their eyebrows rather than
in words, so that when a Mouravanke Rav went so far
as to say "N-nu," that was enough.

The dignity of Rav was hereditary among them,
descending from father to son, and, together with the
Rabbinical position and the eighteen gulden a week
salary, the son inherited from his father a tall, old reading-desk, smoked and scorched by the candles, in the old

house-of-study in the corner by the ark, and a thick, heavy-knotted stick, and an old holiday pelisse of lustrine, the which, if worn on a bright Sabbath-day in summer-time, shines in the sun, and fairly shouts to be looked at.

They arrived in Mouravanke generations ago, when the town was still in the power of wild highwaymen, called there "Hydemakyes," with huge, terrifying whiskers and large, savage dogs. One day, on Hoshanah Rabbah, early in the morning, there entered the house-of-study a tall youth, evidently village-born and from a long way off, barefoot, with turned-up trousers, his boots slung on a big, knotted stick across his shoulders, and a great bundle of big Hoshanos. The youth stood in the centre of the house-of-study with his mouth open, bewildered, and the boys quickly snatched his willow branches from him. He was surrounded, stared at, questioned as to who he was, whence he came, what he wanted. Had he parents? Was he married? For some time the youth stood silent, with downcast eyes, then he bethought himself, and answered in three words: "I want to study!"

And from that moment he remained in the old building, and people began to tell wonderful tales of his power of perseverance—of how a tall, barefoot youth, who came walking from a far distance, had by dint of determination come to be reckoned among the great men in Israel; of how, on a winter midnight, he would open the stove doors, and study by the light of the glowing coals; of how he once forgot food and drink for three days and three nights running, while he stood

THE LAST OF THEM 575

When it was time for the householders to go forth out of the town, to meet the young Charif, the old Rav offered to go with them, and they took a chair for him to sit in while he waited at the meeting-place. This was by the wood outside the town, where all through the week the Jewish townsfolk earned their bread by burning pitch. Begrimed and toil-worn Jews were continually dropping their work and peeping out shamefacedly between the tree-stems.

It was Friday, a clear day in the autumn. She appeared out of a great cloud of dust—she, the travelling-wagon in which sat the celebrated young Charif. Sholom-Alechems flew to meet him from every side, and his old father, the tailor, leant back against a tree, and wept aloud for joy.

Now the old Rav declared that he would not allow the Charif to enter the town till he had heard him, the Charif, expound a portion of the Torah.

The young man accepted the condition. Men, women, and little children stood expectant, all eyes were fastened on the tailor's son, all hearts beat rapidly.

The Charif expounded the Torah standing in the wagon. At first he looked fairly scared, and his sharp black eyes darted fearfully hither and thither over the heads of the silent crowd. Then came a bright idea, and lit up his face. He began to speak, but his was not the familiar teaching, such as everyone learns and understands. His words were like fiery flashes appearing and disappearing one after the other, lightnings that traverse and illumine half the sky in one second of time, a play of swords in which there are no words, only the clink and ring of finely-tempered steel.

The old Rav sat in his chair leaning on his old, knobbly, knotted stick, and listened. He heard, but evil thoughts beset him, and deep, hard wrinkles cut themselves into his forehead. He saw before him the Charif, the dried-up youth with the sharp eyes and the sharp, pointed nose, and the evil thought came to him, "Those are needles, a tailor's needles," while the long, thin forefinger with which the Charif pointed rapidly in the air seemed a third needle wielded by a tailor in a hurry.

"You prick more sharply even than your father," is what the old Rav wanted to say when the Charif ended his sermon, but he did not say it. The whole assembly was gazing with caught breath at his half-closed eyelids. The lids never moved, and some thought wonderingly that he had fallen into a doze from sheer old age.

Suddenly a strange, dry snap broke the stillness, the old Rav started in his chair, and when they rushed forward to assist him, they found that his knotted, knobbly stick had broken in two.

Pale and bent for the first time, but a tall figure still, the old Rav stood up among his startled flock. He made a leisurely motion with his hand in the direction of the town, and remarked quietly to the young Charif:

"Nu, now you can go into the town!"

That Friday night the old Rav came into the house-of-study without his satin cloak, like a mourner. The congregation saw him lead the young Rav into the corner near the ark, where he sat him down by the high old desk, saying:

"You will sit here."

He himself went and sat down behind the pulpit among the strangers, the Sabbath guests.

For the first minute people were lost in astonishment; the next minute the house-of-study was filled with wailing. Old and young lifted their voices in lamentation. The young Rav looked like a child sitting behind the tall desk, and he shivered and shook as though with fever.

Then the old Rav stood up to his full height and commanded:

"People are not to weep!"

All this happened about the Solemn Days. Mouravanke remembers that time now, and speaks of it at dusk, when the sky is red as though streaming with fire, and the men stand about pensive and forlorn, and the women fold their babies closer in their aprons.

At the close of the Day of Atonement there was a report that the old Rav had breathed his last in robe and prayer-scarf.

The young Charif did not survive him long. He died at his father's the tailor, and his funeral was on a wet Great Hosannah day. Aged folk said he had been summoned to face the old Rav in a lawsuit in the Heavenly Court.

A FOLK TALE

THE CLEVER RABBI

The power of man's imagination, said my Grandmother, is very great. Hereby hangs a tale, which, to our sorrow, is a true one, and as clear as daylight.

Listen attentively, my dear child, it will interest you very much.

Not far from this town of ours lived an old Count, who believed that Jews require blood at Passover, Christian blood, too, for their Passover cakes.

The Count, in his brandy distillery, had a Jewish overseer, a very honest, respectable fellow.

The Count loved him for his honesty, and was very kind to him, and the Jew, although he was a simple man and no scholar, was well-disposed, and served the Count with heart and soul. He would have gone through fire and water at the Count's bidding, for it is in the nature of a Jew to be faithful and to love good men.

The Count often discussed business matters with him, and took pleasure in hearing about the customs and observances of the Jews.

One day the Count said to him, "Tell me the truth, do you love me with your whole heart?"

"Yes," replied the Jew, "I love you as myself."

"Not true!" said the Count. "I shall prove to you that you hate me even unto death."

"Hold!" cried the Jew. "Why does my lord say such terrible things?"

The Count smiled and answered: "Let me tell you! I know quite well that Jews must have Christian blood for

their Passover feast. Now, what would you do if I were
the only Christian you could find? You would have to
kill me, because the Rabbis have said so. Indeed, I can
scarcely hold you to blame, since, according to your false
notions, the Divine command is precious, even when it
tells us to commit murder. I should be no more to you
than was Isaac to Abraham, when, at God's command,
Abraham was about to slay his only son. Know, however, that the God of Abraham is a God of mercy and
lovingkindness, while the God the Rabbis have created is
full of hatred towards Christians. How, then, can you
say that you love me?"

The Jew clapped his hands to his head, he tore his
hair in his distress and felt no pain, and with a broken
heart he answered the Count, and said: "How long
will you Christians suffer this stain on your pure hearts?
How long will you disgrace yourselves? Does not my
lord know that this is a great lie? I, as a believing Jew,
and many besides me, as believing Jews—we ourselves,
I say, with our own hands, grind the corn, we keep the
flour from getting damp or wet with anything, for if
only a little dew drop onto it, it is prohibited for us
as though it had yeast.

"Till the day on which the cakes are baked, we keep
the flour as the apple of our eye. And when the flour
is baked, and we are eating the cakes, even then we are
not sure of swallowing it, because if our gums should
begin to bleed, we have to spit the piece out. And in
face of all these stringent regulations against eating the
blood of even beasts and birds, some people say that
Jews require human blood for their Passover cakes,

and swear to it as a fact! What does my lord suppose we are likely to think of such people? We know that they swear falsely—and a false oath is of all things the worst."

The Count was touched to the heart by these words, and these two men, being both upright and without guile, believed one the other.

The Count believed the Jew, that is, he believed that the Jew did not know the truth of the matter, because he was poor and untaught, while the Rabbis all the time most certainly used blood at Passover, only they kept it a secret from the people. And he said as much to the Jew, who, in his turn, believed the Count, because he knew him to be an honorable man. And so it was that he began to have his doubts, and when the Count, on different occasions, repeated the same words, the Jew said to himself, that perhaps after all it was partly true, that there must be something in it—the Count would never tell him a lie!

And he carried the thought about with him for some time.

The Jew found increasing favor in his master's eyes. The Count lent him money to trade with, and God prospered the Jew in everything he undertook. Thanks to the Count, he grew rich.

The Jew had a kind heart, and was much given to good works, as is the way with Jews.

He was very charitable, and succored all the poor in the neighboring town. And he assisted the Rabbis and the pious in all the places round about, and earned for himself a great and beautiful name, for he was known to all as "the benefactor."

The Rabbis gave him the honor due to a pious and influential Jew, who is a wealthy man and charitable into the bargain.

But the Jew was thinking:

"Now the Rabbis will let me into the secret which is theirs, and which they share with those only who are at once pious and rich, that great and pious Jews must have blood for Passover."

For a long time he lived in hope, but the Rabbis told him nothing, the subject was not once mentioned. But the Jew felt sure that the Count would never have lied to him, and he gave more liberally than before, thinking, "Perhaps after all it was too little."

He assisted the Rabbi of the nearest town for a whole year, so that the Rabbi opened his eyes in astonishment. He gave him more than half of what is sufficient for a livelihood.

When it was near Passover, the Jew drove into the little town to visit the Rabbi, who received him with open arms, and gave him honor as unto the most powerful and wealthy benefactor. And all the representative men of the community paid him their respects.

Thought the Jew, "Now they will tell me of the commandment which it is not given to every Jew to observe."

As the Rabbi, however, told him nothing, the Jew remained, to remind the Rabbi, as it were, of his duty.

"Rabbi," said the Jew, "I have something very particular to say to you! Let us go into a room where we two shall be alone."

So the Rabbi went with him into an empty room, shut the door, and said:

"Dear friend, what is your wish? Do not be abashed, but speak freely, and tell me what I can do for you."

"Dear Rabbi, I am, you must know, already acquainted with the fact that Jews require blood at Passover. I know also that it is a secret belonging only to the Rabbis, to very pious Jews, and to the wealthy who give much alms. And I, who am, as you know, a very charitable and good Jew, wish also to comply, if only once in my life, with this great observance.

"You need not be alarmed, dear Rabbi! I will never betray the secret, but will make you happy forever, if you will enable me to fulfil so great a command.

"If, however, you deny its existence, and declare that Jews do not require blood, from that moment I become your bitter enemy.

"And why should I be treated worse than any other pious Jew? I, too, want to try to perform the great commandment which God gave in secret. I am not learned in the Law, but a great and wealthy Jew, and one given to good works, that am I in very truth!"

You can fancy—said my Grandmother—the Rabbi's horror on hearing such words from a Jew, a simple countryman. They pierced him to the quick, like sharp arrows.

He saw that the Jew believed in all sincerity that his coreligionists used blood at Passover.

How was he to uproot out of such a simple heart the weeds sown there by evil men?

The Rabbi saw that words would just then be useless.

A beautiful thought came to him, and he said: "So be it, dear friend! Come into the synagogue to-morrow at this time, and I will grant your request. But till then you must fast, and you must not sleep all night, but watch in prayer, for this is a very grave and dreadful thing."

The Jew went away full of gladness, and did as the Rabbi had told him. Next day, at the appointed time, he came again, wan with hunger and lack of sleep.

The Rabbi took the key of the synagogue, and they went in there together. In the synagogue all was quiet.

The Rabbi put on a prayer-scarf and a robe, lighted some black candles, threw off his shoes, took the Jew by the hand, and led him up to the ark.

The Rabbi opened the ark, took out a scroll of the Law, and said:

"You know that for us Jews the scroll of the Law is the most sacred of all things, and that the list of denunciations occurs in it twice.

"I swear to you by the scroll of the Law: If any Jew, whosoever he be, requires blood at Passover, may all the curses contained in the two lists of denunciations be on my head, and on the head of my whole family!"

The Jew was greatly startled.

He knew that the Rabbi had never before sworn an oath, and now, for his sake, he had sworn an oath so dreadful!

The Jew wept much, and said:

"Dear Rabbi, I have sinned before God and before you. I pray you, pardon me and give me a hard penance, as hard as you please. I will perform it willingly, and may God forgive me likewise!"

The Rabbi comforted him, and told no one what had happened, he only' told a few very near relations, just to show them how people can be talked into believing the greatest foolishness and the most wicked lies.

May God—said my Grandmother—open the eyes of all who accuse us falsely, that they may see how useless it is to trump up against us things that never were seen or heard.

Jews will be Jews while the world lasts, and they will become, through suffering, better Jews with more Jewish hearts.

GLOSSARY AND NOTES

[Abbreviations: Dimin. = diminutive; Ger. = German, corrupt German, and Yiddish; Heb. = Hebrew, and Aramaic; pl. = plural; Russ. = Russian; Slav. = Slavic; trl. = translation.

Pronunciation: The transliteration of the Hebrew words attempts to reproduce the colloquial "German" (Ashkenazic) pronunciation. *Ch* is pronounced as in the German *Dach*.]

ADDITIONAL SERVICE. *See* EIGHTEEN BENEDICTIONS.

AL-CHET (Heb.). "For the sin"; the first two words of each line of an Atonement Day prayer, at every mention of which the worshipper beats the left side of his breast with his right fist.

ALEF-BES (Heb.). The Hebrew alphabet.

ASHRÉ (Heb.). The first word of a Psalm verse used repeatedly in the liturgy.

AUS KLEMENKE! (Ger.). Klemenke is done for!

AZOI (= Ger. also). That's the way it is!

BADCHEN (Heb.). A wedding minstrel, whose quips often convey a moral lesson to the bridal couple, each of whom he addresses separately.

BAR-MITZVEH (Heb.). A boy of thirteen, the age of religious majority.

BAS-KOL (Heb.). "The Daughter of the Voice"; an echo; a voice from Heaven.

BEIGEL (Ger.). Ring-shaped roll.

BES HA-MIDRASH (Heb.). House-of-study, used for prayers, too.

BITTUL-TORAH (Heb.). Interference with religious study.

BOBBE (Slav.). Grandmother; midwife.

BORSHTSH (Russ.). Sour soup made of beet-root.

CANTONIST (Ger.). Jewish soldier under Czar Nicholas I, torn from his parents as a child, and forcibly estranged from Judaism.

590 GLOSSARY AND NOTES

CHALLEH (Heb.). Loaves of bread prepared for the Sabbath, over which the blessing is said; always made of wheat flour, and sometimes yellowed with saffron.

CHARIF (Heb.). A Talmudic scholar and dialectician.

CHASSIDIM (sing. Chossid) (Heb.). " Pious ones "; followers of Israel Baal Shem, who opposed the sophisticated intellectualism of the Talmudists, and laid stress on emotionalism in prayer and in the performance of other religious ceremonies. The Chassidic leader is called Tzaddik ("righteous one"), or Rebbe. See art. "Hasidim," in the Jewish Encyclopedia, vol. vi.

CHAYYÉ ODOM. A manual of religious practice used extensively by the common people.

CHEDER (pl. Chedorim) (Heb.). Jewish primary school.

CHILLUL HA-SHEM (Heb.). "Desecration of the Holy Name "; hence, scandal.

CHIRIK (Heb.). Name of the vowel " i " ; in Volhynia " u " is pronounced like " i."

DAVVENING. Saying prayers.

DAYAN (pl. Dayonim) (Heb.). Authority on Jewish religious law, usually assistant to the Rabbi of a town.

DIN TORAH (Heb.). Lawsuit.

DREIER, DREIERLECH (Ger.). A small coin.

EIGHTEEN BENEDICTIONS. The nucleus of each of the three daily services, morning, afternoon, evening, and of the "Additional Service" inserted on Sabbaths, festivals, and the Holy Days, between the morning and afternoon services. Though the number of benedictions is actually nineteen, and at some of the services is reduced to seven, the technical designation remains "Eighteen Benedictions." They are usually said as a "silent prayer " by the congregation, and then recited aloud by the cantor, or precentor.

ERETZ YISROEL (Heb.). Palestine.

EREV (Heb.). Eve.

ERUV (Heb.). A cord, etc., stretched round a town, to mark the limit beyond which no "burden" may be carried on the Sabbath.

FAST OF ESTHER. A fast day preceding Purim, the Feast of Esther.

"FOUNTAIN OF JACOB." A collection of all the legends, tales, apologues, parables, etc., in the Babylonian Talmud.

FOUR-CORNERS (trl. of Arba Kanfos). A fringed garment worn under the ordinary clothes; called also Talliskoton. See Deut. xxii. 12.

FOUR ELLS. Minimum space required by a human being.

FOUR QUESTIONS. Put by the youngest child to his father at the Seder.

GANZE GOYIM (Ger. and Heb.). Wholly estranged from Jewish life and customs. See Goi.

GASS (Ger.). The Jews' street.

GEHENNA (Heb.). The nether world; hell.

GEMOREH (Heb.). The Talmud, the Rabbinical discussion and elaboration of the Mishnah; a Talmud folio. It is usually read with a peculiar singsong chant, and the reading of argumentative passages is accompanied by a gesture with the thumb. See, for instance, pp. 17 and 338.

GEMOREH-KÖPLECH (Heb. and Ger.). A subtle, keen mind; precocious.

GEVIR (Heb.). An influential, rich man.—GEVIRISH, appertaining to a Gevir.

GOI (pl. Goyim) (Heb.). A Gentile; a Jew estranged from Jewish life and customs.

GOTTINYU (Ger. with Slav. ending). Dear God.

GREAT SABBATH, THE. The Sabbath preceding Passover.

HAGGADAH (Heb.). The story of the Exodus recited at the home service on the first two evenings of Passover.

HOSHANAH (pl. Hoshanos) (Heb.). Osier withe for the Great Hosannah.

HOSHANAH-RABBAH (Heb.). The seventh day of the Feast of Tabernacles; the Great Hosannah.

HOSTRE CHASSIDIM. Followers of the Rebbe or Tzaddik who lived at Hostre.

KADDISH (Heb.). Sanctification, or doxology, recited by mourners, specifically by children in memory of parents during the first eleven months after their death, and thereafter on every anniversary of the day of their death; applied to an only son, on whom will devolve the duty of reciting the prayer on the death of his parents; sometimes applied to the oldest son, and to sons in general.

KALLEH (Heb.) Bride.

KALLEH-LEBEN (Heb. and Ger.). Dear bride.

KALLEHSHI (Heb. and Russ. dimin.). Dear bride.

KASHA (Slav.). Pap.

KEDUSHAH (Heb.). Sanctification; the central part of the public service, of which the " Holy, holy, holy," forms a sentence.

KERBEL, KERBLECH (Ger.). A ruble.

KIDDUSH (Heb.). Sanctification; blessing recited over wine in ushering in Sabbaths and holidays.

KLAUS (Ger.). "Hermitage"; a conventicle; a house-of-study.

KOB TEBI BIESSI (Little Russ.) "Demons take you! "

KOL NIDRÉ (Heb.). The first prayer recited at the synagogue on the Eve of the Day of Atonement.

KOSHER (Heb.). Ritually clean or permitted.

KOSHER-TANZ (Heb. and Ger.). Bride's dance.

KÖST (Ger.). Board.—AUF KÖST. Free board and lodging given to a man and his wife by the latter's parents during the early years of his married life.

"LEARN." Studying the Talmud, the codes, and the commentaries.

LE-CHAYYIM (Heb.). Here's to long life!

LEHAVDIL (Heb.). " To distinguish." Elliptical for " to distinguish between the holy and the secular " ; equivalent to " excuse the comparison "; " pardon me for mentioning the two things in the same breath," etc.

LIKKUTE ZEVI (Heb.). A collection of prayers.

LOKSHEN. Macaroni.—TORAS-LOKSHEN, macaroni made in approved style.

MAARIV (Heb.). The Evening Prayer, or service.

MAGGID (Heb.). Preacher.

MAHARSHO (MAHARSHO). Hebrew initial letters of Morenu ha-Rab Shemuel Edels, a great commentator.

MALKES (Heb.). Stripes inflicted on the Eve of the Day of Atonement, in expiation of sins. See Deut. xxv. 2, 3.

MASKIL (pl. Maskilim) (Heb.). An "intellectual." The aim of the "intellectuals" was the spread of modern general education among the Jews, especially in Eastern Europe. They were reproached with secularizing Hebrew and disregarding the ceremonial law.

MATZES (Heb.). The unleavened bread used during Passover.

MECHUTENESTE (Heb.). Mother-in-law; prospective mother-in-law; expresses chiefly the reciprocal relation between the parents of a couple about to be married.

MECHUTTON (Heb.). Father-in-law; prospective father-in-law; expresses chiefly the reciprocal relation between the parents of a couple about to be married.

MEHEREH (Heb.). The "quick" dough for the Matzes.

MELAMMED (Heb.). Teacher.

MEZUZEH (Heb.). "Door-post;" Scripture verses attached to the door-posts of Jewish houses. See Deut. vi. 9.

MIDRASH (Heb.). Homiletic exposition of the Scriptures.

MINCHAH (Heb.). The Afternoon Prayer, or service.

MIN HA-MEZAR (Heb.). "Out of the depth," Ps. 118. 5.

MINYAN (Heb.). A company of ten men, the minimum for a public service; specifically, a temporary congregation, gathered together, usually in a village, from several neighboring Jewish settlements, for services on New Year and the Day of Atonement.

MISHNAH (Heb.). The earliest code (ab. 200 C. E.) after the Pentateuch, portions of which are studied, during the early days of mourning, in honor of the dead.

MISNAGGID (pl. Misnagdim) (Heb.). "Opponents" of the Chassidim. The Misnagdic communities are led by a Rabbi (pl. Rabbonim), sometimes called Rav.

MITZVEH (Heb.). A commandment, a duty, the doing of which is meritorious.

NASHERS (Ger.). Gourmets.

NISHKOSHE (Ger. and Heb.). Never mind!

NISSAN (Heb.). Spring month (March-April), in which Passover is celebrated.

OLÉNU (Heb.). The concluding prayer in the synagogue service.

OLOM HA-SHEKER (Heb.). "The world of falsehood," this world.

OLOM HA-TOHU (Heb.). World of chaos.

OLOM HO-EMESS (Heb.). "The world of truth," the world-to-come.

PARNOSSEH (Heb.). Means of livelihood; business; sustenance.

PIYYUTIM (Heb.). Liturgical poems for festivals and Holy Days recited in the synagogue.

PORUSH (Heb.). Recluse.

PRAYER OF THE HIGHWAY. Prayer on setting out on a journey.

PRAYER-SCARF. See TALLIS.

PUD (Russ.). Forty pounds.

PURIM (Heb.). The Feast of Esther.

RASHI (RaSHI). Hebrew initial letters of Rabbi Solomon ben Isaac, a great commentator; applied to a certain form of script and type.

RAV (Heb.). Rabbi.

REBBE. Sometimes used for Rabbi; sometimes equivalent to Mr.; sometimes applied to the Tzaddik of the Chassidim; and sometimes used as the title of a teacher of young children.

REBBETZIN. Wife of a Rabbi.

ROSH-YESHIVEH (Rosh ha-Yeshiveh) (Heb.). Headmaster of a Talmudic Academy.

SCAPE-FOWLS (trl. of Kapporos). Roosters or hens used in a ceremony on the Eve of the Day of Atonement.

SEDER (Heb.). Home service on the first two Passover evenings.

SELICHES (Heb.). Penitential prayers.

SEVENTEENTH OF TAMMUZ. Fast in commemoration of the first breach made in the walls of Jerusalem by Nebuchadnezzar.

SHALOM (Heb. in Sefardic pronunciation). Peace. *See* SHOLOM ALECHEM.

SHAMASH (Heb.). Beadle.

SHECHINAH (Heb.). The Divine Presence.

SHEGETZ (Heb.). " Abomination; " a sinner; a rascal.

SHLIMM-MAZEL (Ger. and Heb.). Bad luck; luckless fellow.

SHMOOREH-MATZES (Heb.). Unleavened bread specially guarded and watched from the harvesting of the wheat to the baking and storing.

SHOCHET (Heb.). Ritual slaughterer.

SHOFAR (Heb.). Ram's horn, sounded on New Year's Day and the Day of Atonement. *See* Lev. xxiii. 24.

SHOLOM (SHALOM) ALECHEM (Heb.). " Peace unto you " ; greeting, salutation, especially to one newly arrived after a journey.

SHOMER. Pseudonym of a Yiddish author, Nahum M. Schaikewitz.

SHOOL (Ger., Schul'). Synagogue.

SHULCHAN ARUCH (Heb.). The Jewish code.

SILENT PRAYER. *See* EIGHTEEN BENEDICTIONS.

SOLEMN DAYS. The ten days from New Year to the Day of Atonement inclusive.

SOUL-LIGHTS. Candles lighted in memory of the dead.

STUFFED MONKEYS. Pastry filled with chopped fruit and spices.

TALLIS (popular plural formation, Tallesim) (Heb.). The prayer-scarf.

TALLIS-KOTON (Heb.). *See* FOUR-CORNERS.

TALMID-CHOCHEM (Heb.). Sage; scholar.

TALMUD TORAH (Heb.). Free communal school.

TANO (Heb.). A Rabbi cited in the Mishnah as an authority.

TARARAM. Noise; tumult; ado.

TATE, TATISHE (Ger. and Russ. dimin.). Father.

TEFILLIN-SÄCKLECH (Heb. and Ger.). Phylacteries bag.

TISHO-B'OV (Heb.). Ninth of Ab, day of mourning and fasting to commemorate the destruction of Jerusalem; hence, colloquially, a sad day.

TORAH (Heb.). The Jewish Law in general, and the Pentateuch in particular.

TSISIN. Season.

TZADDIK (pl. Tzaddikim) (Heb.). " Righteous " ; title of the Chassidic leader.

U-MIPNÉ CHATOÉNU (Heb.). " And on account of our sins," the first two words of a prayer for the restoration of the sacrificial service, recited in the Additional Service of the Holy Days and the festivals.

U-NESANNEH-TOIKEF (Heb.). " And we ascribe majesty," the first two words of a Piyyut recited on New Year and on the Day of Atonement.

VERFALLEN! (Ger.). Lost; done for.

VERSHOK (Russ.). Two inches and a quarter.

VIERER (Ger.). Four kopeks.

VIVAT. Toast.

YESHIVEH (Heb.). Talmud Academy.

YOHRZEIT (Ger.). Anniversary of a death.

YOM KIPPUR (Heb.). Day of Atonement.

YOM-TOV (Heb.). Festival.

ZHYDEK (Little Russ.). Jew.

P. 15. " It was seldom that parties went 'to law' . . . .
before the Rav."—The Rabbi with his Dayonim gave
civil as well as religious decisions.

P. 15. " Milky Sabbath."—All meals without meat. In connection with fowl, ritual questions frequently arise.

P. 16. " Reuben's ox gores Simeon's cow."—Reuben and
Simeon are fictitious plaintiff and defendant in the
Talmud; similar to John Doe and Richard Roe.

P. 17. " He described a half-circle," etc.—See under
GEMOREH.

P. 57. " Not every one is worthy of both tables! "—Worthy
of Torah and riches.

P. 117. " They salted the meat."—The ritual ordinance requires that meat should be salted down for an hour
after it has soaked in water for half an hour.

P. 150. " Puts off his shoes!"—To pray in stocking-feet
is a sign of mourning and a penance.

P. 190. " We have trespassed," etc.—The Confession of
Sins.

P. 190. " The beadle deals them out thirty-nine blows,"
etc.— See MALKES.

P. 197. " With the consent of the All-Present," etc.—The
introduction to the solemn Kol Nidré prayer.

P. 220. " He began to wear the phylacteries and the prayer-
scarf," etc.—They are worn first when a boy is Bar-
Mitzveh (which see); Ezrielk was married at the age of
thirteen.

P. 220. " He could not even break the wine-glass," etc.—
A marriage custom.

P. 220. " Waving of the sacrificial fowls."—See SCAPE-
FOWLS.

P. 220. " The whole company of Chassidim broke some
plates."—A betrothal custom.

P. 227. " Had a double right to board with their parents
' forever.' "—See Köst.

P. 271. " With the consent of the All-Present," etc.—*See note under* p. 197.

P. 273. " Nothing was lacking for their journey from the living to the dead."—*See note under* p. 547.

P. 319. " Give me a teacher who can tell," etc.—Reference to the story of the heathen who asked, first of Shammai, and then of Hillel, to be taught the whole of the Jewish Law while standing on one leg.

P. 326. " And those who do not smoke on Sabbath, raised their eyes to the sky."—To look for the appearance of three stars, which indicate nightfall, and the end of the Sabbath.

P. 336. " Jeroboam the son of Nebat."—The Rabbinical type for one who not only sins himself, but induces others to sin, too.

P. 401. " Thursday."—*See note under* p. 516.

P. 403. " Monday," " Wednesday," " Tuesday."—*See note under* p. 516.

P. 427. " Six months' ' board.' "—*See* Köst.

P. 443. " I knew Hebrew grammar, and could write Hebrew, too."—*See* MASKIL.

P. 445. " A Jeroboam son of Nebat."—*See note under* p. 336.

P. 489. " In a snow-white robe."—The head of the house is clad in his shroud at the Seder on the Passover.

P. 516. " She knew that on Wednesdays Yitzchokel ate his ' day '," etc.—At the houses of well-to-do families meals were furnished to poor students, each student having a specific day of the week with a given family throughout the year.

P. 547. " Why had he brought . . . . a white shirt-like garment? "—The worshippers in the synagogue on the Day of Atonement wear shrouds.

P. 552. " Am I . . . . I suppose I am to lie down? "—*See* MALKES.

P. 574. " In a hundred and twenty years."—The age attained by Moses and Aaron; a good old age. The expression is used when planning for a future to come after the death of the person spoken to, to imply that there is no desire to see his days curtailed for the sake of the plan.

The Modern Jewish Experience

An Arno Press Collection

Fineman, Irving. **Hear, Ye Sons.** 1933

Fishberg, Maurice. **The Jews:** A Study of Race and Environment. 1911

Fleg, Edmond. **Why I Am a Jew.** 1945

Franzos, Karl Emil. **The Jews of Barnow.** 1883

Gamoran, Emanuel. **Changing Conceptions in Jewish Education.** 1924

Glass, Montagu. **Potash and Perlmutter.** 1909

Goldmark, Josephine. **Pilgrims of '48.** 1930

Grossman, Leonid Petrovich. **Confession of a Jew.** 1924

Gratz, Rebecca. **Letters of Rebecca Gratz.** 1929

Kelly, Myra. **Little Aliens.** 1910

Klein, A. M. **Poems.** 1944

Kober, Arthur. **Having Wonderful Time.** 1937

Kohut, Rebekah. **My Portion** (An Autobiography). 1925

Leroy-Beaulieu, Anatole. **Israel Among the Nations.** 1904

Levin, Shmarya. **Childhood in Exile.** 1929

Levin, Shmarya. **Youth in Revolt.** 1930

Levin, Shmarya. **The Arena.** 1932

Levy, Esther. **Jewish Cookery Book on Principles of Economy Adapted for Jewish Housekeepers.** 1871

Levy, Harriet Lane. **920 O'Farrell Street.** 1947

Lewisohn, Ludwig. **Mid-Channel.** 1929

Lewisohn, Ludwig. **The Island Within.** 1928